ZON

The End...

Has Come and Gone

Mark Tufo

Createspace Edition

Copyright 2011 Mark Tufo

Discover other titles by Mark Tufo

Visit us at marktufo.com

and http://zombiefallout.blogspot.com/ home of

future webisodes

and find me on FACEBOOK

Editing by:

Monique Happy

Editorial Services

mohappy@att.net

Cover Art:

Cover Art by Shaed Studios, shaedstudios.com

Dedications:

To my wife; we've walked a difficult path these last few months and except for a scratch or two from an errant briar we've come out in pretty good shape. I look forward to the trail we're getting ready to blaze and I love you with all my heart.

To my family both immediate and extended your strength has been a tangible force upon which I have been able to keep myself upright, I love you all.

To Mo Happy, I've asked a lot of you at a time in your life when maybe you needed a break, I appreciate your hard work, dedication and friendship. Your skills will get you far.

To Paul Rumson my best friend for damn near forever, I offered you crappy pay with a worse deadline and still you produced some awesome art. I hope the new life you are forging ahead with brings you immense happiness.

To Craig Ellison, a reader, a fan who stepped up when I was in need of some help. I cannot express the amount of gratitude that I feel. Simply; thank you.

Always to the men and women of the armed forces, police and fire departments, all of you are the reason why this country is so great. Thank you for all that you do and remember that there are more of us thinking about you than you realize.

To those that signed up for the name contest, I told you guys I'd get you in the book one way or another! So thank you to all those listed below.

Jamie Brown, Nick Orlando, Chuck Craig, Paula Baca, Michael Gunn, Rachael Janda, Ash Careme,

Gill Hancock, Mark Brenner Jr, Thayer Janda, Matt Heaps, Landon Vanlandingham, Joe McCormick,

Luke Asquith, Andy Angel, Cynthia Ellstrom-Organ, Paul Half-Orc Harpham, Jason Waugaman,

Therese Morin, Ashley Morgan-Garcia, Van Loggins, Paul Gosling, Rob Horowitz, Raiden Morgan-Garcia,

Greg Jean, Jeremy Holmes, Steve Wright, Jared

Dunn, Ruby Rain Morgan Garcia,
Andre Daniel Uckert, Michael Adams James,
Shannon Love, Reiko Morgan-Garcia, Bobbie Ayala,
Tammy Nguyen, Ryan McNeil, Cindy Martell,
Brandon Hartle, Kara Baker, Steven Clutch Totten,
Ryan Lynch, Jennifer Locascio, Chris Baines, Brian
Wamsley, Ione Bargy, Christy Peery,
Gregory Wendler, Rich Baker, John Harrington,
James Agbey, Laura Underwood,
Gibby McGibberson, Ray O'Connor, Felicita Green,
Jack O'Donnell, Emelda Rivera, Cami Adair,
Jan Wilkins Parchman Grant, Kyle Sell, Steven
Parkin, John Rose, Dave Kolan, Andrea Wimmer Piper,
Siobhan Hayes, Darren Murphy, Crystal Drumheller,
Chris Crinigan Friedly, Paul Green, Jodi Evans,
Jeffrey Hoffman, Gabe Harris, Vinny O'beirne, Talea
Fields, Evan Roy, Hendrik Lagewaard,
Calum Roebuck, Tini Blair, Elina Kelley, Christoffer
Piper, Becky Graveling, Stacie Shular,
Greg Lose, Chris Walker, Rhiannon Graveling,
Robert Burton, Max Ayala, Traci Sellers, Luci Keenagh,
Robert Stocker, Jeff King, Lisa A Dellert, Grant
Tillie, Roselie Bouyea, Jerome Lim,
Joe Deutschendork (Dutch), Gary Mountjoy, Rob
Eichen, Kristie Long, Nate Gipe, Ryan Dobkins,
Stuart Woodruff, Tillman Dickson, Sarah Flores,
Tanya Murphy, Ryan Sanders, Stephen Deese,
Sean Sommers, Jessica Lord, Rich Parenzan, Moo
and Bandit, Gina DiPaolo, Brian Kay,
Zachary Parenzan, Joel Sheets, Stacy Barbour
Stewart, Charles Stultz, Jodi Jackson, Amber Belinski,
Aysha Hackert, Meredith Hampton, Rodney
Lawrence, Patty Quinn, James Fulton,
Shawnda Picraux, Sean Marsh, Commodore Mann,
Jen Haskins, Barbara Jean, Perla Tirado,
Martin Munro, Elizabeth Briscoe, and Nick Reed!

TABLE OF CONTENTS

PREAMBLE

Hi all I just wanted to say thank you for your continued support and your words of encouragement, for always telling your friends and families about these books and for basically just being awesome readers. I have told some of you that this 'series' was basically only supposed to be one book and then I quickly realized that Talbot was WAY too long winded. That first book became a trilogy almost overnight, I was halfway through the third book when I realized the story just wasn't and couldn't be completed in that time frame. So most folks were pretty happy when I said the trilogy was now a four book series, others not so much. I got some hate mail expressing that I was outright deceiving my readers, most of you know that was never the case if you have EVER sent me any type of correspondence you know that I value and appreciate every reader I have. With that being said, as I sit here today (9/29/11) there will be a ZF5 and right now I think that's it, but I will not guarantee that. So dear reader if you are hoping that this is the conclusion to the Talbot saga, not quite yet, most likely the next installment (or maybe not). Is that vague enough? You guys are the reason I write, keep on reading and I'll keep on writing, as always I love to hear from you guys!

CHAPTER 1 - Talbot Journal Entry 1

The End…has come and gone. This is the new beginning, the new world order and it sucks. The end for humanity came the moment the U.S. government sent out the infected flu shots. My name is Michael Talbot and this is my journal. I'm writing this because no one's tomorrow is guaranteed, and I have to leave something behind to those who may follow. Although the chance of humans making a comeback is remote. We have never been this close to the abyss. Oh, who the hell am I kidding, we've already fallen over and are clinging desperately to a small outcropping.

I've lost damn near everything in an attempt to get back to the East Coast Talbots. I watched as two dear friends departed to their families in the south, to never be heard from again. I watched as my neighbor, a valiant warrior named Jen, was shredded by zombies. My daughter's fiancé Brendon died in a rescue attempt for me, BT and Jen. And my adopted son Tommy has gone missing. So now I must leave 'home' and strike out against a relentless enemy named Eliza, who has placed me on the top of her 'to kill' list. The clock is ticking. My son Justin has been infected with a low dose of the zombie virus and for the most part has been able to keep it at bay, although with some notable side effects, one being that Eliza can use him as a spy. While we were recuperating on the banks of Lake Erie in Camp Custer, Doc Baker came up with a serum that Justin has to take daily. It quite literally keeps the Demon out of his head, the problem being is that we only have forty-five or so of these shots left.

So either we find Eliza and deal with her or she'll find us. Come to think of it, both ways really kind of blow.

I'd much rather wait out the end of the world in a nice cozy cabin but now it's personal. She has dominion over two of my sons, and is directly responsible for the death of my future son-in-law.

Day One – T-Minus four hours before departure – Talbot Journal Entry 2

"Is everything all packed?" Ron asked.

"Hell Ron, I'm a Talbot, everything was packed last night," I told him.

"One more thing then," he said. "I need to show you something."

"I'm not a doctor, I don't know what boils on your ass mean."

"It's too early."

"I know, it's just my way of diffusing the stress."

Ron smiled wanly at me as he led me to the back of his bedroom, more specifically into his master closet.

"Holy crap this closet is huge, you could sleep in here," I jibed.

"I have," he responded. When he didn't elaborate, I figured this to be his 'doghouse' so to speak. "I even have cable in here," he finished proudly.

"Get out?" I questioned him.

He moved a duffle bag aside to show a small 19" flat screen set back against the wall. "Sometimes I start a fight when the Sox are on just so I can get some peace."

I was nodding my head. "Brilliant."

"I thought so," he said, smiling modestly.

"This is cool and all but this isn't why you brought me here, is it." It was more of a statement than a question.

"Not so much," he said as he bent over, rooting around and under a small mountain of sweaters. He finally pulled out the prize he was searching for. It was an old suitcase that had seen better days and a box roughly the size of a football, not the shape mind you, just the size.

"Any chance you've got a hand grenade in there?" I

asked him hopefully, pointing to the small box.

"Nothing quite as explosive, literally."

"Figuratively then? Really?"

"I just remembered it and I thought it might be relevant. Dad gave me this box and the suitcase when I was 15. He told me this story about how his father gave them to him to eventually give to his, at the time, unborn grandkids. Grandpa told Dad to never open these and that he should give these to his kids because *they* would know what to do with them."

"Wait, so Papa John gave this stuff to Dad, with the explicit directions not to open them, so that he could give them to his future kids to open?"

"Yeah, that's the gist of it."

"And you've been hauling this stuff around since then? But I've never seen it and I used to snoop around your room all the time."

"Nice Mike, so much for the sanctum of privacy."

I shrugged my shoulders. "Hey, I was just doing what all younger brothers did."

"Yeah, and you weren't my first younger brother. I made the bottom of my closet into a trapdoor."

"Damn, you just keep racking up the respect points. So what else you got hidden in here?" I asked as I started tapping my right foot on the closet floor listening for the telltale sign of hollowness. Alarm flashed across Ron's face. "So you *do* have something here!" I said, redoubling my efforts.

"You tap one more time and I will take the tires off the truck I'm letting you borrow."

My foot hovered in the air. I was close, but I would leave it at that. Who knew what treasure trove he had hidden? I wouldn't doubt it at all if it was gold bullion.

He first opened up the suitcase. There were stacks of notebooks and loose-leaf papers. They looked pretty brittle to the touch. I bent to grab a piece and the corner broke off in my hand.

"Careful," Ron chided me.

"I barely touched it," I said in defense.

"This stuff is almost a hundred years old."

"Ron, I'm not getting the importance, especially now, why you're showing me this stuff."

"Let me back track. Gram Marissa."

"Oh I loved Gram Marissa, she always smelled like licorice and honey," I said fondly.

"She did sort of, didn't she?" Ron said, getting that faraway look in his eyes.

Grandma Marissa had a smile on her face every day up until the day she died; it was a trait I had often desired to emulate but I always seemed to come up woefully short. Either her faith in mankind was much stronger than mine, or much more ignorant. It was better to think the former, it made her seem a much stronger person.

"Anyway," Ron started up again. "Gram Marissa's dad was a doctor, actually a physicist."

"Really? I didn't know that." I was astonished, that was a pretty lofty position and I was fairly certain that I had never heard of the man.

"Stop interrupting me."

"Just because you're my big brother doesn't make you the boss of me."

"What are you, two?"

"Just messing around."

"The whole stress thing?"

"It's what I do."

"Any chance you'll grow out of it?"

"Pretty far in the game now to think about changing the rules."

"Fair enough, you ready for the rest of the story?"

I nodded and twirled my hand around to let him know it was OK to proceed.

"Alright, so Gram Marissa's dad was Dr. Hugh Mann."

"Like *Hu-man*?" I asked.

"I thought you weren't going to interrupt anymore?"

"I never said that, *you* did."

"Fine," He said, a little perturbed. "Yes, like Hu-man, only with a Hugh, H...U...G...H, not H...U."

"Sounds the same."

"Mike, shut up."

I nodded again, I had yet to agree to anything though.

"So Dr. Mann discovered these bugs that under the microscopes of his time bore an eerie similarity to the human form."

"No way, he was the one that discovered Hugh-Mannites? Why aren't we rich or something? I read all about them on the Internet, how they were really just a concocted boogie-man to raise awareness about hygiene back then."

"Oh they were the boogie-man alright, but they weren't concocted. Didn't you read between the lines, the similarity of time lines between the eradication of the dust mites..."

"And the Spanish Flu? Wow, I never put it together until now."

"It's all in these papers."

"Now don't get me wrong, this is super interesting shit, and I'm not even pretending."

"Thanks," Ron said drily.

"Wait," a conspiracy light bulb flickering above my head. "How does this tie into the H1N1?"

"Now you're getting it," Ron smiled grimly. "I started reading these notes right after Dad gave them to me."

I looked questioningly at the brittle parchment. Ron understood immediately.

"I had them photocopied."

I nodded and he continued. "So our great grand dad was one of the first to put it together. When dust mites died so did people."

"So the flu was no flu."

"And they said when Mom dropped you on your head you'd never be right. I thought they might be mostly wrong."

"Keep talking, funny one, just remember I'm borrowing your truck and you won't be there to see what happens to it."

His previous smile fell from his face. "Anything happens to that truck..."

"Whoa, whoa, big brother, I didn't say anything was going to happen, I merely implied it."

"Yeah, that makes me feel SO much better."

"I'm just messing with you, nothing is gonna happen to your baby."

He eyed me unmercifully, we both subconsciously knew my last statement was a lie.

"The doctor realized when the military became interested that his discovery could now be used for nefarious purposes."

"Big word, been using a thesaurus again?"

"Bad, asshole, it means bad."

"Oh I know what it means, it just seems like you were dropping large words just to do it. So even back then the government was a little shady?"

"Remember the USS Maine?"

"Touché. I still don't know if I'm putting all the dots together. So the gummint..."

"Gummint?"

"Yeah, just my white trash way of saying government."

"Whatever, how many times did Mom drop you?"

"So the gov-ern-ment," I said slowly, making sure to over-enunciate each word. "They got a hold of our great granddad's research and they did what any self-respecting government would do. They figured out a way to use the bugs as a means of mass destruction on our enemies. Is that a fair assessment?"

"Well, yes and no. They definitely took an interest after the Spanish Flu wreaked its havoc. There is even evidence to suggest that they ran tests with it around the time of WWII but besides the deaths of 1918 that were caused by accident, there is nothing to suggest that they did anything with it after that."

"Would they wait a hundred years? And why use it against their own..." I stopped mid-thought. "Someone *else* got a hold of it."

Ron put his index finger to his nose to let me know I had nailed it.

"So someone tainted the world's supply of flu shots. But who and for what purpose?"

"Hell, take your pick little brother. The John Birch Society, the One World Government, the Illuminati, the fucking Girl Scouts, any one of them. To what purpose? Well, that depends on which one of the psychotic groups got a hold of it. Just plain anarchy, control of resources, not enough cookie sales. I can't imagine they expected this much collateral damage but there you have it."

"What else do his notes say?" I asked.

"There's a potential for a cure in here, but he never fully perfected it and I'm not sure what effect it would have on the parasite now. Whatever version is running through those zombies out there, it isn't 1.0."

"If the government..."

"Gummint," my brother corrected me.

"Yeah, them." I said. "By the time they got through with it, the parasite has to be a fully weaponized creature."

"Do you think your friend Doc Baker along with his research and these notes would be able to do something?"

"Possibly, but I wouldn't even know where to begin to find him. I don't even know for sure if he made it off the base." I missed the doc and his family; they were good people and I only hoped the best for them. "And Tommy is my priority."

"Above Justin."

"I've been good so far brother, but I don't need any extra pushing. If I thought I had a one in a million shot of tracking down the doc with these notes AND, that's a big AND, I thought he was alive AND could do anything with them I'd change everything in a heartbeat."

"I'm sorry Mike, it wasn't my intention to make you feel like you weren't doing the right thing."

"Oh it probably was but you didn't mean it in a bad way. We have a link to Tommy. There is a potential way for us to track him down, slim sure, but a chance. Doc Baker could be two houses away from us right now and we'd never know it. I promise if I come across a clinical physician I'll hog tie him and won't let him go until he figures out how to make this potential potion."

"That'll have to do."

"Glad you're on board," I said sarcastically. "What's in the box?"

"I'm not a hundred percent sure but I think you'll know."

"Uh oh, I don't like it already," I said, and I wasn't kidding or trying to be funny.

He pulled the lid off the box. The smell of old garlic slammed into my nose. I intrinsically knew, it would have been impossible not to. As he pulled the white gold locket from its case a tremor of unease began in my stomach and wrapped around my spinal column. I was shaking uncontrollably like a bear had wrapped its paws around a small tree and was shaking it violently trying to make the bee hive drop its prize, only the prize in this analogy was my quivering mind.

"Don't," I mouthed silently as he opened the jewelry.

A bolt of power seemed to leap from Eliza's cold eyes as she stared back at me. A small smile pulled up one corner of her lips as she seemed to take a cruel satisfaction in my unease.

"You alright?" Ron asked across a seemingly vast expanse.

"Close it," I said breathlessly.

I'll give him this, he didn't taunt me with it like a big brother is apt to do with an object of fear. Like countless brothers holding a bug up to the frightened gazes of their sisters. Or the glob of spit that is repeatedly drooped in front of the younger sibling's face to only be sucked up at the last moment, or a countless other myriad forms of minor torture. My anguished look of distress was enough to convince him that this wasn't a game.

"That's her then?" he said as he shut the locket.

"Where did you get that?" I asked after I was able to speak again. I reached my hand out, not sure if I truly wanted to touch it.

Ron brought it closer to my hand. "You sure? I thought you were going to pass out just from looking at it."

"Not from the piece itself, only the picture, it has power."

Ron eyed me skeptically. He was not a big believer in what he could not touch or see, but he still reluctantly handed it over.

"Wow, it's so cold," I said as I gripped the chain.

Ron touched the chain to see what he was missing. "It's cool at best, room temperature I'd say. I think it might be in your head, little brother."

"Well there's always the chance of that, Lord knows what else goes on in there, it would fit right in." With my right hand I grabbed hold of the locket, rubbing my thumb over the smooth surface. I pulled back instantly when I felt something prick my finger. "I'm bleeding!" I muttered, looking at the small drop of blood pooling up on the tip of my thumb.

Ron grabbed the locket out of my hands and rubbed every last bit of it. "What the hell did you cut yourself on? This thing is as smooth as buttered silk. Maybe you shouldn't use so much anti-bacterial on your hands, it's making them as dry and brittle as Hugh's notes."

"Funny," I said as I sucked the bubble of blood off my opposing digit.

"Use a different finger and touch it," he suggested, pressing the locket back into my hand.

"Kiss my ass. Rub it on your face first."

And he did just that and nothing happened, no scratch, no mar, no nothing.

I was feeling a little foolish, I angrily grabbed it from him.

"Hold on," he said. "I want to make sure that you're not pulling a scab off or something."

"Fine," I gritted out as I showed him the index finger on my right hand.

You would have thought he was looking for trace evidence at a crime scene the way he analyzed my finger. "Alright, it looks fine."

"So I can continue?"

"Proceed," he said airily.

I rubbed my finger over the face of the jeweled locket. "Ow!" I pulled back quickly, blood was again pooling on a previously unmarred finger.

"Crap Mike."

"I told you the damn thing had something wrong with it."

"I'm not ready to believe that just yet, I think you might be hitting a trigger switch or something that causes a barb to come out. Kind of like an early ages theft deterrent."

"Oh yeah, that must be it," I said sarcastically, now cleaning blood off of my finger and thumb. "Just put the damn thing away."

Ron put it back in its box and then proceeded to hand it to me.

"No way," I told him. "I don't want it."

"Near as I can tell it's yours."

I shook my head in the negative like a six year old child being accused of stealing cookies. My face was covered in chocolate and in my hand I still had half a cookie but still I denied ownership.

"Gram Marissa was kind of vague, like she was remembering the details through a veil. But the boy with the incredible baklava told her that this locket was somehow linked to his sister, that it had some power."

Goosebumps the size of small gooses, (geeses?) rippled up my forearms. "Gram Marissa met Tommy?"

Ron stopped to think for a moment. "I think she said the name 'Tomas' but I guess that makes sense from everything you've told me."

"Why is our family the center of this shit storm, Ron?" I asked in despair. Just when I adjusted to the extra weight of a particular event, I seemed to pick up some extra baggage. Eventually I would get to the point of breaking, maybe not today but I could feel it coming like a locomotive in a dark dead-ended tunnel. There would be nowhere to run and by then I don't think I'd want to.

He shrugged his shoulders. "I wish I knew Mike. But I think we need to think of these items as weapons in this war. They were obviously important enough that Tomas came into our grandparents' lives to keep them safe and let them know what they had, at least to a degree."

"A book of directions or maybe an instructional DVD would have been awesome."

Ron laughed. "Let's get the rest of your stuff."

I could feel the chill of the locket in my heart as I gingerly rubbed the outside of the box.

*   *   *

Talbot Journal Entry 3
Day One

Outfitted with a new truck, plenty of ammo, weapons and food, Tracy, Justin, Travis, my brother Gary and I headed out to find Tommy. My previous injury to my shoulder has nearly healed to completion. I came to Maine hoping for the best and expecting the worst. The East Coast Chapter of the Talbots have suffered some losses, notably my brother Glenn in North Carolina and my niece Melanie who lives, (lived?) in Massachusetts. But for the most part, paranoid delusional Talbots or as they are now known, 'survivalists,' have stayed relatively strong.

My spirits should be much higher than they are, but I just can't get it out of my head that this is a one way trip. We've been driving for four hours, and Tracy has yet to say one word. Her head has been resting against the passenger window, and she's just been staring blindly out at the passing scenery. Leaving her mom Carol behind was actually a good thing. She wouldn't be on the run any more, she'd be able to rest and find some semblance of normality, if possible, at the Talbot compound. Leaving Nicole behind was another matter. Our daughter is pregnant and Tracy wasn't going to be there for it, and that above all else was weighing heavily on her. Well, that and the fact that some dumb ass named Michael Talbot was dragging her two sons back into harm's way.

I didn't quite see it that way. 'Harms Way' seemed to now be a main thoroughfare that intersected regularly with our 'Life's Path.' The only noise in the truck was Gambo's (my brother Gary) checking and rechecking of his magazine clips. I appreciated the thoroughness, and the obsessive compulsive disorder of it, I really did. But four or five times should be the max!

"You about done back there?" I asked Gary.

"With what?" he asked back.

"Admitting your problem is the first step to recovery," I told him.

"What problem?"

"Forget it," I said, too tired to even sound exasperated.

Gary started unloading and reloading his magazine clips again.

"I thought BT was gonna kick your ass, Dad, when you told him he had to stay behind," Travis said from the backseat.

"Yeah, he got pretty close to your head with his crutch," Justin said smiling in remembrance.

I absently rubbed my cheek where the rubber bottomed tip of the crutch had brushed across me. BT had been swinging for the fences, lucky for me he had foul tipped or I'd be back at my Dad's nursing a concussion. Although how bad would that be, really?

"Yeah, that was close," I said, forcing myself to sound cheerier than I felt. It fell flat. The interior of the truck once again slipped into silence, interrupted only by the repetitive sound of bullet scraping against bullet. How the hell that became a comforting noise was a mystery to me.

"What the hell is that smell?" Travis asked, grabbing his nose.

Justin sheepishly raised his hand. "Aunt Lyndsey made me try her breakfast burrito."

The smell was horrific but it wasn't this which caused my already depressed mood to implode. It was the remembrance of Henry. I had felt it best to leave him behind also. Besides not having my furry friend and companion along, I no longer had a viable alibi when my lactose intolerant bowels fired off a fiery discharge. "Oh, Henry," I mumbled under my breath.

Gary rolled down his window, the howling wind masking his sounds of gagging.

"Wonderful," Tracy said as she rolled down her own window. I was thankful that at least now she couldn't rest her head in that melancholy way. It was breaking my already shattered heart.

We hadn't seen much in the way of zombies yet. I figured there were a few mitigating factors. Maine was sparsely populated, number one, number two the area was so economically depressed that if the infected flu shot wasn't being given for free not many people here were going to spend the twenty to twenty-five bucks to get one no matter how virulent the bug. Who cares if you're sick if you don't have a job to go to anyway.

"How are you planning on finding Helen?" Gary's voice came from the back seat.

Tracy slowly turned to look at him. "Who?"

"You know, the werewolf chick," he replied, never

looking up from his magazines.

"You know you're talking out loud right now, Uncle Gary?" Travis asked in concern.

"Dad, there aren't any werewolves, right?" Justin asked.

"Hon, do you have on any silver jewelry?" I asked Tracy.

"You can't be serious. And even if I did have some on, you wouldn't be making any bullets out of it to kill a beast from faerie tales," she said, placing her hand protectively over her obviously gold chain and crucifix.

"Was that cross blessed?" I asked her.

"How should I know, you bought it for me for our anniversary."

"You sure?"

"No, that's right, it must have been my other husband." Her glare should have stopped me in my tracks, unfortunately I was paying too much attention to the roadway to heed the warning.

"Well, did *he* get it blessed?" I asked her.

Her hand would have connected with the side of my head if the G-forces from my hard braking hadn't flung her forward. Thank God she was wearing her seat belt.

"What the hell Mike?" she asked hotly.

Travis nearly crawled over his seat to get a better look at what had brought us from 60 to 0 in record time. A full grown two thousand pound moose was galloping full speed towards us, and he had no clue whatsoever we were in his way. The zombie latched on its back and the one on its left rear leg had absorbed all of its attention.

I was in such a rush to throw the truck into reverse, I slammed it into park. The engine was taching at 5000 rpms and we weren't moving.

"Mike, you're going to want to back up," Gary said, his eyes never straying from the charging beast.

"I think he's right Dad!" Justin threw in for good measure.

It was taking long seconds for my racing mind to catch up to my ill-timed action.

"Mike!!" Tracy said, placing her feet on the dashboard and bracing for impact.

Travis sat back down and refastened his seatbelt. Wise move, I thought to myself.

The moose was within fifteen feet by the time I figured out how to drop the gear into reverse. That transmission got the workout of its life as I slammed the gas pedal down. We were moving but the moose was still gaining.

"Not gonna make it!" I said aloud.

The moose's front hoof clipped the bumper, momentarily taking our rear wheels off the pavement. Between my furtive glances to the rear to make sure we weren't going to hit a wayward semi, and back to the front and possible death by Bullwinkle, I noted that the moose's next step was going to take him half way up our hood which would result in certain destruction with death being a possible consequence. Zombies saved our lives, yeah, write that line down, *zombies saved our lives.* (Sure, we would have never been in this situation if it wasn't for them, but that's just splitting hairs.) The one that had latched on to the rear of the moose took that opportune moment to hamstring the giant critter. The moose dropped like a brick, his head slamming into the hood and grill. So much for the resale value. Ron was going to be pissed.

I laid on the brakes again almost as hard as I had the first time. For twenty seconds I sat there, sweat accumulating on my forehead. The pops and groans of the overworked engine were drowned out by the mewling of the moose as it was being eaten alive. The sad sound pierced the air and my heart, so much so that I got out and killed the zombies as they feasted and then put one into the moose's terror stretched eye. It was then that I noticed the torn tendon on the hind leg still hanging out of the zombie's mouth. Tracy and Travis had come up to get a better look. Justin was rubbing Gary's back as he puked behind the truck.

"We should go, Mike," Tracy said, grabbing my arm.

This opening act to our quest seemed an ominous premonition of things to come. I could not stop staring at the brain matter as it oozed from the moose's eye wound.

"Dad, how did they catch a moose?" Travis asked.

'By hunting it down relentlessly,' I thought. "They must have stumbled on it while it was sleeping," I lied.

We had narrowly escaped death by deaders just a week ago, how far would we have gotten if it had been speeders? As a survivalist I had prepared and trained for the day when the world was going to take a giant shit on itself, but I had no idea how much luck was going to factor into my family's continued existence. I did not like it. Luck was a fickle bitch.

I finally turned from the gruesomeness; Gary's retching had subsided slightly. Justin was no longer rubbing his back as the puddle of bile began to spread and he didn't want to get in the splash zone.

"Big moose," Gary said from his hunched over position, brown drool hanging in stringy rivulets from his mouth.

"Big moose," I echoed. "You ready to go?" I asked him.

"Just about," he answered, immediately followed by his biggest purging thus far.

I popped the hood of the truck to see if the contact with the beast had damaged anything internally. Besides a bumper that would never pass inspection and a hood with a two foot long crease, we were in pretty good shape. Ten minutes later I gave as wide a berth to the carnage in the roadway as the two lanes would allow. It wasn't near enough. Gary's persistent gagging in the back brought me to the edge of my own expulsion. Another ten minutes and I was almost able to convince myself the whole thing was just some elaborate nightmare induced by my sister's chili. Then I saw the drops of blood on the hood and they sliced effectively through that illusion. Oh yeah, did I express how pissed off Ron was going to be about his truck?

CHAPTER 2 – Mad Jack's Backstory

Mad Jack aka Peter Pender until recently was a Technical Adviser for the Department of Defense. It was his primary responsibility to view all the aerial photographs and satellite data and determine viable threats from a hundred different rogue countries, and every major terrorist cell on the globe. He was so adept at his job that within three short years he went from an Analyst Assistant I to the Department Head. He had stopped six major attacks on American soil and at least a dozen other minor ones. Unfortunately, nobody had thought to take a picture of a crate filled with flu vaccinations or quite possibly this latest disaster could have been averted.

Peter was not well liked among his peers, shooting stars seldom were, but he was well respected. Peter's home life revolved around one thing: HALO. His gamertag was Death by Murder667 (he thought he was one better than the devil). Those that had crossed his path on Xbox Live had a 98% mortality rate. He was a legend in the gaming world, a not well liked but well respected gamer. Peter had set up residency in his parents' home for the first twenty-seven years of his life. The basement was his dominion, and he probably would have spent the next twenty-seven years there also if his father had not gently chided his son that it might be time to fly the coop. Only then could George Pender finally realize his dream of a man cave, resplendent with a six-seat home theater.

Peter traveled almost across the whole Pender backyard before he set up his new domicile in the apartment above the garage. The independence was invigorating. Between work and wreaking ruin on the minions within the

HALO universe, Peter had very little time to deal with the fairer sex. It wasn't that he didn't think, dream, eat and sleep about them, it was just that they were a mystery that defied explanation. He could glance at a black blurry box the size of a foot locker photographed from 2,400 miles away and let you know with stunning detail the threat level that it imposed. Women he couldn't decipher with a Cray super computer. HALO was easy in comparison, kill or be killed, no right no wrong, no double meanings, no games. It was straight forward and linear, whereas women were all dangerous curves.

Liver had saved Peter's life, not directly mind you, but the effect was the same. The day his division was scheduled to receive the flu vaccine, his favorite restaurant Ma's Grill and Home Cooking (the slogan being 'the food tastes just as good without all the nagging!') was having a special on liver and onions. This was hands down his favorite meal on the planet, which confused the hell out of his parents because they had never once made it for him while he was growing up. Ma's was slow, the smell of the liver keeping her normal customers at bay.

"I thought you guys would be packed," Peter said excitedly as he placed his order at the counter.

Stan the cashier, a young man doing his best to not let the smell affect him, could only shrug his shoulders in reply.

The only other customers in the restaurant were seated as far away as possible from the grill, although it didn't help. They were unhappily shoveling their food into their mouths as fast as they could in an attempt to be out and away into the chilly air of Kansas City.

"I thought you said this place was good?" Peter overheard the woman ask her male companion in the booth. "Everything tastes like liver," she said in distaste, roughly placing her sandwich down on her plate.

To Peter that sounded like the most wonderful thing in the world. "See, that's what I mean about women, there is just no figuring them out," he said silently to himself, shaking his head.

Stan had hastened to the back of the store to crack open the door and allow some carbon dioxide from the Fed-Ex truck parked in the alley to enter in. It was heavenly in comparison to the stench of grilled liver. Stan reluctantly closed the door just as a man approached from behind the open door which had effectively blocked Stan's view. Had Stan been able to see he would have noticed that a fever ravaged man was approaching, red lines radiating out from his scalp and crisscrossing on his sweaty cheeks. Blood and drool combined to flow freely from his mouth; the smell of liver which he had hated his entire life all of a sudden it smelled like sweet ambrosia, and right now he didn't care if it was off the grill or out of a body. One of his last coherent thoughts was ironically wondering where his last thought had come from.

Peter took his time returning to work, reveling in his great lunch. It wasn't until he entered the lobby and saw the sign: FLU SHOTS HERE >>> that he realized his mistake.

"Dammit," he whispered as he ran down the hallway to the conference room that was set up just for this occasion. Peter dreaded being sick, mostly because his mother thought she made the best chicken soup this side of the Mississippi, when in fact she didn't make the best soup west of her own kitchen. But primarily he hated it because it slowed his reflexes and his HALO kill ratio would take a hit. He skidded to a stop right outside the door just as the nurse was putting the waiver forms back into her bag.

The nurse heard and then saw the man; his features let her know how disappointed he was. "Don't worry sweetie, we'll be back tomorrow for the 4th floor, just get in line and we'll take care of you."

But that was a lie, the nurse did not return the next day, and neither did 90% of his department who had missed work.

"What a weird day," Peter said to himself as he walked home from the bus stop. The streets of Kansas City looked deserted, barely anyone had showed for work and Ma's Grill was closed. The bus which was generally standing room only had only one occupant and he was a bum with a bus pass. He was on the bus every day. He just rode it all day long in the winter to stay out of the cold. Peter sometimes wondered why the homeless man didn't just buy a ticket to Atlanta, seemed like it would have saved him a lot of time. What Peter didn't know was that the man lived for the here and now. The future was the big unknown, a doctrine that the rest of the surviving human race was to become very familiar with.

Peter stepped onto the gravel of his parents' driveway and turned to watch the streetlight turn on. "Ha, beat you this time!" he shouted to the indifferent fixture. He noticed the lights on in his parents' house but did not see any movement. "Probably watching a movie," he said aloud to somehow dispel the dread that was building up.

He looked up and down the street uneasily before entering his tiny abode. It was never Grand Central around here, but it was quitting time and there should be and was always more movement as folks returned from work, errands, school, whatever. Realization did not completely sink in until he logged on to Xbox Live and noticed there was somewhere in the neighborhood of 20% of the usual volume of games being played. He had no explanation for the increased beating of his heart or the sweat that started to build up on his forehead and palms.

He looked out his window and across the yard into the large bay window that dominated the back of his folks' home. Nothing looked unusual except for the lack of movement. His mom was usually a whirling dervish of activity, preparing dinner, doing laundry, playing with their two Maltese dogs. Peter picked up the phone to call his parents, but the phone alternated between a fast busy signal and the three tone warning of a downed line.

"Should probably go and check on them," he mused, still gazing out the window, the phone chirping in his hand.

He wouldn't have gone if he had stopped to turn on the television. Early stories were already reporting mass riots involving cannibalistic mobs. He walked down the stairs, the air seeming oppressively heavy. The clicking of the phone was drowned out by multiple sirens caterwauling a few blocks away. Peter moved his hand up to his face, studying the handset he carried, suddenly wishing it was heavier and had a longer reach. "Now why would I need a weapon?" he asked himself. "I'm going to my parents', not Detroit."

Each step got heavier and heavier as he crossed the yard. "Come on Mom, just walk by the window, just once," he pleaded. More sirens joined the fray and for the life of him he could not figure out why his parents weren't checking out what the fuss was about. 'They must really have Breakfast at Tiffany's cranked,' he thought, looking for humor and finding none. The sirens which had violently been pushing the silence away cut off as if on a timer as his foot hit the first step on the back porch. The vacuum of sound was immediately filled in by the frantic barking of Chip and Dale, his mom's dogs.

"Chip and Dale never bark," Peter said aloud. "Mom dotes on them too much for that." He never noticed as the phone slid from his grip and cracked on the cement. His eyes were fixed on the door handle. For reasons he could not explain, he was more afraid now than that time he had stopped a barge three miles off the shore of Florida that carried two nuclear warheads. This was far worse, this was quite literally happening on his own doorstep. Retreating into the alternate reality of HALO right now seemed like the wisest course of action. And he was close to that decision, he wanted to put this made-up nightmare behind him and go try out the new game armor he had purchased.

He had actually started to softly close the screen door and turn to walk away when Chip's or possibly Dale's barking changed into a high pitched howl. "Never heard that before," He said, frozen in indecision, half in and half out of the entrance. He gripped the door handle and pulled back quickly. "Whoa, that's freezing!" he said, blowing air into his palm. Even the dog's change in tone was not enough to force him into action. It was the three shambling strangers that had just entered into the circle of light at the base of his driveway that sealed the deal. "You guys don't look so good," he said as he twisted the knob and prayed to the patron Saint of All Who Opens Things that the door was not locked.

He was in and had quickly shut the door before the smell assailed him. His first thought was that he was wearing the same shirt he had worn for yesterday's luncheon special and had possibly taken home far more than his fair share of cloying liver and onions' odor. Although that would have been heavenly compared to the aerial blast of assification that filled the room. Chip, the lighter colored of the two dogs came running down the hallway, tail tucked between his legs. He stopped right in front of Peter and began to piss all over the floor, something he could not remember the dog doing even when he was a puppy.

"What's the matter boy?" Peter asked, lowering himself down to the dog's level. Chip was shaking violently and he pulled back when Peter tried to comfort him. Peter stood back up; Chip ran and hid behind the couch. "Mom? Dad?" Peter said so softly they might not have heard him if they were in the same room. Peter wanted to check the basement first because it was on the opposite side of the house from where Chip had run out from. "Not very logical," he chided himself. "Or courageous. Come on, what would Death by Murder667 do? Well, first off he'd have an M392 and about 25 hand grenades, so that's not going to work so much considering I don't even own a squirt gun. But Dad does. Yeah, and it's down the exact hallway you'd rather not go down. And who the hell are you talking to?"

Peter started slowly down the hallway and turned back to where the small dog had hidden. "Any chance of some back up?" Not so much as a whimper. "Solo mission then," he said, steeling himself to go down a path he'd traveled at least ten thousand times in virtual reality. The atmosphere, the stink, the feelings of dread all intensified. Each step became a chore, a vastly distasteful chore.

He could hear something tapping in his parents' bedroom. It was a discordant sound that more than anything had Peter on edge. The door was half open but no light spilled out, and the ambient light from the hallway did little to pierce the darkness beyond.

"This sucks," Peter said hardly a register above silent. The tapping grew louder and more frantic and then suddenly stopped. The tapping which he had found ominous was light years better than the ensuing quiet. Something stirred in the darkness. Peter involuntarily checked his chest for his trademark hand grenade bandoliers. "Yeah, that's how most people solve their problems, throw a hand grenade in their parent's bedroom."

A face materialized out of the gloom, it was familiar yet unrecognizable. His mother looked through Peter with opaque eyes. Blood lined her mouth, entrails emblazoned her night shirt, a jagged strip of flesh was torn from her forehead where dirty white bone shone in the light. If his mother had not slipped on the remains of Dale, Peter would have died that night, frozen in fright. His last thought as he fled from the house was that the tapping noise had been Dale's toenails hitting the wall in his death throes.

Peter spent the next two days barricaded in his apartment, only occasionally stealing glimpses of the chaotic outside world. Hundreds of zombies had passed by his house, this he could tell by the smell alone. The windows were shut and duct tape sealed every crevice, and still the stench bled through. Gun fire gave him grim hope that not all was lost, but by the end of the second day the frequency of shots was becoming less and less and the smell was getting worse. He was able to do the math in his head on that one. Sleep was infrequent and always ended abruptly when the ruptured skull face of his mother crept in on him.

Seventeen diet 7 Ups, half a bottle of ketchup and something that might have been a corned beef sandwich lined the barren shelves of Pete's fridge. "Always ate dinner with Mom and Dad," he choked out. Pete understood the irony of starving to death in his apartment or becoming dinner for the abominations that walked outside. 'It's an eat or be eaten world,' he thought sourly and with no humor.

Three days later and even with strict rationing he was down to one 7 Up. The previous night he had stripped most of the bluish-green mold from the mystery meat sandwich. His stomach had cramped something fierce but it was worth it. The 7 Up and ketchup soup just wasn't cutting it anymore. He didn't dare drink any of the tap water until he was sure that wasn't the agent that had caused this epidemic or whatever it was. Hunger and depression was making him lethargic, and leaving the couch was becoming increasingly difficult.

He was like the frog put in a slowly boiling pot of water; he would never leave this apartment. Starving to death was a slow painful process and was worlds better than the alternative. If not for the smell of smoke that was exactly what would have happened. Fire was the mitigating factor. Pete could think of no worse way to die except for maybe having rats eat his eyeballs while he was strapped to a table, but that was a completely different nightmare. Pete did not want to burn, charred blistering skin peeling back from his hands and face as lava hot smoke burned through his chest, exploding his lungs and torching his throat. The fluid in his eyes would sizzle and explode, his mouth forever pulled back in a smile of death like the victims of Pompeii.

He peeked out the window, the first time in a while he had cared enough to bother. Two streets away, in the general direction of where Susan Payne had lived (the first girl he had ever kissed), the sky was completely enshrouded in thick black smoke. Fine filaments of the sooty substance were bleeding through under his door and even around the uneven edges of the duct tape. He momentarily considered throwing up another layer of tape and sticking a towel under the door, but to what end? All that would accomplish would be allowing the fire time to catch up and roast him alive instead of suffocating him to death. Neither way was a savory means to his end.

The fire storm had one benefit, the things that were human once wanted as little to do with the fire as any other living creature. Squirrels, cats, dogs, and what he would come to know as zombies all made hasty retreats in the opposite direction from the impending doom.

"Now or never Pete," he told himself, taking one last glance over at his parents' home. He absently wiped a tear away from his eye. The fire had jumped to the street parallel to his own. He could see the flames as they licked the edges of the homes. God had turned his back on man, hell had been unleashed on earth, the proof was now devouring the Almstead house. The fire was a vengeance, a scouring of all that was wrong with the world.

Pete walked slowly through his apartment taking mental images of a home he would never return to, then left with nothing more than the clothes he was wearing. He ran to the driveway to get the white van his father used for his in-town delivery service. He went directly to the back of the van, feeling around the juncture where the bumper met the frame until he found what he was looking for, the spare key. His mother had made Pete's dad get the magnetic contraption after his dad had called the locksmith for the third time in three months because he had once again locked the keys in the van. Funnier still was that in the twelve months since he had the spare key attached to the bottom of the van, he had never again locked his keys in the car.

Pete adjusted the captain's chair and turned the ignition over. His heart skipped a beat when he peered into the kitchen window and saw his mother staring back at him. He threw the van into reverse heedless of whatever might be behind him. He nearly took out the privacy fence that encased his parents' yard. He never took his eyes off that window as he stopped and then placed the car into drive; his mother's gaze never wavered as her milky white eyes followed his treacherous departure.

CHAPTER 3 – BT

BT watched as Mike rolled down the gravel driveway. Surrounded by people, BT had never felt more alone. He draped his huge arm around Nicole as they walked back up into the house.

Nicole was crying, partly from hormones run amok, mostly from watching her family drive away. "Will we ever see them again BT?" she managed to ask through her sobs.

"We'd better, because I don't know how long I can survive your aunt's cooking," he said, trying to lighten the mood. It worked for a moment, and she silently thanked him for it.

Carol had stayed in the kitchen opting not to watch the departure. BT came over to see how she was doing.

"Was it wrong of me to not see them off?" she asked the big man. She never gave him an opportunity to respond before she started talking again. "It just felt like that would have been too final, do you know what I'm saying?"

BT nodded because that was exactly how it felt. He didn't tell her that it felt that way no matter where you stood. That wouldn't have helped. Carol then did something unexpected, she turned and gripped him hard in a bear hug, her hands not making it halfway across his broad back. BT was not used to being thrust into the mode of comforting people, not many people looked to a 6'8" 350 pound bear of a man for solace, it just didn't happen.

"There, there," he said, patting her back gently. He thought that he had seen this technique once in a movie and it had seemed to work. He looked more like a person who doesn't like dogs and taps the tops of their heads gingerly, hoping they'll go away.

Tony Talbot took this opportune time to enter the kitchen. BT wouldn't swear to it, but Tony and Carol had seemed to hit it off. Maybe not romantically, not yet anyway, but there was something to be said about being around someone your own age. They had an uncanny ability to ease the mind of the other, shared experiences possibly or maybe even shared worries, didn't matter. Whatever it was they each found peace in the contact. BT was grateful when Carol broke the hug and acknowledged Tony's entrance.

BT left the kitchen to go to the living room that overlooked the now empty driveway. Ron, Mike's older brother, stood looking out as if expecting guests.

"How's the leg?" Ron asked without turning around.

"Feels better," BT said aloud. But he thought to himself 'it hurts a lot' was only shades better than 'hurts like hell,' or maybe it was the other way around.

"When are you planning on leaving?" Ron asked, now looking directly at the big man.

"A day or two at the most."

"How are you planning on following him?"

"Just follow in the wake of destruction, it's usually pretty cut and dried with Mike. He doesn't leave much to chance when he goes somewhere."

"A shortwave radio transceiver might make your life a little easier."

"How many of those things do you have?"

"Five, I bought three and convinced the store owner to throw in two for free. Didn't think I was actually going to need all of them but it's nice to be prepared."

"You sound like Mike, or does he sound like you?" BT asked with a grin.

Ron laughed. "Let's get you some supplies."

BT followed slowly behind Ron as they descended into the basement. Ron entered into a room that housed the water heater and furnace. Behind those fixtures was another door. Ron opened that and flipped on a light switch.

BT could not believe what he was seeing. It was a huge room that dwarfed the size of the house it sat under. Metal shelves were lined with canned goods, bags of rice, coffee, flour, sugar, fuel, candles and every other imaginable necessity that people waiting out Armageddon might or might not need.

"Ron, this is like having your own Wal-Mart."

Ron beamed. "Took me twenty years to gather all this stuff, so who do you think sounds like who now?"

"I'd bow to the King of the Crazies if it didn't hurt so much."

"That's alright, I appreciate the sentiment. And I've got something that will fix you right up." for that."

"You truly are a scholar and a gentleman."

CHAPTER 4 – Talbot Journal Entry 4

We stopped that first night off of the Mass Pike at a rest stop. The combo Dunkin' Donuts, Mobil Gas Station and Papa Gino's had long ago been ransacked but the building itself was in remarkably good shape and easily defendable, two sought after qualities in this brave new world. I had everyone exit the truck and pulled it up so close to the front door only an anorexic zombie would be able to fit through, and I had yet to find one that fit that bill. Gary grabbed the radio out of the back and set it up on one of the red and white checkered pizza joint tables.

"Is it time yet?" Gary asked.

"He said he would keep it on all the time, so I would imagine any time would be fine," Tracy answered.

"Breaker one nine, breaker one nine," Gary started. "This is Hammer of the Gods, breaker one nine, Hammer of the Gods over."

"Hammer of the Gods?" my wife mouthed the question to me. All I could do was shrug my shoulders.

"Can you hear me Mount Olympus? This is Hammer, over?" Gary asked.

An out of breath response came through almost as clear as if we were next door and not two states away. "I thought you were kidding about those call signs," Ron said.

Gary seemed instantly relieved when Ron spoke. It was a connection to normalcy, or at least the Talbot version of it. "Mount Olympus, this is Hammer, the Chariot of Fire has suffered some damage."

"Chariot of Fire? Gary, speak English. Wait, the truck! What happened to the truck? Get Mike on the horn!"

Ron yelled.

I was backing up, my arms outstretched, hands waving back and forth in the negative. "Tell him I'm not here," I told Gary.

"I can hear you, you little pecker, get on the mic!" Ron said from three hundred miles away.

"Balls!" I said resignedly. "You and me are going to talk, Gary," I said softly but with force.

Gary looked taken aback but there was also something else there, something underlying and subtle; it was humor. The ass was loving it. 'That's fine,' I thought to myself, 'revenge is a two lane highway, and we still had plenty of roadway left before this dance is over.'

"Yeah Ron, this is Mike," I said with forced cheerfulness.

I had to step back from the speaker as Ron's yells bellowed forth. "That truck is brand effen new, you've been gone for one day. What the hell could you possibly have hit? There's not even anybody out there."

"Well, there was this moose..." I started.

"You hit a freaking moose? What were you doing, did you take the damn thing off-road?"

"See, it's more like the moose hit us."

"Forget it!" Ron yelled. I could picture him throwing his hands up in the air the way my mom had so many times before when I was a kid and trouble had somehow found me and then followed me all the way home, and sometimes even inside. "Is everyone alright?" he asked, finally getting down to the important matters.

"Don't you think that should have been your first question?" I taunted.

"Don't try me little brother."

"A little shaken up but no worse for the wear, you're going to lose your security deposit though."

I could hear him groan. "That's fine," he said grudgingly. I could tell he was struggling within himself to not go ballistic and from this distance it was funny, any closer and not so much. "What are your plans for the night?" he continued.

We had decided before we left that we would check in at least once a day, preferably at the same time, and that I would let him know where we were at and what we planned on doing the next day. There was an innate comfort in somebody knowing where you were at all times. It wasn't like he could send in the cavalry to rescue us, but maybe, eventually, he would be able to find what remained of us and give us a proper burial, provided of course there were any remains to be found.

"We're off the Mass Pike, mile marker 70, holing up for the night in a rest stop. Then we're going to go a little further west tomorrow into Pennsylvania and maybe south depending on if I get any hunches."

"Mike, for the fiftieth time, is this what you want to be doing? The U.S. is huge, how are you going to find one woman?"

"No, this isn't what I want to be doing," I answered a little snappishly.

"You know what I mean."

"Ron, I don't know how it will happen, but it will. I *will* find her and I *will* kill her." I was much more confident about the finding part than I was the killing, but this I would keep to myself.

"Alright little brother, you guys have a good night and stay safe. I'll talk to you tomorrow. And one more thing."

"Yeah…?" I said hesitatingly.

"You mess my truck up any more and you're going to need Eliza to protect your ass from *me*."

I wanted to tell him just to get another one, what was the big deal. I decided that discretion was the better part of valor and instead said, "Hey bro, don't want to waste any more battery, over and out."

"Wait you litt…." I took this opportune time to shut the transceiver down.

Gary was about ten feet away, his face split with a shit eating grin.

"Not cool man," I said, pointing my finger at him. I might have done something more than threaten him but just then the sound of metal scraping on metal caught all of our attention. The sounds of multiple firearms being readied dominated the landscape for the next four seconds. Travis was coming up behind me, shotgun at the ready. I put my hand on his shoulder as he drew up alongside. I pointed to my eyes and then motioned for him to watch our backs. The building, which I felt had been an ideal resting spot just moments earlier, now seemed more like a trap. We were in the dining area in the middle where long gone customers used to sit and try to digest all the processed food they bought at the gas station store on our left or at the pizza counter in front of us. The Dunkin' Donuts had never opened the fateful day the zombies came, either that or the last employee to ever work there had had the foresight to close shop and run. That heavy gauge metal screen had been pulled down in front of the counter. You know the kind, you can fit your fingers through and almost reach the plastic mugs. What the hell you're going to do with it once you get it in your grasp is beyond me, they won't fit through the gaps, not that I had tried... lately.

No other sound emanated from the gas station store, but I still brought my gun up out of an abundance of caution. Out of the corner of my eye I could see Tracy tense up. Gary for all his comedic endeavours was now all business. He came up beside me as we advanced on the store. Justin went up to the front doors and peered out. I stole a glance towards him. His thumbs up assured me that our one avenue for escape was still clear.

"One chance," Gary said loudly, startling the hell out of me.

I hated giving potential enemies any sort of heads up. Maybe that was how they had done it when Gary was in the Air Force. Marines? What can I say, we don't fight fair, we fight to win.

"Did you hear me?" Gary asked again. "I said *one chance*."

"Dude," I said impatiently. "You already gave them their one shot, enough already."

"We're coming in!" he added just for good measure.

I stopped and let my gun slack down. "Really? Are you kidding me? Should I get some flyers printed up, with our arrival date and time?"

"Well I don't think *that's* necessary," Gary answered.

"Don't shoot!" came from the far corner and of course the dimmest lit section of the store.

We both swung our guns and trained them on that spot, advancing even slower.

"Don't move," came from our immediate right.

"Text book," I said quietly.

"What?" Gary asked.

"We just walked into a trap."

Why Gary looked down at his feet I don't know, maybe he was looking for a tripwire.

"Not that kind," I told him.

"Put your guns down," came the voice from the corner.

Like gasoline to a fire Travis came running up to the store entrance. "Drop that fucking gun!" he yelled.

"No swearing!" Tracy said reflexively from the food court.

I could hear the metallic sound of the action being moved on the pistol that was aimed at my right side. I started going through the laundry list of vital organs exposed to that potential shot, any of them being damaged was not something I wanted to deal with today.

"Hold up!" I yelled. "I'm putting my gun down. Travis, do not do anything."

"Dad, it's just a girl," Travis said. I don't know if he meant he could take her down quickly or 'it's just a girl and what the hell do I do?'

"How big is the gun?" I asked evenly as I bent over very slowly to place my rifle on the floor.

"Fucken huge," he said with some awe.

"No swearing!" Tracy said again.

"Angel, you alright?" the voice from the corner asked.

I couldn't believe it. The girl apparently holding a rhino killing pistol started to giggle. "I'm alright Eyean. But he looks scared." And then she started to giggle again.

I had placed my rifle on the floor and stolen a glance at my captor as I stood back up. She stuck her tongue out at me when she realized I was looking at her. A six year old girl holding a .44 magnum had gotten the drop on me. "Wonderful," I said in self-disgust.

She put on her meanest face, probably the one reserved for when she found out that the Hannah Montana episode on that night was a repeat. However, it was no joke when she motioned with the gun for me to put my hands over my head. Gary had already put his gun down and was lying prostrate on the floor.

"Dad?" Travis asked.

"Put the gun down. I'd rather get shot than ever shoot a little girl." Visions of a Wal-Mart loading bay blazed across my memories. "Again," I added.

"Eyean, all their guns are down," Angel said, putting her hand over her mouth to stifle another giggle.

"Eyean, why would you send this girl out here to do this?" I was enraged.

"It's *Ryan*, she's never been good with the 'R'," a skinny kid maybe 15 or 16 years old said as he came out from behind a NASCAR display. "She was in the bathroom when we heard you come in. I *told* her to stay there."

"Any chance we could convince her to put that gun down before anyone gets hurt? And considering I'm the only one under aim at the moment, it would most likely be me."

"Mister, I'm sorry," Ryan said. "But we don't know you at all."

"Stranger danger!" Angel said excitedly.

"Wonderful, so now what?" I asked.

Ryan didn't seem so prepared to answer that question.

Tracy came up cautiously to the front of the store. "Why she's just a little girl Talbot, what's the matter, did she trap the big brave men?" she asked condescendingly, laced with a bit of humor. I don't know how she pulled it off. It was magnificent and it also had the added bonus of diffusing a potentially bad situation.

"Hi pretty lady," Angel said, waving the hand that was not holding the magnum. How the hell such a little girl was keeping that cannon trained directly on me I don't friggen know.

"Hi, Angel is it?" Tracy said, getting a little lower to be on eye level with the Bonnie (of Bonnie and Clyde fame) wannabe. That might seem harsh to you but I was the one being held at gunpoint. Give it a whirl sometime and let me know what you think of it.

"Yes," the girl answered coquettishly, lightly kicking her left foot forward.

"You're very pretty Angel," Tracy said softly.

"Thank you pretty lady," Angel answered. This would have been an awesome Disney flick if that cold steel huge caliber weapon wasn't pointed at me.

"It's Tracy," Tracy answered.

"My mom's name was Alicia," Angel answered back. We all noted the key word 'was.'

"Oh honey," Tracy said, standing back up. As she walked forward she opened her arms wide.

Angel didn't give a crap about me as her gun clattered to the floor and she ran into Tracy's outstretched arms. I was thankful it didn't go off, especially considering the first action of the dual action revolver had already been engaged. When I walked over to retrieve the weapon I increased my embarrassment level exponentially. I opened the revolver only to realize that she had no bullets.

"What now mister?" Ryan asked, cautiously watching

his sister as she sobbed heavily into Tracy's chest.

"Nothing, come on out." I looked down. Gary hadn't moved. "Umm, you can get up now brother."

"All clear?" he asked.

"You could say that," I answered, showing him the empty revolver.

"Oh, I knew that all along," he said seriously.

I couldn't tell if he was being truthful or just trying to save face. Ryan stepped hesitantly up to where we were.

"You're fine, kid, we probably don't fit the definition of Good Guys but we sure as hell aren't the bad ones."

He seemed to relax a bit, especially when he saw how Angel had taken to Tracy.

"Can we come out Ryan?" another voice from the shadows asked.

I grabbed my rifle and slung it over my shoulder.

"Can they mister?" Ryan asked warily.

"It's Mike and yes, this is *your* place, we're the ones intruding."

I could tell Ryan was feeling more comfortable, not completely trusting yet but not fearful either.

"It's alright guys," Ryan said.

Three more kids came out from behind the end aisle cap. They were all roughly the same age as Ryan. One was a little taller and looked to be suffering greatly from their gas station food diet. Drakes Cakes were playing hell on his acne. I hadn't noticed before but Ryan, Angel and the other three castaways were filthy, they looked like orphans from 18th century France. Apparently 21st century America wasn't as far removed from those troubled times as we had hoped to believe.

"How many more of you are there?" I asked Ryan.

"This is it," he said with downcast eyes. "Benny and Chirp went home when the end started and they haven't been back. Dizz and me," he said, pointing to the aforementioned face-pocked tall kid. "We went to look for them a couple of weeks ago and maybe see what happened to our parents," he added softly. Angel had finally unburied her face from Tracy's chest and was listening intently.

"How far away do you live from here?" I asked.

"Not very, from the back of this rest area you go through the fence, a small woods and then we're about two streets away. "Half mile maybe?" he asked his friends, looking for validation.

One of the dirtier kids (who was aptly named Sty) just shrugged his shoulders. "Guess so," he answered in that typical dripping with contempt teenager way.

"What were you guys doing out here?" I asked, just to change the subject. He had lost at least two friends and his parents and probably didn't want to rehash that again.

"We were sledding, there's an awesome hill right at the fence," Ryan said with a ghost of a smile on his face.

"And this store used to have the best chocolate milk," Dizz added a little melancholy.

"I drank the last one," Angel said. "Dizz gave it to me. Thank you."

"You're welcome," Dizz said, a little embarrassed.

"Our mom was going to get her hair done," Ryan said. "She told me I had to take Ang with us if I wanted to go out."

"Daddy wasn't feeling good, he was cranky and had gone to sleep," Angel added for good measure.

My immediate thought was that he had been infected. Ryan must have been able to see the wheels spinning in my head, he nodded in assertion to my unspoken words.

"I had just come back up the slope and was waiting for my turn when I heard a bunch of horns and some skidding," Ryan said.

"And then a lot of crashy noises," Angel said, placing her hands over her ears as if it was happening now.

"Zombies just started walking out into the roadway. I mean, we didn't know they were zombies then. It was horrible, trucks and cars were just plowing into them or crashing into the guardrail or each other trying to avoid them.

But that wasn't the worst part."

"Don't Eyean," Angel begged, trying to bury her head and her thoughts deep down.

"Well anyway," Ryan started back up, leaving out the gorier details for the sake of his sister, and I guess for all of us actually. "We watched, we just couldn't believe what was happening." Angel groaned. "Customers and people that worked here they all left, I mean in a hurry, and the zombies pretty much followed them. I know it was wrong but we," and he made sure to point at all of the guilty parties. "We just had to come in and take a look."

An untended store as a teenager, that's a no-brainer. I would have ransacked the hell out of the place. It's in my nature.

Ryan looked at me to see if I was holding judgment over his actions. "I would have done the same thing," I told him, and he seemed relieved. Now to clarify, just because I would have done it *definitely* didn't make it right, but I decided to not tell him that.

"We were still in here messing around," he continued.

"And eating stuff," Dizz added.

Ryan looked over at him crossly. "And yeah, I guess, eating some stuff."

"A lot of stuff," Angel said with a big grin.

"I get it, you ate a bunch of stuff," I said.

"A bunch," Angel agreed. "And then the army men came."

"Yeah, they were using huge trucks with plows to push all the cars out of the way," Dizz said.

"We thought they were coming for us," Ryan said.

"Yeah, it's a Capital Offense to steal a Slim Jim," I said sardonically.

Angel started crying. "Nice one Talbot," Tracy said, trying to comfort the girl.

"I was just kidding Angel," I said, trying to placate her. "And how do you know what capital offense means?"

"So we were scared," Ryan continued. "We hid until

they had gone by, it was completely dark by then and the power was out. Couldn't see anything here because there was only a little bit of moonlight. We heard some wicked fighting down the road."

"Guns, grenades, missiles, everything," Dizz said in fond remembrance. "The sky was pretty bright because of it."

"And smoky," Angel interjected.

"Yeah, definitely smoky," her big brother said.

I was going to ask them why they hadn't gone home at that point. But this wasn't a difficult puzzle to piece together. The power was out everywhere, no fun being out and about when you can't even see your hand in front of your face, much less whether zombies are after you. I wouldn't have taken that chance either.

Ryan continued his narrative. "The next day, early on, we saw some army guys heading back the way they had come and then nothing. No cars, no fighting, nothing. Benny and Chirp said it was time to go." Ryan looked down at his feet. "Mister, I was scared, for… for my sister."

'Nice recovery,' I thought. Can't ever show weakness in front of your friends, *especially* not your friends.

"We had been safe in the store the night before, there was no way of telling what was happening outside. They called me chicken but promised they would send help back."

"That was a long time ago," Angel added softly.

"And have you tried to go home since then?" Tracy asked, her arm still wrapped protectively around Angel.

"Me and Dizz went down the hill and to the edge of the woods a few weeks ago, but all we saw were zombies. I'm pretty sure we could have made it to either of our houses, but I didn't want to know by that point. My mom knew where we had gone, if she was…" He paused as Angel looked at him. "Um, well, she would have got us if she could, that's all I meant."

"And you haven't had any zombies come here?" I asked incredulously.

"Early on there were a few outside, but none ever

tried to get in. And then they just started leaving like they were being called or something."

Chills ran up my spine.

"What now?" I asked Ryan.

"Don't know," he said, shrugging his shoulders.

"What do you mean Talbot? We can't just leave them here!" Tracy said hotly.

"You think taking them with us is the wisest choice?" I said, matching her tone. "You know where we are going, right? Into the damn teeth of the enemy!" Tracy flinched at my outburst. "I think that they're light years safer here than with us!"

Angel started crying. "You're an asshole Talbot!" Tracy said as she turned and walked away.

"Whatever, I've been called worse by better!"

"Dick," she added, flipping me the bird over her shoulder.

"Geez mister, you sure do have a way with the ladies," Sty said in wry admiration.

Ryan looked dejected that we weren't the cavalry. "I'm sorry kid," I told him. "You do *not* want to go where we are going."

"The Summoner?" he asked apprehensively.

I involuntarily staggered back a step as if he had given me a physical blow. "How... how could you know?"

"She keeps showing up in my dreams,"

"Yeah. Ryan's kind of psychic," Dizz said half-jokingly and half with awe.

"Psychic?" I asked Ryan. "Anything else you could tell me?"

"Yeah," he said solemnly. "You shouldn't follow her."

CHAPTER 5 – BT and Meredith

"I'm going with you," Meredith, Ron's second oldest told BT as he placed some ammo cans in the back of the SUV.

BT stood up, towering over the girl. "I'm more the solo type," he told her sternly.

"Oh, you're all lone wolf and shit?" she said sarcastically.

"I am a giant man. I know this, so why are all you Talbots not afraid of me?"

"What time are we leaving?" she asked, not in the least nonplussed.

"Your father isn't going to let you go."

"I'm 23, I'm pretty sure I can make my own decisions," she said, poking a finger at his sternum.

"Wonderful, looking forward to the company," BT said without much conviction.

* * *

BT would have left hours earlier if not for the fight that raged in the Talbot household. Meredith had made her decision known and Ron had snapped.

"I am 23 years old, Dad. I am by all conventional methods of societal acknowledgement an adult."

"Don't go pulling that psycho-babble mumbo jumbo you learned in college, that I paid for by the way, on me. This isn't telling me that you're going to Paris for the summer. It's war out there, Meredith, people are dying!" Ron yelled.

"Yeah and Uncle Mike is going to try and do

something about it!" she yelled back. "And I want to be part of it!"

"I understand wanting to be a part of something bigger than yourself, I really do," he said, taking it down a few notches, going with the reasoning approach. "But getting yourself killed is not a solution to the problem."

"Is that what you think is going to happen with Uncle Mike?" Meredith asked. Ron's ensuing silence answered her. "Then he definitely needs my help."

Ron could only shake his head. BT stood at the doorway to the living room as Meredith passed by.

Ron turned to BT, eyes red rimmed with worry.

"I will not let anything happen to her," BT said. "I promise you."

Ron nodded once, emotions choking his thoughts. Words would have pooled with tears if he had tried to speak.

Ten minutes later the SUV was packed and ready to go. Meredith climbed into the driver's seat before BT could protest.

"You remember to call me every night. Do you understand?" Ron asked leaning into the driver's side window.

"We will, Dad," Meredith answered impatiently.

"BT?"

"Yes Dad," BT answered.

"Two smart asses, fantastic," Ron said as he stood back up.

"You're letting her go?" Nancy, Ron's wife asked incredulously.

"I tried to stop her, I did. You know how strong-willed she is."

Nancy could only nod. Even from an early age Meredith had been an independent soul. Nancy had never won an argument with her daughter, but they had from time to time come to a mutual agreement that they would stop fighting. Nancy placed her head on Ron's shoulder as she watched her daughter prepare to leave.

Meredith waved to her assembled family and placed the truck in gear. She looked over to BT and kept staring.

"What?" BT asked.

"Seatbelt."

"What about it?"

"I'm not going anywhere until you put yours on," she said stubbornly.

"Are you kidding me?"

"Do I look like I'm kidding?"

BT stared at her long and hard. When he realized intimidation wasn't going to work, he reached behind him and grabbed the buckle. He pulled it across his chest and down towards the locking mechanism; it came up 4" short of its goal. "Can't," he said triumphantly.

"Suck your gut in," Meredith told him.

"I'm not forcing this thing, it'll cut off my circulation!"

"Then you might as well get out now."

"Something wrong honey?" Nancy asked.

"Yeah, apparently someone liked home cooking a little bit more than they should have, Mom!" Meredith yelled back.

"Fine!" BT said, driving the buckle into the lock.

"You look like you're wearing dental floss," Meredith chuckled. "Don't you feel safer now?"

"Just drive," BT said through gritted teeth.

"You're no fun," Meredith said as she took her foot off the brake. She could not help but feel that they were the cavalry and they would get there in the nick of time. She hoped history would prove she was right.

Eliza and Tomas - Interlude

Tommy sat alone in the dark. The room was preternaturally cold; the radiator he was chained to gave forth no heat. Blood and snot intermingled on his top lip, pooling before running into his mouth. The thick liquid did little to quench his insatiable thirst. Fear pressed in from every angle, insidiously worming its way into every exposed crevice in his unnaturally strong mental armor.

"Hello Tomas," a dark voice issued forth from a darker recess in the room.

He knew he was slipping, he had not even noticed when his sister had entered the room. Tomas had stopped pleading with her days ago when he realized the entity that looked like his sister carried none of her legacy traits.

"It is time," Eliza told him.

"God is mad, Lizzie," Tommy sputtered.

When Eliza laughed, a cruel thin metallic sound issued forth. Tommy did not fight when she gripped the top of his head and forced it to the side. As she leaned down, Tommy's screams filled the night.

CHAPTER 6 – Alex, Paul and Company

"Marta, are you alright?" Alex asked his wife with concern. She had been tossing and turning for hours and now moans of despair where coming from deep within her chest.

"NO I WILL NOT!" She said forcibly, sitting straight up.

"Honey it's me. Mi amor."

Eyes wide open, lips pulled back, teeth clenched; terror strained her features. Marta took a half-hearted swipe at Alex before realizing who he was. She stiffened when he hugged her.

"Are you alright?" Alex asked, breaking the embrace to look into her eyes.

Marta's head sagged down. "My head hurts Alex," she said, rubbing her temples.

"Do you want me to get some aspirin Marta?"

"It's a deeper pain than that Alex, I don't know how to explain it. I used to have migraines when I was a teenager, those don't even compare. I feel like something deep in my mind has decided it wants out and it is going to crack my head wide open to do it."

Alex was alarmed. Marta sometimes had a flair for the dramatic but he was not picking that vibe up right now. That she was in immense pain was clearly evident, the whites of her eyes were filled with red lines and he felt powerless to do anything about it. Paul had come up to the doorway of the room the Carbonaras were staying in. The abandoned school that they had sought refuge in had been a perfect fit. Plenty of room and plenty of canned goods in the cafeteria, although there was a reason school food was so horrible, it was of extremely low quality. The words 'Grade E but edible' adorned more than one label.

Paul wore a look of concern. Marta's headaches had become more frequent and more intense. His initial thought was 'tumor' but he didn't think their chances of finding a neurologist were so good.

Much like a migraine, all that seemed to help Marta was extreme dark and extreme quiet. Alex met Paul at the doorway and closed it behind him. Before they had walked more than a pace, Marta's voice floated out to them and froze them both in place. "The darkness matches the void where her soul should be."

Paul could not contain the shiver that started at the base of his spine and like an insidious spider crawled all the way up to his brain stem, all eight legs caressing his creep factor.

"She does not know what she is talking about," Alex told Paul, an insincere smile splashed across his face.

Paul thought otherwise.

CHAPTER 7 – Talbot Journal Entry 5

"Honey I'm sorry," I told Tracy for the fifth time. Dammit, I hate groveling, well maybe I actually love it, I put myself in enough of these situations where it's my only avenue of escape. "Hon, look at me. I feel for these kids, I really do, that's why I don't want to take them with us."

Tracy did finally look at me. "You're right."

She could have punched me square in the gut and not gotten the same effect. We had been married twenty something years and I could count on one finger how many times she had told me I was right. "Wait, what? Could you maybe say that again?"

"Don't push it Mike," she snapped.

Gary was nodding behind her.

"They need to go to Ron's," she said triumphantly.

It was a brilliant idea. Ron would take them in without even blinking. "Hey, which of you guys has a driver's license?" I asked the three boys hopefully.

"I have a permit," Dizz answered, obviously feeling self-important.

"Mike, that's not what I meant. How much have you driven, Dizz?" Tracy asked.

"I pulled out of the driveway once. Clipped the mailbox and then my dad made me get out, he was *not* happy," Dizz answered, his inflated importance quickly deflating.

"Dad!" Justin yelled from the front doors.

"Company?" I asked.

He nodded in return.

Gary grabbed his gear and ran to the front. "Fifteen,

nope sixteen." I could see him doing quick calculations in his head. "Scratch that, eighteen, oh where'd that one come from, nineteen. Does a crawler count, because that would make it twenty,"

"I get it, there's a bunch,"

"Yeah, 'bunch' will work," Gary said, staring out the window intently.

"Couple of speeders, mostly deaders though," Justin clarified.

"Thank God for small favors," I said resignedly.

"Hi pretty lady. Can I get back in your arms?" Angel asked Tracy.

Tracy reached down and plucked the small child up. "Mike, I am not going to entrust these kids to a kid whose driving experience involves backing up in a driveway."

"Umm, it's a very long driveway," Ryan said, trying to help his friend recover some of his lost ego.

"Okay, so his main experience is driving down a very *long* driveway and into a mailbox,"

"That hurts, lady," Dizz said.

"Twenty-five yards, Dad," Travis said as he took position next to his brother and uncle.

"We need to take them, Mike," Tracy told me.

That was the most sound idea, it really was. But I felt like Big Ben was ticking in my head, that elusive concept called time was slipping through my fingers. I, we, could not afford to lose the two days it would take to get them back and then us back on track. 'Crap,' I thought angrily. Leaving these kids here was a death sentence plain and simple. Bringing them forward was a painful death sentence. Bringing them to Ron's was their only chance.

I loved Tracy for a myriad of reasons. She knew the math I was going through in my head, so she solved the problem for me. "I'll take them back."

I was elated, I was depressed. The kids would be safe, my beloved would be safe, we would never see each other again. I hugged her just as our defensive gunfire erupted.

Twenty zombies, three skilled marksmen, they should be able to make short work of it.

"Alright you guys," I said, turning to the kids. "Grab all the crap you want to bring with you. We're getting out of here."

Angel jumped down from Tracy's arms and into her brother's arms. "We're going home Eyean!" she said excitedly.

CHAPTER 8 – BT and Meredith (Plus One)

BT and Meredith had not been on the road more than a couple of hours when Meredith looked over towards BT for the fifth time, each time rolling her window down an inch or two more.

BT on as many occasions stole a sideways glance towards Meredith. He grimly did his best to cover his nose discreetly during the more noxious outbursts.

By the sixth time he could not take it. "What did your aunt make you eat? Damn it girl!"

"Excuse me?!" she answered indignantly.

"Smells like pickled weasel in here. What the hell did you eat?"

"Me?? I thought that seat belt was so tight it was cutting your large intestine in half and it was leaking."

"So it isn't you?" BT asked.

"God no! I thought you must be dying!"

"Pull over, I know of only one thing on this planet that could do *that*."

Meredith pulled over, a look of confusion on her face. BT ripped the belt buckle from its harness, guaranteeing that it would never work again. He opened the door and took heavy intakes of untainted air before opening the back door to look for their stowaway.

"Well son of a bitch. Hi Henry!" BT uttered genially.

Meredith was peering over the seat. "How the hell did he get in there? Should we take him back?"

"Naw," BT said, affectionately rubbing the dog's proffered belly. "I've got a hunch he's supposed to be here."

CHAPTER 9 – Talbot Journal Entry 6

Gary, Travis and Justin came in a few minutes later. "All set?" I asked as I finished packing up the radio. "Yeah," Travis said, a little flushed.

Gary responded by turning his head and vomiting into a convenient trash receptacle, and Justin resumed his vigil at the front window.

"Won't be too long Dad before we get some more company," Justin said.

"Yup, time has her finger in everybody's pie," I responded, my thoughts clouded with worry and anger.

Justin looked at me funny.

"Did I say that out loud?" I went outside, the putrid stink of the dead assailing my nostrils. "Oh yeah, *that* never gets old," I said sarcastically. I walked over to the gas pumps looking over the abandoned cars. The third one I looked at was perfect, mainly for the reasons that the keys were hanging in the ignition and the tank was mostly full.

I had thought foolishly a few months ago that the parting with Paul and Alex was bad. That was topped tenfold when I left the East Coast Talbots, but that paled in comparison to what I was feeling now. I am not a perfect man, I do not claim to be. I am rife with shortcomings and my own sets of insecurities, but somehow Tracy has always been able to bring my better qualities to the fore. For twenty-three years she has been the vital piece that allows me to function correctly in a dysfunctional society. We were parting as cleanly as a rock breaks under the assault of a sledge hammer. There would be, there could be no reunion, we were now two separate parts..

"Mike, you come back to me," she said, grabbing the front of my jacket. I couldn't look her in the eyes, mine were rimmed with tears. "Mike, you bring my boys back," she said, softly beginning to sob. I met her eyes and she saw the truth. She let go of my jacket and stepped back, an inaudible gasp flowing past her clenched mouth.

"Mike you have to promise me!" she said, raising her voice.

"I can't Tracy, it would be an empty one. I will not let my last words to you be a lie."

"Stop! You will promise me! Or I won't go!"

I looked at her and over towards the kids who were waiting expectantly. Would a lie be so bad if it saved six others? "Tracy, please." I wanted her to let me off the hook.

"Listen Talbot, you stubborn bastard. I do *not* want an empty promise. I want a promise that you will not break. I have known you long enough to know that you would rather go to hell, come back, and maybe revisit one more time before you would break your damn word. *That* is what I want from you, not this death march mentality I see in your eyes."

I looked away marshaling my reserves. The best part of me was leaving and she wanted me to be a better man than I was. "How?" I said so softly Tracy did not hear.

"I'm waiting," she said, arms crossed, foot getting ready to start tapping.

"Dad," Justin said. "Multiples coming." Just the way in which he said it implied that this was a major battle about to take place. Saved by zombies, again! I was going to have to send them a Thank You card.

I started to turn to judge the new threat. Tracy grabbed my arm. "Don't even think about it."

I coalesced the scared little boy inside of me. I drew on all the best parts of me that Tracy saw. I reached down, figuratively not literally, and grabbed my balls. "I promise you, I will do all that is within my power to bring all of us home," I told her with conviction.

She stepped in and pulled me close; we kissed. No

further words were needed.

"Um, Mike we gotta go," Gary said as he stepped away from the window.

Tracy quickly told Justin and Travis how much she loved them and that they needed to watch out for each other and especially their dad.

I walked over to a darkened corner. Crying was a solitary endeavor for me; I did not want an audience. Gary grabbed some gear off the table and walked over my way.

"Wanna talk about it?" he asked.

I quickly rubbed away the incriminating evidence from my cheeks. "Do I look like I want to talk about it?" I told him without looking to face him.

"Well I don't know, that's why I asked, and you didn't turn around, so how would I know?"

"It's a good thing you know how to shoot," I said as I brushed by him.

"What's that mean?" he asked as he struggled to catch up to my quick pace.

Speeders were bearing down, we had half a minute tops to get out of here. After that it would take a major gun battle and a shitload of ammo I didn't want to waste on these flunkies. No, this ammo was being especially saved for the queen bee and her minions.

Travis let fly some well-aimed lead. The closest zombie's forward momentum brought his headless body skidding to a halt. Travis' next shot ripped an arm from the elbow down clean off its victim. The zombie did not slow a beat as thick half congealed blood dropped in fat globules from the wound.

Tracy hopped into her new Subaru hatchback after she made sure all the kids were in and secure. She gave me one long look and mouthed words to me which were unmistakable. "You promised."

Gary, Justin, Travis and I set up a small firing line to give Tracy some safe clearance from our pursuers. Legs crumpled, heads disintegrated, blood arced, and still they came. Injuries that should have sent our attackers shrieking into the night had absolutely no effect to the throng. They trampled over their fallen without pause or hesitation, their need to feed far surpassing any other feeling they might possess. But something was happening here, wasn't it? The mere fact that they hunted together implied some sort of cohesion, a hive mentality maybe? Could these ones also be under Eliza's control? How far did her powers extend?

These were all higher functioning questions that I ran through as I took a breath, aimed, fired, reacquired, took a breath, aimed, fired.

"I can do this all day motherfuckers!!" I screamed. They didn't care.

Travis and Gary were running to the far side of the truck as Justin tugged on my sleeve.

"Dad, time for a hasty retreat!" Justin yelled over my death dealing cycle.

I dropped two more before I let my self-preservation kick in. Tracy hadn't been gone more than three minutes and I had almost broken my promise. Yeah, this was starting off just the way I wanted it to.

'I miss you my love, but not as much as I will,' I thought.

CHAPTER 10 – Tracy

"Pretty lady. Why are you crying? My mom says crying makes your asscarrots run," Angel said.

Tracy could only look at the small child in confusion.

"Angie, no swearing!" Ryan berated her from the back seat.

"What?" Angel asked indignantly. "I only told the pretty lady her asscarrots would run! I did not say a bad word!"

Tracy understood now. "Did you mean mascara? My mascara would run?"

Angel nodded as if this is what she had said all along, then she turned around to stick her tongue out at her brother.

"Thank you sweetie. I needed that," Tracy said. "I was crying because I miss my family."

"Like I miss my mommy and daddy?" Angel asked.

"Just like that," Tracy answered her.

"Oh. I don't like that feeling," Angel told her matter-of-factly.

"Me neither, sweetie."

"Will you ever see them again like I will see my mommy and daddy again?"

Tracy wanted to tell Angel that absolutely NOT like that. If Angel's parents were still alive there was a good chance they had been participants in the mob of zombies that had been attacking the rest stop. Tracy was glad they got out of there when they did. She had been fearful that they might have spotted people that the kids had known.

Tracy was vague but Angel only heard the words she wanted to hear. "Someday sweetie, we will all be reunited with the ones we love."

Angel might have missed the subtleness but it was not lost on Ryan. He knew what Mrs. Talbot was trying to avoid saying but wisely thought better of calling her on it. 'I guess this is what it means to grow up,' he thought to himself sourly.

The hours droned on as Tracy drove, deep in her own thoughts. The boys occasionally horsed around in the back seat but it was more of a remembered activity, something they were supposed to do as opposed to wanting to do. They were seeking ways to strive for normalcy in a screwed up world.

It was Dizz who said something first, although Tracy had seen it a few seconds earlier.

"Is that a car?" Dizz asked, leaning over the front seat.

Tracy's heartbeat had accelerated. Absolutely no good came from dealing with zombies, and the odds were near to that bad when dealing with humans, post-apocalyptically speaking. And even a lot of times beforehand now that she thought about it.

"Angel, you scoot down under the dashboard. Boys, I want you to sit up and puff yourselves up. You need to look as big as possible."

Angel didn't argue, she quickly picked up on Tracy's trepidation. Dizz and Sty were a little slow on the uptake.

"What's going on?" Sty asked. He was nervous and now he didn't know why.

"Just do it!" Ryan said, folding his legs under his butt to gain some height.

Tracy wanted to laugh when she looked in the rear view mirror and saw that Ryan was turning varying shades of red as he took in large breaths of air in an attempt to gain bulk. She wanted to tell him to stop before he hurt himself but he was trying and for that she silently thanked him.

The cars were on opposite sides of the highway, hurtling towards each other. Tracy kept her eyes locked forward, not daring to glance over and possibly let them see any signs of weakness.

Dizzy had no such compunction. "Oh my God!" Dizzy said, fear twanging his voice two octaves higher, which immediately had the added effect of de-pubertizing him.

"What?" Tracy asked. She could only picture the worst. Red Neck Number One was alive, jaw-less and seeking revenge. Or it was Eliza herself come to finish them off personally. "Fine!" Tracy steeled herself. "I'll finish the bitch off myself." The words flowed out easier than she would have imagined. Now if she could only infuse some belief into her words she'd be all set.

"I just saw…" Dizz started.

"A man with no jaw?" Tracy finished.

"Ooooh gross," Angel said from under the dashboard. "How does he eat licorice?"

In spite of her fear Tracy still managed a grin at that statement.

"A man with no jaw? No, and I agree with Angie, that *is* gross," Dizz said.

"What did you see?" Tracy asked as she saw red brake lights flare to life in her side view mirror.

"I just saw the biggest man I have ever seen in my life!" Dizz said with amazement.

"What color was he?" Tracy asked. Durgan might be under control to not kill Mike, but she didn't think that extended to the rest of his family or whoever else he might run across.

"What?" Dizz asked. "Oh. He was black."

"You're sure, Dizz?" Tracy asked.

"Positive, and the driver was a white girl. So what?" Dizz asked.

"Can I get out from under here? It smells like feet," Angel giggled.

"Yeah, come on up here sweetie and get your seatbelt back on," Tracy said as she took the Subaru over the grassy median.

*   *   *

BT and Meredith

"Did she see us?" BT asked as he tried to fit his immeasurable bulk under the console. His success rate was much, much less than Angel's.

"Umm let's see. She just crossed over the grass and is now heading this way, so my guess is yes."

"Does everyone in the Talbot family have to go to a special 'smart ass' class before they can be considered an actual family member? I mean, do you guys have to get certified or something?"

"I don't think you're going to fit," Meredith told BT.

"Is she still coming?" BT asked without turning around.

"No, no, she thought better of it. It looks like she's heading the other way."

"Really!?" BT craned his neck around to confirm this new information. "What? She's not turning around!" BT said, more than a little miffed.

"You've known my uncle how long?"

"Hilarious, drive. Let's get the hell out of here."

"I am not driving away from my aunt," Meredith said as she pulled over, placing the car in park and getting out.

"What are you doing? We have to leave!" BT said in alarm.

Meredith peeked her head back in. "You scared of Aunt Tracy? I mean, you should be, she's probably a good buck ten, buck fifteen tops."

"How long you known your aunt?" BT asked in disbelief.

Meredith actually stopped to think about that point. "I guess you have something there. If she has to deal with Uncle Mike then I guess she must have some serious brass tacks."

"Of that I can assure you," BT said, slowly getting

out of the car, dreading the confrontation that was about to ensue.

"Meredith, BT?" Tracy asked as she pulled the car up alongside them and quickly hopped out. "What are you guys doing here?"

"I guess we could ask the same of you," BT said. "Is everything alright, where's Mike and the boys? Okay I get it now," he said after looking over the precious cargo she was hauling in the small hatchback. "Where'd you pick up the vagabonds?"

"We are not bagavonds!" Angel said coming out of the car, yelling at BT's knees. "Mommy says we're Protestants!"

"Holy crap mister, you're huge!" Dizz said, slowly approaching BT as if he were a carnival attraction. Ryan grabbed his sister before the giant inadvertently stepped on her.

"You first," Tracy said, circling back to her original question.

"What do you think?" BT said.

"I wanted to help, Auntie," Meredith said. "I was kinda also hoping that we'd come across Melanie and I could let Dad finally grieve instead of holding onto any false hope."

"And *you*, BT?" Tracy pressed.

"I owe your husband my life Tracy, probably a couple of times over." BT looked at her defiantly for a moment then off into the distance, obviously hoping she would let it slide.

Tracy immediately looked away when she noticed a stubby tail wagging from the rear of Meredith's car. "Henry?" Tracy walked over to open the door and pet the dog.

"See, I told you he was supposed to come," BT said, nudging Meredith. "He just saved my ass."

Henry licked Tracy's face, leaving a trail of saliva down her cheek.

"Oooh gross!" Angel exclaimed as she came up to pat

Henry's broad face. Henry turned his attention to the girl's sticky fingers. Angel squealed in delight as Henry began to clean up all the sugary goodness left behind.

Tracy stood back up, wiping the slime from her face.

"We didn't know he was in the car when we left," BT said, preempting the next question Tracy was sure to ask.

"Yeah we didn't realize he was there until I just didn't think any living human could possibly make that stench, not even BT," Meredith said, pointing towards the big man.

"The more I get to know you Meredith, the funnier you get," BT said.

Meredith did a small curtsy and grinned at him cheekily.

"How do you know where to go? Tracy asked.

"Ron gave us a radio. The plan is to have Mike do his nightly call and then Ron lets us know where he's at."

An idea rapidly began to formulate in Tracy's head. "Meredith, I can't make you do anything you don't want to, but I can ask you."

Meredith's attention was rapt, but Tracy hadn't even begun to ask before Meredith had figured it out. "You want me to take these kids to Dad," she said, her voice full of resignation.

"My kids and husband are out there," Tracy pleaded. "I can't leave them, I can't."

"I understand, Auntie, my sister is out there too though. Even if I don't think she's alive I want to find her."

"I understand, I do. I'm sorry," Tracy said with the full impact of reality striking her square on the shoulders.

"Why don't we all take these kids back and with the two of you driving we'll be able to catch up in half the time," BT reasoned.

Tracy and Meredith both thanked the big man enthusiastically for his idea. Meredith could rid herself of the guilt and Tracy could latch on to hope. Within five minutes they were both heading east on I-90 back towards Ron's.

CHAPTER 11 – Talbot Journal Entry 7

We had been on the road for an hour or two. I was feeling much more subdued than I had been in a long while. We were now a lean band of four, a high powered fire team. I mostly had what I wanted, my wife, daughter and Henry were safe. That stupid adage, be careful what you wish for, came to mind. The dramatist within me always thought Tracy would be stroking my head as I lay dying on the battlefield. Strange thought, obviously, I just figured that would be the way it would play out. The thought of Gary filling in for Tracy just didn't have the same dramatic effect.

"Dad, I really have to piss," Travis said from the back seat.

"How many Dews did you have?" Justin asked his brother.

"Three maybe. I was VERY thirsty," Travis told him.

"Alright," I said noncommittally. I should have just pulled over, there wasn't another car for days and there were plenty of trees. But old habits don't die easily, especially when you aren't paying any attention to them. I drove another five miles to the next rest stop.

Travis nearly popped the hinges off his door in his haste to relieve his floating bladder. Gary got out of the passenger seat. There was an audible 'pop' from his back as he stretched.

"Getting old, huh?" I asked him.

"Why Mom didn't put you up for adoption when she had the chance, I'll never know," he said as he walked away to investigate our surroundings.

"That's not funny," I said to his back.

"Wasn't trying to be," he retorted as he made his weapon ready.

"Nothing quite like family to put you in your place," Justin said humorously, noting our exchange.

"Go keep an eye on your brother before I kick your ass," I said good naturedly.

"DAD!!!" Travis screamed.

Justin and I paused for a second to look at each other before we bolted in the direction of the cry. Gary was already at full tilt. I flipped the safety and placed my finger outside the trigger guard. Something was about to die in a most unnatural way.

My gut was sinking as I ran. I had not heard Travis scream like that... ever. Two football seasons ago he broke his collar bone and fractured his nose all in one play. Blood had streamed from his face and the bone in his collar had been protruding outwards once his shoulder pads had been removed. I had waited by the sidelines, anxious as any parent that watches their child injured on the field. The team trainer had brought out the dreaded golf cart to bring my son to the sidelines to be worked on further.

Travis had shook his head in the negative when they tried to get him to sit on the cart. He walked off the field in an ovation to the injured. His first question to me while we were in the car driving to the hospital was how many games did I think he was going to miss. The bulge in his collar told me the rest of the season, but I let the doctor break the news to him since I had still been within arm's reach of his unbroken side. Even with the broken nose, the broken collarbone and the heartbreak of his season coming to a crash, he hadn't so much as shed a tear. I knew he was bummed by the way he threw his cleats across the waiting room once his x-rays came back, but other than that he took two Advil a day until the pain went away.

Gary was first on the scene. I saw him grab Travis by the shoulder and physically pull him out from the entrance to the small gas station.

"Oh boy," he said as Justin and I met him there.

That I was breathing hard was really bad, the smell that emanated from that open door was a physical assault upon my senses. Why Gary hadn't toppled over I don't know. I veered away before I took in one more pull of the obnoxious odor. The one guy that had survived Armageddon and who arguably had the weakest belly stood there, mouth wide open to the scene laid out before him, and he wasn't puking. Travis walked past me possibly in shock. His face was pale and I don't imagine that he was thinking about the piss that had presented such an urgent need mere moments before.

"You alright?" I asked him, my hands on my knees in the classic, 'I'm about to heave' pose. Jets of saliva weren't quite coating the back of my throat yet in preparation for stomach evacuation but they were calling in all available volunteers to man the pumps.

He waved his hand back at me as he walked slowly towards the truck. He had already gotten back into the truck and was vacantly staring in our direction before I was finally able to stand upright without the immediate impression that I was going to let loose a torrent of bile. Justin had also decided he had seen enough, either that or he wanted to console his little brother. I'm not sure which but he was hightailing it back to the truck too.

"What do you make of this?" Gary asked from the doorway.

I could not get enough air or nerve for that matter to get much closer than the ten feet distance I had now. "I'll be right back, I'm getting the Vicks."

Gary waved at me much as Travis had earlier, but he did not move away from the scene in front of him.

I don't know what I was thinking, the only way Vick's was going to mask the smell from the gas station was if I swallowed the entire container, choked and then died on it. No, this was primarily a futile exercise in stalling. The point seven five seconds during which I had seen the gruesomeness on the floor was all I would ever need or want to see of that.

Tens, dozens, maybe a hundred, (I'm not Rain Man, I can't count that quickly) zombies were piled like cordwood. They were neatly stacked like a farmer would lay out his fire wood for the upcoming harsh winter. They alternated head to toe. What were once men, women and children were laid out like the world's largest funeral pyre. Thick black viscous fluid at least an inch thick lined the entire floor, the only thing keeping it contained within the gas station was the door stop.

"Could you hand me the Vick's?" I asked Justin.

He was leaning in the truck talking to Travis. "You're going back?" he asked as he fumbled around in the first-aid box for the smelly concoction.

"Definitely not out of morbid curiosity. I think there may be some answers there," I told him.

"Let me know what you find out," he replied. He was the smart one that wasn't going back.

I'm pretty sure the label on Vick's warned against what I was about to do, but I'd take my chances. I shoved a wad of it up each nostril. It burned like hell and I was pretty sure I would never smell anything ever again and right now that was just fine with me.

"Let's get this over with," I said to psych myself up.

Gary took one step in to give me access to the doorway. Corroded humans melded into each other, it was difficult to tell where one zombie ended and the other started. Blood, muscle and tendon were all intertwined with their neighbors.

"You think people did this?" Gary asked me. "I mean as a message maybe?"

"A message to whom? Zombies don't care about their brethren. Who would take the time to stack them so neatly?" 'Neatly' just didn't feel like the right word to use. I mean if I was to save Henry's shits and then one day stack them all on top of each other, would you use the word 'neatly' or would you just say, 'Hey there's a huge pile of shit!' I know Henry would have a different take, to him it would be his 'life's work!' his 'Grand Masterpiece.' But that's a different story.

"Eliza then?" He asked.

"It seems like something she would do for some reason. But I don't know, she cares about them less than they care for themselves. I think we're missing something here,"

A small tremor spread through the molasses thick semi-congealed fluid on the floor, a ripple spreading out like a pebble had been thrown into split pea soup. I was watching the small wave as it gently washed over the tow of Gary's boot. "Did you move your foot?" I asked him, looking up at his face.

"No," he said, never taking his eyes off the meat pile in front of him. "Do you think they died? Wait, you know what I mean, did they expire?"

"You sure?" I asked.

"About what? Asking you a question?"

"No, your boot."

"What about it?" he asked a little peevishly because I was not responding to his repose query.

"You didn't move it?"

"Mike, what is wrong with you?" Gary asked, tearing his gaze from the macabre view in front of him. "What the hell is up your nose? You did not shove Vick's up your nose did you? Did you read the damn label? It's people like you that made McDonalds have to put 'Caution , Contents Hot' on the outside of their coffee mugs for Chrissakes."

Another ripple crashed into Gary's boot. "Did you see that?" I asked him as I pointed to the floor.

"I think the Vick's is eating your brain away,"

"Great, maybe the zombies will stop chasing me then," I told him, never peeling my eyes from the floor. "Gary, I think we should get out of here, um probably now. I think they're moving."

"Come on little brother," he said with a condescending lilt. "They're done for, it's just bloating or decomposition, or most likely both of those processes together."

"Would decomposition make an eye open?" I said, taking a quick step back and pointing at the one rheumy gray eye peering longingly up at us.

"Well, maybe," Gary said, matching my hasty withdrawal.

By the time the zombie's arm reached up, Gary and I were in full on retreat.

"Get in the car!!" I yelled to Justin.

"What's going on?" Justin yelled back.

"Is anything behind us?" I yelled to Justin, running at the same time. I was entirely too spooked to look over my shoulder to verify it for myself. "Wish there was a Jumbotron I could look up at to check."

Gary looked over at me but did not question my statement. Running for one's life tends to take precedence over asking questions that aren't directly involved to said Life.

"No, nothing is... ummm, yeah, you guys should run faster!" Justin yelled, hopping in to the truck cab.

We reached the truck. I fumbled with the handle for a split second, long enough to imagine the deep seated pain involved with a bite to my shoulder. The windshield picked up the reflection of zombies hurtling in our direction. No deaders in this chase. As I opened my door I peered back towards the gas station to see tens, dozens, maybe a hundred zombies heading our way. They were in such a rush to get to us that they were jamming up in the doorway like an old Three Stooges scene that took this inopportune time to come to the forefront of my mind.

The truck started and I hauled ass out of that parking lot just as Gray Eyes slammed into the front quarter panel. "You tell Ron about that and you'll be walking home," I stressed.

Gary was too busy white knuckling onto the truck off-road grips to pay me much attention. Within a hundred yards we were safe, but none of us visibly relaxed for another ten miles. Travis kept looking in the rear window, apparently convinced that the zombies were somehow going to be able to keep up with us. I'll be honest, I kept stealing my own glances. I was under the distinct impression that we had just encountered Zombies 3.0 and we as of yet did not know their new and improved powers. Hopefully it was more like most household products bought at a grocery store that *promised* new and improved features but delivered only a higher price tag.

"Dad, what was that?" Travis asked, turning back around from another peek through the looking glass.

"I think they were in stasis," Gary answered, never taking his gaze off the road ahead.

"Hibernation?" I asked for clarification.

"Maybe, that's my guess," Gary said.

"What would make them do that?" Justin asked. Travis was busy looking back again.

"Well bears do it for food, or lack thereof," I said, more talking out loud than to answer his question. Once I friggen said it, I wished I could have pulled it back in.

"Lack of food?" Travis asked, paling. "People you mean? There's not enough people left for them to eat?"

I nodded, sorry I had opened this can of worms.

"How long can they hibernate?" Travis asked.

"Bears can go about three to four months. But fleas can go for like six months and then I think that bedbugs can stay in a stasis state for years, and then there is the Moroccan…" Gary pontificated.

"Enough," I told him. "You're scaring the boy and you're freaking me out."

"Is there any way we can use this to our advantage?" Gary asked.

"Well, the obvious is that there will be less of them just roaming around. And if we can stumble on an orgy of them, we have a couple of minutes of opportunity where we could burn a ton of them, I mean before they awaken and chase us."

"Burn them. Sounds good," Travis said with a slight shiver, as if he wanted to heat himself over the roasting of the zombie pyre.

"What now?" Gary asked me.

"Well, now we find a gas station that is not inhabited by the dead and we use Ron's handy dandy hand pump to fill up a bunch of gas containers. So the next time we'll be prepared," I told him determinedly.

"That's as good a plan as any," Gary said.

"It's about time I had one," I told him.

"Amen to that," Travis said, stealing one last backwards glance.

CHAPTER 12 – Alex and Paul

North Carolina was a balmy 58 degrees, and the trees were resplendent with early spring greenery. Life was burgeoning. Well, that's an untrue statement, *plant* life was doing wonderfully and would absolutely flourish in this new world as man's poison-laced waterways and smoke filled air finally gave way to the pristine, as nature had always intended. Man's brains had removed him from nature and now ironically it was this very same brain that was going to return the earth back to its rightful owners.

The small band of survivors had wisely avoided Charlotte, instead taking the beltway to the outer limits of the city. Paul knew of what he thought would be a perfect haven. Furniture City Warehouse turned out to be just that. It was a large corrugated blue steel building, one main entrance for customers and then loading docks in the rear for them to pick their purchases up.

"It's locked," Paul said, turning back to the throng.

"Were you expecting a 'Welcome' sign?" Mrs. Deneaux asked him in her usual acerbic manner.

"You really are tough to get along with," Mad Jack said, stooping to get a closer look at the lock.

"Do you have a hammer?" Alex asked Mad Jack.

"Even better," Mad Jack told them. He patted down all of his pockets until he came across what he was feeling for. It was a lock picking device that looked much like a small pistol. "Working for the DoD sure had its perks," MJ said, placing the picking device into the lock. He began to rapidly pull the triggering mechanism.

"That standard issue?" Paul asked skeptically.

After another ten seconds of fiddling with the device, Mad Jack stood up with a satisfactory 'Aha' sound.

"Is it open or not?" Mrs. Deneaux asked. "Do you need all the theatrics?"

"Oh, put a sock in it," Joann told Mrs. Deneaux as she pulled the door open.

"Hold on!" Alex told her. "We don't know what it's like in there."

"It's a furniture store. And an inexpensive one at that. So unless zombies have started eating vinyl we should be fine," Mrs. Deneaux said, although she did not volunteer to go in first.

Joann's initial haste to get indoors was quelled at the idea that the dark store could be hiding a variety of nightmares.

"We should be safe," Paul stated. "No food means no people, no people…"

"No zombies," Little Eddy finished the sentence.

"You got it," Mad Jack said, pulling a flashlight off the utility belt he was wearing and heading into the murkiness.

The majority of the group huddled behind that one light as they checked furniture display after furniture display looking for anyone or more importantly anything that didn't belong. The only notable exceptions were Joann and April who were standing guard by the front doors and Mrs. Deneaux who had found a Lazy Boy Recliner and had fallen fast asleep.

It took over an hour to go through the entire showroom floor, the loading bays and the offices, but it was well worth it. There were four fully stocked vending machines with all sorts of snacks from nuts to licorice. Eddy was at first ecstatic to come across an ice cream machine and then severely depressed when he realized he was standing sneaker sole deep in the melted treats.

"Do you think anything's still in there?" Eddy asked Erin.

"Oh honey, I don't think so," she told him and then hugged him before he started to cry again, something he had been doing a lot of since his mother had executed his family and then turned the gun on herself.

"You going to use your fancy lock picking device on this?" Paul asked, pointing to the vending machine.

"Step aside," Mad Jack told him. The loud splintering crash as he threw a display vase through the glass awoke the slumbering Deneaux.

"What the hell is going on in there!" she yelled from across the floor.

"Everyone's fine!" Paul yelled. "You old bat," he said much more softly.

Mad Jack giggled like a schoolgirl. "She really is, isn't she?" he said, stating a fact more than formulating a question.

"See," Paul started. "Mrs. Deneaux is proof to me that God has one hell of a sense of humor. End of the world, and the crankiest 75 year old bitch that can't shoot, can't run, can't fight, couldn't make a friend in a whorehouse on payday and *she* survives. Armies of the finest men and women on this planet have been ground to dust and yet that cantankerous hag still mouths on."

"Don't hold back Paul. Tell us how you really feel," Alex said, coming up to pat his friend on the shoulder.

"She just gets under my skin." Paul shook his head.

"Like a rash?" Eddy asked.

"A lot like that," Paul laughed. "Come on kid, grab the stuff you like the most," he said as he lifted Eddy up to a bird's eye view of the treats in front of him.

"I think we're safe for the time being," Mad Jack stated. "I'm going to lock the front doors, unless anyone has an objection to that." He waited for a few beats before heading off.

Alex cleaned up some of the stray glass around the machine and started surveying what his kids might want and that might be somewhat healthy, not an easy task when dealing with vending machine food.

"Alex, can you hold the baby, I'm not feeling so well," Alex's wife Marta asked.

Alex was midway between deciding on licorice or peanuts when he turned to honor his wife's request.

"Marta, what's wrong?" Alex asked in alarm. The lighting was not good but it could not hide the fact that his wife was as pale as a cold winter moon. Black crescents ringed the bottom of her eyes, and her eyes themselves were as dark as craters.

"Mi Dios!" Alex exclaimed as he grabbed the baby and almost simultaneously his wife as she very nearly collapsed.

Erin quickly took the baby as Alex eased his wife to the floor. "Marta, what's the matter?" Alex fairly cried. Marta did not look well and the transformation from bad to worse was happening right before their very eyes. Paul was watching it too, he thought it looked like those time lapsed photographs they sometimes showed for some special effects make-up make-over. This was much scarier than watching Lon Chaney become a werewolf, this was real.

"Alex, let's get her to a bed," Paul said.

Alex looked up and nodded, then picked his wife up in his arms. "You're so cold, Marta. Talk to me mi amor."

"It's in my head," she whispered in his ear.

A spike of iciness plunged down the middle of his back. "Who's in your head Marta? Eliza?"

She shook violently, with a force that almost caused Alex to drop her. "Much worse, it's Tommy!"

CHAPTER 13 – Tracy's Car

"That guy was huge!" Dizz was telling Sty, as if Sty hadn't been there to witness it himself. "His bicep was bigger than my thigh," Dizz added with amazement, as he sized himself up.

"Yeah, like that's hard to do? Mrs. T's arms are probably bigger than your spindly legs."

Tracy and Dizz simultaneously yelled out, "Hey!"

"I meant no disrespect to you Mrs. T," Sty added slyly, leaving Dizz out of the response.

"Hey pretty lady we should have taken the doggie," Angel said to Tracy. "I would have been able to hold him in my lap."

Tracy looked over to the small girl. "Honey, I think he's bigger than you. You would have had to sit in *his* lap."

"Dogs have laps?" Angel asked in wonderment.

"It's a figure of speech," Ryan said from the back seat.

"I've got your finger of speech right here!" Sty said, flipping his friend off.

"Oh, I'm telling!" Angel said, catching a glimpse of the 'dirty finger,' as her mom used to call it. When she realized there was no one she could tattle to even though she was only playing, she started to go back down the path of sadness.

Tracy watched the girl's head bow. "Plus it wouldn't have been safe to bring Henry in this car," Tracy told her.

"Why, is he mean?" Angel asked. "Does he have big teeth?"

"No, way worse."

"Way worse?" Dizz asked with concern. "Does he have rabies or something?"

Tracy shook her head in the negative.

"Come on Mrs. T, what gives, does he turn into a werewolf or something?" Sty asked, getting sucked in.

Angel sat up straighter so that she could look through the windshield at the car they were following. Henry was seemingly staring straight back at them. Angel ducked down under the dash to be out of his line of sight. "I think he knows we're talking about him," she whispered to Tracy.

All three boys followed Angel's lead and peered into the lead truck. "Does he know?" Dizz asked, getting himself a little spooked.

Tracy was a moment away from dismissing the thought, but the more she looked at Henry the more she thought that maybe on some level he did know.

"Is that why he's dangerous?" Angel asked. "Because he can read thoughts? If I think of dog biscuits will he like me?" Angel scrunched up her face. Tracy imagined that she was thinking hard about dog cookies.

"Henry's dangerous because of his *farts*!" Tracy said, emphasizing the last word.

Angel's deep thought lapsed as she started to laugh out loud. The desired effect Tracy was shooting for was met.

"Really?" Dizz asked. "Because right now he looks mad," he added, pointing to the back of the truck.

Of course they couldn't hear him but Henry was barking up a storm. Tracy was left to wonder if maybe the dog had another trick or two up his sleeve.

* * *

Meredith's Car

"We really should have made Henry ride in Tracy's car," BT lamented as he pulled his shirt over his face. "You should call your dad and let him know we're coming back."

"You do realize I'm driving, right?" Meredith told

him through clenched teeth, hoping that she would be able to filter some stink that way.

"Fine, but if I pass out from the fumes, it'll be on you," BT said, turning around to fumble with the radio.

"I'm willing to take that chance," Meredith told him.

"Yo, crazy Talbot number one!" BT yelled into the handset.

"Damn! You get any louder and he'll pick up your echo."

"Sorry," BT said sheepishly.

"BT? This is Ron, you're early, everything okay?" Ron asked.

"Yeah, Tracy found us out and is bringing some kids back," BT told him.

"What? Okay BT, let's start as if I'm not there and I have no idea about what you're talking about."

BT spent the next few minutes laying out all that had transpired that day.

"Man, I'm glad you've got Henry," Ron said.

"I'm not," BT said.

"I've been looking for him for hours. Mike would have killed me. How long before you get back here?" Ron asked.

BT turned to Meredith for an answer. "Three hours tops according to your pain-in-the-ass daughter."

"Yeah, try living with her for the better part of twenty-three years," Ron voiced.

"Dad?!" Meredith exclaimed.

"Love you honey," Ron said. "See you guys in a few hours. Out."

"I think I can come to like that guy," BT said with a smile on his face as he sat back down. "Wake me when we get there." He folded his arms and rested his head against the headrest. As his eyes closed he was nearly asleep, Ron's pain pills taking full effect.

"BT, wake up!" Meredith said, shoving his arm as hard as she could. He barely moved. "BT, get your ass up!"

Meredith yelled this time.

"Damn girl, you made good time, we there already?" BT asked as he stretched his arms out.

"Not quite. We've only been driving about an hour and a half."

"Why isn't the car moving?" BT sat up straight. He followed Meredith's line of sight. About a quarter of a mile up the roadway was a roadblock.

"It's cops," Meredith said.

"Doubtful," BT finished.

Tracy had pulled up alongside Meredith's car on BT's side. She rolled down her window. "What do you guys think?" Tracy asked. Angel was peering over Tracy's lap to get a better look at the mountain of a man.

"Even if they were cops once, which I'm not inclined to believe, I don't think that they are out right now 'to serve and to protect.'"

"Kind of what I thought," Tracy agreed.

BT thought she looked scared. 'Makes sense,' he thought, 'I am.'

"Any ideas?" Tracy asked hopefully.

"What's the worst that could happen?" Meredith asked.

"I know you didn't just ask that," BT said.

"BT, I don't want to go guns all a blazing with the kids in the car."

"Hey pretty lady, the policeman turned his lights on," Angel said, pointing up the road.

"Yeah and the other one is waving for us to come up there," Meredith noted.

BT turned to the backseat and grabbed a rifle to make sure it was loaded, then turned the radio back on. "Ron, this is BT, over."

A few moments later a response came forth. "Hi BT this is Mark, did you find my sister yet?" Ron's youngest asked.

"Not yet buddy, is your dad there?" BT said, looking

over his shoulder to see if the police were advancing.

"We had another zombie come up this morning, almost got to the house because Gary wasn't there to guard anymore," Mark said.

"Yeah, I heard that before," BT answered, paying absolutely no attention to Mark. "Hey Mark, I need your dad, it's pretty important,"

"He's outside, he's setting up some fencing."

"Don't care kid, GO GET HIM!" BT said with force.

"Ass," Mark said as he let the mic drop and hit the floor. BT and Meredith jumped from the loud noise in the cab of the car.

"The second cop just got in his car," Tracy said with alarm.

"Meredith, grab the binoculars and see if there are other people in those cars," BT told her, clutching the microphone. Any harder and he was going to have a handful of plasticized dust.

It was a stand-off at the moment, Tracy and Meredith's cars versus the two cop cars.

"Twice in one day, to what do I owe this honor," a slightly out of breath Ron asked.

"Got some issues Ron. We're about an hour and a half away from the homestead and we've come up on a roadblock."

"Military?" Ron asked.

"I wish, cops or at least guys pretending to be cops. They have the cars and they have the uniforms but it doesn't feel right."

"Dad," Meredith said loudly. We just got off of 95 at Augusta and we're on Route 3."

"I know where you're at honey. Listen BT, that's a great place for an ambush, there's nowhere to turn off. Have they seen you?"

"That would be an affirmative," BT said.

"Okay, how far away are you from them?"

"Quarter mile tops, and they've both entered their

cars, so by the time we whip a U-turn and get out of here, they'll be right on us. And to make it even funner, they look like they're driving the old school 442 Interceptors, we can't outrun them,"

"Why would we want to outrun the cops?" Angel asked BT.

"Ryan, get your sister's seatbelt back on, please," Tracy requested quietly.

"Come on sis. Sit back down." Angel fidgeted and squirmed but finally acquiesced to her older brother.

"This is so cool, we're going to run from the cops," Sty said with a glint in his eye.

"Shut up you idiot," Ryan said as he punched his friend in the arm.

"You're on a straightaway BT, they did it on purpose," Ron said. "My suggestion is to go straight at them. I'll get in my truck now and head your way. With the speeds we're going to be going you only need to hold them off for forty minutes before some help gets there."

"That might be thirty-nine minutes too late. They're rolling, Ron." BT said softly.

"I'm leaving now," Ron said. "I have a radio in the truck, stay in touch, tell Meredith to stay on Route 3 even when she gets to the Route 1 turn off. Let's see if we can give these assholes something to think about. Out."

"You hear that, right?" BT asked Meredith. She nodded. "Glad you came now?"

"Not so much," Meredith told him honestly.

BT turned to Tracy. Her knuckles were glowing stark white on the steering wheel. "Tracy," BT said. She turned towards him. "When they get within a hundred feet or so, I'm going to give you the signal to go. Once we get past them, I'm going to have you stay in the lead and Maria Andretti here," he said tapping Meredith on the shoulder, "is going to stay between you and the cruisers. You got that?" Tracy nodded imperceptibly. "Just stay on Route 3, don't slow down for anything. If anything happens to us you keep going, you understand? You keep those kids safe." Tracy's face nearly matched her knuckles. "This might be nothing,"

"Do you believe that?" Tracy asked BT.

"Not at all," he answered.

The two cop cars rolled to a halt within a hundred or so yards from Meredith and Tracy. "Citizens. this is Officer Gibson of the Portland Police Department, I am going to need to have all of the occupants of those two cars exit and lay flat down on the pavement," the authoritative voice issued forth from the megaphone mounted under the hood.

"I can see the barrels of a couple of rifles in the first car," Meredith whispered. "It's like they're hiding or something."

"I'm pretty sure they can't hear you," BT said. "But on a worse note, only people that are doing something wrong need to hide."

"Citizens," Officer Gibson's voice said again. "Flash your headlights if you heard and understand my instructions."

Meredith looked over to BT. He nodded. Anything that bought them a few extra moments was fine. She flipped her headlights on, as did Tracy.

The first car crept up another hundred yards. 'Officer Gibson' stepped out, the car microphone still in hand. "Red Subaru, I want you and your occupants to exit first. Slowly," he added.

Tracy looked over to BT. He nodded in the negative.

"NOW!" Officer Gibson shouted through the megaphone.

BT got out of Meredith's car, puffing himself as large as possible trying to impose fear. It worked. Officer Gibson took an involuntary step back and placed his hand on the hilt of his holstered weapon.

"I said the Subaru first," the officer said sharply.

"Yeah, they aren't much in a complying mood!" BT shouted.

"This isn't a request!" the officer shouted, putting his

microphone down. "We are the law!"

BT laughed. "Where have you been, man! There IS no law!"

"I'm going to ask you one more time," the cop shouted in warning.

"And then what? You gonna take the *law* into your own hands?" BT mocked him.

"This is a checkpoint and we are authorized to search every car that comes this way."

"Then I can solve all of our problems, we'll just turn around and you can search the next *citizen* that comes along!"

"I'm not going to tell you again, *NIGGER,* get your ass on the pavement."

"Go fuck yourself pig wannabe," BT answered, remarkably calm. "I think that went well," BT told Meredith as he reentered the car.

Meredith's eyes were huge. BT was under the impression she didn't think it went quite as spectacularly.

"You ready Tracy?" BT turned and asked her.

"Kids, you keep your heads down," she said, staring at each one of them until they gave her a sign that they would do what she asked.

"Meredith when I tell you, I want you to head right for the illustrious Officer Gibson and hopefully we'll get lucky."

"You… you want me to hit him?"

"Oh no hon, I want you to run his cracker ass over," BT told her with a smile on his face.

"I think I'm going to be sick."

"First things first. GO!" He shouted at Meredith and Tracy simultaneously.

The rear tires on the truck momentarily spun in place before leaving black skids. Tracy's Subaru struggled to meet the initial thrust of Meredith's truck. Meredith started to creep over to the right to avoid the cop car. "Hit him Meredith," BT said calmly.

Officer Gibson was a doughnut away from becoming road kill. As it was, he was fairly certain his ankle had been shattered as the giant's girlfriend's car slammed into his door and slammed it into his leg as he dove in a futile attempt to get out of the way.

"FUCK!" Officer Gibson shouted.

"You all right Aaron?" the lone male occupant in the back of the car asked, sitting up.

Gun shots rang out as the two cars sped past the idling cruisers.

"I think my damn ankle is broken," Officer Gibson gritted out through his teeth as he plowed through the contents of his middle console. He found the prescription bottle he was searching for and immediately downed three Oxycontins, courtesy of the last car they had pulled over. The occupants of that ill-fated voyage now found themselves lying face down in the grass not a mile from this exact location. The bitch had wailed when Officer Gibson had taken her pills, something about chronic back pain. 'Yeah, well, now you've got chronic face pain,' he'd said as he drilled her hard in the face with a right hook. The four men he was with had all laughed as Mrs. Pinchant fell to the ground, blood flowing profusely from her split lip and the gap where her tooth used to reside. Her husband cried equally as hard after the third member of the rogue police force lined up and punted his balls up into his sternum. After Mr. Pinchant died from the blunt force trauma, the men proceeded to piss on his body.

The real 'fun' came as they placed his head by the rear wheel of the cruiser. Two of the men held Mrs. Pinchant's heaving body still so that she could watch as Officer Gibson slowly ran over Mr. Pinchant's head. The tire gripped the front portion of his face, and his cheek and nose began to pull away from his face under the pressure. For a moment the heavy car started to 'climb' up his face, but gravity was not on Mr. Pinchant's side as bone after bone began to crack and shatter from the pressure. The back of his head started to swell to almost twice its normal size before it burst under the strain. Brain matter shot nearly 30 feet away from the back of the cruiser and the men laughed. Mrs. Pinchant had long since passed out from the strain. The two holding her released her. Her head bounced off the ground teeth first, shattering four or five of them in the process. She regained consciousness five minutes later, shrieking in pain and horror as she was placed next to her husband's deformed, deflated head.

"Job! Shut her up!" Officer Gibson said as he cupped his hands over his ears. "She's louder than that stupid Cockatoo my wife just had to have."

Job walked over to her and placed one round through her right ear. He stared for a few seconds longer before commenting, "I guess what they say is true," then turned and walked away.

"What's true?" Kyle, the third member of the gang asked.

"That the longer a couple stays married the more they start to look alike," Job said with a wicked grin.

Kyle walked over to the dead pair and tried to find any similarities. "I don't see it Job."

"Don't worry about it," Officer Gibson, the man in charge said. "Drag these two off the street and let's see what this car has to offer."

Kyle did what he was told, studying both people as he did so. When the task was finally complete he went over to a lounging Job. "I get it now, it's because both of their heads are blown up."

Job winked, clucked his tongue and tapped his head.

"I knew it!" Kyle said, happy he had figured the puzzle out.

"What now, Boss?" Wes, the fourth of the deadly horsemen, asked as he piled up the belongings of the Pinchants' car into the trunk of the cruiser for sorting, "This is sure easier than going house to house looking for stuff."

"And funner," Job added.

"Now we wait," Officer Gibson said, getting back into his car. He slowly rubbed his temples as one killer of a headache began to let its true intentions be known. "And find me some damn aspirin!" he barked.

"Even better Boss!" Wes said as he shook the bottle of pain pills in front of the quickly blurring vision of the officer.

"Give me those," Gibson said, grabbing the bottle out of Wes' hand before the rattling noise threatened to split his skull. "And stop calling me 'Boss.' You're not on a Southern chain gang!"

"You got it Bos… Aaron," Wes said as he left before Aaron could let lose a tirade.

Wes was already forgotten as the officer opened the bottle of meds. He couldn't see clearly enough to make out what the medication or the dose was, but he figured two seemed like a safe amount on top of the three somethings he had taken earlier. Little did he know that there weren't enough pills in the bottle to cure the true cause of his pain, arteriovenous malformation, unless of course he took ALL of them at once. The good officer's head was leaking internally and without some serious medical attention he would be dead in three weeks. The pain pills did what most good pain pills do; they allowed him to drift off into a pain free sleep environment. But even his sleep was haunted with pain, pain of a different kind, but pain nonetheless.

*   *   *

"Hey hon, I'm home. Left a little early, that friggen' headache was starting to come on. We got any liquid pain killer?" This was Officer Gibson's joking way of referring to beer. "Hon?" he asked as he placed his duty belt on the hook by the door. The house was quiet. That wasn't too unusual, his wife Wendy was often out with their 4-year-old son Aaron Jr. But he could hear the television in the family room and the kitchen light was on. Wendy was very particular about conserving power, her contribution to the green movement. She would even admonish him if he stared into the fridge too long without grabbing something.

Cops are nothing if not paranoid, and that quality had saved more than one during their careers. Aaron grabbed his 9mm Walther out of his duty belt. He quietly chambered a round and slowly walked towards the family room. He attempted to regulate his heartbeat as he moved past the kitchen, but this wasn't some punk perp's house, this was his home. Wendy and AJ were his world; he was a cop so he could do his part to make the world a better place for them. But if the scum of the planet had somehow made way into his private sanctuary, hell would not have enough in its coffers to pay the note.

"Wendy?" He asked softly, barely loud enough to be heard past his mouth. The sound waves would never make it down the hallway, much less around the corner and into AJ's bedroom where more light was spilling from. He decided to forgo the family room and check AJ's first. "AJ?" Aaron's heart was now threatening to rupture through his rib cage. His cop sense was pegged out; all was not right. He slowly maneuvered down the hallway, keeping his pistol in front of him. Silently he moved his feet forward, hoping he would find Wendy rocking their child to sleep, instead of the images of so many crime scenes that kept flashing through his head.

"They're both asleep," he said softly, his right foot moving ahead of the left. "He was cranky and just needed a nap." His left foot pushed past his right. "And Wendy was tired also." His right foot came to rest by the entrance to AJ's bedroom. "So she took a nap too." He took a big breath to try and quell the panic that threatened to overtake him. Small sounds were escaping through the doorway. They were not the comforting sounds of Wendy's heavy sleeping breaths or the mumbling chatter that AJ sometimes made during his naps. It was a clacking noise that reminded him of the old toy monkeys that would crash the little cymbals together. But that wasn't it exactly, that noise was too tinny. This had a sound more like two dice crashing together. Officer Gibson took that final step from the hallway into the threshold of the bedroom and out of the realm of sanity forever.

"AJ?" Aaron asked. His 4 year old son was standing with his back to his father over the prone body of his mother. Wendy was lying face down on the floor; an ever expanding pool of blood encircled the pair. The fatherly part of Aaron wanted to put his gun down and rush to the aid of his wife and son. The cop part of him hesitated. "AJ?" he asked again. AJ acknowledged his father's presence this time. He turned, his face bathed in blood, strips of flesh hanging from his mouth. His hands were covered elbow deep in gore.

"AJ, what did you do?" Aaron asked his son. AJ took a step towards his dad. Aaron backed up until his back was against the far hallway wall. AJ kept coming. "AJ, please. Please stop," Aaron said, his gun shaking wildly. AJ teetered a step, almost losing his footing in the slick liquid that coated the flooring. "That's a bad boy," Aaron said. AJ was beyond caring about his father's approval and relentlessly pressed on.

Aaron closed his eyes as he sprayed the immediate area with three pistol shots. The first shot popped into the doorframe sending a shower of splinters into his child's room. The second shattered his son's left leg and the third completed the deed. The round entered to the left of the child's nose and exited at the base of his skull. The sound of the bullets being shot could not compete with the solid thud of impact as AJ's body met the floor. Aaron spent a few more seconds looking past the lifeless body of his son to that of his wife. There would be no recovery from the 3 inch wide, 2 inch deep wound in his wife's neck; blood had already ceased to flow.

He shut the bedroom door, walked down the hallway, grabbed a beer out of the fridge and sat down in his favorite chair. His headache had begun to crystallize into a white hot inferno of pain. He pressed the cold container against his head before taking long pulls to quench the sickness that begged to issue forth. Within minutes he had fallen asleep.

When he woke, Aaron Gibson, respected policeman, loving husband and doting father would never view the world in the same way again. The bleeder in his head, his dead wife and the son he killed would never allow it. He didn't remember lighting his house on fire, but as his police cruiser pulled out of the driveway and he took one last glance at his house, it sure did seem like the right thing to do.

*   *   *

"Company!" Wes said, startling Aaron out of his drug coma.

"Why they sitting there?" Kyle asked.

"Because they're smart," Officer Gibson replied as he took out his binoculars and looked at the car and truck that were a quarter of a mile or so away. "Looks like they got plenty of stuff in there too."

"Any women?" Wes asked.

"Hell," Job said. "If you were so horny why didn't you hook up with that lady?" he asked, pointing to the approximate location where Mrs. Pinchant's body rested.

"I've got my standards," Wes said sardonically.

"What about the women's standards?" Kyle asked, laughing.

"Shut up. All of you," Officer Gibson said. The constant talking got to him sometimes, but when his head was throbbing like it was now he couldn't take any of it. "It looks like there's at least two of them and plenty of stuff from what I can tell." His vision had cleared somewhat since his nap but it wasn't the 20-20 he was used to.

"Let's play this cool." Job told Wes. "And maybe you can fuck a live woman this time."

"She was still warm," Wes said in his defense.

At one time Officer Gibson would have just put a bullet in the degenerate's head. Now, he just didn't care. The world was anarchy and he was doing his part to keep it that way.

*   *   *

BT had tried to place some well-aimed shots in the second cruiser as they passed it by but Meredith had nearly lost control of her car after she slammed into the police car.

"Okay, I know you act a lot like your uncle, do you need to drive like him too?" BT half wailed as he pulled the rifle back in.

"Sorry," she replied softly. "I… I just tried to kill a cop."

"No you didn't, you tried to save our lives. Now drive faster!"

Tracy had passed on the left as Meredith fought to regain control. The two cars came close enough that sliding anything thicker than a folded piece of paper between the two vehicles would have been impossible.

Dizz's eyes had grown to twice their size as he watched BT get closer and closer. "That would have been bad," he said as Meredith slid further back.

"I think I crapped myself," Sty revealed.

"Please tell me he's trying to be funny?" Tracy asked as she pressed harder down on the accelerator.

"Not so much!" Ryan yelled as he pinched his nose closed.

"Sty pooped himself!" Angel said happily from underneath the dashboard. "Poopedy-poop!" And then she went into her own made up song that was drowned out by the sound of the wind whipping through the car as all four windows were opened to capacity as they sped down the highway.

It took five full miles, but even at speeds in excess of 100 miles per hour the 'cops' soon caught up to their prey and they were pissed.

Shots began to ring out but at these speeds nobody was in a rush to stick their head out for too long and take a well-placed one. Meredith had scooted so far down she looked like a 99-year-old osteoporosis sufferer.

"There is no way you can actually see where you're going," BT told her.

"I can see enough," she answered, her hands almost above her head on the steering wheel.

"Meredith, BT! This is Ron, what's your status?" blasted from the radio.

BT reached his arm over the bench seat to grab the handset. He took the cue from Meredith that maybe a low profile was a good idea.

"Hey, Ron!" BT yelled over the noise of the road and the percussions of the bullets. "We've got two very angry cop cars on our ass, we're topped out at about a hundred and five and I don't think their cars are even laboring. We won't be able to do this for very long, her heat gauge is already starting to move up."

"How far until you get to Route 3?" Ron asked.

BT looked over to Meredith.

"Twenty minutes Dad!"

Ron's heart dropped as he listened to the anguish in his daughter's voice. "When you get to Route 3 remember to keep going straight, but you're going to have to slow down, I'll never be able to catch up."

"Speed is the only thing keeping us in the game, Ron," BT explained. "How far are you from there?"

"22 to 25 minutes," Ron said. Even over the airwaves BT could hear the rev of Ron's truck tach up an extra thousand or so revolutions.

"What if we start to slow down now?" BT asked.

Ron immediately grasped the implicit meaning.

"Ambush?"

"You got it."

"Dad, hurry!" Meredith threw in at the end as if that wasn't already a foregone conclusion.

"I'm coming honey," Ron reassured her.

"Ever watch Nascar?" BT asked.

"Are my front teeth missing or something?" Meredith

shot back.

"Okay, point taken. Listen, I want you to drop down to around 70 or so. When you do that, Tracy is going to start to pull away and I guarantee you that one of those cop cars is going to try and get her."

"Uh-huh," Meredith said slowly, taking in the information.

"You're not going to let them though."

Meredith stole a glance over towards BT as if to see if he was bullshitting her, "Um, how am I supposed to do that?!" she fairly cried.

"Well, see, if you watched car racing you'd know," BT said with a smile he didn't feel.

"Um, excuse me, *you* don't look much like a Nascar follower yourself."

"You're right, more of an Australian rules football fan myself. Brisbane Lions are my team."

"You're kidding me right?" Meredith shot him an incredulous look.

"Never about the Lions."

"Fine, what do I need to do?"

"Just stay in front. When they swerve to get over, *you* swerve to block them."

BT knew it was an exercise in futility, but it would buy Tracy and Ron a few very precious minutes. Eventually the two trailing cars would see the ruse and instead of following in a line they would come up side by side. No matter how much Meredith swerved, she would not be able to block both at the same time.

"I'm scared, BT," Meredith said as she took a deep breath.

"I don't know if it's appropriate right now, but somehow your crazy Uncle Mike convinced me that this was sound logic and I fell for it. We were surrounded by zombies, no hope of rescue, and low on bullets. He looks over at me, his face serious as a heart attack and he shrugs his shoulders and goes, 'What the hell BT, you only die once.'"

Meredith mulled it over for a few seconds and then looked over at BT and started laughing.

"That's exactly what I did! Ease up now," BT cautioned, placing his hand on her arm.

Tracy began to rocket down the roadway. In a few more minutes she'd be a fading memory.

It didn't take Officer Gibson long to see the ploy for what it was. He grabbed his police radio. "Job, get up here and get that other car before it gets good and gone. This one is mine," Aaron said as he tapped the bumper of the slowing truck.

"He hit us!" Meredith yelled.

BT was thinking they'd be lucky if that was all he did. BT didn't hesitate as he blew out the back window with rifle shots.

Officer Gibson swerved to the left as a bullet came dangerously close to his ear. "He shot at me!" he yelled to Wes as if that was beyond the realm of any conceivable possibility. "Wes?" Aaron looked over to Wes and saw a gaping wound in his chest pulsing blood. Wes looked over towards Aaron, the hiss of air as it escaped his punctured lung louder than the air that came in through the damaged windshield.

"I think I'm hit, Boss," Wes said without any volume to the words.

Aaron was amazed Wes could even speak; his body was hissing like a blown out tire. "Wes, I know we went to the Academy together but I've never really liked you."

Wes looked more hurt from the words than the wound. His breath started to hitch as he struggled to get elusive air into his system. Blood and carbon monoxide were becoming his biggest enemies, but none of them could compete with Officer Gibson.

Aaron removed his pistol from his holster and drilled Wes straight through his outstretched hand and into his forehead. He was dead before what was left of his head collided with the passenger side window. "Now I'm going to have to clean that!" Aaron shouted as the gore from Wes' head streaked down the window and the upholstery.

BT watched the entire exchange, hoping that the wounding of the cop's partner would take him out of the game. When it didn't he turned to Meredith, "You should probably speed up now."

"Make up your mind!" Meredith screamed, partly because of the voluminous amounts of air that were cascading in from the rear but mostly because she was scared shitless.

"Definitely faster," BT said as he started to reload his magazine, fingers fumbling nervously with the shells. 'If the cracker was crazy enough to shoot his own friend that doesn't leave much room for doubt with what he'd do to us,' BT thought.

* * *

Aaron stopped long enough to push Wes from the car.

"Jesus, Aaron. What the hell happened?" Job asked as he pulled his car next to the other cruiser.

"Did I tell you to stop?" Aaron screamed.

Job rolled up his window and floored it.

"Dude, I watched him shoot Wes," Kyle said, looking nervously back as Aaron got back into his cruiser. "That man is crazy, we need to get out of here."

Job looked at his rear view mirror. Aaron was gaining rapidly even though Job himself was doing 95. "I think you're right, he's been acting crazier than an evangelist on acid."

Kyle stopped looking back to look over at Job. "What does that even mean?"

"How the hell do I know? I was under pressure for an analogy and that was the best I could do. But think about it."

"Yeah, I guess that would be pretty bad."

"He's almost on us. No, don't turn around, he might suspect something. Let's just have some fun with these people, kill them and then we'll maybe leave tonight. When he takes   those pills he'll be out for hours."

"Good plan, then hurry and catch them because I want to get away from him as soon as possible."

The cruiser easily climbed to 110 and Job had his foot only about three-quarters of the way down.

*   *   *

Tracy ripped onto the Route 3 off ramp, tires squealing like live pigs shoved through a deli counter slicer. All the occupants were thrown to the left, threatening to overturn the car with the inertia. Angel was damn near in Tracy's lap. Dizz, Sty and Ryan were pressed so tightly together they could exchange undergarments and nobody would be the wiser.

"Damn, lady!" Sty said as he tried to pry his mouth away from Dizz' elbow. Ryan was closer to another man's junk than he ever hoped to be for the rest of his life. He almost tore a muscle in a straining attempt to keep his hand off of Sty's thigh. His face hung dangerously close to plopping straight down into Sty's lap.

"Like what you see?" Sty said, smiling slyly as Tracy finally hit a straightaway and the g-forces of orbital release were removed.

"Kiss my ass, Sty," Ryan said as he turned bright red.

"I think the left side of my head is flat," Dizz said, referring to where he made contact with the window.

"Didn't Mountain Man say we were supposed to stay on that other road?" Sty asked.

"I saw a chance for us to get away, it's called improvisation and I learned it from my husband," Tracy explained briefly, looking through her mirrors for any sign of pursuit.

When she turned forward, her heart lurched at the sight of the approaching truck until she realized it had to be Ron. She frantically waved him forward; she did not want him to stop as he barreled to intercept the cops. To his credit, he slowed slightly to look but immediately regained his forward momentum and hurtled on.

"Where are we going, Pretty Lady?" Angel asked.

"That's a good question, sweetie," Tracy answered. "I don't know." And she didn't, should she follow Ron and see if she could help, or hide somewhere around here and wait for whoever remained alive to drive by. Or did she just keep driving and go back to Ron's?

She knew she couldn't go back into the fray with the kids. The whole reason BT had done what he had was so that she could get away with them. She damn well couldn't go back to Ron's house without the rest of them. What would she say?

She pulled into an Arby's parking lot. It had a ring of juniper trees that encircled the entire place. Only the most prying diligent eyes would see the car. Then Mike's paranoia crept in on her thoughts. 'Yeah, but aren't cops very prying and very diligent?' "You suck sometimes, Mike," she said out loud. Tracy parked the car behind the building and started to undo her seatbelt.

"Whoa lady, where you going?" Sty asked, grabbing her shoulder.

"Are they open?" Angel asked, looking up at the big Cowboy Hat sign. "I like curly fires."

"Fires?" Tracy questioned the girl.

"She means fries," Ryan explained.

"I don't think they're open sweetie," Tracy told the little girl. "I'm going to the front of the store and see who passes by. You guys need to all stay in the car."

"Wait! Out here? By ourselves?" Dizz looked on the verge of a panic attack.

"Eyean, do they have Happy Meals here?" Angel asked her older brother.

"I don't think so sis," he said and watched as her face sank in resignation, "But we can check." She immediately perked up.

"Absolutely not," Tracy said, "Nobody is leaving this car."

"You are," Sty pointed out.

"Except for me," she said, shooting him a withering glance.

"Pretty lady just told *you*!" Angel squealed with delight.

Sty sat back hard; teenage brooding came to the fore.

"Eh," Tracy said. "You've got nothing on my daughter," she finished mockingly. "I'll be right back. Dizz, you get in the driver's seat. If anything happens to me, you get out of here. Understand?"

"God help us all," Sty said sarcastically.

Dizz looked sick although he nodded once in acknowledgement. Tracy was out of the car and had taken a step away. "Dizz, I meant now."

He gave her thumbs up, swallowed back some gorge and got into the front seat. Angel immediately got serious. She sat up straight in her seat and allowed Ryan to buckle her in with absolutely no extra added squirming.

"Which way is reverse?" Dizz asked, looking at the shift box.

Tracy turned back around. "Get out," she told him. A look of relief flooded his face as he extracted himself from the seat that he was so reluctant to take. Tracy turned the car around and backed up into the parking spot.

"You crossed over the white line," Dizz told Tracy, referring to her less than stellar parking job.

"Better than most times," she said looking down. "Now get back in."

"I'd rather go with you lady," Sty said. "It's way safer."

"Blow me," Dizz said as he determinedly got behind the wheel.

"Like a pinwheel?" Angel asked.

"No, he actually..."

"Dizz!" Tracy and Ryan yelled.

"Sorry," he said sheepishly.

"I'll be right back. Okay?"

Dizz' thumbs up reply was about half mast.

"How about a little more enthusiasm?" Tracy asked him. He brought two thumbs way up and the cheesiest false smile he could muster. "Better, but not great," she said as she went around to the front. Even behind an 8' high, 4' wide juniper she felt completely exposed. 'Didn't even bring my gun. What the hell is wrong with me?' She was torn between standing at her post or returning to get her weapon.

Dizz solved her problem as he came walking around the side of the Arby's. "You forgot your gun," he said. "So I brought it to you," he added needlessly.

"Dizz, you were supposed to stay in the car!"

"I figured you were going to need this," he said defensively.

Angel and Ryan rounded next.

"Guys?" Tracy asked exasperatedly.

"Eyean said he would look to see if they had any toys," Angel said excitedly. Ryan didn't look Tracy in the face. He figured his sister could do the dirty work.

Sty came around last. "Don't look at me lady, I wasn't gonna stay in there by myself."

"Fine! Dizz, give me the gun," Tracy said, "We'll all go in and see if there's anything we can use in there and then all of you are getting back in that car!"

Dizz looked thrilled that he didn't have to go back just yet.

Tracy hoped the store was locked as she approached. The sun was at high noon and was doing little to shine any light into the store. The interior looked darker than it had a right to. It didn't feel menacing, but 'inviting' was also another adjective she would not have used as a descriptor. The door swung open easily as she pulled on it. "Of course," she said sourly.

It was when she opened the second set of doors that reality made itself known. The air that poured around the group was thick with stench. Tracy was physically repelled; she stepped on Sty's foot as she retreated. He didn't seem to notice as he was doing his best to get away also.

"Never really liked roast beef," Dizz said, almost removing himself to the other side of the parking lot.

"I don't really want a toy Eyean!" Angel said as she rushed to meet up with Dizz.

Sty and Tracy pushed the first door closed in an attempt to stem the tide of poisoned air. Ryan placed his hands on the glass of the store front. Head bowed, he did his best to calm the currents in his stomach. He spat puddles as his salivary glands were working overtime.

Sty went over to egg his friend on and see if he could push him over the edge. "Man, that was almost as bad as if you went into a porta-potty and started dunking your head in for turds."

Ryan gagged again. Sty was loving it, a little more and victory would be his!

"It's like someone blended old moldy fish with road kill cat and then made…" Sty stopped short as Ryan's hands bounced off the glass from the impact of the zombie that slammed into the partition from the other side. Ryan jumped back.

"FUCK!" Ryan yelled in surprise, his stomach's earlier unrest completely forgotten.

"Eyean, Mom says you can't say Fuck!" Angel yelled across the lot.

The zombie slammed into the glass again. Tracy came up beside with the boys. Another zombie came up to the glass. This one didn't slam up like its partner. Its eyes slid over towards the door.

"Whoa!" Sty said. "Did you guys see that? It looked over towards the door!"

"Did we pull or push that door open?" Tracy asked as she started to grab the kids' shoulders and herd them back to the car.

"Pull," Dizz said as he grabbed Angel's hand.

"Thought so. Kids, run for the car NOW!"

The kids bolting for the car triggered some subliminal remembrance in the zombie's rudimentary brain. Chase and pursue. The hunt for food, the most basic of all animalistic instincts and zombie thought. Tracy was rooted to her spot as the zombie met her in the eye – and then it bolted for the door.

'Great, speeder!' Tracy thought as the zombie began its pursuit which triggered in her the second oldest response known to all living kind, the need to save one's own ass!

Tracy didn't stop to check on the advance of her enemy but the smell as it escaped the now defunct fast food restaurant told her all she needed to know. This was going to be a lot closer than she had hoped.

*   *   *

Ron watched as Tracy's car passed by. "She must have been able to get away," he said to his dad. Tony nodded once.

"Meredith and that big son of a bitch BT will be fine," Tony said. "We'll make sure of it."

"Thanks Dad." 'The old man is determined, I'll give him that,' Ron thought.

Ron was within a minute or so away from the Route 3, Route 1 interchange. "Dad, can you get on the radio and see if they've passed yet?"

Tony did as he was asked. When no response was received, Ron's hope began to spiral downward. If he drove forward and they hadn't passed yet, he would not be able to lay a trap. If he waited and they were already gone, he didn't want to dwell on that thought.

As they drove up the on ramp, Tony saved him the trouble of making a difficult decision. "Is that a cop car?" he asked.

"I don't even see a car, Dad, much less what kind," Ron responded. "Oh wait, there it is. How the hell did you see that?"

"Vitamins," Tony answered.

Ron stopped the truck and opened his door so he could prop the barrel of his Winchester 308 on the windowsill. Tony got out and placed his Browning 30-30 on the hood.

"Wrong family to mess with," Tony said as he adjusted his scope for the outgoing projectile.

*   *   *

"Is that them?" Kyle asked Job, pointing to the truck parked on the ramp.

"Yeah dipshit, she traded her red Subaru in for a silver pickup," Job said.

"Really?"

"No, not really." Job didn't like this at all. He was traveling well over a hundred miles an hour; there was no margin for error. He could not maneuver at this speed, and something about the way that truck was just waiting there was unsettling. "Probably nothing," Job said, doing his damnedest to keep his eyes on the road, on the silver truck, and look for the car he was chasing.

Kyle noticed it first. "They got guns, Job," he said as he gripped the dashboard roll handle. "Turn around man, I don't feel good about this," he said in a near state of panic.

"I can't, by the time I slow down to a safe enough speed we'll be sitting ducks."

"Job, I don't want to die a virgin."

Job couldn't help it. With everything that was going on, he had to a spare a second to look at his friend. "No way, what the hell are you talking about? You went out with Vickie Johannsen for almost a year."

"She was saving herself for marriage."

Job knew that was a lie. He had bedded Vickie on more than one occasion and most were while his friend was dating her. Kyle may have made a startling revelation, but

Job felt no such compulsion.

"We'll get through this…" the live Job started to tell his friend. "…buddy," was what his incorporeal soul finished. Job exited the world of the living and into the plane of the dead so fast that he did not even realize there was a transition.

He watched from the roof of the car as his own head was thrust back, the right side having caved from the impact of a high velocity 30-30 hollow tip round. His cheek was the first to accept the molten metal. Next, muscle and nerve endings separated as the bullet burrowed further. The impact into his jaw shattered it in four places. Eleven teeth crumbled under the assault and still the bullet pushed on. The back of his skull finally released the offending impact as the bullet came to a stop in the head rest.

Job watched with some detachment as his friend first screamed frantically and then tried to wrest the wheel from the twitching hands of the steering corpse, Job's foot had lodged down on the accelerator, causing the car to top out at 130 miles per hour. The essence that was Job moved a few feet higher from the scene just as the car began the first of its twelve somersaults. It was the fourth spin that sent Kyle hurtling away. Job was finding it more and more difficult to relate to the events that were unfolding before him. A higher calling was beckoning. And then he found himself in the Field of Flowers, an inner peace that every man strived for settled on him like a warm blanket. He took two steps to the comforting light before the serenity was ripped from his shoulders. Light faded to Dark. He ran as far and as fast as he could away from the hate, the pain, the misery, and the torment, but it was not quickly enough as his world faded to black.

*   *   *

Ron watched in awe as the police car finished the last of its death throes, screeching metal succumbing to the pissed off caws of disturbed crows. He didn't know what they were bitching about, they'd dine well tonight.

Tony ejected the spent shell casing from his rifle and with the bolt action drove another into place.

"Dad! Wow!" Ron said with true amazement.

"Keep your focus, your daughter is still out there."

"Yeah, but still…"

"We'll celebrate when this is over," Tony told his son. It had damn near been sixty years since he had shot a human and it sucked now as much as it had then. The Japanese on Tarawa had been a ruthless enemy committed to the extermination of the Americans who had the audacity to land on their soil. Tony and a platoon of fellow Marines, due to intense shelling from the Japanese, had become separated from the larger battle group they were assigned to. For four days those forty men had held on to a knoll roughly the size of a football field. The Marines had not slept the entire time as the Japanese sent everything they could at the detachment.

The Marines had bloodied their hands as they dug down as deep as they could with their small shovels. Mortars, grenades and withering machine gun fire rained down on their position almost the entire time. The only breaks in the devastating arsenal assault were when the Japanese would launch a charge. Seven times they came and seven times the Marines had rallied. Their dogged persistence and crippling marksmanship repelled the Japanese.

After the third assault, grumblings of Tuefelhunden came to the fore in the ranks of the Japanese troops, the German word for Marines which quite literally translated into Devil Dog. For what demon must they be fighting that could survive the shellings and the hundreds upon hundreds of Japanese soldiers that kept assaulting their position.

Tony, a mere corporal, found himself in charge of the remnants of his platoon as his lieutenant was killed and the gunnery sergeant was incapacitated by a gunshot wound to his abdomen. The snot-nosed 19-year-old was going to do his damnedest to keep the remaining twenty-two of his fellow

Marines alive. He kept his word to fifteen of them. A battalion of Marines had finally pushed far enough inland to encapsulate the 'Fighting Fifteen' as they became known in the papers back home. The Japanese initially feared that the gates of Hell had been ripped open as thousands of Marines poured out of that small hill; they turned tail and ran as if their very souls depended on it. Tony had always hated the moniker the newspaper thrust upon them. Twenty-five of the finest men he had ever known had lost their lives in a land God had forgotten, and apparently so would the people back home.

*   *   *

"I see Meredith!" Ron said excitedly.

Tony once more brought his eye down to the sighting aperture.

Even at 110 miles per hour, Officer Gibson took in all the information around him. He had been a good cop once and those skills made the leap into psychosis with him. He first noted the pickup truck strategically parked on the on-ramp. He also noticed the smoldering wreckage that was Job and Kyle. Most disconcerting though were the two riflemen taking aim on his position. He had absolutely no hope of returning any sort of covering fire, his only hope was to use the car in front of him as a shield.

"There's Dad!" Meredith exclaimed.

"Not yet girl!" BT yelled as Meredith pulled a hand off the steering wheel to wave at her father. BT looked back at the cop, hoping that he had been too focused on them to notice the cavalry, but it wasn't to be. The cop car started to shift over to Meredith's left, and then the cop gunned it so that his front quarter panel was even with Meredith's rear.

"BT, I'm sorry he got past me," Meredith said frantically as she looked at the police cruiser in her side view mirror creeping up.

"Let him," BT said coldly.

"You said to not let him," Meredith responded.

"If I learned nothing else from your uncle, I will now be able to go the grave with the ability to adapt."

"The grave?"

"Figure of speech. I hope," BT mumbled.

"Did you just say, 'I hope'?"

"I did not say that out loud."

"You're right, I just made that up. I'm driving 110 miles per hour down a highway with a psycho cop chasing our asses and I needed to add a little more flavor to the mix."

"Sorry," BT said, looking over his shoulder at the cop car which was just a few feet from pulling even.

Officer Gibson liked his position, he was damn near parallel to the bitch and her black boyfriend, another quarter mile and they'd be past the other pick-up truck. Then he'd shoot the life out of the both of them, repeatedly. He'd be long gone before that other truck would ever be able to catch up. Screw it, maybe he'd wait for them too, death did not discriminate. "Should almost be past them," he said to himself, doing the calculations in his head. The bigger truck to his right had him completely shielded.

*　　*　　*

"NOW!" BT shouted.

"Now what?!" Meredith screamed, looking around for some new threat.

"Slam your brakes! Put your foot through the floor board!"

"Don't you yell at me!" Meredith shot back, even as she used her entire frame to stand on the brake pedal. The truck bucked, the ass fishtailed, tortured brake pads melted under the intense heat. BT had to brace himself against the dashboard from the forces applied to his body. Smoke shot out from all four braking points and the rear end threatened to come completely off the ground.

*   *   *

Officer Gibson took a second longer to react as he was already enjoying the mythical killing fields. As the front end of the truck slid past him he was awarded the view of two of the largest rifle barrels he thought he had ever seen in his entire life. "Fuck…"

*   *   *

The smell of burnt pads hung in the air as Meredith's truck limped to a stop. The screech of metal on metal thankfully came to a halt in another three hundred feet. The right rear wheel having completely seized up contributed to the quickness of their stop.

Meredith was first out, running to her father. Ron put his rifle back into the cab and met his daughter halfway. Tony, not knowing if the initial threat was over or if another threat were to soon present itself, grabbed the rifle from the bench seat.

"I thought I taught him better," Tony said, shaking his head as he went up to check on his granddaughter.

*   *   *

Tracy could hear the distant sound of a horrific car crash but it might as well have been the miniscule pleadings of an ant under a sun intensifying magnifying glass for all the attention she paid it. What was magnitudes louder was the slap of bare feet on pavement as her pursuers chased her down. At 5'2", Tracy was never going to be a world class sprinter, but the prick behind her sure was.

Tracy could tell from the faces of the children in the car staring back at her that she wasn't going to make it. She first saw her reflection in the glass and then that of the tortured soul that chased her. Ryan, Dizz, Angel and Sty were all pressed up against the far side of the interior, wide eyed expressions of fear on their faces. Tracy could feel the pull of fingers that grasped out to latch on to the hood of her sweatshirt. Angel squealed and buried her head into her brother's shoulder. Tracy knew she would never be able to open the driver's side door and close it before the damn track star got in with her, and then she'd be exposing the kids to danger. Either way the kids were doomed as she felt the press of the keys in her right pant leg; Dizz had given them to her when he had gotten out of the car.

Tracy almost ruptured her ankle as she got within two feet of the car and thrust off to the right with all her force. Her ankle screamed in pain. 'I will not be a cheap B movie heroine that sprains an ankle and gets pounced upon by (insert movie monster here). I lived with Mike too long,' was her next thought.

The zombie slammed headlong into the car. The door creased significantly to the point where it might never be able to open again. The zombie did not stop or even address the injury to its leg. Its knee cap had shattered in three places and what remained had shifted a full two inches to the left. Tracy was saved by this very damage. The zombie's left leg had locked completely up. His decathlon days were gone, but that wouldn't stop any of his peers from cutting in line.

Dizz hopped into the back seat just as Tracy opened the driver's side door. The car rocked from multiple zombie impacts. Angel shrieked with each one, Sty only every other. Tracy slid over as far as she could and still remain in the driver's seat. Zombies were pressed up against the glass. She could not keep her eyes from them as she tried in desperation to start the keyless car.

"Hells bells!" she said as she raised her butt off the seat to fish the almost forgotten keys from her pocket. 'This is where the B Movie Queen drops the keys,' she thought sourly. "Mike, stop it!!!" she yelled.

Diz was scared shitless. It looked like their driver lost her mind and now he was going to have to drive. They might as well open the doors; it would be quicker and less painful.

Tracy's inner ramblings did not come to fruition. The implosion of the window masked the sound of the engine. Eager fingers reached in just as Tracy jerked back and placed the car in drive, not knowing whether it was running or not. Blood-crusted broken nails clawed through the air seeking to gain purchase, but were denied as the car leapt forward. She almost crashed headlong into the junipers and that would have been the end. The small Subaru would have hung on the large plants like a shiny bulb on a Christmas tree. Fortunately she jinked at the last moment and floored it. A small contingent of zombies chased them as Tracy headed back towards Route 3.

Eliza and Tommy - Interlude

"Do you feel it brother?" Eliza asked as she ran her fingers through his hair.

"I feel pain, Lizzie," Tommy answered back.

"Yes," Eliza answered, reflecting back in reflection to a time long past. "Isn't it wonderful?"

CHAPTER 14 - Talbot Journal Entry 8

Gary had been driving for the last fifty miles or so and was reveling in it. He had lost his license about two years prior to the zombpocalypse, something about trying to run over a judge's flower bed. I never got the full story and to be honest, I really didn't want to know. I've had enough close brushes with the law that I didn't want to know any information that could possibly get me in trouble as an accessory to the fact or some other bullshit. Suffice it to say, Gary was enjoying the end of the world in ways many of us couldn't understand. His whistling had at some point become less of an annoyance and more of a regular rhythm of the road. My startling awakening had nothing to do with him breaking into song in full on a cappella mode.

I sat bolt upright as a fairly strong shock was sent through my body. I almost jumped when I felt a hand on my shoulder.

"Dad," Justin started.

I turned back. He looked like I felt. "You felt it too?" It was phrased as a question but it just as easily could have been a statement.

"It wasn't Eliza," Justin said, bowing his head.

"No, it was Tomas." I don't know why I went back to his old name, but whatever had reached out and made contact was not the Tommy I had known. It felt like a malevolent presence and it was searching for us. I don't think I can explain it any better, but it was as if Tomas had cast a wide net but the holes within it were big enough for us to wriggle through. It would only be a matter of time before he sealed the holes up and we would be trapped like dolphins in a tuna net.

"It didn't feel right, Dad," Justin said, still clutching the sides of his head.

"I agree."

"He was looking for somebody, but I don't think it was us," Justin finished as he rubbed his temples.

"You got all that?" I asked him. All I had felt were the greasy fingers of evil as they had brushed over my scalp.

"I think it was his aunt, I'm thinking he was maybe even calling to her."

"Like a summoning?" My heart started to freeze. Alex and his family were in extreme danger. Eliza and Tomas, like twin vipers, had turned their deadly gazes towards them and we were powerless to help before they struck. We had a general idea of where to go, but my actual hope had been that Eliza would track *us* down, not the other way around. I already know that was a horrible plan, you don't need to remind me. I can't imagine a buck *waiting* for, or even *wanting*, the hunter to find him. That is not how the deadly game is played.

I could only hope that Paul and Erin were finally home. Would thanking God for small favors for only having half of your loved and cherished friends destroyed be a bad thing? I couldn't even begin to think about how many transgressions I had with the Big Man, what's one more? And then the stupid straw that broke the camel's back analogy decided to rear its ugly damn self.

Gary had still been doing his best 98 Degrees or Back Street Boys impression. I can honestly and thankfully say that I did not know which one it was. Although I figured I lost a few man points just by knowing the names of those bands.

"Right now you feel like you could never love again, now all I ask is for a chance
to prove that I love you…" Gary's voice had risen as he sang. Cats in heat would have been preferable.

"Gary!" I shouted. I had awoken Travis, although the

fact that he slept through that caterwauling was impressive.

"… from the..." Gary trailed off as I shook his shoulder. "Hey Mike," he said with a large grin.

"Having some fun there brother?" I asked him.

"Who doesn't love a good love song?" he asked in response.

"Depends on who is singing it," I barbed back.

"I guess that's true," he answered, thinking about it. I could tell though that not once did he question the validity of his rendition, "What's up?"

I started flipping through the atlas and alternating between road signs trying to find out exactly where we were. After a few moments of quietude, I could tell Gary was getting antsy to start up his song. I had to stop him before he got going, at all costs.

"All right, in about another fifty miles we'll be coming up on Route 77. I want you to take that heading south. It looks like eventually in South Carolina it will hook up with 95 and then we can take that into Florida."

"Mike," Gary said in all seriousness. "We could have saved a lot of time if we had just taken 95 all the way out from Maine."

He was right and I regretted my poor decision, because in all likelihood people I loved would suffer because of it.

Travis stretched and groaned. "Wouldn't have found the kids then," he said, rubbing his eyes.

Out of the mouths of babes, although who was I kidding? At 17 years old, he was bigger and faster than me. "Good point," I told him. If all else completely went to hell, which was a more likely scenario, we had at least saved those kids and I could go to my beratement from God knowing Tracy was safe.

Gary nodded his head once and went straight back into his song like he had never missed a beat.

CHAPTER 15 – Alex and Paul

The furniture store proved to be worth its weight in gold after Paul and Erin had tried to go home, Asheville, North Carolina was a vast wasteland. It looked like the entire region's National Guard had decided to make their final stand here. The only thing that stood taller than ten feet was the church in the center of town. Like a stalk of corn in the eye of a tornado it stood, righteous and untouched. At least it looked that way. The small caravan pulled up to the stairs that led to the massive oak doors to search for signs of life.

"Are you sure about this, Paul?" Erin asked her spouse as he started to ascend the stairs.

"I was until you asked," he responded back.

Mad Jack was following behind, struggling to hold up a box that was roughly the same shape and size of a 25 inch old school television and looked twice as heavy.

"What is that thing and do you want some help with it?" Paul turned to ask.

"I'm good," MJ puffed out. "Is she watching?" he asked in between heavy breathes.

"April?" Erin asked. "You know giving yourself a hernia to show off in front of a woman is not appealing," she told him.

He shrugged with a grimace.

"Are you sure you don't want any help with that thing?" Paul asked, smiling.

"This *thing* you refer to..." MJ took a breath, "is a prototype."

"A prototype? It's not going to blow up is it?" Paul asked, grabbing Erin's arm and pulling her a few steps away.

"Blow up? Why, do you know something I don't?" MJ asked in alarm. He looked like he was about to place his burden down and make a run for it.

"Is it a bomb?" Eddy asked, following the trio.

"He wanted to come with you guys!" Joann yelled from the cab.

"Shhh, Auntie Jo!" Eddy yelled back. "They don't know I'm here!" he yelled.

"It is most certainly not a bomb," MJ said, addressing Eddy. "And all indications are that it most likely will not blow up," he finished, looking at Paul and Erin.

"Comforting," Paul said sarcastically as he headed back up the stairs.

The huge door swung open effortlessly as Paul pulled on it, the all too prevalent waft of death his only reward. "Does it suck that I've smelled worse?" he asked a rapidly greening Erin. She did not respond as she moved off to the side in pursuit of more breathable air.

"That wouldn't happen to have a fan?" Paul asked as he stepped away and tried to help MJ carry the box up the last few stairs.

"Is she watching?" MJ asked.

Paul wanted to tell him that he was pretty much a shoe-in with April considering that he was the only available male in their party, but it seemed important to the kid so he played along. "Yeah, she sure is," Paul said with a wicked smile.

"I've got it then," he said as he marshaled his reserves and hefted the box the rest of the way.

"Good, 'cause that thing looks heavy," Paul said under his breath, while also giving his balls a necessary adjustment from the mere thought of carrying whatever the hell was in that thing. Add to that fact that he would have to holster his pistol to help out and he couldn't find any plusses.

Paul held the door as MJ got one foot in. He went immediately to the right and out of eyeshot of the semi and damn near smashed the container in his haste to get it out of his overtaxed arms.

"Heavy?" Paul asked sardonically as he placed a handkerchief over his face. MJ could only manage a weak one fingered response as he leaned over to catch his breath. "Gotcha," Paul laughed.

Erin had secured a scarf around her mouth and nose and now was at the entry way to the church. Paul admonished himself again for his lack of caution. 'One of these times this is going to bite me in the ass, literally.' He quickly did a visual sweep of their immediate surroundings as MJ fiddled with some switches and dials. Paul just figured it was all for show as MJ caught his second wind. Eddy slammed into Erin's legs in his rush to get in and check out something new. Joann was right behind him and scooped him up in her arms, all too aware of the danger that could be behind that door.

Eddy stopped squirming when the stench invaded his nostrils. He now looked more eager to remain with the rest of the troupe in the truck.

"Paul, is this worth it?" Erin asked, watching as Eddy and Joann descended the steps much more rapidly than they had ascended them.

Paul had stopped listening the moment he spotted the altar. It wasn't that he was ignoring his wife; it was that his senses could only handle so much input at any one time. A high pitched squawk from MJ's box brought him out of his self-induced trance. "MJ you scared the hell out of me!" Paul said, rubbing his ears.

"Sorry, just calibrating," MJ said, not really sorry. He was used to apologizing for experiments gone awry and had learned long ago that appeasement was sometimes the bastard brother of technological advancement.

Erin gave a deep scowl to MJ who did not even look up to acknowledge the slight, which made Erin even madder until she followed her husband's line of sight. "What is that?" she asked, trying to catch up to Paul.

"It's people," he answered, never breaking stride.

"You sure?" she asked, her own steps faltering.

"I mean, it has to be, doesn't it?"

"Why are they all piled up like that? Paul we should go, there's nothing we can do for them now," Erin said, reaching out to grab his sleeve.

"Maybe it's religious. Some sort of sacrifice?" Paul answered more to himself than to Erin's query.

"MJ, maybe we should go," Erin begged, looking back towards the door. An even louder box squawk was her only response from that direction. She was halfway through the large church and Paul was halfway again that much closer to the altar. "Paul, please!" she near silently screamed.

He turned to her and pressed his index finger to his mouth to quiet her.

"They're dead Paul, aren't they?" she whispered. That they were dead was preferable to them being in that ungodly clothed pile on the altar, alive.

Paul slunk another five feet closer, every fiber in his flight reflex telling him to get the hell out. He ignored it like most people ignore a yellow light, confident in the fact that yellow is more of a 'travel advisory' than an actual warning to pay heed to.

Another footfall forward and Paul had unwittingly tripped a silent alarm. Well, more like a dinner bell but the result was the same. First one set of brown green goop encrusted eyes opened to be followed by another and then a third. It was the fourth set belonging to the priest of the church that caught Paul's attention. The priest's piercing blue eyes snapped open, did one complete revolution into the back of his head and then solidly met Paul's gaze. There was no hesitation on either side as Paul turned and ran and the priest disentangled himself from his congregation in hot pursuit.

Verbal commands were unnecessary for Erin as she watched the entire event unfold. But Paul's shout of "GO!" spurred her on even faster.

"MJ, gotta go!" Paul shouted as he passed the halfway mark in God's house.

"Just a couple of more adjustments," MJ answered

merrily, unaware of the danger sweeping down the aisle.

"MJ NOW!" Erin screamed as she passed his position and ran out into the daylight.

Alex had seen that look of terror on enough folks' faces lately to realize it was time to hit the road.

Mrs. Deneaux climbed up into the bed of the truck by herself, not willing to wait for somebody to offer a hand, her cigarette still lit and shaking wildly in her hand.

MJ stood up to look at Paul as he approached. A throng of flesh worshippers followed closely, led by the leader of the congregation. Paul stumbled a bit as he did the familiar horror movie faux pas of looking behind him. His foot caught on the edge of a pew and nearly dropped him on his face. MJ moved forward to help.

Paul stuck his hand out. "Forget it man, I'm good, let's go!" Zombies filled the center aisle and both sides of the pews. Some were the traditional shufflers, most however were not, and the distance between Paul, the door, and death was closing rapidly.

"I can't leave the box!" MJ yelled.

"It's not worth getting eaten." Paul said as he got to the main door.

MJ paid no heed and turned around to get the device; thick cords on his neck bulged as he strained to pick the device up. Paul took a millisecond to scan the events. He would JUST make it if he opened the church door and pushed it shut. "Dammit!" he said as he ran to MJ's position. "This stupid heavy thing better be worth it!" he shouted as they lifted it into the air. MJ's side dipped as he struggled with his grip. "How did you carry this thing alone?" Paul struggled to get out through clenched teeth. He shifted the load so that he could get his hand on the door handle and open it. His mind had been doing rapid calculations and he figured by now the priest at least should be on them. He was too scared to even look back. Just then sunlight streamed into the church. Alex was at the front door, rifle in hand. "Come on you crazy gringos! What is it with white boys always trying to play the hero?" he shouted. Alex had the rifle raised, poised to shoot at anything moving that wasn't alive.

"Get over here!" Marta yelled from the truck cab.

Paul could not understand why Alex' rifle was not firing as they quickly moved off to the side to give him a better vantage point.

"O mi Dios," Alex softly breathed out.

Paul almost dropped the box, expecting some new horror to come bounding out of the doors a la Resident Evil. He hoped there were no zombie Doberman Pinschers. "What is it Alex?" Paul said as he struggled with himself whether to drop the stupid box and run or stand his ground with Alex.

"They're just standing there," Alex said, not daring to put his rifle down.

Paul craned his neck. Alex was right, about fifteen feet from the door the zombies were crowded around as if they had hit a force field. MJ lowered his corner a bit so that he could peer past Paul.

"I'll be damned! It works!"

"What works?" Paul asked. "This thing?"

"Yeah, it's a frequency modulator. It…" MJ started.

"Fascinating, really," Paul said, "but I'd rather you told me all about it later when we're safe."

"We're quite safe now," MJ said in rebuttal.

"You know what I mean," Paul answered.

"Guys, let's get out of here. This is not how I wanted to spend my afternoon, in a Mexican standoff with zombies," Alex said.

"That's funnier because it's true," Paul said.

"Hilarious. Let's go," Alex motioned with his rifle.

As MJ and Paul descended the stairs, the zombies moved that much closer.

"Paul, we need to put this thing down. My shoulder is killing me and I have a bad grip."

"You're lucky you don't have a hernia," Paul answered as he put his corner down on the stairs.

With the box on the ground MJ wiped his brow. Paul

kept an eye on the zombies.

"Really guys? This is where you want to have a siesta?" Alex asked nervously.

"Relax Alex, it's fine," MJ said, resting against the side of the box. The zombies at the top of the stairs were not moving. The sunlight was not kind in its exposure of the monsters. Shredded gray skin gave way to gray-green ropy muscle, which in turn showed in some extreme cases yellowing bone. Then the unthinkable happened. The priest moved but the box hadn't, from fifteen feet away to twelve. His followers did what followers do, they followed.

"What's happening?" Paul asked as their circle of safety diminished.

"Huh, must be the batteries," MJ answered absently.

"Couldn't think to put in fresh batteries?" Paul asked.

"Can't expect me to think of everything," MJ answered him, a little miffed.

Zombies began to spill off of the stairway as the overcrowding became too great. The ones that had not damaged any parts vital to locomotion began to encircle the trio.

Within seconds before the trio could react, a twelve foot wide bubble of zombies encircled them. Then it was ten feet.

"This isn't fun anymore. I'm thinking we should leave," Paul said as he grabbed the edge of the box.

"In agreement," Alex said. Sweat alternated between running in rivulets down his back and freezing in place.

The circle had become eight feet in diameter by the time MJ got his side up.

"This is going to be a little closer than I thought," MJ said as a red LED light began to flicker on the top of the box.

"Let me guess," Paul said. "Low battery indicator."

MJ could only offer a weak smile in reply. Alex' rifle now went off as the circle became six feet around. The damage the bullet did to the human form from this distance was devastating. Pink gray, brackish brain matter exploded onto their brethren as Alex started to weed out the non-believers in the Power of the Bullet.

And still they pressed on. Paul and MJ kept shuffling backwards. They were careful to make sure that the zombies behind them were given enough time to react to the repelling effects of MJ's box. By the time the three were in front of the truck, a yard stick could have been held to the priest's forehead to measure the space. Black gore stained teeth gnashed wildly as saliva flowed from both sides of his mouth like a rabid dog. Alex had his back pressed up against the side of the box now as the three moved to the cab.

"Careful dude," Paul said as Alex almost jostled the heavy burden from their hands.

Alex didn't comment as he shoved bullets into the magazine well.

"Screw it dude," Paul said as they got to Alex' door. "Won't help much now anyway."

Alex nodded.

"Get up there man!" Paul labored.

Alex was hesitant to go first, but he wasn't holding the zombie repeller and this way he could, in theory, cover MJ's and Paul's retreat. Alex scurried up into the cab.

"Okay MJ, put your edge of the box on the step and get in the cab. Can you make another one of these?" Paul asked before MJ could get into the cab.

"Yeah, I've got everything already in my van."

"You mean the one over there?" Paul said, motioning with his head to the van now swathed in zombie kind.

"Yeah, that one," MJ said, bowing his head, "All that beer…" he said resignedly. "You're going to want to hurry," MJ told Paul as he jumped in, passing Alex on the way into the sleeper cab. Brown fingernails were separated from Paul's face by millimeters Paul eased his edge of the box onto the wide step. The box teetered precariously as Paul used the remaining strength in his arms to haul himself in and dive past Alex. Alex fired off two quick rounds at the closest zombies and immediately shut the door. The box fell to the ground as the big rig lurched forward.

MJ watched sadly as the van became a distant memory.

CHAPTER 16 – Tracy and Company

Tony turned his rifle in the direction of the oncoming sound of an engine at high rev. Meredith slid behind her dad, fearful of what this new threat might entail. BT walked up to Ron, gun clutched in his hand. BT's heart had just begun to take on a relatively regular rhythm from the preceding events and seemed a little reluctant to begin such a frenetic pace again.

Henry had climbed over the middle console and let himself out from the passenger side of the now nearly useless truck. With his two front legs in front he bowed his back and stretched. His mouth gaped wide as he yawned, his tongue lolling to the side.

"Rough day Henry?" BT asked.

Henry, in traditional form, did not acknowledge the big man. He walked over to Ron's truck and unceremoniously christened the front tire.

"What the hell Henry?" Ron chided the dog.

Henry walked past Ron and placed one paw on the running board, then looked over his shoulder.

"Is he serious?" Ron asked BT.

"Oh, very much so," BT responded.

"You know, if you lay off the gravy maybe you'd be able to get your fat ass into the truck by yourself," Ron huffed as he picked the dog up and placed him back in the cab.

Ron had no sooner put the dog down on the seat when Henry let out some voluminous flatulence. Even with the sound of an approaching car, BT could not keep from laughing.

"That'll show you to tell that dog off," BT said.

"Should've remembered that was Mike's dog," Ron said, ineffectually sweeping a hand past his face to make the disagreeable smell go away quicker. He had the feeling that the smell had somehow stuck to his hand and all he was doing was continually waving it past his face.

"It's Tracy," Tony said, putting his rifle up, the clenching in his jaw subsiding.

"I don't think she's going to stop in time," BT said as he stepped away from the truck. Tracy's tires screamed in protest as she took the on ramp at double the legal limit.

"Not another truck," Ron lamented, hoping that Tracy didn't rear end him.

The front of Tracy's car dipped down as she laid heavily on the brake. She was barely going 2 mph when her front end collided with Ron's truck, the thud of impact did little structural damage, but Ron's truck could no longer be considered pristine.

"Dammit," Ron said softly as he looked at the seven inch scrape on his chrome bumper.

"Gives it a little character," his dad told him with a smile on his face.

"I liked it just fine without character," Ron answered him irately.

"Hi mister!" Angel said, getting out to survey the damage. "Sure was a nice truck."

"Sorry," Tracy said, hugging her brother-in-law.

"What's your name little miss?" Tony asked Angel.

Angel looked up at the grizzled man and that was it, love at first sight. She stretched out her arms, and Tony handed his rifle to BT in order to pick the little girl up. She was nearly asleep before her head hit his shoulder.

"That's my sister, Angel," Ryan said.

"You kids alone?" Ron asked the trio.

They all nodded in their various ways.

"You boys did good," Tony told them, "keeping this little one safe."

Ryan puffed his chest out. There was something about the older man. He had a calming effect on those around him. Ryan could sense something deeper but was too young to put words to it. If he had been able, he might have said Tony had an air of resolve about him. If pushed, this man would push back tenfold. There was a calm but it cloaked a tempest. He very much wanted to be on the good side of this man.

"You Mike's dad?" Ryan asked him.

Tony nodded, not wanting to speak and possibly wake the little package in his arms.

"Thought so," Ryan said beaming. Tony reached over and tousled his hair.

"We should go." Tracy said, relating the story of the zombies at the Arby's.

"Alright, let me pull up to Meredith's truck. We'll get the supplies and get the hell out of here," Ron said.

"Tony, you want me to take her?" Tracy asked.

"No, we're good hon," Tony answered. "I think we both could use the company," he said, gingerly getting into the truck. Henry looked over from the rear of the cab. "No farting, you!" Tony laughed as he scolded the dog lovingly. Henry licked Tony's face, leaving a three inch swath of spit down his cheek. "Thanks." He dragged his free arm across his face to remove the slobbery kiss.

Henry seemed satisfied as he lay back down. Meredith scooted Henry over so she and Ryan could get in. BT walked back over to the other truck and started dragging stuff out to put in the back of Ron's truck bed. Dizz and Sty kept a vigilant look out for the zombies.

"Do you think they stopped following us?" Dizz asked Sty.

"Maybe they never even started," Sty told him, neither one taking his eyes from the on ramp. When monsters were real, it was worth paying attention. This wasn't algebra, attention deficit disorder wasn't going to be a problem.

"I think I see one!" Dizz yelled.

Ron came over. "Just the one?" he asked.

"Yeah, it's a shuffler!" Sty said.

"Shuffler, huh? I like that. Alright, one slow one shouldn't be too big of an issue. Let me know if any of his faster friends try to crash the party."

"Don't you think that's kind of weird?" Dizz asked his friend.

"What?" Sty asked as he threw a stone at the oncoming zombie, not even coming relatively close.

"I mean just the one zombie and a slow one at that."

"Probably not even from the same bunch," Sty said, humming another rock in the general direction of the zombie.

"Maybe you're right," Dizz said, turning to see how the rest of the group was doing.

Sty bent over, looking for a suitable rock to throw at their guest. As he stood back up, Dizz and Sty's looks of astonishment mirrored each other's almost perfectly.

Sty's 'shuffler' was now in full on sprint mode, while Dizz watched dozens of zombies swarm onto the freeway from the west bound side.

"Zombies!" they screamed in unison.

Tony gently placed Angel in the shotgun seat. Thankfully she was still fast asleep, although that was likely to change in the next few moments. Tony got out with his rifle. "If I didn't know any better," he said to BT, "I would think they were trying to ambush us."

"I think your 'knowing' is just fine. Ron, it's your call, but I'd really like to rid the world of a few of these maggot breeders," BT said with some vehemence.

Ron did a quick mental count of the assaulters, distance and firearms available. "Let's do it," he said calmly.

"Dizz, tell me when that zombie behind us gets to within a hundred yards," BT said as he shouldered his assault rifle and let loose a volley towards the oncoming horde.

"Dizz, Sty, get in the car," Tracy said. They didn't need much encouragement. Dizz immediately turned to follow the progress of the zombie that he now realized was only the diversionary tactic.

Fifteen or so zombies had made their way up the embankment on the far side of the highway, but none of them made it past the median. The one that had staged the diversion actually made it the closest only to have his goal wiped out from under him as he met a chunk of high speed lead with his head. It really was never much of a contest as his skin split first, met immediately by the eighth of an inch of tissue that did little more than lubricate the projectile with blood as it passed through this small layer. Next came the fragmenting of the much thicker skull. Bone shattered like a hollowed out Easter egg under the foot of a petulant child who had not received a Nintendo 3DS for the rising of Christ's day. The bullet, much flattened from its impact with the brain casing, still slid easily through the black-gray diseased matter that had once entertained thoughts of becoming a restaurant owner and asking Alicia Barker to marry him. As the projectile came into contact with the rear of the zombie's head, it significantly slowed from its initial impact and gathered some inertia as it sought to fight its way out of the dark enclosure and back into the sunlight. The mushroomed bullet broke through the back of his skull leaving a hole roughly the size of a baseball. Any thought he might have still harbored of leading anything resembling life crashed to the ground in shattered bits of past memories, pains and joys.

"Well that was gross," BT said, shouldering his rifle. Ryan agreed adamantly.

"And a little disturbing," Ron added. "They are showing the ability to deceive and to employ tactics. Does this somehow tie back to Eliza, or is it just a natural progression of the zombies?" Ron asked the group. Nobody answered. There was no answer anyone could conclusively give.

"Just what the world needs, smart zombies," Tracy said. "Hell, we've already got men, that seems like overkill."

Ron arched an eyebrow. Meredith went over and

high-fived her aunt.

"Cute, real cute," BT said. "Can we get the hell out of here now?"

"Yeah, I agree. Let's get home," Ron said

"BT, what do you want to do?" Tracy asked.

"What? NO!" Ron said. "We are heading home."

"Ron, I'm not," Tracy said softly. "My boys, *all* of my boys are still out there. I can't go sit this out."

"We got unbelievably lucky here," Ron sputtered.

"Well, I wouldn't call it luck," Tony said as he rubbed his fingernails on his chest. "Skill is what I'd call it," he added, trying to throw some levity into the next few difficult minutes he knew were coming.

"Tracy, you don't even need to ask," BT answered her original question, "By your crazy ass husband's side is where I want to live or die."

Tracy nodded her thanks.

Henry was looking for some assistance down from the truck seat. Meredith helped him down. "Dad," Meredith started.

"Not a chance!" he said vehemently.

"I started out to do something," Meredith said.

"Yeah, and it damn near got you killed!" he shouted. Meredith flinched, but didn't back down.

"I have to do this," Meredith told her father.

Tracy wanted to try to convince Meredith to stay with her father. Enough people were already in harm's way, one less would be better. But she could also see the determination that Meredith held. This war was going to be won by the ones that took it 'to' the enemy and not 'from' the enemy.

"I don't think I can handle another good bye," Ron said, turning away from his daughter if only in a vain attempt to hide his tears.

"Dad, I'll be back," Meredith croaked out past her own eye leakage.

"You'd better be," he said. Meredith came over to hug him fiercely. She then circled the truck to give her grandfather a kiss on the cheek and a hug. Water flowed freely from all involved.

"Wow, Talbot men sure do cry a lot," BT said as he got into the car. It was not lost on Tracy as he discreetly pulled his sleeve up to wipe his face.

"BT, you hold to our original deal," Ron said, pointing a finger at the big man.

"Always," BT answered, quickly putting on his sunglasses.

"Missed a spot," Tracy said with a smile as she wiped a tear away on his cheek.

"Damn you woman," BT said.

"I won't tell anyone," Tracy told him.

"I saw it too and I'm not promising anything," Meredith said smugly.

"Wonderful, what could I have possibly done in a past life that I deserved to be in a car for a cross country trip with TWO Talbot women? Did I shoot the Dalai Lama or something?" He asked the heavens.

CHAPTER 17 – Alex and Paul

Marta was shivering uncontrollably even under the small mountain of blankets that Alex, Paul and Erin had gathered for her. Alex was pacing around the bed as Erin administered a cool damp paper towel to Marta's forehead.

Erin directed her statement more to Paul but it was meant for Alex also. "She's burning up."

"What did she mean 'worse' Tommy?" Paul asked Alex. "Tommy's on our side, right?"

Alex looked over to Paul, his eyes tortured with pain.

"Is she being used like Justin was?" Paul asked hesitantly.

"The creepy kid?" April asked as she brought more wet towels for Erin.

"That can't be it," Alex pleaded. "We know Tommy. The kid is always smiling."

"My husband used to say 'Never trust anybody who smiles all the time, they're up to something,'" Mrs. Deneaux said, throwing her two and half cents into the fray.

"Guess your husband never had to worry about you then," Paul said meanly.

"Paul!" Erin said.

"No, he's quite right," Mrs. Deneaux said, nodding towards Paul. "I always thought of smiling as frivolous behavior and my husband appreciated that right up until he decided to sleep with his secretary."

"Alright, way too much information," Joann finished. "I think we need to start figuring out what to do. I can feel the heat coming off of Marta from here. We should probably get her some antibiotics or something. And if Tommy is in her head and if, I'm stressing IF, he is on the other team now, are we in danger?"

"Well, I think we're always in danger," Mad Jack said.

"No existential crap please," Joann moaned.

"Sorry," MJ said, "I just thought it was worth saying."

"You know what I meant, all of you," Joann said. "How much more danger are we in now than we were twenty minutes ago?" That question hung somberly over their heads. Alex and Paul both had family that they were trying to get home to. The rest had thrown their lot in with them thinking they would be safer being away from a zombie homing beacon. Now that fundamental premise was being questioned.

"Go then!" Alex shouted. "It's what you're all thinking, we've already done it once, what's another time? Your soul can only get stained so many times before one transgression becomes indistinguishable from the next!"

"Nobody said that," Paul said, trying to diffuse the situation.

"No one needed to say it Paul," Alex answered, his earlier anger ratcheted down a notch.

"I was thinking it," Mrs. Deneaux said. Paul shot her a fierce glance. She didn't so much as flinch. "Oh, you can't be that naïve Mr. Ginner. Altruism is a wonderful trait, it truly is, but it is for the misguided. Why should one risk their own life for that of another with no promise of significant gain for the action?"

"Real humanitarian you are," MJ spoke up.

"Pah," Mrs. Deneaux spat, waving her arm at him.

"How much time do we have?" April asked as she looked towards the front door.

"That's the ten thousand dollar question, now isn't it?" Paul responded distractedly.

"No matter what decisions we come to," Joann stated, "I think we need to get Marta some medicine first. Who's in?"

"Me," MJ replied, raising his hand, "but only if we stop at a Radio Shack too."

"Me too," April said, looking over lustfully at MJ who for the moment was not paying her any attention.

"I'm in," Paul stated.

"Paul," Erin said. Implicit in that one word was the question, 'Why do you feel the need to risk your life and leave me here?'

Paul shrugged his shoulders as if to say, 'Look who's going, someone has to watch out for them and it might as well be me.' Paul laughed a little; sometimes being married was a trip. They had just had an entire conversation, mostly unspoken.

"I will go too," Alex said dejectedly.

"No, you will stay here my friend, by your wife's side," Paul said, placing his arm around Alex' shoulder. "It'll be fine," he added hollowly.

"You really believe that?" Alex asked, calling him out on his statement.

"I have to," Paul answered him. "What's the alternative?"

"Fair enough, but hurry up or I'm going to throw Deneaux outside on her ass," Alex said with a small smile.

"What's the cut-off point?" Paul asked, looking at a non-existent watch.

"I'm going to lock the door on our way out," MJ said.

"That would be wise," Alex told him.

"That means you'll be locked in," MJ said as if he was talking to a five year old.

"I think he gets it," Paul said, grabbing MJ before Alex had the chance to lose his cool again.

"I just wanted him to be aware of that," Alex heard MJ say as Paul led him away.

Mrs. Deneaux walked over to the far side of the store to the recliner section, and with a loudly audible sigh sat down in an oversized EZ Boy.

"I think her fever's breaking," Erin said excitedly as

she pressed her palm to Marta's head.

Marta's eyes fluttered open as she uttered one word. "Demonio."

Alex made the sign of the Holy Trinity. Erin looked questioningly over towards him. "Demon," he offered in translation.

"Got it," Erin answered with a shiver. Marta's eyes closed as a more restful sleep ensued.

CHAPTER 18 – Ron - Searsport

As soon as Ron got home with his dad, Nancy took the kids to get them settled in. Their initial fears of being in a new place were put quickly at ease by Nancy as she got them cleaned up, fed and showed them where they could sleep. For now she set up a bunch of sleeping bags and pillows in the family room in the basement. She had a hunch that, at least at first, they would feel much more comfortable if they were all within arm's reach no matter how much testosterone the three boys pretended to throw around.

"They going to be alright?" a wiped out Ron asked his wife as she came up the stairs.

"As all right as any kids can be when they lose their parents," Nancy answered him solemnly. "I had hoped Meredith would come home with you," Nancy commiserated as she placed her hand on Ron's arm.

"Me too," Ron said, using his other hand to try and wipe the exhaustion from his features. Ron related all of the events that had transpired throughout the day. As he wrapped up, he thought that he most likely should have glossed over a few of the stickier details. Nancy was looking a little less hale than she had been a few minutes before. "The old man is a rock," Ron said, referring to his father.

"You've got more of him in you than you know. I'm going to check on the kids." Nancy needed desperately to take her mind off of just how close to a disastrous end her daughter had come. She was still mourning for one of them. She could not compound those feelings; her soul was already feeling threadbare.

All was quiet as Ron sat on his couch reflecting back

on the day. His hands nervously twitched. He did not notice.

"Eagle's Nest, Eagle's Nest, this is Valkyrie," Mike said through the airwaves.

"What is wrong with you?" Gary asked, "It's Mount Olympus. You can't just go making stuff up."

"How many people do you think he has checking in?" Mike asked his brother.

'More than you know,' Ron thought as he got up to talk on the handset.

"That's not the point," Gary said a little peevishly. "If you're not going to follow protocol…"

"Protocol?" Mike cut his brother off, "Are you kidding me? Chariots of Fire my ass, I still haven't forgiven you for ratting me out. You know that moose wasn't my fault."

"Maybe if you had driven a little better…" Gary needled his brother.

"You're blaming my driving skills now! Maybe if I wasn't so distracted by your attempt at singing, or whatever you call that…"

"Boys!" Ron shouted through the microphone. "Am I going to have to put you two in a time out?"

"He could probably use it!" Gary shouted. A loud crashing sound immediately followed.

"I've got your time out right here!" Mike shouted to the most likely retreating back of his brother, but over the headset it was deafening.

"Mike! I've already got a headache. It's been a hell of a day," Ron yelled.

Mike immediately turned all business, "Everything all right?" Mike held his breath waiting for a response. "Tracy make it back?" Fear was coiled in that question like a compressed spring.

Ron took a breath, he hated lying this big to his brother. Oh, there were times when it was necessary like on the Risk board when he would tell a mistruth about how many turns they would stay allies, but this was of a much higher magnitude, life and death to be exact.

"Ron?" Mike asked, fear threatening to overcome all of his senses rendering him useless.

"She's fine, Mike." 'Not so much a lie there,' Ron thought.

"Whew," Mike said in relief. "Can I talk to her?"

"She's sleeping, they had a close call on the way back." Ron had learned from his earlier revelation to his wife that it was best to limit the amount of details. "She's fine, Mike," Ron reiterated to stop the next barrage of questions. "As are the kids."

Ron could picture his younger brother wiping the dampness from his eyes as he collected himself.

"Dad, everything alright?" Travis asked on the other end. Ron's vision must have been spot on.

"Good," Mike choked out. "Just relieved. Your mom is safe."

'Dammit.' Ron thought. 'Didn't actually say that.'

"It's a little early for a call in Mike. What's going on?" Ron asked. He didn't get a sense that there was any urgency to the call but this was not a time in history where assumptions should ever be taken.

"Well, I was calling to check on Tracy and to let you know that we're heading south a little quicker than we thought," Mike told him.

"What's changed?" Ron asked, intrigued.

"We've got reason to believe that Alex, and possibly Paul if they are still together, are now the objects of Eliza's attention."

"What? Did she send you a text?" Ron asked sarcastically.

"Just about," Mike answered back seriously.

"I don't even want to know," Ron told him.

"Probably better off."

"Are you going to be able to find them? South is a pretty vague direction."

"I've got an idea, not sure if it will work. Just

something I've been thinking about on the fly."

"The last time you thought of something 'on the fly' it cost me three hundred dollars to bail your ass out of jail," Ron jibed.

"Don't go getting all riled up, I paid you back for that."

"No you didn't."

"You sure?" Mike asked. "I'll get right on that when I get back."

"Yeah, a lot of uses for cash these days. Just get your ass back here and we'll discuss repayment."

"I'm not aligning with the Allegiance of Darkness on the Risk board if that's what you have in mind."

"Well, that was partially it, but we can figure something else out," Ron said smiling now. "Alright, call me when you hunker down for the night."

"Roger that, tell everyone there that I love them."

"Will do."

*   *   *

Ron waited a minute before changing the frequency. "You catch that?" he asked BT.

"Got it," BT said.

"You'd better be careful or you'll end up passing him by."

"That would serve him right if I did and then saved the day, so by the time he got there I had Eliza's head on a pike. I'd be drinking the last ice cold Molson on the planet and he'd get stuck having to kill some crippled ass old zombie and drinking a piss warm Schlitz."

"Umm, still a little pissed that he asked you to stay behind?" Ron asked.

"Does it show?" BT asked seriously.

Ron decided wisely to not answer. "You know the drill. Next time he calls, wait a few, then switch to frequency two and we'll discuss what we want to do going forward."

"What I want to do is kick his…"

"BT!" Tracy said.

"Fine, we'll be in touch," BT said menacingly.

"Always a pleasure," Ron responded.

A loud growl came over his headset. He truly hoped it had something to do with the curvature of the earth as it came in line with sunspots, as opposed to any sound emanating from a human being.

Ron stood there a moment longer basking in the quiet of his home. He hoped that someday soon the quiet would be replaced by the noise of the living, many of the living.

CHAPTER 19 – Talbot Journal Entry 9

"All right Justin, I know this was partially my idea, but I'm not feeling all that great about it," I said to my son.

"Dad, we've already decided that I can skip one day of shots without any ill effects. This is just one more day and it means that they will last longer," Justin answered. He had a brave face on, but I wasn't completely convinced. Hell, I was scared and the bitch wasn't in my head nearly as deeply as she was within his. I could feel her on the periphery of my consciousness but that was it. Kind of like a mosquito on the other side of a screen door, somehow we now shared a link from the 'kiss of death' she had given me before the downfall at Little Turtle. But it was more a knowledge of something bad than actually being bad.

As the effects of Justin's shots wore off, it meant that Eliza could begin to hold sway over him. It was not a comforting thought. We sat at the edge of I-95 for a few hours waiting; we actually saw a few cars pass by. It wasn't rush hour by any stretch of the imagination, and they were about as friendly as Yankees fans after losing to the Red Sox, but it was still nice to see actual living breathing, not trying-to-cut-my-throat people.

"Oh Dad," Justin said with a moan. "I'm beginning to feel her." He began to scratch his arms like a junkie.

"It's not worth it," I said, digging through his bag for a shot.

He seemed to rally his reserves. "It's alright, I can do this," he said, taking a big breath of air. "I *need* to do this." He sat there a few moments longer, eyes closed, body shivering even though it was a fairly balmy 40 or so degrees, which after this winter seemed like the tropics. Gary and Travis were busy having a snowball fight, oh how I wanted to join them.

"Do you think we should maybe try this at another time?" I asked Justin. A cold chill wind buffeted my back, although I think the chill was more internal than external.

Justin opened one eye. "She's least active during the day. This is our best chance to go unnoticed."

Unnoticed under Eliza's watch? I didn't share in the optimism.

Justin seized up, his entire body going rigid. I grabbed him, fearful that he was going to topple like a redwood tree.

"Found her," he meted out.

"Wonderful." To those of you that might possibly find this journal having not read the previous three, here is just a brief moment of explanation. 'Wonderful' in this context is primarily meant as a term of sarcasm. I in no way relished any more contact with Eliza than was absolutely necessary. "And?"

"Not yet," he said stiffly. "It's not like there's a set of directions."

"Sarcasm returned." I didn't know it was even possible but Justin seemed to stand even more ramrod straight. Gary caught a snowball with his ear hole as he turned to watch.

"Uh oh," Justin said.

"Uh oh is bad Justin, what's going on? The last time I said uh oh I had… yeah, I think I'll just hold on to that thought."

Even under the heavy concentration, Justin was able to spare a moment to give me a sidelong glance. I smiled weakly.

"Whoa, I thought she felt me. It's good now though. I don't know how much longer I can keep this connection without her feeling me though. And I'm still no closer to reaching out to Marta."

"Forget it then. There's no sense in giving her a heads up about us especially with no upswing."

Justin looked as if he was just about inclined to agree, "Wait… wait… she's there!!" he said excitedly.

All I could figure was that it was Eliza. I damn near panicked and shoved the shot in his sternum.

"Marta?" Justin asked. "It's me, Justin," he said touching his chest. "I can't stay long, but we're coming to help. Where are you?"

Travis, Gary and I were now in a semi-circle watching the birth of a potential new means of communication. Is this what it was like when Edison invented the telephone? Talk about a Smart Phone!

"We're on our way, stay strong!" Justin said beaming, "Hold on, my dad has one quick message for Paul." Justin relayed the message exactly as I had given it to him even if he now wore a panicked expression on his face. "Dad, *she's* coming! Hit me!"

I was momentarily lost in the reverie of marketing the new telecomm age, but that quickly changed as I watched elation turn to fright in the span of a blink. I plunged the needle in and the fear in him receded slowly, but the taint of evil took much longer to leave. He spent the majority of that day huddled in the back seat with a couple of blankets on him. Eliza needed to be dealt with quickly.

Eliza and Tomas Interlude

"I am intrigued, brother," Eliza said coolly. "Why is it that you would allow our enemies to converse?" she asked as she arched an eyebrow. She feigned indifference but it was clear her brother had upset her.

"Does it not make the task at hand easier if they are all together?" Tomas asked.

"Perhaps, my brother, but I do not yet know if I trust you."

Tomas smiled as he walked away. That smile lay somewhere between conniving and triumphant. Even Tomas did not know to whom he had given the benefit when he allowed Justin a moment to communicate with Marta.

CHAPTER 20 - Alex and Marta

Marta's arm shot up as she grabbed Alex' forearm. "They're coming!" she said excitedly.

'She's gone,' Alex thought sourly. 'She's finally lost it.' Alex was wondering how he would be able to live out the remainder of his days without her.

Marta watched the sadness in her husband's expression as it traversed across his face. "No," she said tenderly. "Mike is coming!" she said softly but excitement punctuated the words.

"Oh Marta, you cannot know this," Alex hitched. It was one thing to witness the destruction of one's body, a completely different form of torture to watch one's mind disintegrate.

"The boy who was scratched," she said as she wet her fever dried lips.

"Justin?" Alex asked.

"Yes, Justin," she answered, putting her head back on the pillow. "He says that we are in danger and that they are coming to help."

Alex had a look of astonishment on his face.

"He says that he, his brother, Mike, and Mike's brother are coming here and that we should not go anywhere."

"I do not know what to believe," Alex nearly cried.

"Believe me, dear husband," Marta said as she fell back into a much more peaceful sleep.

Alex did seventeen laps around the store alternating between outright joy and terror, never becoming fully comfortable with any one thought. He was on the far side of the store on his eighteenth lap when he heard Paul and MJ coming back from their expedition. He was met with stares of concern as he ran down the center aisle to meet them.

"Everything alright?" Paul asked, scanning the warehouse for any signs of trouble. "Is Marta okay?"

"Mike's coming!" Alex rushed out. He was all out of breath and covered in a sheen of sweat, the exertion of his power walk showing.

"Catch your breath buddy and maybe start from the beginning," Paul suggested concernedly as he escorted Alex over to a chair.

MJ already lost interest and was pushing his shopping cart full of electronics to the desk section for assembly.

"Hey, maybe work on improving that low battery indicator," Paul said to MJ before turning back to Alex. MJ was too deep in thought to catch the slight.

"Marta says that Justin spoke to her, and that Mike is heading this way," Alex reported, looking at his friend. It sounded much less sane when spoken out loud and to one that had not witnessed the event.

"And she's sure it was Justin?" Paul asked, not willing to believe just yet.

Alex nodded.

"And she was sure of Justin's intent?" Paul asked. He didn't say it, but they were both thinking it. When they parted company with Mike, Justin was already feeling the effects of Eliza's power and was slipping further away every day. It did not seem that the elapsed time could have done him better. The exact opposite was more likely the case.

"Paul, she looked happy after she 'talked' to him."

"Far as I know Alex, Justin was not born with the ability to speak psychically. I think that's Eliza's specialty."

Alex bowed his head. "But why, Paul? Why bother?"

"To keep us off guard, maybe just to raise our hopes so she could be there when she smashed them. I don't know, who can tell what such a malignant mind might find worthwhile." Paul's thoughts ran deeper and darker. 'If,' and

Paul truly believed that was the case, 'If Justin was now an agent for the enemy, that meant that more than likely Mike had not made it to Maine.'

"If Justin *is* one of them," Alex said, verbalizing Paul's thoughts, "then Mike is dead."

Paul's knees suddenly felt weak, and he sat down next to Alex. A torrent of memories flooded through his senses, from the first time they met, through high school, college and ultimately until they parted. "I'll miss you my friend," Paul said to the heavens. A more pressing thought came to the fore. "We've got to leave," he said, wiping his eyes. "I'll start rounding people up," Paul said as he stood up. Alex still had his head in his hands. Even false hope hurt when it was ripped from your soul, like a fish hook through a cheek.

Erin was walking down the aisle way when Paul stood. "Hi baby," she told her husband, glad to see that he was safe. "Marta woke up for a second," she told Alex. He turned to see if it should be anything to be concerned about. "Now this may sound weird, but I'm only repeating what she said." Paul and Alex looked expectantly at her. "All right here goes. 'Dad wasn't sure if Paul is still with you guys, but if he is, ask him what he thought of Pete Townsend's piss.'"

Paul damn near choked on his laughter. "Mike's alive!" he said, pumping his fist in the air.

"How... how do you know?" Alex asked, not quite yet willing to grab onto the thread of promise.

"Inside joke," Paul said beaming.

"Referring to...?" Erin asked.

"Uh," he stalled, "College, window pane... acid," he coughed out. "A case of beer and some unbelievable amounts of laughter."

"That doesn't really explain the reference to the Who's lead guitarist's urine," Erin said quizzically.

"Didn't you catch the part about the acid?" Paul said, still smiling.

"Fine," Erin said, "but some day you are going to fill me in."

"And this isn't a trick?" Alex asked.

"No way," Paul said, "There's no way Mike told any of his kids about that night."

"Please, just tell me that it had nothing to do with that man's piss," Alex fairly begged.

Paul started laughing again. "No, no, nothing like that... well kind of... but not what you're thinking. We were talking about Pete Townsend and how he probably had fans who worshipped his piss." Alex had a blank stare, but Erin walked away. She decided she'd heard enough. "Trust me," Paul said slapping his friend on the shoulder, "It's hilarious when you're tripping your trees off."

"I'll take your word for it," Alex said, "So we're staying then?"

"I guess for now, this place is a little bigger than I'd like it to be, but as far as defending against zombies our only real concern would be the front door. We picked up some canned goods while we were out, so food will be a non-issue for a few days. What the hell, I say we hunker down for a bit, recharge our batteries, and let Wonder Boy over there finish up his zombie stopper," Paul finished off by pointing over towards MJ.

"Will she let him?" Alex indicated April, who was nearly tripping over her tongue as she hovered around MJ.

"It's kind of funny the 180 he's done since he first laid eyes on her. The more she talks the less interested he becomes. April has yet to figure that equation out. She rambles on like a meth-head at a rave. All that beauty and not an iota of brain to go with it," Paul laughed.

"Meth-head at a rave? That gives me a headache just thinking about it. I like the idea of resting for a few days. I don't, however, like the idea of my wife being the human equivalent of a cell phone. And I'm having a hard time reconciling how close in proximity Tomas' message was to Justin's."

"It does make for some interesting pondering, I'll give you that. But I'm telling you Mike would no sooner tell his kids about his drug experiences than he would tell his wife about his sexual exploits."

"Oooh, I get your point." Alex cringed just thinking about how that conversation would go do with his own betrothed. He inadvertently covered his testicles.

"Yeah, pretty much just like that," Paul said, catching the involuntary motion.

"We wait then." Alex rose from his chair and headed back down the aisle to where his wife was resting.

Paul headed back to the front doors. "I'll keep a watch out," he told Joann, who was all too happy to let him.

"Storm's brewing." She pointed up to the blackening shroud of clouds.

"Sure is," he told her. 'And I don't think it's the only one,' he thought. 'Hurry up Mike.'

CHAPTER 21 – Talbot Journal Entry 10

I drove most of that day alternating between looking at the road and readjusting my rear view mirror to keep an eye on Justin. This was a dangerous game we played with a lethal enemy; it was the equivalent of playing with a Black Mamba and seeing if we could inject the anti-venom before the neurotoxin had an opportunity to stop the beating heart. Justin noticed me looking on occasion when he wasn't resting. I saw no sign of the duality from before the shots, but he still did not look well. The expense of that call might not have been worth it, even AT&T in their heyday didn't charge that much.

"I'll be fine, Dad," Justin said as he smiled weakly. "And stop looking at me, you're kind of giving me the creeps."

"All right, but you let me know if you need anything," I told him as I adjusted the mirror back to its intended view of the road behind me.

"Who is Easter Evans?" Travis asked.

"What?" I asked him back.

"The sign right there says welcome to Virginia, home of Easter Evans," he clarified.

We almost passed it by, it was your standard State sign, but painted very neatly below it was 'Home of Easter Evans.' This wasn't your standard issue graffiti, someone had taken painstaking detail to make this look as professional as possible, and I didn't like it. Anyone that thought themselves important enough to make sure everyone knew about them was not anyone I wanted to know.

"I don't like it Mike," Gary said.

"It's just a sign," I said, half convincingly.

"Yeah, so is that." He pointed to a much different 'sign' a few hundred feet further down the road. Hanging from a highway exit sign were the bodies of three people.

"What does that sign say?" I asked, squinting my eyes to try and get a better look. I knew it wasn't going to be anything good. I mean it wasn't going to say, 'These were very bad people that did very bad things.'

Gary pulled out a small pair of binoculars. "Sinners, it says sinners."

Well, maybe I was wrong. It actually did kind of say what I thought it might. Now the question was what kind of sins did Easter Evans think were hanging offenses. You would have to step very far out of bounds with me to get that type of response, but who knows if Easter might be of the ilk that thought chewing gum was a hanging offense.

"I think I would like to go *around* Virginia," Gary said conversationally as he put the binoculars back in their case.

"Great idea, can't afford the time delay though," I told him.

"Figured you'd say that," as he put his seatbelt on.

Travis took the lead from his uncle and did the same.

"Could you get Justin's?" I asked Travis as I strapped myself in.

"Kind of like a Bible Belt." Gary tugged on his harness to make sure it was secure.

I drove slowly as we approached the bodies hanging above us. I hoped that they were zombies, that would almost make sense. Not that the zombies cared, it wouldn't be much of a deterrent for them but it would somehow still make sense. I stopped the truck within a few feet of the swaying dead people, one of which looked like a woman, or was merely a victim of crows dining on its tenderloins. I walked completely around looking for head wounds.

The bodies were bloated and blackened from exposure to the elements but they were still intact enough to tell that there were no gunshots to any of these poor souls' heads.

"Mike, any reason why you wanted to stop? This isn't really a photo-op," Gary stated nervously.

"Was trying to see if they were zombies or not."

"And?"

"Not so much."

"Even more reason that we should probably get going."

"My sentiments exactly," I told my brother.

"Still planning on going through Virginia?" he asked.

I didn't answer him as I put the truck in drive.

It wasn't five minutes later that we became the victims of a rolling blockade. Cars, trucks, vans and SUV's poured in from the off ramps on our right and left. Trucks that were bigger and cars that were faster, and all of them were packed with Easter's true believers. Apparently Easter thought very well of arming his flock so when the first car pulled up alongside and a mutton chopped man pointed to the side of the road, I saw no way out that didn't involve a lot of carnage, a great amount which would occur in our truck.

"Turn the truck off," came Mutton's voice as he pulled alongside. "If you could be so kind as to hand the keys to Brother Wilkinson, I would greatly appreciate it."

"Well he sure sounds nice," Gary said. "I'm thinking West Virginia would have been a lot better state to go through though."

"I think I would have to agree with you," I said as I handed over to the keys to the guy who I could only assume was Brother Wilkinson. A small platoon of cars and trucks completely encircled us. The scene in the Godfather with Sonny at the toll booth was going through my head. I could only hope that these people had good aim. I didn't want to dance around like a marionette as I was riddled with bullets.

"Now friend," Mutton started up again. "I would like for you to put all of your weapons outside of your truck."

Gary was imperceptibly shaking his head in the

negative. "I'd rather go out like the Bon Jovi song."

I looked at him questioningly then asked, "What? 'Livin' on a Prayer?'"

"No dumbass, 'In a Blaze of Glory.'"

"Great."

"Dad, what are we gonna do?" Travis asked, not nervously, but if we were going to start shooting it needed to be sooner rather than later.

The people outside were starting to tense up also. If anything was going to happen it was within these next few crucial seconds. I took a second to look at Justin's peaceful sleeping face, at Travis, and then my brother. "Not this time guys."

"You sure you know what you're doing Mike?" Gary asked me with a false smile on for our onlookers.

"Of course not," I told him softly. I opened my door slowly; fingers on triggers applied an ounce more of pressure. "Nobody get happy fingers on us, I'm putting our guns outside."

"Hold," Mutton said through a strained smile.

Within another minute the four of us were up against the car and getting a more thorough pat down. I felt it was good news that they hadn't just opened fire.

"All clear, Father Easter," Mutton said as we were allowed to turn from our 'assume the position' stance.

A stately man of about 60 came out from one of the cars in the back; it looked like a Caddy but I didn't have the best angle. He was dressed all in black with a hat which was in direct contrast to his shock of white hair and beard. He looked like any pastor might down in the South, almost affable, but his eyes belied him. His true nature he could not hide, his eyes burned with what? Insanity? Rage? Tyranny? All of the above?

"Good day citizens," he said politely as he approached. "What kind of man be ye?" He asked Gary.

"I'm not sure of the answer, sir," Gary told him honestly.

"Well!" Easter boomed. "Do you walk in the light of the Lord or do you not!"

"I would like to think I walk in the light," Gary told him.

Gary tensed as Easter placed his hand on Gary's chest. I didn't know what was happening but I didn't friggen' like it.

"Pious!" Easter shouted.

"Praise be to God!" His followers shouted.

He next touched Travis and repeated the same word, followed immediately by the chorus.

"And you?" he said as he got so close I could smell his tobacco laced breath.

"I have strayed from the path on occasion, but only to see what lay in the shade. Always was I within the reach of the light."

"Praise be to God brother, it is better to have lost one's way and found the path back to righteousness. It shows true character." Easter placed his hand on my chest. I felt damn near the same sensation when I first picked up Eliza's locket. A small current of energy coursed through me. His hand stayed there moments longer than it had on Gary and Travis combined. He looked me in the eyes before he spoke. "I see that you walk with one foot in the light and one foot in the dark, Mr. Talbot."

"How do you know my name?"

"Be quiet son. I am divining your nature. You have a darkness in you that you have warred with valiantly to keep at bay. I think that someday you will lose this battle, but for now, I will grant you the chance to keep fighting. Pious!" he shouted.

"Praise be to God," rang out around us.

"Can we go now?" I asked Easter.

"Perhaps," he said, eyeing Justin suspiciously, "The boy is not well?" It was phrased as a question but the answer was evident.

Justin nearly fell backwards as did Easter when the

divining touch was made.

"Seize them!" Easter said as he struggled to get his breath. "This one is marked!" Mutton and two other men closed in.

"Wait, please!" I shouted before the situation spiraled even further downhill. "He's my son, he needs help."

"Nothing that a short rope on a tall tree won't cure," Brother Wilkinson sneered.

"Easter, he's just a boy," I pleaded.

He had not yet fully recovered from his encounter. "And yet he is stained deeply. He cannot continue to exist. He is an abomination!"

"You yourself just called the three of us pious men. Would we so willingly align with the darkness?"

"Evil can take on a great many forms. Most cannot see it until it is too late and it has led us very far from our path. It can bring even the mightiest among us to our knees."

A bunch of "Amens" and "Hallejulahs" rang out.

"What if we," I said, pointing to Gary, Travis and myself, "as men of righteousness, what if we are using the evil within him..." Justin's face sagged, I felt sorry for bruising his feelings but our literal necks were on the line. "...to serve a higher purpose."

I don't think we had won anyone over, but Easter was at least pondering my suggestion.

"You three may go forward," Easter said, "and I will attempt to exorcize the demons from the boy. If I can, he will be allowed to live among us until you return or he wishes to go after you."

"And if that doesn't work?"

"He swings," Easter answered bluntly.

"What if we don't go?" Travis asked. "He's my brother."

"You will all suffer the same fate as Eliza's pet," Easter said, motioning to Mutton to round us up.

"Then just leaving is out of the question?" I tried one more time.

"I would no sooner let loose a scorpion in a baby's crib and hope it did not strike," Easter said over his shoulder as he walked away.

"That's a 'no' then?" I asked. Mutton smacked me upside the head.

"Should have left when you had the chance, veil walker. I've never seen Easter give anyone the chance to go with a taint of darkness in them." He shoved me forward but not menacingly.

"Well that's me, always the uninvited guest, first to come, last to leave."

"Boy, are you sure that you're right in the head?" Mutton asked.

"He's my brother," Gary said. "He's always been a little like this."

Travis nodded in agreement.

Mutton looked us over. "Really wish you three hadn't come this way," he said, not including Justin who was now being led in a different direction. "He'll be fine for now, Easter will do what he promised, but after…"

He let it lie.

We were driven back down the off ramp and within a few minutes we came to a stone building structure with a large ornate sign that read 'Robert E. Lee Middle School.' I looked over at Mutton.

He shrugged, "It's our town hall slash prison slash housing. It's easily defendable, all of the windows have metal grating over them."

I understood defendable. We were led up the two first floors. We passed the gamut of human suffering, from hollow eyed victims to the sunken defeated. This was the last harbor in which their drowned souls could seek refuge. Some would recover, some would fade away. Mutton opened a locked door which led us up a small set of wooden steps. At the top was another door and I didn't need the sign to realize this was the supply closet, it smelled of bleach and mimeograph solution. It was a very nostalgic smell and it instantly brought me back to my grade school days when the biggest drama of the day was when Billy Allen stole my lunch dessert. I should have kicked his ass.

"Go on up now," Mutton motioned. "Don't cause any trouble and none will be brought to you."

"Mutton..." I started. "Umm...?"

"The name is Talisker," Mutton/Talisker said.

"Talisker, who is Easter Evans?" I asked. I truly expected to hear how the man was the second coming of Christ himself wrapped around a crap load of Praise Be to Jesus and maybe a Can I Get a Witness, with a side dose of some serious pontification.

"He used to work within these walls," He answered me. "Before the wrath of God was unleashed."

I could understand a principal taking charge in a moment of crisis, it was almost a natural progression in lieu of any other formal type of government.

"He was the janitor," Talisker finished up, completely shattering my thought process. The look on my face must have been amusing, "Yup, that's pretty much what we thought at first. But the man had an uncanny ability to organize us when everything was falling apart." I momentarily thought of Jed. Would I even be here now if it wasn't for that man?

"Easter fought house to house to gather the pious," Talisker continued. "My first words to the crazy old man covered in blood on my doorstep were 'Fuck Off.' He smiled and told me that he thought I'd say that. Then he placed his hand on my chest and my doubt and worries disappeared. I grabbed my wife and kid and we've been here ever since. My house burned down that night. If not for Easter, my family would be dead," The stoic Talisker looked away for a second as he composed himself, "Seventy-seven houses we fought our way to before the zombies got so thick I swear we could have stepped on their heads to get back here. I won't say that the zombies made a path when Easter Evans walked towards them, but it seems to me that they really wanted to be somewhere else when he was around. Unfortunately, his influence only spread so far and the rest of us had to fight our way back. Some fell, most lived. None of us would have made it though if not for Easter. He's a good man that just might have been elevated to greatness due to the end of times."

"What of the three people we came across that were swinging from a highway sign?" I asked Talisker, looking for some sort of weakness in the armor he had placed protectively around Easter's character.

"The Bowdoin brothers, always were petty thieves. Mostly shoplifting and vandalism. I believe that one of them did time for stealing a car, nothing overly serious though."

"Did they not fit into Easter's view of a Utopian society?"

Talisker did not rise to the bait, if he even noted it at all. "About a month ago, Easter came to me and told me to get three strong men with tight mouths. We had an errand to perform. I didn't question the man. We drove a couple of miles out of town. When he told me to park and that we'd walk from there, I shut the truck off and got out. A mile later we were on the front porch of the Bowdoins' run-down house. "Take them alive," he told us, "they must atone for what they have done. They must first face God before they are eternally damned." I was scared, I had no idea what we were getting into. Easter had turned around and was looking up to the sky, his bible clenched in his hands. Tears streamed down his face. I kicked the door in, probably could have leaned on it and it would have broken open it was so termite infested. Damn near fell into the living room but I recovered quick enough. The first of the Bowdoins, Les, came running from the kitchen. He had no drawers on, but so far no law had been broken as far as I could tell. How a man wants to dress or not in his own home is no concern of mine. Felt somewhat bad as I used the butt of my gun to drop him to the ground."

Talisker's full tone, easy demeanor and his honesty

made for a very captivating story.

"And then his other two brothers, Donny and Lyle, came running from the kitchen. But the funny thing, at least that was what I thought then, I'd change my mind soon enough, was they were also without trousers. I was thinking that it just wasn't warm enough to be running around like that, and I mean technically we were still at war. Who the hell wants to get caught with their talliwacker hanging out?"

I laughed, I agreed. "When I die I want it to be with a gun in my hand, not my penis."

"I like you Mike," Talisker chuckled.

"How does everyone know my name?"

Talisker continued on with his narrative, disregarding my question altogether. "The three guys with me quickly rounded up the other two brothers. Easter told them to 'make them unconscious, that they did not deserve to see the light of God's day.' Donny almost died that day when the black flashlight Red was carrying crashed down on the top of his skull. His legs flopped around like a puppet controlled by a palsy victim. The batteries flew out as the metal casing ruptured from the assault. 'Alive!' Easter shouted at Red and then Easter placed his hand on the man's head. Now, I'm not saying he healed Donny, but those legs stopped flopping around. What came next was the worst thing I had ever seen in my life."

"Talisker, I don't think I want to know."

"You don't want to know," He answered honestly, "But I can see it in your eyes, why am I blindly following a man who a few months ago was barely making a living wiping up kiddy puke in the cafeteria and cleaning toilets, so now I'm telling you. There was a boy, maybe seven, maybe eight, too tough to tell. They had him tied to the stove and they were using that boy in ways that go against all the laws of man, nature, and the Bible." Talisker began to cry now, silent tears leaking down his face unnoticed. "And in between them taking their turns on the boy, they would burn him. It looked to be mostly grease; the boy was just all burned skin and blood. He died in my arms the second I released his bonds, almost as if he had been waiting for sweet release. I cried more that day, I believe, than I have my entire life. Even as my hands bled as I dug the grave, I cried. I wept the entire walk back to the truck and almost the entire ride into town. Easter calmed my tortured soul as we headed home. He said some things can never be forgotten, and they shouldn't. But there comes a time when we need to move on, that God had told him we have more to do. I have a heaviness that I will hold in my heart until the good Lord takes me from this life and lets me enter into the next, but for now I will do all that it takes to rid the world of the blackness that has descended among us."

"Damn, Talisker." What argument did I have against the man at this point?

"When we got the Bowdoins back into town, we gave them a trial. They were completely belligerent, ranting about their rights to do as they pleased. Shouting that it was the end of the world and who gives a rat's ass about one little boy and besides someone else had told them to do it. If I had been allowed to bring my gun in that day, I would have just shot them all dead and hoped that God would forgive me. When it was all over and the verdict came down as guilty, none of them showed any remorse. It was never about the boy's rights, it was always about their own self-serving needs. They started swearing and threatening to kill everyone in the courtroom. Easter had a couple of the bigger guys restrain Donny. Easter then walked up to the man and placed his hand on his head. He then told the two guys holding Donny to let him go. At first Donny shrugged them off and then it was like someone had taken a 220-volt live exposed wire and shoved it up his asshole."

"Which he would have deserved," I threw in for good measure.

"Which he would have deserved," Talisker echoed. "He stood so rigid, I thought Easter must have stopped his heart. He looked like a plank of wood, and then he arched over backwards so that his face was pointing straight up into the sky. I damn near shit a brick when Donny uttered just one word and it was a question. "God?" And as I stand here and tell you today, blood began to fall like tears from Donny's eyes. His brother Les started screaming that Easter had poisoned his brother and that he was gonna kill everyone here and then rape their rotting bodies. Donny heard none of it as fat globs of blood began to pool on the ground. Besides Les' ranting, the rest of the room was quiet. Oh, we were all standing and watching, and I've got to think that everybody was as scared as I was. Donny then stood straight back up and slumped back into his chair. Les asked him if he was alright. How Donny saw anything I don't know, his eyes were burnt. Where there should have been his blue irises were now just red burned husks. And no, it wasn't blood covering them up. The entire eye was the color of a cinnamon ball like you used to get in the gumball machines. 'I've seen God,' Donny told his brothers, 'and he isn't the loving and forgiving kind, he's a vengeful and demanding God.' I think Les and Lyle were now beginning to see the errors of their ways. Lyle started running. He didn't get too far with leg irons on and all. It was the same thing when Easter touched Lyle's head. Within a minute he was next to Donny, they were completely subdued. Donny was crying normal tears this time and Lyle just kept mumbling how sorry he was. Les was going nuts, swearing that Easter had better not lay his poisoned hands anywhere upon him. Then he did something that even Easter wasn't prepared for. Les began to say the Lord's Prayer in reverse. That courtroom darkened and there wasn't a cloud in the sky. Easter might have faltered for half a heartbeat, but he recovered and slammed the heel of his hand into Les' head. The room immediately flooded with a light a hundred times brighter than I think we should be able to see and not go blind. It was like a super bright flashbulb, it was that quick. Les broke his back, he was flung so violently backward. He lay on the ground as he gazed upon his maker. He did not cry or beg for forgiveness. He seemed to want to go to the one upon whose allegiance he had sworn. We hung them that day."

I didn't know what to say, how do you dispute what the man witnessed?

"There's some canned goods up in the far corner," a much more morose Talisker told us as he motioned for us to go through the door before he shut and locked it.

"Do you buy it Mike?" Gary asked as he rummaged around in the box until he found something that sounded good to his palate, a can of Mandarin oranges, "I mean, you're the cynic and all."

"Well, *he* believes it, that's for sure," Travis said in a subdued voice.

"Mass hallucination?" Gary asked.

"I hate that term, that's a Government term if I ever heard one. They invented that to cover up any number of eyewitness accounts of something they didn't want people to see," I said. "I'm more inclined to believe in Les' theory."

"Poison?" Travis asked.

"Really?" Gary asked, so perturbed that he dropped an orange in his lap.

"It's a possibility for sure, but the event as explained by Talisker seems just as real of a possibility."

Gary stopped, his hand mid-way to his mouth with the orange.

"I've been witness to a lot of events recently Gary that I can't explain," I told him bluntly.

He thought about it for a moment longer and then finished the action of bringing the succulent fruit to his mouth.

"Either way, I'm not sure where that puts Justin," I said.

"Or us." Gary smacked down another morsel.

"Any more of those?" Travis asked, heading over to the box.

"How can you guys eat?" I said as I paced the room.

"Easy, we're hungry," Gary answered.

Travis nodded.

By the time Talisker came to get us a few hours later, I had polished off two cans of oranges and one of pears. My stomach grumbled from all the fruit, might as well have eaten a three-alarm burrito for all the fireworks that were going off in my plumbing. I was going to make a great impression when I started releasing some of the internal pressure, so to speak.

We were not led to a classroom, but rather what was once more likely the teacher's lounge which had now been converted into Easter's living abode. I was relieved we weren't on trial, but not quite comfortable. We were still waiting to be judged and by ultimately Easter's sole authority.

Justin seemed to have had better accommodations than us. He was sitting on the couch, a half-eaten sandwich and a small bag of chips off to his side on an end table. He even had some comic books on his lap and a blanket wrapped around his legs.

"Comfortable?" I asked him, relieved to see that he was alright.

"Not so bad," he said with a sincere smile. I could still see a sense of nervousness etched in his features, but he was unharmed and that was a good way to be.

Easter came in through another door that attached to the cafeteria. "Welcome," he said as he spread his arms. "Please sit. That will be all Talisker, thank you." Talisker nodded once and walked out. He did not go far, however. I could see his shadow in the frosted windowpane.

"Ah, Mr. Talbot, I can almost see the wheels spinning in your head. You're wondering if you should overpower me and tie me up, or take me as a hostage until such time that you can safely let me go."

He caught me off guard but I recovered quickly. "Well, you pretty much got everything right until the part where we 'safely' let you go, as you put it."

"I feel that I should almost be intimidated," Easter

said with a jovial laugh. "Perhaps a few months ago I would have believed you."

"What changed, Easter?" I asked, truly wanting an answer.

"I can tell you before the End of Times came I was not a religious man. I had perhaps been in a church a dozen or so times in the last twenty years and those times were either for weddings or funerals. I did not see much sense in worshipping a deity I could neither see nor understand, I guess would be the correct phrasing. An omnipotent being that was threaded through all of our lives absolutely made no sense to me. I understood the comfort others got from His perceived presence, but that was as far as it went. Something happened the night the zombies came. It altered me in ways that I have not come to understand quite yet. That there is a God is no longer of doubt to me, that He is not the kind forgiving God of the King James version I find troubling, but I do not question His will."

"So you are merely a vessel? So if my son is not deemed to be 'saved' you will rid him of his life as you will ours?" I asked angrily.

"You were given the opportunity to leave of your own accord when you found that you were traveling with one that is marked. When you chose not to go, I believed that as free beings you wanted to be with him. Evil can be blinding in its own right."

I was livid. "Justin is not evil!" I spat.

"Sit, Michael," Easter said calmly. "I know this, but he has evil *in* him."

I could not argue with that. I was well aware of that fact.

"If the boy were evil, we would not be having this conversation," he said, his back to me as he poured a cup of tea. "Head still churning with thoughts of escape I see," he said as he turned back around.

"Busted," I told him. "And how do you know my name?"

"Easily," he said without hesitation or doubt. "It is stamped on your soul. Shall we begin?"

"And if what you are doing here should fail, do you think I will idly stand by as you prepare to do harm to my son or the rest of us?" I asked him openly.

"I am trying to help you," he said as he walked over to the sink. I watched as he applied a liberal amount of disinfectant soap to his hands before he scrubbed them vigorously and washed off the residue in a small flood of water. "I wouldn't want anything untoward to get on the boy."

"So much for the poison theory," Travis said.

"One final time I will ask you Michael," Easter said.

"What about my son and my brother?"

"Their will is theirs to do with as they wish… right now."

"Not a chance, Mike," Gary said.

Travis had a look of steel set in his eyes. "No, Dad."

I turned to Easter. "If Travis leaves this room?"

"He would be welcome to stay or leave at any time he saw fit," Easter said as he pulled up a chair next to the couch Justin had been reclining on since the conversation started. "There was a mild sedative in the milk I gave him, whichever way this goes it will not be pleasant for him," Easter explained as he pulled the blanket up from Justin's legs and covered his chest.

"Alright, one more scenario," I stated. Easter waited patiently. "Travis leaves the room, this thing with Justin does not go well. Gary and I fight our way out of here. Maybe we make it, maybe we don't."

"Yes, yes Mike, Travis would still be welcome."

"Dad, I'd rather take my chances with you," Travis pleaded.

"But your leaving is not a chance, Travis. I believe Easter, no matter his inner convictions, to be an honorable man and would do as he said here."

"Thank you, I think," Easter replied mildly.

"Dad, he's my brother."

"And he's my son, as are you. I cannot, I will not put the both of you in harm's way if it can be avoided. If this does not work out, do not do anything. Do you understand me? I can tell you're listening but the set of your jaw is telling me a different story."

"I will do what I can," Travis promised, but in which direction did the promise lie?

He shut the door slowly. With one final glance back, he looked at me like I had just told him Santa wasn't real AND that the fat man that played him at the mall had earlier that day also pissed in his cheerios. It was a withering assault; his mother had taught him well.

"Go!" I yelled through the door when I didn't hear his footfalls echoing down the hallway. I heard a fairly good attempt at deception steps. "Not bad, now do it for real."

"I'm telling Mom," he muttered.

"God, please, I hope that you do," I said in a soft prayer.

"Didn't make you to be a believer," Easter said.

"When I perceive it to be for my benefit, I'll give him the benefit of the doubt," I told him.

"Then you might want to start praying now," Easter said as he placed both his hands on Justin's chest.

I did, too. Hypocritical? Sure, but when you're playing Texas Hold'em and all you're holding is a ten high, what can it hurt?

Easter looked over at me, fat droplets of sweat beginning to form on his forehead. His mouth became a thin line, almost imperceptible as it got lost in his white beard, as he began to speak: "The evil within this boy will relinquish its right upon his being."

"Have you done this before?" I asked Easter. His forearms rippled from the strain he was feeling.

"This darkness has a strong hold. And I know Talisker told you what I used to do before. I've seen vomit that looked possessed and children that probably had small demons inside them, but I have never before tried to exorcise a demon. I never had much reason to believe in the men of the cloth, although I played one on television."

"Seriously!?" I asked.

"No, boy!" Easter said sternly. "Did your momma drop you on your head? Now stop asking me questions while I'm trying to work."

"I think I actually saw her do it on more than one occasion," Gary said.

"What?" I mouthed, not wanting to disturb Easter.

"Drop you on your head. I think I saw her do it more than once," Gary finished.

"Do… you… mind!" Easter said under some heavy duress.

Gary and I both pointed to each other like third graders in trouble but at least neither of us spoke this time.

"Come forth!" Easter shouted, "so that I may see who I cast aside!"

I was thinking that wasn't such a good idea. Better to just kick her out before she had a chance to realize what was happening.

"Who dares to tinker with my pet?" came out of Justin's mouth but it was not his voice. I had heard the same arrogant tone once before coming out of Durgan's mouth.

The locket hung around my neck. The chain stayed relatively body temperature, but the skin where the locket made contact with my chest began to burn from the cold.

Easter tried to remove his hands from Justin, but in less than the blink of an eye Justin grabbed his forearms in a strength that was being intensified through supernatural means. The room was cool but Easter looked like he was baking under the Sahara sun. Easter pulled for all he was worth to get away. He might as well have been super glued to Justin. Justin was now sitting up and staring intensely at Easter.

"Charlatan! What kind of two-bit magician are you?" Eliza asked Easter.

"Let me go, the power of Christ compels you!" Easter shouted.

"The power of Christ? Your God is a false prophet to whom I will never bow down," Eliza answered menacingly.

"Then who do you worship?" Easter asked her. I thought that we all knew the answer to that, but Eliza surprised us once again.

"Why myself, of course," she said slyly. Eliza turned Justin's head to scan the rest of the room. "Michael, so good to see you again. I sense that you possess something that belongs to me, although what it is I cannot determine," she said with a sneer. "Ah, and who is that with you, he bears a family resemblance, a brother perhaps? Is it not good to be reunited with family?" She asked, obviously sticking a dagger in my already broken heart with the loss of Tommy.

Easter was frozen. A look of sheer terror creased his features. Myself, I was ready to run. Eliza had a way of making me feel like a jack rabbit and she wasn't the sly fox, she was the rabid wolf, so big was the difference in my perception of her.

Gary seemed the least disturbed by the situation. "So that's Eliza?" he asked me. I could barely nod in reply. "Yeah, she's a mean one," he said solemnly.

"You think?" I gritted out.

"And what of this man, Michael?" Eliza asked as turned back to Easter. "I fear that he means you harm."

"And that bothers you somehow?" I asked her incredulously, not believing that we were having such a conversation.

"That death befalls you is of a main concern of mine. That it is by my own hand and in my own way is of the utmost importance. What good would it be if I did not first destroy everything that was dear to you, and then crush the broken shell of your existence? And do not be flippant with me again, Michael, I can easily turn Justin against himself. Would you like to watch as I make him tear his own eyes out?"

"Wait Eliza, we will have our confrontation!" I told her, putting my hands up. I hoped she would take heed of my words and not hurt Justin.

"What of this man!" she spat, shaking Easter's still form. "He calls himself a Holy man, but he is a trickster. His wizardry lies in chemistry and staging."

"How has he reached *you* then?" Gary asked.

"Michael, I grow weary of this encounter," Eliza said, ignoring Gary's question. "He will not let you go. I can easily stop his beating heart and be rid of him."

"We are prisoners, if you kill him, they will kill us," I told her.

"If only the revenge was not going to be so sweet, I could be rid of you now. What do you propose?" Eliza asked.

This was surreal, I was talking tactics with Eliza. "Can you make him answer questions?" I asked her.

"All men have a way of answering truthfully when I threaten to rend their genitalia from their body and make them eat it. Only once did I have to completely follow through. He died choking." She actually let out a small laugh at the remembrance of the event.

"Easter," I said. "You need to answer me truthfully, do you understand?" He nodded jerkily. "Eliza is not one for idle threats." He gulped once. I took that as an affirmation of my words. "What is really going on here?"

"God…" he began. Justin/Eliza grabbed Easter's manhood in what I could only imagine was a vise-like grip by the way he reacted. "I was…" he labored to speak. "I am a chemist and … and…" I think Eliza was squeezing harder just for the sheer cruelty of it. "And an electronics hobbyist."

"But yet you're a janitor at a middle school?" Gary asked disbelievingly.

"I… I… I got burned out." He vomited from the pain.

"He lies," Eliza said coldly. "I would like to crush his reproductive organs now."

"Wait," Easter said, trying to yell but not having enough breath to do so.

"Eliza, could you please ease up so that he can talk?"

"I will do so, but for the last time Michael, if he lies again, I will crush what I hold in my hand and you will have to do what you can to honor your promise of our final meeting."

"Fair enough," I told her.

Easter bent forward slightly as Eliza let up somewhat.

"This is it Easter, you tell the truth like a man or die as a eunuch," I cautioned him.

"I like to be around children," he said. "I'm disgusted with myself. I've never done anything but I wanted to," he cried.

"So you set something up with the Bowdoin brothers," I said, linking the pieces.

He looked up at me wondering how I got that information. His head bowed as he answered, "I couldn't go through with it. And by the time Talisker got there with his men they had gone too far. I did not want them to harm the boy."

"Why take them alive?" Gary asked, "Didn't you risk them exposing you?"

"They did not know who they worked for. I had contracted them to do this before the zombies came. It was all set up through chat rooms and dummy email accounts."

"How long did they have that boy?" I asked with disgust.

"Weeks at least, perhaps as long as two months," he dispensed.

"Sweet Jesus," Gary choked, covering his mouth in fear that he might make an involuntary discharge.

"I did not know that they had gone through with it," Easter said in defense. "Not until right before I sent Talisker to get them."

"Well that makes you a friggen saint doesn't it?" I yelled at him.

Talisker pretty much crashed through the door. "What is going on?" he said, drawing his gun. I had a suspicion that he might start firing first and wait for the answers later.

"Tell him to stop, Easter," I said.

I watched as the squirrelly man started to weigh his chances. Apparently so did Eliza as she redoubled her efforts on his what now must be considered his mushy privates at this point.

"Put the gun down, Talisker," he wheezed. Talisker did without as much as a beat of hesitation.

"You're going to want a seat for this," I said as I pushed him the chair I had originally been sitting in.

Easter spent a moment to retell the sordid depraved tale. Talisker looked like he was the one getting nut punched.

"But what of the trial, the bleeding eyes, the visions of God?" Talisker asked, not believing that the savior that walked among them was a devil dressed in black.

"Hallucinogens, the power of suggestion and Anistreplase," Easter said breathlessly.

"The pious tests?" Talisker asked, grasping for straws.

"Taser leads in my gloves. Please make her stop," Easter begged me.

"What of the zombies not attacking you? There has to be some truth in there somewhere?"

"Certain sound oscillations seem to have an effect on the undead. I discovered it quite by accident."

"Now that's some information we could use," I said excitedly.

The screaming that pierced the room next was inhuman, maybe even inhumane if it wasn't being uttered by the creature known as Easter. Eliza had crushed his testicles. It would be hours, maybe days before he was in a state of mind that could help us with the sound machine he had mentioned.

I will never know how Easter said what he said as he writhed in agony. But the words or at least the vast majority of the message is transcribed below.

"*Is animus has haud inherent macula salvifico unus*

vos have largior super is, ut libri of revelations civitas, vos have haud vindicatum in is animus quod mos relinquish totus vox prurigo."

Talisker stood up and placed the barrel of his pistol against Easter's head and blew his brains across the room.

"He was in misery. He was speaking jibberish," Talisker said. "And he betrayed me, he betrayed the entire community." He wiped his free hand across his eyes. "And no one else needs to know."

I had my hands halfway raised, fearful he would turn the gun on the rest of us.

"You are all free to go," Talisker said as he approached the door.

"Wait," I said. "Can we look for this machine that he says can repel the zombies?"

"You will leave now," he said, not leaving any room for doubt that we had no other options in the matter. I heard his melancholy footfalls as they faded down the hallway, and then what had to be Travis' as they rapidly approached.

"Well that was entertaining," Eliza laughed. "You have your other son with you I see," Eliza commented as Travis ran in the doorway.

"Dad?" Travis asked.

I held up a hand to hold off any further questioning.

"It amazes me how malleable the human mind can be to the power of suggestion."

"Eliza, what did you do?"

She laughed. "I have given you your way out and maybe rid the world of a small piece of evil, or a small piece of light."

"I will kill you, Eliza."

"Perhaps Michael, only the great enemy of mortality will tell. Since I have been banished from this host, the next time we talk will be face to face." With those last words she released Justin.

"Holy crap," Justin said as he looked at the slumped over body that was Easter Evans. "What happened?"

"We either took part in a great good or a great evil," Gary explained briefly. "Let's get out of here before we figure it out."

Talisker was true to his word. Our truck and all of our belongings were waiting outside of the school building. Nobody was in sight as we got in and drove off. We were ten miles out and the whole scene just kept playing over and over in my head like a movie on auto rewind.

"Justin, how did Eliza come out past Doc Baker's shot?" I asked.

"Mike," Gary cautioned.

Justin looked from his uncle to me. "Easter drew her out."

"Mike, enough," Gary said forcibly.

That was not normally Gary's role, but I deferred to it.

We drove through the remainder of Virginia without incident and in silence.

"He wasn't wearing gloves when he touched my chest," I said aloud.

"Mike, I will kick your ass!" Gary shouted.

"You were in the Air Force, how is *that* going to happen?" I mocked him. He held up one finger right under my nose. "All right, all right," I told him, more than willing to let it go at this point.

Extra Journal Entry: I stopped at a Barnes and Noble store a few hours after our encounter with Easter and grabbed a Latin to English translation dictionary. I knew it was Latin, seems that only very holy people or very evil use the language anymore. Looking back, I wished I had just left good enough alone. Below is a rough translation of the words he spoke the day Justin was freed from the shackles of Eliza's hold.

"This soul has no inherent stain except for the one you have bestowed upon it, as the Book of Revelations states, you have no claim on this soul and will relinquish all rights to it."

CHAPTER 22 – Tracy, BT and Meredith

"Who do you think Easter Evans was?" Meredith asked.

BT opened one eye to look at the state sign. "Don't know, but he must have lost his social standing because they crossed it out."

"Or his life," Tracy said.

"You didn't need to go there. I was trying to keep it light," BT said.

Tracy smacked the big man's arm. He immediately sat up. Arm smacking was her signal for danger. "You do know those rings hurt every time you do that, right?"

"Mike used to say that. I always thought he was being a baby."

"Probably got nerve damage," BT said as he rubbed his arm.

"BT look," Tracy said, pointing to a large caravan of trucks, cars and motorcycles.

"They all have their headlights on like a funeral procession," Meredith said, as they came up on the last vehicle in the line. The young woman in the car was most definitely crying and paid absolutely no attention to Tracy as they passed on by. Different car, same results. A white hearse led the long line of vehicles. A man with mutton chops drove the car, a grim set of determination on his face. They noted that of all the occupants in the cars, he was the only one that did not shed tears.

Tracy punched the accelerator to be rid of the reminder of the fate that awaits us all, although, most likely in this day in age without as much pomp and circumstance as the man in the back of the hearse was receiving right now.

"Mike you think?" BT asked, jabbing his thumb behind him in the direction of the hearse.

"Cause that? Naw," Tracy said unconvincingly.

CHAPTER 23 – Paul and Alex

Paul was moments away from getting someone to replace him on watch. It was MJ's turn, but the man had not stopped working on his zombie box in the last four hours. Movement caught Paul's eye as he swung back around to look out the large dual glass doors.

"Zombies it's always zombies," he said softly. "Zombies!" he yelled to alert the rest of the group.

"How many?" Alex asked, hauling half their arsenal to the front of the store.

"I'd say roughly all of downtown Asheville," Paul said as he moved away from the doors. "MJ come on, we've got to get some heavy stuff in front of these doors."

MJ looked up, smoke from his battery operated soldering iron swirling around his head. In his haste to help he inadvertently put the still hot iron down on his unfinished and delicate circuit board. Paul moved over to an oak chest and hutch set that together easily weighed in excess of three hundred pounds. Moving it was extraordinarily easy over the tiled floor as the three men used their adrenaline testosterone fueled muscles to get it going.

"Wait," Alex said as they pushed it up against the doors. "If we moved it this easily won't the zombies be able to also?"

"We've just got to keep stacking stuff here until it becomes impossible," Paul said, already moving on to the next closest item, a butcher block kitchen table that was on clearance because someone had seen fit to drag a key across the surface and mar the finish, deeply in some places.

The thud of the first zombie impact pushed the hutch

almost a half inch away from the door it had just been placed against.

"Uh oh," MJ said, looking at the spider web of broken glass that emanated from the collision zone. "Guys, we'd better move faster."

"What the hell are you talking about?" Alex asked him, "You're not even moving."

"The glass is breaking," MJ pointed out.

"Come on!" Paul urged as he pushed the table into place. "Let's get that book case!"

The thuds kept coming, but each one was of a slightly less jarring impact as the zombies began to run into their brethren that had reached the doors first. Within half an hour, the small ten foot wide hallway that led to the doors was stuffed with more contents than would fit in a standard U-haul truck.

"That's going to hold them?" Joann asked Paul anxiously.

"It never does," he told her.

"Maybe we should figure out how to get on the roof," was Alex's reply to Paul's words.

"Good call," Paul said, clapping him on the back. "Joann, can you keep an eye on the doors while me and Alex check out the roof?"

She nodded tersely.

"Dammit!" MJ yelled, his sweat soaked back to the trio.

"You alright?" Alex asked.

MJ turned towards them and held up a circuit board with a soldering iron clearly infused with the green plastic.

"Can you fix it?" Paul was concerned. The sound box had saved them once and there was no reason to think it couldn't do it again if MJ could get it to work.

"I can't fix this," MJ said in disgust, pulling the iron away from the plastic casing. "I can rebuild it but I lost all that time."

"Then why are you wasting more time talking about

it?" Joann asked.

"You know, not everyone likes a New York attitude," MJ said to her as he sat back down and began to get the pieces he needed out of his Radio Shack bags.

"I can help," April told MJ.

"I'd rather you watch the door with Mouth over there," MJ said peevishly.

April stomped away and Joann laughed. "I think I got under his skin," she said to Paul and Alex.

"Whatever gets him working," Paul said. "We'll be right back. Grab a gun, if we hear a shot we'll stop whatever we're doing and be here as quick as we can."

Mrs. Deneaux walked up the main passageway, cigarette in hand as if she were on stroll through the streets of Paris, grabbing a small revolver as she walked past the weapons Alex had deposited on the couch in his haste to help rearrange the furniture.

"You know how to use that thing?" Joann asked her.

"Don't be silly, I was the State Champion in 1964," Mrs. Deneaux replied, yellow tobacco stained teeth showing in her attempt at a smile. It looked more like a dog getting ready to strike with her teeth clenched that tightly together.

"That smile looks kind of painful," Alex remarked.

"Go and find us a way out of here." She motioned them off with the wave of the gun.

"Got another cigarette?" Joann asked.

"Oh honey, of course I do, but I'm not sharing," Mrs. Deneaux said as she took another long drag, making sure that the majority of exhaled smoke went in Joann's direction.

A narrow cement staircase led to a locked door which ultimately led to the roof. Paul lined up his gun to remove the lock.

"Crazy one, what the hell are you doing?" Alex asked his friend in alarm.

"I'm opening the door," Paul answered with a look to match Alex's for the question asked.

"You're shooting at a metal lock attached to a metal

door encased within a narrow landing surrounded by cement, but you don't see anything wrong with what you're doing?"

"Dude, I'm just trying to open the door, I've seen this done a hundred times."

"Those were movies Paul, make-believe stuff."

"Do you want me to get MJ?" Paul asked, a little hurt that his try was being rebuffed.

"First things first," Alex said as he turned the lock.

"Wouldn't have thought to do that," Paul said as he stepped out into the muted sunshine. Black ominous clouds hung overhead and the stench of the dead wafted up from below. "Shaping up to be a wonderful day it is," he joked in a fake Irish brogue.

"Damn," Alex said, looking up at the sky while simultaneously holding his nose.

"Come on, let's see what we're dealing with," Paul motioned as he stepped away from the doorway.

Alex placed a small piece of slate between the door and the jamb, just in case.

"Good call," Paul said looking back at his friend.

Alex gave him a thumbs up with his free hand, not yet willing to take in any more breaths than he had to. They were still a good twenty yards from the edge when they began to see the outer fringes of the enemy below, with still more making their late entry into the fray. And yet they kept marching forward, like lemmings to the abyss.

"Wow," Alex stated. "Zombies don't really care so much about personal space, do they?"

Paul doubted that if it began to rain any of the water around the zombies would touch ground. Zombies were packed tighter than Legos snapped together. This brought 'close' to a whole other level. "Do you think they might just crush themselves to death?"

"That would be great, but it would be better to heed the advice of my Mee-Maw."

"I'm waiting," Paul said as Alex got lost looking at the wall of moving death below them.

"Oh she used to say, 'If the shit hits the fan, unplug it before it gets all over the place.'"

Paul thought about it for a moment. It had a ring of truth to it but he couldn't see how it fit the present situation, "Any chance you could elaborate?"

"I never knew what it meant either; it's just something she used to say. How many you think there are?" Alex asked looking back down.

"Five, six hundred, probably be a thousand in another hour."

"Escape?"

"Not by the truck that brought us here," Paul pointed. It was nearly consumed by the sea of zombanity that surrounded it. "Let's go see what's going on at the back of the store."

"Who parked it that far away?" Alex asked a little miffed.

"MJ parked it, but I should have known better," Paul said.

Alex shook his head. "No sense in slipping in spilled milk."

"Another Mee-Mawism?" Paul asked.

"What's wrong with that one?"

"Nothing. Come on, let's see if there's still a way to get out of here which doesn't involve sleeping on the roof."

"Yeah, especially since it looks like the heavens are going to open up."

Shots rang out from the front of the store. Paul and Alex ran for the doorway and made a quick descent down the stairs. Had they waited a few moments more and gone to the far edge they would have noticed that it was still clear of zombies and they could have made a hasty retreat. That fact would radically change over the next few hours.

Joann was firing blindly into the stacked furniture, wood splintering as bullets crashed into table legs and hutch casings. Mrs. Deneaux sat idly by smoking another cigarette.

"What's going on?" Paul shouted as he ran up the

aisle way.

Joann was firing blanks by the time he got up to her. He placed his hand on hers to remove the empty weapon.

"Joann?" Alex asked, catching up.

Her eyes were stretched wide in fear. "The… the furniture is moving," she cried.

"Yes," Mrs. Deneaux said between puffs. "So she thought it worthwhile to kill the divan."

Paul and Alex both looked at Mrs. Deneaux harshly. She didn't care. "I think she may have gravely wounded the lounger also," she went on with a dry coated rasp.

The movement was almost imperceptible; the strewn furniture pile vibrated slightly as if a semi passed close by. Paul's attention was drawn back to the front when a couch cushion landed at his feet.

"MJ, how much longer on your wonder machine?" Paul asked.

MJ hadn't even looked up at the sound of the shots being fired less than fifty feet away.

"MJ!" Paul shouted.

"What! Can't you see I'm working!" he shouted back, still not looking up.

Paul walked over towards his work station. "Listen, I understand dedication, I really do. But we've got a situation here. How much longer do you think this is going to take?"

MJ finally looked up and noted the concern in Paul's features. MJ's face sagged as he spoke. "Possibly forever with what I have here. I fried some vital components that I don't have replacements for. Is there a chance we could make another run out to Radio Shack?" he asked hopefully.

Paul shook his head, leaving no doubt in his answer.

"Alright, there's still an outside shot I can do it with what I've got, but it's not going to be as powerful."

"Fifteen foot gap between us and them?" Paul asked optimistically.

MJ shook his head.

"Ten maybe?" Paul asked, grasping at straws.

MJ's head hadn't stopped moving from the previous question.

"Dude, how much then?" Paul asked in alarm.

"Three feet max," MJ answered with a sickly smile.

Alex had come up and was listening to the whole exchange. "That's less than a few inches at most from an outstretched hand."

"Yup," MJ said apologetically.

Paul's stomach got queasy. "And you're only talking three feet from the transmitter of that box, with all of us huddled around that thing, that three feet is gone."

"Hadn't even thought of that," MJ said, removing his protective goggles.

"Well," Alex said grasping on to another hope. "What if he finishes it, we move the furniture, and place it by the entrance so that the zombies will stop trying to get in?"

"I like the idea in theory. But first off he isn't done, and if the furniture is moving I've got to believe that they have already broken through the doors. We could be speeding up our demise instead of holding it at bay."

"Paul, I do not want to get trapped on that roof," Alex said. "Sure it's spring and all, but it's still cold at night and it looks like it's going to rain."

"And yet that is the choice before us."

"That sounded very Mike-like," Alex said with a sick grin of his own.

"Yeah I liked that, I've been working on it. Listen, while we've got time, let's see how much warm stuff we can get up on the roof and if they have any types of sales banners we can use as tarps to keep the rain off."

Joann was still watching the pile as if she expected an evil leprechaun to pop out at any second.

"How did Mike do this stuff?" Paul asked aloud. Alex looked at him questioningly. "You know, keep everyone in line. Get them to doing stuff as opposed to blanking out," Paul said as he pointed to Joann.

"He's got crazy eyes," Alex said jokingly, "He made

us more afraid of him than the zombies."

"You might be right. Joann, come on, let's grab April and haul some stuff upstairs. Mrs. Deneaux, you alright watching the door by yourself?" Paul asked the old bat.

She waved him off with her cigarette laden hand. "And I'll be sure to put the lounger out of its misery," she cackled.

"Hilarious," Paul mumbled as he walked away.

CHAPTER 24 – Talbot Journal Entry 11

"Gary, slow down," I told him.

"I'm not even going fast," he answered back.

"Something's not right, slow down," I said, sitting up a little bit in my seat to get a better view.

"We've been through this Mike, you do not have Spidey sense," Gary said with a smirk.

"STOP THIS TRUCK!" I screamed. He damn near threw me through the windshield as he slammed on the brakes. The truck came to a fishtailing halt.

"Happy? You woke the boys."

Justin and Travis were both removing their faces from the front headrests.

I quickly got out of the truck, rifle at the ready. Our front tires were literally resting on the front edge of a spike strip.

"Damn," Gary said getting out of the truck. "You saw that from way back there?"

A rifle shot rang out from the tree line fifteen feet away on the driver's side. Gary jumped over the hood and deposited himself on my lap. The boys were out the door before the echo of the shot was complete.

"I take it that was a warning shot!?" I yelled.

"It's twenty feet at the most, how could I have missed?" came the disembodied voice from the trees.

"You could have been prior Army," I shouted back. Why do I provoke? I don't know, we all have character flaws, but why do mine seem to always have the potential to get me killed?

"That's funny, just so happens that I am."

"Always with the snappy line," Gary admonished me.

"Semper Fi," I yelled back.

"You don't say? A lot of people know that slogan."

"Okay how about, 'this is my rifle, this is my gun, one is for killing and one is for fun.'"

"Better," the voice said. "But Full Metal Jacket is a personal favorite of mine."

"Alright, how about this, the unofficial Marine Corps motto."

"I'm listening."

"Lie, deny and counter blame."

"Fine, I believe you to be a jarhead now but that sure as hell doesn't make us friends."

"But maybe we shouldn't be enemies either. What do you want?" I asked.

"That should be obvious, we want your truck. Our car broke down a few miles ago and this walking crap is for the birds."

"Now I know you're an Army dog and all, but what makes you think we carry four spare tires around with us?"

"Well, hadn't really thought it out until you said that."

"There's gotta be ten thousand cars in the general area, why take ours?"

"Well we DID think of that," he said defensively, "but we keep coming across these hives of zombies and if you get anywhere near them they get real hungry real fast."

"Been there, done that!" Travis shouted.

"Gary, hold my rifle. I'm standing up! I would greatly appreciate it if you didn't shoot me."

"I'll do my best."

"Comforting."

"Don't worry we aren't the Air Force," the voice said mockingly.

"Hey!" Gary said as he stood up. "I was in the Air Force! It was a very honorable branch of the military!"

"Don't get your feathers ruffled, friend," the voice said apologetically as its owner emerged from the tree line, rifle in one hand off to his side.

"How many of there are you?" I asked as Gary handed me my rifle and I placed it over my shoulder.

"Four," he answered. "Two on this side and two on the other. Yeah, you were pretty much goners."

All of the people came out of the woods looking like they had just come from a camouflage expo.

"It's not what you think," our initial contact person stated. "All of us know about camouflage but we're not those crazy survivalist types."

"You say that as if it's a bad thing," I told him.

"Yeah, I guess there's nothing wrong with being alive," he mused, "This whole thing started while we were in cami's so we figured we should stick to what works. We were up in the hills, a place called Oak Ridge Hollows, it was a company sponsored paint ball event. Hell, we were having a good old time, drinking beer, barbequing, shooting our bosses multiple times with paint balls."

'Oh, what I wouldn't have done to have been able to do that," I thought wistfully.

"And this one guy, Sully, he starts getting sick. I mean violently. It was shooting out his mouth and his ass. I could see his trousers stained in crap and blood. I just thought the fat bastard was getting sick from running around all over the place. Most exercise he probably ever got was when he squatted on the shitter and made a toilet baby. Somebody thought to call an ambulance, but hell, we were forty minutes out of town, it was going to be a wait. So everyone kind of sat in their cars or branched off in small groups. A few were with Sully, but you didn't need a medical degree to figure out that he wasn't going to make it. I'd seen guys in combat with limbs blown off that looked better than he did. He died twenty minutes before the ambulance even got there. That was kind of the end of the event."

"Yeah, I could see how that would put a damper on things," I told him.

"You from Boston?" he asked.

"Yeah, the accent gives it away," I told him.

"No, it's the sarcasm, had two guys in my unit from Southie. Their accents were a little thicker than yours and just about everything was 'Wicked Pissah.' But the sarcasm man, they just never let up."

"Yeah, that sounds just about right for Southie boys."

"Still, I was pretty sad when their Hummer got blown up. The camp lost a lot of color when they moved on."

I took my hat off to pay my respects.

"Anyway," he said, trying to pull himself away from that unhappy thought, "You remind me of them."

"Yeah, but in a live way right?" I said to him.

"Yeah, but in a live way," he reiterated. "So a bunch of people start heading home. I mean, what the hell else could they do? But Sully was in my department and for some misaligned sense of duty I figured I should stay with him. My girlfriend here Cindy, Cindy Martell and my buddy Jack O'Donnell and his girlfriend Perla Tirado, we all stayed behind with most of the bosses. Me and Jack were sharing a smoke a few feet away when Cindy came up the large entryway to the playing field, she and Perla were leading the ambulance in. I threw my cigarette down and started walking over to where Sully was and by now it was dusk. The red and blue lights of the ambulance were making everything dance. I looked down to the cigarette wondering if Jack had laced it with anything because Sully was up and the fat bastard was eating, he was eating Lipstein. I mean literally gnawing through his neck."

I don't know why he thought I needed extra explaining. It wasn't like I was going on the faith of his words alone.

"I don't know what the hell I was thinking, but all I had on me was my paint ball marker. I started running towards the scene, pelting Sully with yellow and green balls. He didn't even look up as blood spewed out of the side of Lip's neck. The other higher ups had just taken off, left their own to die. Jack comes running up beside me, asking me what the hell I'm doing,"

"Thought I was going to puke," Jack said succinctly.

"Yeah, that's the usual state of affairs when you first come across them," I said to him, sharing in his pain.

"I guess I finally pissed Sully off when I nailed him in the eye. He dropped Lip and started heading my way. I kept pulling the trigger but what was the use. Jack pulled me out of there."

"We were in Fallujah together," was all Jack said, and that really summed it up. Looking out for your buddies was the main thing you did in combat.

"I don't know what happened to Sully," our 'host' said. Cindy wrapped her arms around herself and shivered, remembering the events of that night. "So that's about it, the four of us have been on the run ever since. Oh yeah, and my name is Brian, Brian Wamsley."

"Dude, I don't need last names," I told him.

"Is it because you don't know us well enough and if we die you can keep yourself emotionally distanced from us that way?" Perla asked.

"Perla," Jack said. "We don't know them at all, I'm sure he has his reasons."

"It's pretty basic reasoning actually," I told them. "I'll just never remember them."

Cindy laughed. "Yeah, the 80's were a great time. So what's your story?"

I gave her the super stripped down version that did not contain Eliza or Tommy, and even that was a pretty far-fetched scary tale. Friggen' hate when I give myself the shivers.

"So now you're going to try and get to your friends?" Perla asked.

"That's the idea, we think they might be in trouble," Gary said.

"How would you *know* any of this?" Brian asked suspiciously.

My story had gaping wounds that you could drive a

Mini-Cooper through. I had watched knowing exchanges passed between Jack and Brian. I didn't have time to appease their suspicions.

"Listen, I've... we've got someplace we need to be," I told the foursome. "I will be more than happy to drive you somewhere until you get a set of your own wheels and then we've got to go," I told Brian directly, basically telling him that I was done answering his queries. We owed each other nothing and I was holding good to that.

"What if we went with you to this rescue?" Jack asked, "And then you helped us find some wheels."

"Listen, everyone here knows that I didn't tell you half of the truth." Gary nodded, I smacked him in the arm. "What's going on with the zombies is horrible, but being around us is not something most would want to do willingly."

"Yeah, we're sort of trouble magnets," Gary said.

"That's one way of saying it," I added, agreeing with Gary.

"We're in," Brian said with conviction.

"You speak for everyone?" I asked him.

"We're thrill junkies," Cindy said as she hopped into the back of the truck.

"I don't think you're getting it," I said.

"Ooooh, *zombies*," Perla added, throwing her hands up in the air. "Dammit, I think I chipped a nail," she fake whined as she climbed into the truck bed.

"Jack," I said grabbing his arm. "This is no joke."

He looked me straight in the eye. "Nothing better to do. Can we go now?"

I let his arm go. "I thought *I* was nuts," I muttered as I climbed into the driver's seat.

"Oh you are," Gary said wisely. "But apparently you're not alone."

"Comforting," I said as I was about to put the idling truck back into gear. "Gary, we're just about the same height but I've got to adjust the damn seat every time. Why do you like to drive with your knees in your face?"

Gary shrugged.

"DAD!" Justin yelled.

I jumped. "Boy, you almost made me crap myself. What's the matter?"

"Spike strips!" he yelled.

"That would have sucked," I said as I got out of the truck to remove the pointy bars.

"Whoa, that would have sucked," Brian said as he looked over the edge of the truck bed.

"You want these things?" I asked him, holding them up.

"Not so much."

I tossed them as far from the road as I could so that some other unsuspecting traveler would not find their forward progress hampered by them. It wasn't nearly as far as I would have hoped, and leave it to Travis to let me know.

"Nice toss Curt," he mocked from the back of the cab, referring to the great Red Sox pitcher Curt Schilling.

Tracy would kill me if she had seen this, but I flipped him off. He laughed as I went to make sure the strips were off the roadway.

"Zombies!" came the shout.

"Well, forget the strips," I said as I got back into the truck and got going, "Speeders," I said looking into the rear view mirror. "I hate speeders."

"We would have been screwed if I hadn't remembered about the strips," Justin said boastfully.

"Yeah, you definitely deserve a pat on the back for that one," I told him. We would have been FAR better off dealing with the twenty or so that were following than the hundreds that were in the process of surrounding the furniture store, but then again I hadn't a clue what we were driving into so I forged ahead.

Brian tapped on the glass window that separated the crew cab from the truck bed. Travis slid it open.

"So how far to the rendezvous point?" Brian shouted

to be heard over the sound of the wind and the road.

Gary pulled out the Atlas and tried to get a bearing from our surroundings. "Damn," was the only thing he said.

"Did we pass the exit?" I asked him.

"Not yet, but if Brian hadn't of asked we would have."

"You're the navigator, you're supposed to be watching out for this stuff."

"Well, technically, I'm still supposed to be driving."

"Yeah, well, that was before having your knees all up in your face nearly hindered your view of the roadway and you almost gave us four flats."

"That's one way of looking at it I guess. About an hour," he turned to Brian to answer the original question.

My stomach began its internal churning, bile mixed with acid. Oh boy, yum! I didn't get flashes of images for my prescience, no, nothing quite so noble. I got to feel like I was going to either throw up or crap myself when I felt like we were getting into some trouble.

"Brian!" I yelled. He stuck his head through the small window. "You sure about this?"

"About what, Mike?" He asked. "Listen, you guys are the first folks we've run across in a long while that I feel even remotely comfortable around. That you guys are risking your lives for your friends says a lot about your character. We're in for a while Mike, and unless you prove me wrong, who knows man, maybe you'll be stuck with us for the long haul too." He pulled his head back through, satisfied that he had spoken his peace.

"Brian!" I shouted again to stop him from completely extracting himself from the cab's window. I pointed my ringer over my shoulder right at him. "Do not EVER say that I did not give you fair warning."

He laughed. Travis closed the window as Brian got his head out.

"I don't think he gets it, Mike," Gary said seriously.

"He's gonna shoot me when he does."

"I've got a feeling it'll be Cindy you have to worry about," Gary warned, turning back from looking at the passengers in the truck bed.

"She does look like she knows how to use that thing, Dad," Travis piped in.

"Just tell me when we get to the exit and feel free to keep your opinions to yourselves," I told them. Of course they wouldn't listen but I might get at least a ten minute respite.

It ended up being more like five.

CHAPTER 25 – Tracy and BT

BT was looking at the grass causeway as Tracy hurtled down I-95. He barely registered the spike strips as they passed by his field of vision.

"Zombies," Tracy said flatly a few minutes later.

BT pulled his field of vision in and looked straight ahead. Thirty or so zombies were running full tilt down the highway in the same direction. They nearly took up the entire width of the roadway. Tracy slowed the car down.

"Whatcha doing, Auntie?" Meredith asked.

"Was thinking of going over the grass and just avoiding them," Tracy responded.

"Do you think they're following Mike? We could be pretty close," BT said.

"We could roll on up on them and ask," Meredith grinned.

"I hate Talbots," BT murmured under his breath.

"There's no reason to fight them, right?" Tracy asked.

"Besides ridding the world of them, no, not right now anyway," BT answered her.

Tracy drove over the grass in the median, the car bouncing around on the rough ground.

"I like where God put my kidneys, woman," BT said, bracing himself with one hand on the roof and one on the door.

"He really is kind of a big baby, isn't he Auntie?" Meredith asked, needling BT.

Tracy laughed as she got to the edge of the roadway and looked both ways for traffic before she pulled out.

"Don't say it BT," Tracy said pointing her finger at

him, "It's a habit!"

"How many times have you crossed a highway median?" BT asked.

The zombies turned as one when they heard Tracy's car coming down the roadway. Without hesitation they began to run directly at her.

"Good thing they don't have the concept of cutting us off or this would be close," BT said, once again bracing himself.

The zombies were running to where the car was, not where it was going to be. They had to keep readjusting their trajectory as Tracy pressed even harder down on the accelerator, the zombies were losing crucial fragments of time during each repositioning. Tracy blew past them somewhere in the neighborhood of 90 mph. The zombies fell back in line, full on sprinting after their retreating prey.

"I hate zombies Tracy, I really do, but you know what scares me more?" BT asked a leading question.

Tracy turned to look, full seconds elapsing as she waited for a response. Icy beads of sweat fell from BT's forehead.

"*You* driving at high speed, dammit, look at the road!" BT yelled as he kept pumping on brakes that he did not have access to.

Tracy turned back to the roadway, and then looked at her instrument panel. "Wow, I had no idea I was going that fast."

"We did, Auntie," Meredith said, clutching on to the seatbelt.

"I'm not *that* bad of a driver," Tracy said grumpily, looking into the rear view mirror.

"Please, I'm so young," Meredith pleaded. "I've always wanted to have a family of my own."

"Oh for goodness sakes," Tracy said as she eased up on the accelerator. "Bunch of babies. I'm going to get back onto the other side unless there are some complaints from the peanut gallery."

"No, we're good now," BT croaked as they approached a more respectable 70 miles per hour.

Once Tracy had crossed back over she crept the car back up to close to 80 miles per hour. She knew she was close to Mike; she could damn near smell the sanitizer.

"I think I saw a glint," BT said pointing straight ahead.

Tracy flooded the engine with gas.

"This doesn't mean you need to speed up," BT said in all seriousness, "We don't know what we're heading into."

"Oh come on BT, I can almost smell rubbing alcohol and bleach. It has to be Mike," Tracy said, her heart thumping wildly in her chest.

"I think I smell it too," Meredith sniffed as she stuck her head out the window.

BT shook his head. "Listen, you're already gaining on them... him." He changed the word when Tracy looked over at him glaringly. "Let's just make sure we don't plow into him, that's all I'm saying. You're not listening to a word I say, are you?"

"You still talking?" Tracy asked.

"You weren't born a Talbot, what happened to you?" BT asked her.

"It must be infectious."

"Great, when can I expect the conversion?"

"Oh, it's already deep into your bones by now, big man, won't be long at all," Tracy told him cheerfully.

BT absently scratched his arms. "Feels like I've got spiders crawling on me."

"In, not on," Meredith added helpfully.

"There are people in the truck bed," Tracy said as she shielded her eyes.

BT grabbed his rifle.

"Is that Dad's truck?" Meredith asked, peering over the front seat.

Tracy took a moment to respond. "It's the same color, that's all I can really tell from here."

"Mike's not really one for picking up passengers," BT said, really only as a pronouncement and not a query.

"We still don't know if that's the right truck yet, so let's try not to adopt Mike's philosophy of riddle with bullets first and then solve the puzzle."

* * *

Brian tapped on the window. "We've got company."

"Yeah, I saw them a few seconds ago," I told him.

"You want us to light them up!" Cindy asked excitedly.

"Don't they have medication for that condition?" I asked. Thankfully the buffeting wind knocked my response clear from her ears.

"Did he say 'Yes?'" Cindy asked Brian as she started to check her magazine.

Perla popped her head up. "What's going on?"

Cindy pointed to the approaching car, rapidly gaining on the truck.

* * *

"Well it looks like we've been noticed," BT grimaced.

"They're pointing weapons at us," Tracy said as she eased up on the gas.

* * *

"No shooting!" I yelled.

"No offense Mike," Brian said, "but I'm feeling mighty exposed sitting here in the back of a truck."

"This doesn't feel right, Mike," Gary said. "We can't just go blasting folks because we have a 'funny feeling.'"

"Agreed, big brother." I began to slow the truck down.

"What's the plan?" Brian asked poking his head in.

"I'm going to pull over. You guys jump out and use the truck body as cover, no firing until we are fired upon. Fair enough?"

"Fair enough," Brian agreed.

*   *   *

"Tracy, I see brake lights. You should slow down, they'll be able to hammer the hell out of us if we drive by them," BT said with a little alarm, remembering the last time they had gotten into a broadside attack with a truck full of errant rednecks. His leg twinged in sympathy.

Tracy mirrored the truck in front of her, as it slowed so did she. When it came to a stop she was moments away from stopping herself. "Now what BT?" Tracy glanced over at him.

*   *   *

"Foh!" Cindy yelled. "That is the biggest man I have ever seen in my life!"

I was busy checking my magazines when Cindy's exclamation sank in. "What color?" I asked sharply, bringing my head up. "And what the hell does 'foh' mean?"

Cindy swiveled her head to look at me like I had asked her if she wanted fries with that. "It's Shakespearean."

"Oh, okay that explains everything." I answered.

"Mike," Jack said, "He's big, black, and he's walking this way. Looks like he's carrying a Browning Fully Automatic but it looks like a matchstick in his arms. He opens up on us with that thing and we're in trouble."

"Where did BT get a Browning?" Gary asked.

"Ron held out on us." I wanted to cuss heatedly.

"BT?" I threw my gun back in the cab and started to jog towards the small car stopped behind us. I could see the big man grin as I approached.

I heard Perla ask Jack why they had hooked up with a

crazy man. I laughed and picked up my pace. I almost tripped and fell to my knees when Tracy came out of the driver's seat. BT was an unimaginable surprise, but when my beloved showed too it was almost more than I could bear. Now I know it had only been a span of a couple of days since I had last seen Tracy, but you've got to remember I truly believed in the depths of my heart I had said my final goodbye to the woman I shared the deepest connection with on this world. I faltered before once again gaining momentum.

I looked over at BT with a huge grin as I ran past and swept my wife up into my arms. I spun her around once, still too caught up in the moment to give her any crap about following us. I put her down and kissed her once. Then I turned to embrace BT in a hug and I was met with a fist roughly the size of a half ham. I crashed to the deck before my body could even begin to register the oncoming rush of pain.

BT was standing over my prone body, finger roughly the size of a Johnsonville Sausage pointing in my face. "You ever leave me with your crazy ass family again and it will be hours before you're able to get your ass up off the ground."

"BT!" Tracy yelled.

I put my hand up, "It's all right, I deserved that." BT grabbed my hand and hoisted me up.

"Good to see you man," BT said grabbing me tight.

There was something comforting about being embraced in steel cabling.

"Mike, everything all right?" Brian asked breathlessly as he and Perla came running up with weapons at the ready.

"Who are these fools?" BT asked, letting me go.

"Replacement friends," I told him. He looked down on me with a frown. "They don't punch me."

"Come on, I barely touched you," BT groused.

"And yet I found myself on the ground," I told him.

"Not my damn fault you didn't like your greens when you were growing up."

"You know not everyone had their collard greens

infused with Human Growth Hormones."

"What can I say? My momma loved me."

Brian pulled up a little short when he got closer. I think that was the only way he could get all of BT in his field of vision. "Mike?" he asked cautiously.

I rubbed my jaw. Eating anything with more chew to it than peas for the next few days was going to be a chore. "BT, this is Brian Wamsley, another military man."

"Oh for the love of God, where do they all come from, do they breed them with rabbits?" BT said.

"Nice to meet you too," Brian said.

"Oh it's nothing against you personally, it's just that recently I have found Marines to be the least likely to think before they act and that always leads to trouble. This shitbird here has been trying to get me killed for the last four months. And when he couldn't succeed, he left me with his clinically insane family to see if they could push me over the edge to do myself in,"

"I wasn't in the military," Perla said smiling. "So I should be okay," as she came up to shake BT's hand.

"Yeah, but you're hanging out with them so it's crazy by proxy," BT told her.

"Don't listen to him, he's this friendly with everyone," Tracy told Perla and Brian.

"Hey, Uncle Mike," Meredith said diffidently; she had been standing behind BT and I had missed her completely.

"Oh no, there is *no* way your dad knew you were coming. I am so screwed!"

"Glad to see you too!" she cried back.

"No, no, that's not what I meant."

"See, this is what I'm talking about, typical Marine. Screw up first and then try to correct later," BT threw into the mix. I pointed a mean looking finger at BT. "Get that straw outta my face, what are you gonna do, make me a milkshake?"

"Meredith no, it's awesome to see you. It's just that

this isn't like a family reunion-type setting, it's pretty crappy out here."

She didn't seem appeased. "I think I have a pretty good idea of how bad it is out here, we were all almost killed a couple of times," she blurted out.

Tracy was holding up her hands trying to hold back the flood of words as Meredith graphically and in rich detail laid out all the events of the last few days. I thought Perla was going to collapse.

Unfortunately it seemed an all too standard relating of unfolding events to me. That it happened to my wife, niece and closest friend while I was not there to help almost made my rail-running heartbeat slide off the tracks. I was about to lay into Tracy about why she had put herself and everyone else in danger by coming back when she stopped me dead in my tracks with her next words.

"I wasn't ready to say goodbye."

What do you say to that? What can you possibly say that doesn't make you sound like a big asshole?

"I, uh, yeah, we should probably get going, looks like a storm is brewing."

"One more thing Mike," Tracy said as she opened her door. My fat bottomed fawn colored Henry came padding out from her side of the car. His huge tongue was lolling as he ran to me, oversized jowls flapping in the wind like the useless wings on a dodo bird.

"No way!" I said as I nearly cried, dropping to my knees. Henry bowled me over like I was a lone bowling pin and he was going for a spare. Drool coated me from goatee to my forehead, and I loved every gross part of it!

*   *   *

As Tracy got into the car and they got rolling again, BT looked over at her and laughed. "Wow, you hit harder than I do."

"Damn Aunt Tracy, I will never underestimate you,

you rock!" Meredith told her.

"How hard did you hit him?" Tracy asked with her own smile.

"Oh, I smacked the hell out of him," BT laughed.

They drove up to where the pick-up was parked so that brief introductions could be made and Tracy could give and get hugs from her boys. Mike still seemed to be reeling, whether from the physical blow or the psychological one, she didn't know.

*   *   *

Perla and Cindy got into Tracy's car. Our next stop was going to be the very next exit where we would find some sort of transportation for Brian, Jack and the women. First off so they could get out of the rain that was about to hit, and second it would be yet another opportunity for them to go their own way. I had my doubts they would do so, but it would ease my conscience. I had yet to disclose everything so they were not making a completely informed decision.

We had no sooner pulled off the highway and there were a couple of fast food joints. Oh for some onion rings. And a boot outlet store with ten or so cars and trucks in the lot. Brian motioned for me to go in there.

When I pulled in I got out of the truck. Tracy pulled in behind, my heart still tripping at the sight of her. "You know how to hot wire a car?" I asked Brian.

"No, but Jack's got an idea," he told me vaguely.

Jack walked up to the doors of the boot store and when they didn't open he gave them a .223 caliber reason to do so. The shattering glass rivaled the percussions of the bullets.

"Army men!" BT said exasperatedly. "Do they remove the brain stem BEFORE or AFTER boot camp?"

"During," Brian replied.

Jack's boots crunched over the smashed glass. "Hostiles!" he yelled. He motioned with his free hand first five and then another three.

Within seconds Travis, Justin, myself, BT, Brian, Cindy and Perla had him completely flanked. He backed up to be within our firing line as opposed to being in front. We stayed about fifteen feet from the front of the store and then they came, a worse looking lot of zombies we would have had a difficult time finding. Flesh was sloughing off their faces; the putrid smell of feces and decomposition wafted from the store. Perla took a moment to put her stomach into check, but everyone else stood firm.

The first zombie out was a girl maybe in her early twenties. Her green tinged skin made age identification an impossibly difficult feat, it had more to do with her clothing. She had on a sun dress, a leather jacket and boots. I think it was Cindy who took the first shot, drilled her right in the head, most likely more for the fashion infringement than for being a zombie.

Two or three employees came out next. This was easy to tell from their Smacker's Boots and Belts smocks. Two cowboys came out, big brass belt buckles and all, how the hell they still had their ten gallon hats on amazed me. Listen, I know I have issues and if the world is ever once again dominated by humans I promise I will be the first to get in line to get checked. But all I could think when those two came through the door was Brokeback Mountain and how damn disgusting would it be for two zombies to be getting it on. Would maggots make good lubrication? Would the friction cause the skin to peel off? Would 'love bites' take on a whole new meaning? Would the other zombies frown on a male on male relationship? I know brains are just a mixture of chemicals and connections, but apparently I'm missing a synapses or two.

"What are you smiling at?" Cindy asked me as she placed another magazine into her Israeli made Uzi.

"It would be best if I kept it to myself," I told her, never easing up on my grin.

"Cease fire," Brian said, holding up his fist.

Would be easy enough for me, I don't think I ever fired a shot.

Jack walked over and started checking the bodies for keys. Eight dead bodies and five sets of keys, pretty good plan I thought.

The blue Mini-Cooper would have been my first choice in a perfect world. A 78ish Datsun that looked like it was barely able to hold off the effects of gravity was also dismissed. The best out of the lot available was a late year Chevy, it wasn't pretty but it ran, had close to a full tank and would fit them all comfortably enough.

"Alright, this looks like the one," Jack decided.

"Ready to saddle up Mike?" Brian asked me.

"Alright, so now you've got your own wheels and you're not in as much dire straits that you need to forcibly take my traveling direction. I think we need to take a minute so I can fill in a few holes to the story I told you. Then you can make an informed decision about whether you want to join us or head as far away in the opposite direction as possible."

"Lay it on us," Brian said, truly not believing that I could offer anything too far off the beaten path as to dissuade them from their present course of action.

I went back to Day One and our first introduction to Tommy, who even then seemed more than he portrayed. To our first encounter with Eliza in the field and to my biggest mistake for not letting Justin blow her demented skull clear from her tainted body.

'It's all right Dad,' he interjected.

I gave them a recap of everything we had been through. It still wasn't the in-depth exposé they deserved, but the clouds that had been threatening all day finally began to release their loads and I still had a sneaking suspicion that Paul and Alex needed our help and soon.

"Wait," Perla asked. "So you're saying that not only are there zombies, there is a Vampire Princess who rules them all?"

"I'm pretty sure I never said the word 'princess' but yeah, she holds sway over them. I don't know if it's every zombie or if she has to be within a certain proximity, but that she can control some of them is without doubt."

"So I'm confused," Cindy started. "The kid from the Wal-Mart roof was, I mean 'is' her brother, and now he's with her? Couldn't you tell?"

"It's not like he hung a sign on his neck that said he was a 500-year-old half vampire," I told her.

"I'm having a real hard time believing this," Jack said.

"Yup, you nailed me, the zombie invasion wasn't a big enough challenge for me and my family. We figured we'd drum up a few more nightmares and see if that could hold our interest."

"That's not what I meant," Jack said placating me. "I'm wondering if you're trying to get rid of us."

"Truth is, guys, I would never turn away any help, least of all experienced ones, but you need to know what you're getting into."

"Cindy?" Brian asked, she nodded. "Cindy and I are in."

Perla nodded without any prompt. "So are we," Jack said.

"Well see, this is where you guys, not thinking before you act actually worked out in our favor," BT said.

Three exits later and we were pulling off the highway again. I had no sooner hit the off ramp when I brought the truck to a skittering halt. Tracy, her usually attentive driving self, almost slammed into us.

"You didn't tell me you were going to stop!" she shouted irately as she got out of the car.

"Hon, those red shiny things in the back let you know what I'm doing," I told her calmly.

"Mike, any chance I could ride with you?" an ashy faced BT asked.

"Traitor!" Tracy yelled at him.

"There is nothing wrong with being a selfpreservationist," he said loftily.

Brian came to a stop and our small caravan idled by the side of the road. "What gives?" he asked.

I walked over to the guardrail. Because of our elevation from the outlying areas it afforded us a decent view of the shops below, one of which was a furniture store.

"Oh my God!" Perla gasped, placing her hand over her mouth.

"That would obviously be where we need to go?" Jack asked me.

I nodded once. The warehouse parking lot was entombed by the living dead. I hadn't seen this great an assembly since the fall of Little Turtle.

"What the hell Mike?" Tracy asked in disbelief.

"They're already dead," Brian said absently.

"Alex risked his entire world to save my family, I owe him the same chance. He did no such thing for you. You don't know him and you barely know me, you're not under any obligation to stay here."

"Relax friend," Brian said. "I wasn't saying it as an out. It just was kind of a voiced thought."

"Oh," I nodded. "I could relate to those."

I blasted off a couple of rounds, not sure if the sound would break through the distance or the dampening effects of the rain, but maybe it would give them a small measure of hope that help, no matter how little of it there was, had arrived.

"Alright, it's almost dark and it's raining like hell. Why don't we find some shelter and see if we can come up with some sort of plan," Gary said, momentarily taking charge. I appreciated it because the scene laid out before me looked like something from Dante's circles of hell and I had yet to assimilate it all.

*   *   *

Paul was exhausted after what seemed like his fiftieth

time up and down the stairs. They had brought mattresses and chairs. Anything that resembled a tarp, all the contents of the vending machine and anything that could help them wait out an extended stay on an exposed roof top. It was on one of the last trips up the stairs that Paul began to ponder this last strategic weak point.

The stairs weren't going anywhere; they were constructed of a giant poured block of concrete. The railing, however, was only attached with hex head bolts. Removing the railing wouldn't necessarily keep the zombies from making it up the stairs but it could keep a great many of them from staying there. The more zombies that tried to crowd on the stairwell, the more that would keep getting pushed off the edge. If they could never get a big enough thrust to work on the door leading out to the roof, the survivors would have a much better chance of waiting it out and potentially receiving some help.

Finding tools was easy enough, the loading bay was full of tool boxes where some furniture had to be assembled before making its way onto the show room floor. Paul and Alex started the removal process. MJ came to help when they got down to the final two bolts. The railing was in two sections of about 20 feet long, with the second top piece having an 'L' bend to accommodate the landing. The lower piece came off without much of a hitch. As the last screw came undone, it was then gently eased to the floor. The second piece was a little more difficult, Alex and MJ held it in place while Paul unscrewed the last bolt down by the bottom, his arm hanging through the railing as he sat on the stair trying to get more leverage. MJ did not fully realize the weight of the railing he was supporting from the top landing. When the bolt came free below, he nearly went head over heels off the landing. With only the concrete floor to stop his fall, his injuries most likely would have been severe. Just as he neared the breaking point which would decide whether he could continue to hang on a little longer or topple over, MJ let loose of the railing. The force pulled the slick metal from

Alex' hands and the resulting crushing force of the railing as it came down almost broke Paul's arm in half. The ear splitting sound of two hundred pounds of metal slamming into concrete was immensely louder than rifle shots.

Joann and Erin came running in. MJ had a mild look of shock on his face, while Alex was checking on Paul who was clutching his arm to his side.

"Paul, are you all right?" Erin screamed from the bottom of the stairs just as the sound finally stopped its incessant echoing from concrete wall to concrete wall.

"Whew, that was close," Paul said to Alex's questioning stare.

"I'm so sorry," MJ said, coming down to the middle of the staircase. "I guess I didn't realize how heavy it was going to be. You alright?" he asked hopefully.

"Yeah, I think I'm fine. I could feel the railing, it just about caught my arm and then I pulled it in real quick, tweaked it a bit but nothing serious. Scared me more than anything," Paul said as he flexed his arm out.

Alex grabbed his elbow and gave a squeeze, "Does that hurt?"

"I'm good, just a little hyper-extended. Could you have set it if it was broken?" Paul asked, concerned now because he had not thought of it before. Could any of them survive what was once considered a basic injury?

"Be thankful it wasn't," was Alex's reply.

Erin came up the stairs to hug her husband.

"Everything's fine honey, just a close call," he reassured her.

Eddy took this opportune time to come screaming into the loading bay where the staircase was located. "Mean lady says the zombies are almost in!" he screamed.

Alex was gone like a shot, going to grab Marta and his kids. MJ was right behind him going to grab his tools and box. To each his own.

"Hey Erin, why don't you and Joann see if there is anything else in this general area you think should go up. I'm going to go lay down some covering fire with Mrs. Deneaux."

"Don't wait too long," she told him and gave him a kiss.

"Just long enough for Alex and MJ to get back and up." Paul hugged her fiercely then let her go and bounded down the stairs.

Shots rang out from the front of the store and, unlike Joann's wild shots a few hours earlier, Paul was under the impression that these were finding targets. He ran to the front of the store. Mrs. Deneaux was furiously puffing on a cigarette while reloading her revolver. Furniture had been pushed back into the store a good fifteen feet. Five zombies lay in a pool of brackish goo.

"Oh, I know what you're thinking," Mrs. Deneaux mouthed the words around the cigarette. It looked like something she had been practicing for many a year. "Six shots five kills, not bad."

Paul hadn't actually had enough time to access the situation, but now that she brought it up, yeah, that was pretty friggen' good.

"Well, you're wrong, because the sixth one is behind the big purple love seat, you just can't see him." And then she cackled.

'That is pretty good,' Paul thought. He just couldn't bring himself to verbalize it. He began to open fire with his rifle. Zombies as a whole had not yet completely figured out how to run through the maze, but they were beginning to leak through like blood through splayed fingers covering a wound. The flood was being held at bay but this was now a game with a timer attached.

"Start heading back!" Paul shouted to Mrs. Deneaux. MJ had already grabbed his stuff and was almost halfway to the back of the building.

"One more revolver full!" she shouted gleefully. "It's been a long time since I've done anything so fun!"

Paul shook his head. Blowing holes in zombie heads

was not supposed to be anyone's idea of a good time.

Mrs. Deneaux' facial muscles screamed in protest as she forced them into a pose they had not mustered in decades.

'That is one hideous smile,' Paul thought, 'but the bitch sure can shoot.'

"Six shots, six kills, huh!" she yelled, "Okay, I'm out of here!"

She wasn't particularly sprightly as she headed away but there was a definite hop to her step as she retreated down the hallway.

Paul waited for three more zombies to appear, dispatching them easily from this distance before hurrying to catch up with Mrs. Deneaux. They had just reached the far wall when the mountain of furniture avalanched down. Zombies streamed through, nothing short of two Gatlin Guns was going to keep them out now.

"Where you at Mike?" Paul asked aloud as he took one final glance back as the enemy poured in. 'Although I don't know what the hell even he's gonna be able to do,' he thought glumly.

The nine of them sat on the rooftop as the rain began to splatter down, the fat droplets incredibly loud under the banner that read 'Sale.' Whether consciously or not, they were as far away from the access door as possible. Alex had set the lock from the inside and there was no access to the mechanism from the roof side. He then propped up some boards to add as a heavy set door stop. It would stop the zombies for now, but it was a temporary fix at best. They now had no egress to the ground. Zombies surrounded the store and a large number were also inside. Life would be measured in moments.

It came as no surprise but it still startled the hell out of each and every one of them when the first resounding thud came from the roof door.

"Our dinner guests have arrived," Paul said sourly.

"That was horrible," Joann answered, fairly close to

crying.

Eddy was the only one that seemed somewhat immune from the depressing void that surrounded the rest of their band. He wasn't old enough to verbalize it, but it was the reason he left the relative dryness of the banner to stand by the wall facing the highway. The soaking from the depression weighed much more heavily than rain. Eddy watched the muzzle flashes as a series of gunshots went off not too far in the distance.

"Did you guys see that?" he asked enthusiastically. He should have known the answer just by the way they were all sitting in a huddled circle with their heads bowed. They would have missed a fireworks show like that.

"What did you see, little man?" Alex was able to ask with an almost decent rendition of a smile.

"Gunshots!" Eddy answered happily.

"You saw gunshots?" MJ asked analytically.

"Well, I didn't SEE the bullets, I'm not Superman," Eddy answered as if MJ were the biggest dolt on the planet. And who knows, the human population was so low at the moment it very well could be the case. "I saw the bright flashes!" he clarified.

"You saw the muzzle flashes of guns?" Paul asked, now perking up a bit.

"Yeah, over by the roadway there was like five of them and they were pointing up in the air."

"Like a signal?" Alex asked Paul.

"It's gotta be Mike," Paul said with a relieved grin.

"Oh, not that insufferable one," Mrs. Deneaux said, but no one paid her much attention.

"Who else would signal their whereabouts with a legion of zombies around?" Paul asked rhetorically.

"Yes, that does sound like Mike," Mrs. Deneaux said, but not in a complementary way.

"And you're sure the guns were pointed in the air?" Paul asked Eddy.

Eddy looked at Paul the same way he had at MJ only

seconds earlier.

"Alright, alright, I get it," Paul said, a true smile now creasing his features.

Alex grabbed Paul's arm and pulled him out in to the burgeoning rain storm. "Listen, hope is a powerful thing and right now even mine is surging, but what is Mike going to be able to do if it really is him?"

"Don't know," Paul said still smiling, "but he isn't going to let us rot up here."

CHAPTER 26 – Talbot Journal Entry 12

We drove a few more miles away from the furniture store than we probably had to, can you blame me? We came across a few zombies that were still making their approach to the siege. Some were so completely damaged, the fight no matter which way it went would be long over before they ever made it. Jack and Brian shot a few of the Johnny and Susie come-latelies, I didn't have the stomach for it. I've been over and over this. I know they're not humans and never will be again, but they were once. If they aren't bothering me, then I'll return the favor. Although wouldn't that be pretty crappy if I went out and got bit by an ankle biter? That's irony right? And why am I asking my journal? Which is basically like asking myself. Which actually is something I do regularly. But enough of this internal musing.

The old apartment building was a four floor, low-rent-looking tenement but it looked weather proof. Some bullet holes dotted the lower level, as if a small battle had been played out here, but maybe if we were lucky it involved something more mundane like a drive by shooting. No lights shone in the windows, either candle or lantern. We'd have to take our chances that any occupants still in the building would not feel the need to bother us in whichever hovel we borrowed for the evening.

Perla started heading right for the front door like she owned the place.

"Uh, I wouldn't do that if I were you," I told her.

"Why?" she asked, looking a little perturbed.

Screw this, I can get into trouble with my own woman quick enough, I didn't need to go looking for it. Jack was busy grabbing some gear out of the back of the truck when I walked up on him. "Jack," I said. "I would consider this an urban combat environment, wouldn't you?"

He nodded his head, "Yeah, so?"

"So would you send one of your team in alone and not even locked and loaded?"

"Perla? Again? The woman isn't happy enough with our present threat level, she always feels the need to up it." He hastened away from the truck to a defiant Perla who was now opening up the front door. "STOP!" he yelled.

"Oh stop Jack, you're always thinking the worst," Perla shouted over her shoulder.

"Do not move! I can see the trip wire from here!" Jack yelled.

"Everyone away from the door!" I shouted.

"Jack, I heard a click," Perla cried. "What do I do?"

I could see her shaking and I was fifteen feet away behind the truck. Tracy, the boys and BT were by my side.

"You ever do demolitions?" BT asked me.

"Hell no," I told him, not taking my eyes from the doorway. "I like to blow things up, not the other way around."

"What the hell is the other way around?" BT asked me. "Unblowing? Is that a word?"

"Perla, what exactly do you see?" Brian asked.

"There's… there's a silver wire leading to a little box and the… the box has a red light on it," she stammered out.

"Claymore mine?" Cindy asked Brian.

"Not with a light on it," he answered her.

"Did she say there's a light on it?" I asked from the relative safety of the truck.

Brian was about mid-way from us to the door way. "Yeah, you know what it is?"

"No, but I've got an idea," I told him.

"Talbot?" BT and Tracy said in startled unison.

"It's all good," I said, walking over to Brian and then past him.

"What are you doing?" Jack asked with alarm. And who could blame him? His girlfriend was a motion away from potentially becoming wet dust.

"I got this," I said, putting up a hand.

"I hate when he does this," Tracy said.

"I heard that," I told her.

"You blow yourself up Talbot, and I'm never going to see if you can crap out gold pieces," BT yelled, and then clarified that it was an 'inside joke' when Jack, Brian, Cindy and even Perla looked over at him.

I placed my hand on the door right above Perla's, making sure to match her pressure before I spoke. "Run," I said calmly.

"Are you sure?" she asked, so wanting to bolt but not willing to trade my life for hers.

"Do you see any reason why the two of us should make final arrangements tonight?"

She took off, and within two seconds was in the arms of her boyfriend. She was sobbing uncontrollably. "He... he sacrificed himself for me," she cried.

"Mike, what are you doing?" Tracy asked with concern. She was pretty sure I knew what I was doing, but not entirely convinced. I winked at her reassuringly and she folded her arms grimly. There would be hell to pay later, her eyes promised me.

I was much more sure of myself when I had been walking towards the door than I was now that I was potentially holding a bomb at bay.

"I... I don't know how to thank you," Jack was fairly crying now.

"You could find me a beer," I told him as I looked over all of the workings of this trap.

"You got it man," Jack said, wiping salty droplets from his face. "I'll always dedicate a beer to you."

"No, that's not what I meant," I said as I pushed the door all the way open. I watched everyone go into duck and cover mode. The 'trip wire' which was actually an antenna was attached to an old school boom box.

"How did you know?" Cindy asked.

"Never came across a bomb yet that announced itself," I told her.

"That's it?" my wife yelled. "You bet everything on a little red light! How many bombs have you come across in your life?"

Man she was pissed, see how easy I can get into trouble?

"No time, Tracy. This thing still has juice so somebody was here recently and they know they have company, and just because this wasn't a bomb doesn't mean they don't have something much more real." All I had done was delay the inevitable. She would remember this long after the mountains had crumbled to the sea. "Just keep piling them up, don't you Talbot," I said under my breath. Hey, I was a good 54% sure that thing wasn't a real bomb.

"Why did I feel the need to leave Maine and follow your crazy cracker ass again?" BT asked irately as I came back to the truck.

"Apparently you felt that I was a little more sane than the Talbot collective," I told him as I patted him on the shoulder and grabbed a few more ammo magazines.

"I was going to go to King Soopers that day," BT said wistfully.

"Huh?" I asked him.

"That day when you came into the Safeway store. I had planned on going to King Soopers the night before. In fact, I had gone but they were all out of buttermilk."

"Buttermilk?"

"Yeah, I like buttermilk pancakes in the morning and I make them from scratch."

"Well aren't you just the Galloping Gourmet," I told him as I stuffed my cargo pockets with more gear.

"Just one carton, one stupid little carton of buttermilk, that's all they had to have and I'd be waiting this whole thing out in my penthouse apartment off of Leetsdale."

I stopped what I was doing. "Wait, you lived in a penthouse suite?"

"Yup, private entrance and everything," He said with regret.

"Why the hell didn't you say anything? We would have been way better off there," I said looking right at him.

"I didn't want you guys messing my crib up. I heard about what you did to your own place. And anyway I checked it out the day you went to the armory, that buttermilk saved my life twice. The building was in ruins, most of it was burnt and zombies were wandering around everywhere. I think I could have gotten to my suite but I'm not sure if I would have made it out. And it wasn't like I had told anyone where I was going. Even you wouldn't have come and tried to rescue me."

"Yeah, you're probably right," I told him, heading back to the door way.

"Well, you don't have to be so cavalier about it," he yelled to my retreating back.

"You know I love you man. Travis, Justin come on, let's find a suitable room. I'm exhausted."

Brian came up to me just as I got the entrance. "Do we sweep the whole building?"

"I don't think so, that sounds too much like Russian Roulette. Eventually we're going to come across an apartment with a loaded gun." He nodded but I could tell he didn't like my reasoning. "I know man, it doesn't make for a secure perimeter, but I'm really hoping that if we leave them alone, they'll leave us alone."

"I think that's asking a lot," Perla said as she came up to our small meeting. "I mean, this is their home and all."

"Would you rather get in a fire fight?" I asked her crossly.

"Maybe we should just find someplace else," Cindy said.

"This one is empty!" Jack yelled about three doors down the corridor.

"Good enough, let's park the cars right up against the doors and get the supplies in. Let's take a breather and then we'll sit down and see if we can get a game plan for tomorrow," I told the group.

Within a few trips all the ammo and food were in our temporary abode. I was going back to the truck for one final look to make sure I didn't miss anything when I heard Cindy talking to someone.

"What's with all the sani wipes? There has to be about twenty containers of them," she asked curiously.

I was coming up to the building exit when I heard BT's laughter. "Oh that's rich," he said. "That's Mike's secret stash, the Lean Green Fighting Machine is afraid of germs. Can't stand the thought of touching other people. I still haven't figured out yet how he conceived children, either it was a stand-in or Immaculate Conception."

I walked through the exit with a scowl laced on my face, hoping to put an end to this conversation. My presence sparked a hint of embarrassment on Cindy's face. She dropped the container she was holding as if it was about to burst into flame. BT thought my timing impeccable.

"I was just talking about you," he guffawed.

"Yeah, I heard."

"Want a drink of water?" he asked, placing his bottle damn near on my lips.

It was all I could do to not push the thing away, thus confirming his accusations to Cindy.

"You're a pain in the ass BT," I told him; he smiled and pulled the bottle back.

"And it's not even because I'm black," BT told a shocked Cindy as he took a long swig of the water.

"That's good I guess," she said hesitantly as she retreated to be back with people she understood.

"I think we should post a guard in the hallway," Jack said as we all sat around the apartment. The light from a half dozen emergency candles made it almost light enough to read by.

"Too exposed," I said.

"I don't like being canned up like this," he replied.

"I've got an idea, help me find some paper and something to write on," I told him. Ten minutes later I was taping a note to our door: "To whom it may concern, We mean no one any harm we plan on being here for a day or two at the most. We are well armed with meager supplies, nothing here is worth dieing for, if you feel like talking just knock. PS Zombies not welcome."

"I think you need an editor," Cindy said as she read the note.

"I'll get one as soon as I can," I told her.

"Is the last part really needed?" Perla asked.

"I'm not putting anything past them at this point," I told her. "And if that dissuades just one of those smelly bastards from coming here then it was worth it."

She shrugged her shoulders. "Can't hurt."

We went back in and I turned the deadbolt. I sat down heavily on a musty but comfortable futon couch. The only other occupant was BT and still I barely had enough room.

"Any ideas for tomorrow?" I asked the room.

"Do you think the furniture store is completely surrounded?" Tracy asked. "Maybe there's a weak point."

"Encircling seems to be their primary means of attack," I said. "But they're not always consistent with how many are at any given point."

"Assault the thinnest area then?" Brian asked.

"Yeah, but as soon as we start shooting we become the center of attention," Travis filled in with his own experience.

"A diversion then? Some start shooting, wait to pull the zombies away, and then another group goes in," Justin suggested.

"I'm not sure we'd be able to pull enough away," I told him. He deflated slightly. "It's a good thought," I said, trying to pump him back up. "It's just that we never tried something like that with this many. I don't know that enough of them would even get the message that something was going on."

"I've got an idea," Brian said. "But I need to scope it out a little better tomorrow when we can see the layout."

We were all looking at him expectantly.

"It's just a thought," he started back up. "In the southeast corner of the parking lot there was a fast food restaurant. It was on a grade about six feet higher than the furniture store parking lot."

"Wasn't there a fence?" I asked, trying to picture what he was talking about.

"There should be, or a retaining wall, something, or otherwise people would go rolling down the hill. I'm thinking we could set up a ladder."

"It has to be at least a hundred fifty feet from that parking lot to the roof. I'm assuming that's what you mean?" I asked.

"That's what I'm talking about, but as for the ladder I'm thinking on a grander scale."

"A fire truck!" BT blurted out.

"How far do those extend?" Tracy asked.

"A hundred feet?" I threw out there.

"I think some of the bigger ladder trucks can get to about a hundred twenty feet," Jack said. "I used to work in the motor pool and I've done some maintenance on emergency vehicles."

"That's still a hell of a gap," I said, "Let's hope my math is off."

Our impromptu meeting adjourned, we chose sticks for the order of guard duty. I got the fourth shortest which put me at just about the worst spot. Late enough that I'd be well into my REM sleep when I got interrupted, then I'd do my duty and not have enough time left over before we got going in the morning to make going back to sleep worthwhile. Great, I got to look forward to an entire day of having heavy lidded eyes. My head had just hit my couch cushion when I was shaken awake. Jack's face was unfamiliar and the darkness from the room made my heart skip a beat; I instinctively reached for my sidearm.

"Friendly, Mike, friendly!" Jack said, putting his hands up. "It's your turn for watch."

The shading of his face gave him the appearance of a wraith. I stared long and hard before the image of a floating skull dissipated and I was once again able to reconcile the parts of his face into a known entity. "Scared me," I told him, releasing the grip on my pistol.

"Yeah well, you did a number on me too. You Marines always so jumpy?"

I dragged my hand across my eyes. "Get some sleep," I said as I sat up. I shivered as Jack retreated into the shadows of the far corner of the room. I could not shake the feeling I had just seen a dead man.

I was in the midst of a very uneventful guard watch when I first heard the shuffling noise. It was so faint I thought I might be imagining it. It could have been a rat or even one of our party with a particularly nasty itch. That was, of course, until I saw a shadow play under the door to the apartment. Something was out there. Now the true question, was it alive or dead? There was no peep hole through which to look, and if somehow Sir Licks A Lot had made the journey I might have finally slipped over the edge I was holding onto so precariously.

I was standing no further than a foot from the door, stuck in a thought loop. Open the door, confront our guest whether friend or foe, or sit and wait and see if they tried to enter. Whoever it was had stones the size of Mount Rushmore and they weren't zombies. I watched as they turned the door knob which spun freely, but when they pushed up against the door the dead bolt held fast. I gripped my rifle tight, wondering if I should just pop a few rounds through the door. There was no way I was missing from this range.

"Michael," came a voice through the door. It was low and throaty and downright terrifying. Cold sweat broke out across my entire body. It wasn't a question, it was a statement.

This wasn't happening, Jack hadn't really yet awakened me for my shift. "I'm dreaming," I said aloud. But I wasn't, I remember what I had been dreaming. Travis and I had been playing the Wii, Mariokart to be specific, and I had been winning so I had KNOWN that it was a dream.

"Michael, I know you're there. I can hear you." The voice, definitely female, came through the door and drilled me in the heart.

"I'm not here," I mouthed.

"Open the door, invite me in."

My hand was working on its own volition. I slowly brought it up and it was now resting gently on the dead bolt. I turned the lock, the resounding click disengaging the mechanism.

"Dad?" Justin asked as he came up behind me. "What are you doing?"

As I was about to turn to look at my son, the shadow under the door vanished. "Am I sleeping?" I asked him in all seriousness.

"Well if you are, so am I," he said smiling. "Dad," he noted with concern. "It can't be more than 50 degrees in here and you're covered in sweat. You getting sick?"

"I think I might be," I told him as I walked away from the door.

Justin passed by me to reengage the lock, a quizzical look on his face.

"What are you doing up?" I asked him at the end of the short entryway.

"Woke up a couple of minutes ago. I was having a bad dream that Eliza found us. She wanted me to invite her in. You alright? You're looking a little pale."

"It was just a dream," I told him with absolutely no conviction, and he saw it for the falsehood that it was, just empty words.

"Who was at the door?" he asked uneasily.

"Avon, I think." I just spit it out; it was my way of diffusing the terror. "Sorry," I said when I saw his frustration. "I'm not sure if anyone was there," I told him in all truth.

"But there might have been?" he questioned further.

"Maybe," I said, licking my lips.

"Was it…?" he asked the unimaginable.

"You should go back to sleep," I told him. Of course I didn't sleep another minute the rest of the night, wondering if I had just come that close to the end of my mortality.

The morning brought a bustle of activity as we planned our strategy. Everything came to a halt when Jack opened the door.

"Someone is messing with us," he scowled as he held my note up. Someone had scrawled "Death Awaits" in a suspiciously red-colored medium, with the added effects of drips and all. "Anybody hear anything?" he asked the room.

Justin and I gave each other a quick knowing glance which fortunately went wholly unnoticed. What was I going to say? "Yeah, this vampire chick who wants to kill me and everyone I know was at the door last night and wanted in. Funny thing is I almost let her." That probably wouldn't go over so well.

*　　*　　*

"Well that's a cluster," Brian said, looking through his binoculars at the furniture store from the same vantage point as the evening before.

"I think I can smell them," Travis said disgustedly.

"Definitely looks like your friends set up camp on the roof," Brian said as he surveyed the area.

I walked over to the truck. "You tell Ron about this and you'll be walking home," I told Gary.

"About what?" he asked suspiciously.

I pushed the passenger side view mirror back and forth until it snapped off.

"He is going to be *pissed*," Gary said shaking his head.

"Do you do this stuff on purpose?" BT questioned me.

"I've got my reasons." I lined up the mirror with the early morning sun, trying to see if I could get some reflection to the people on the roof to let them know we were here.

"Do you know Morse code?" Jack asked me.

"Just S.O.S," I told him truthfully.

"I know a little," Perla said sheepishly. The entire group turned to look at her. "When I was 15 my boyfriend and I learned it so that we could message to each other when it was safe to either sneak out or sneak in." She gave Jack a weak smile.

"You never cease to surprise me," he said as he kissed her forehead.

"Doesn't matter though, I'm pretty sure nobody over there would know how to read what you signal," I told her.

"So you basically just ripped the mirror off for nothing?" Tracy asked with one raised eyebrow.

"Et tu Brutus?" I asked.

"I knew it was a mistake when they took you off the Lithium," Tracy laughed.

"She's kidding, right?" Cindy asked with a frown.

"Mostly," I told her.

Travis had grabbed the binoculars from Brian, "Dad, they see us I think. They're waving their hands." I grabbed the binoculars, "Do you think they know it's us?" he asked me.

"I don't know how. I can barely see their faces with the binoculars and it doesn't look like they have a pair up there."

*   *   *

"Wish we had a telescope or something," Paul said. "I mean, I'm pretty sure it's them but I'm not a hundred percent sure."

"Well, they're signaling something," Alex said as he shaded his eyes. "Long, short, short, short, break, long, long. Is that Morse code?"

"Hell if I know," Paul replied. "I've known Mike a long time, he's never said anything about knowing it, but that doesn't necessarily mean he doesn't. But he's got to know that I don't know it."

"Maybe he's hoping someone up here does," Erin said.

"Wait, let's reason this out," MJ said coming up to the edge of the roof. "You're pretty sure he doesn't know Morse code and he would be fairly confident that you don't either. Now considering that it is a pretty archaic form of communication, we've got to think that he doesn't believe anybody up here would know it. But yet he keeps repeating the same signal."

"Well, what is it brain boy?" Mrs. Deneaux sniffed disdainfully, sitting in her chaise lounge chair as if it were a throne, smoking another cigarette. Joann looked like she wanted to throttle the old lady if only to get a hold of one of those coffin nails.

"What if the long dash equates to a five and the short dashes equal a one," MJ said, basically talking out loud as he tried to figure the logic puzzle out.

"Eight and ten?" Joann asked, "What the hell does that mean?"

"What if they represent letters in the alphabet?" Alex asked.

Erin started counting the letters off her fingers. "H and J? Still doesn't make much sense."

"More like old school Risk board game pieces," Paul added, completely from left field.

"Any chance you could elaborate?" MJ asked.

"The long is a ten and the short is a one," Paul said excitedly.

"Thirteen and twenty, so what?" Joann asked.

"M and T," MJ said.

"Mike motherfucking Talbot!" Alex said, high-fiving Paul.

*   *   *

"I think your message got through, Dad," Justin said. "Paul and Alex are both fist pumping the air."

"'Bout time, let's go find a ladder truck," I said to everyone, motioning that we should get going.

*   *   *

"They're leaving!" Joann said with dejection.

"They just wanted to let us know they are here. Now we wait to see what kind of plan they've come up with," Paul said.

"Well, I do hope they hurry up. I'm down to my last five or six packs," Mrs. Deneaux said loudly, making sure Joann would catch it.

"I'd throw you over the edge, you old crow, if I thought the zombies would actually eat you. They'd probably just think that you were already one of them," Joann said as she stalked off.

Mrs. Deneaux cackled wildly.

Eliza and Tomas - Interlude

"I told you they would come, Sister," Tomas said from the doorway of the furniture store.

Eliza said nothing as she watched the 'rescue party' depart.

"Mistress please, allow me to go now and finish him off," Durgan said from Eliza's left.

"I do not believe that you possess what is necessary to defeat him," Eliza replied, never turning to address Durgan personally.

Durgan's body shook with rage and impotence. "Yes

Mistress," he said mildly, nearly choking on his hatred of Talbot. Tomas turned and smiled at him which enraged him more. He knew Tomas was kin to Eliza but his allegiance was in question. He would keep an eye on the demon, but the power the boy exuded rivaled that of his sister and therefore he needed to proceed with caution.

"Please, at least allow me to go onto the roof and dispatch of them. They mean nothing to you," Durgan pleaded

"Do not presume to know what is and what is not of consequence to me," Eliza said coldly.

"Yes, Mistress," Durgan, said bowing his head.

"Although it could be an entertaining distraction," Eliza mused coquettishly.

Durgan's head shot up, a glimmer of anticipation on his face, partly because he might get to kill someone but mostly because he loved to please his master. Durgan had always been a leader but he found himself relishing the role of follower, although slave was closer to his title. To be this near to her and her power was intoxicating. Why she wasted so much time and energy on the pissant Talbot he could not begin to fathom. In this world she was without limits, she had command of vast armies, countries would bow to her and he would be by her side. Now that Tommy's blood had cured her she was once again immortal. Talbot would fall eventually, if only to the greatest enemy of mankind: Time. 'FUCK HIM!' he screamed in his head, his missing leg still aching.

"There is the chance, Sister, that Michael will not come to the rescue if no one is left alive," Tomas counseled her.

'I'm going to kill you the first chance I get,' Durgan thought to himself. He froze when Tomas looked directly at him as if in response to his thought.

"You wouldn't be trying to protect your friends now, would you Brother?" Eliza asked as she caressed his face.

"I have no friends," he answered in an even tone.

"And what of me, Brother?" Eliza asked smiling.

"Least of all you, Sister."

CHAPTER 27 – Talbot Journal Entry 13

It was Perla who came up with the idea to break into a Best Buy and grab a Garmin. Within a few minutes it had located a satellite and after a query for Fire Stations we soon had five pulled up within a twenty mile radius. The closest was devoid of all equipment, they had definitely been out on a call when their fate befell them.

"I think we're going to have problems," Brian said dejectedly as he kicked a helmet across the empty fire station floor.

"First responders were doing what they were supposed to be doing," I said.

"Hey!" BT yelled from the truck. "This shows which stations are volunteer based."

"So what?" Jack said a little perturbed, this roadblock souring his mood.

"Real bright," I said as an aside to Jack. "You've seen how big he is right? You always go around poking bears, dumb ass?"

"I'll 'so what' right upside your head you dumb cracker," BT said, struggling to get his bulk out of the truck.

"He knows not what he says my friend," I said coming over to keep BT from ripping Jack in half. "Although this is kind of cool. It's much better that he's the object of your hostility as opposed to me."

BT barely even heard me as he kept trying to get by me. I danced around him, trying to block his path, "Talbot, I swear if you get in my way again, I will beat him to death with your body!" he thundered at me.

I wisely stepped aside. "On your own, Jack."

"Wait, I didn't mean anything by it," Jack said, putting his hands up.

"That's kind of the same pose you use with BT," Tracy said as she came up beside me.

"Am I that pathetic?" I asked as I watched the drama.

"Oh even worse I think," she smiled.

"I used to have dignity," I told her.

She put her hand up and rocked it back and forth. "Debatable."

"BT, could you please not kill him, he knows how to operate the ladder truck," I asked BT's back.

BT had Jack backed all the way up against a wall, "Listen, you little twit!" BT said, pressing his finger on the top of Jack's head. "A volunteer fire department means that they weren't necessarily at the station when the end went down and more than likely never had the chance to get there."

"I get it!" Jack said. Although I think he would have said that even if BT was teaching him quantum physics and he didn't have a clue.

"You wouldn't have thought God would have been able to squeeze a brain in around all that muscle," I said with a smirk.

"Holy shit Dad! He's going to kill you!" Travis said.

"No swearing!" Tracy and I echoed each other.

"Did he hear me?" I asked Travis softly.

"I heard you Talbot!" BT shouted from across the room. "So many crackers, so little time," BT said to the heavens.

The Cherryfield Station Fire House was a disaster. I don't know what happened but the LEAST unsettling thing was the Dalmatian pinned to the wall with a hatchet. What could have possibly necessitated that? Perla waited outside after her third volley of puke left her virtually empty. Dried blood coated the floor. It was at least a quarter inch thick, we kept cracking through the top hardened layer into the thicker still wet and sticky portion. I pretended it was the top surface of frozen snow. The illusion was difficult to hold onto because it was close to fifty out and this snow was a red, black hybrid, oh yeah, that and the metallic smell that human blood tends to give off.

If you've only ever given yourself a paper cut then you most likely have never experienced this phenomenon. I learned of the smell in a much more difficult manner. My unit was on a two hour alert, which basically meant that we could not be anywhere further than two hours away from base should we need to muster. I was boogie boarding on a private Marine Corps beach at the Marine Corps Air Station in Kaneohe Bay, Hawaii when the base siren went off.

I was a lance corporal, pretty wet behind the ears and had no real clue what the hell the siren meant. I saw a few Marines on the beach waving at everybody to come ashore. Now I was concerned, sharks were always a present danger in the warm tropical waters. I grabbed my gear and hightailed it. The idea of being food scared the hell out of me. Who knew that was going to be the state of the world in a few more years?

"Sharks?" I asked the Sergeant as I turned to look at the few remaining folks in the water making their way ashore.

"Have you always been a dumb ass, Marine?" the sergeant asked me.

"Nope, saved it especially for you, Sergeant," I told him.

Two hundred and twenty five push-ups later he kindly informed me that the siren was the muster call. The North Koreans were threatening our allies to the South and we were heading there as a show of force and solidarity.

It was well known in the Corps that the Koreans were fierce determined warriors that might be a suit or two shy of a full deck. I did not look forward to the deployment. Two and a half hours later, I and ninety other Marines were flying across the Pacific Ocean in a C-130 Hercules. It was a quiet flight. No one spoke, more so because it was damn near impossible to hear anything else over the noise in the uninsulated body of the aircraft.

The monster plane landed some five or six hours later. I'm not sure, I slept the majority of the ride, there wasn't a whole bunch else to do. We waited on the tarmac as at least another twenty to twenty-five planes touched down, and there were already a bunch of jarheads on the ground when we arrived. A convoy of troop trucks, 'deuces' we called them, picked us up. We were shoved in like cattle. I felt like I had paid my 500 pesos and was now trying to sneak across the border with the other forty slobs I was packed in with. It was so tight we couldn't even sit. Where were the cops when you really needed them?

We were generally doing what all Marines do, grousing and complaining. That was, of course, until we began to hear the chatter of small arms fire. The heavy staccato bursts of the AK's were unmistakable. This was no drill, the North Koreans were firing. The trucks came to an abrupt halt and the tail gate was slammed down by the corporal that was at the rear of the truck.

"OUT!" came the cry from Sergeant who had moments before been in the shotgun seat. "Keep your heads down or I'll write your mothers and tell them you died a coward!"

"Nice guy," the Marine behind me said.

I laughed if only to still the screaming terrified kid in my head.

The exodus was semi-organized right up until rounds began to ping off the front of the truck, then it became a free-for-all. I almost met my demise as I was pushed from behind just as I approached the exit, almost landing on my head. The only thing that saved my ass was the Marine that had spoken up earlier.

"Thanks man," I told him in earnest.

"You'd do the same." Those were the last words Corporal Meera said as his chest puffed out. The high velocity 7.62 round broke through his back and out his sternum, passing between my arm and my chest. I was able to catch and break his fall as I twisted out of the truck, landing on the soft dirt below.

"Medic!" I shouted as a blossom of blood spread and soaked his entire torso. Blood spewed from his mouth as his ruptured lungs drowned in the viscous fluid. A haunted look came over his eyes as he looked at me. He tried to say something, but between the lack of air in his lungs and the blood in his throat, it wasn't going to happen. It was the smell that stuck with me all these years. It was a rich earthy smell, the iron of his blood burned into my olfactory senses. I will forever associate that smell with death, the wounded do not bleed like that. The medic came just as Meera took his final tortured breath. Thankfully he closed those eyes that I thought might have held a hint of an accusatory stare. Was my stumble enough to delay him? I would dwell upon it at times, but I have come to learn that there is no great manifest destiny, there is no universal order. Chaos will always reign supreme. There is no more order to the world than the falling of a leaf in a stiff fall breeze. That it will fall eventually is a truth, but which route it will take and where it will fall are the great mysteries that evade us all.

This almost forgotten buried memory broke free from the shackled recess it had hidden in for many a years as the earthy smell once again assailed my nostrils.

"You alright Talbot? You're looking a little frothy," BT asked, coming up beside me.

"Old memory my friend that I really wish had stayed where it was hidden."

"There's nothing here to worry about Mike. Why don't you go see how Perla is doing?" he said, placing his hand on my back.

I found Perla in the back seat of Tracy's car. She had Henry on her lap and tears were streaming down her face.

"Who would do that?" she asked me. Well actually she never did look up at me as I approached. She could have just as easily been asking Henry.

"Hey Perla," I said.

She looked up and stared for a moment. "I think you look as bad as I do," she smiled softly.

"Oh, I wouldn't worry about that. I'm pretty sure I look way worse," I told her.

She smiled again, "Thank you for that," as she buried her face again in Henry's neck. "You know, this just might be the best dog ever," she said as she squeezed him tight. Henry turned and licked her forearm.

"You're probably right," I told her as I stroked Henry's huge head. We all turned as the large diesel engine of the ladder truck roared to life. The front of the truck poked its head from the fire station, splatters of a much darker red staining the majority of the vehicle. My mind was working furiously to find an alternate reason to explain away the blotches and was failing miserably.

Brian was driving the truck and Jack was sitting up on the ladder apparatus smiling like a kid who had just received his favorite toy for Christmas. "All aboard!" he shouted.

With a grim determination I walked back into the station. I just couldn't stand the thought of leaving the dog pinned up against the wall. I had no sooner walked in when Meredith came sliding down the brass fire pole. I was happy that she could at least find a moment's relief and enjoy the short thrill ride down, but the look on her face did not speak of any joy.

"Nest..." she barely eked out. I didn't actually hear the words spoken, the blare of the ladder truck's horn almost deafened my already battered ears.

"NEST!" she screamed just as the echoed reverberations of the blast were finished.

Zombies began to fall through the hole just as Meredith vacated the area, more followed down the stairs at the far corner.

Travis' sixth sense was in high gear that day. He came around the corner, the Mossberg in his arms jumping as twelve gauge deer slugs ripped through the barrel. Zombies were launched off their feet; most would never regain a vertical position. Justin was next, quick to drop the cigarette he was smoking and chamber a round in his rifle. The three of us stood abreast, the rapid rate of fire tearing through our enemy but still we were losing ground.

Jack turned from his lofty perch, the smile literally running from his face. "Too many!" he screamed. "Coming around the other side!"

Perla had moved Henry aside and was running towards us. I could hear the blasts of her rifle and was none too pleased. I never did much like having someone shoot past me from the rear. Way too many chances for an errant shot. And Lord knows I'd pissed off enough people in my life that 'friendly fire' was always a personal concern of mine. I turned to look and possibly shout a few choice expletives at her, but she wouldn't have seen me. She was shooting over to our left. I followed her line of sight. Zombies were coming at us at full tilt.

"Back!" I shouted, putting my forearm on Justin's chest.

Brian was honking the horn on the truck and waving frenetically at us to get on. Cindy had climbed up by Jack and they were both concentrating their fire at the targets Perla was shooting at. My firing line was still oblivious to the danger on our side. Travis was jamming rounds into the Mossberg's port with a speed I could barely register. I tapped him on the shoulder just as he shouldered his weapon. His eyes grew twice as wide as he looked over my shoulder at the approaching nightmare. His rifle swung over as he began to acquire new targets.

I shook my head in the negative, "Let's go!" Meredith dropped the magazine she was loading into her rifle as I almost lifted her and Justin off their feet to get them in motion. Perla swung over to cover our retreat. I was now infinitely grateful that she was shooting over our heads. Funny how that change happened, I guess it's just a matter of perspective. The zombies were close. I was waiting for the drag of a nail down my shirt, or a bite in my back, the green slimed teeth sinking deep into my flesh, or the black encrusted broken jagged nails scraping through the fragile layers of my skin. Always knew I should have used more moisturizer as I was growing older. It would have given my skin more elasticity and less chance of splitting when a zombie tried to scrape the life out of me. Yup, random thought as I fled for my life. At least it didn't involve sex, maybe I was finally maturing. And then I began to think of the other uses that lotion could be used for and realized that maybe I was not as far along as I had originally thought.

I had a moment of panic as I looked at Henry in the front seat staring back at me. If he had inadvertently locked the door, which he was prone to do, I was a dead man. I couldn't even count the number of times I had let him in on the passenger side only to have him come and greet me on the driver's side and push the lock button down. Then he would just sit there with his huge panting grin wondering why I wasn't joining him inside. I wouldn't swear on it but I think he did it on purpose. I had taken him on dozens of car rides and never once had there been a problem. The day I had to take him to the vet for some shots he locked me out of the car. Two hours and a missed vet appointment later, the lock smith came and opened the car door.

"Hey buddy, you really should make a spare," he told me as I wrote him a check for a hundred and ten dollars.

I told him to blow me, he laughed.

Five days and four uneventful car rides later, I was able to secure another appointment at the vets. This time I made sure that as soon as I put Henry in the car I ran around to the other side to get in. I slipped a little in the gravel by the front end and by the time I recovered and was able to get a hand on the door handle, I heard the telltale 'click' of the lock being engaged. There was no denying it this time. Henry was full on smiling at me. It was no damn pant. I was cursing loudly as I headed into the house.

"Talbot, did that dog get the best of you again?"

Tracy asked, smiling almost as widely as Henry.

I was beyond pissed as I made sure to pick a different locksmith lest I get the same smart ass as before. I paid the extra twenty to have him make a key on the spot. This guy was an hour and a half quicker than his competition and so I was still able to make it to the vet. Henry was not a happy camper and let me know by leaving an extra heavy puddle of drool on my seat. The twenty minutes it took to drive home was excruciating as the thick saliva soaked through my jeans and onto my left butt cheek.

There was no way he could have known, right? In the hundreds of car rides we had taken together he had locked me out four times. Two were for the vet, once when I wanted to get his picture taken with Santa. The last time had been the summer before. It had been an unbelievably hot day, for some reason I thought it might be cooler at the dog park. Henry had been hesitant to leave our air conditioned home. I had to pick him up off his doggie hammock and physically put him in the car. I had no sooner placed him in the passenger seat when he stood up. He crossed the bridge between the two seats, lifted his left front leg and pushed the lock down with his paw. I watched in amazement. He wasn't running around crazy and just happened to hit the lock, it had been a deliberate action. He had told me in no uncertain terms that he didn't want to go. I reached up under the frame of my jeep, grabbed the key I had hidden with the magnetic box, opened the door and let Henry find his way back to his hammock where he stayed the majority of the day. He occasionally got up to drink and eat, but for the most part he and the hammock were a fused entity.

I now had to hope, with my life on the line, that Henry's actions had ALWAYS been that of a fully cognizant being and not those of an over exuberant puppy/dog. Henry jumped into the back seat just as I got to the door. Travis and Justin who were quicker than me had already gained entry. I pretended for pride's sake that I was covering Meredith's retreat, which technically I was, but she was also quicker than I. This was a blow to my ego. I could smell the gunpowder of the expended rounds as they came dangerously close to my back. The zombies were within striking distance. If they could breathe, I would have felt their exhalations on my neck.

Meredith, Justin and Travis had made it in. Henry had not locked us out after all, but that still did not quiet my hammering heart as my hand wrapped around the cool metal of the handle. If I lifted up and it did not disengage the locking mechanism, there would not be enough time for anyone inside to help me out. I know Henry didn't lock me out now I had to hope that good old Detroit engineering didn't pick this most inopportune of times to fail. The handle pulled up with that satisfactory tug and the door swung outward just as my head jerked backwards. A zombie had grabbed a handful of the hair on the back of my head and was pulling for all it was worth.

"Zombie's got you Dad!" Justin shouted, pointing.

I wanted to shout 'Really?' but there is a time and a place for sarcasm and I certainly didn't have the time for it. I had a variety of none too pleasant sensations all happen quicker than the blink of an eye. The first being the razor sharp burn of pain as a bullet scraped against the side of my head, the second was the separating of a fair portion of hair and skin from my scalp as the zombie behind me suffered a fatal head shot; his hand spasmed closed even tighter, and as he fell he took a part of me with him. The third was my shoulder getting slammed by the car door as BT used our other ride as a battering ram. Zombies shot out at odd angles as the ton and a half projectile slammed into them. I could see Tracy holding on for dear life in the passenger seat. Gary was in the back seat and he spared me a side-long glance as they passed by. BT had bought me a few precious seconds and I would not squander them. My head initially dragged even further backward from the clutch of the zombie and then shot upright as my scalp finally let go of its prize. I didn't even bring up my right hand to see how deep the wound was from the bullet. It wasn't like I was going to be able to do anything about it right now and I was too scared to check anyway.

"Oh my God!" Meredith screamed, "You're bleeding from your head!"

"You've been hanging out with Justin too long," I told her as I shoved the car in gear and screeched the tires out of the parking lot. BT and the fire truck were not far behind. Neither were the zombies for that matter.

Blood was accumulating in my lap at an alarming rate. "How bad is it?" I asked Meredith. If I was to solely base her answer on the expression she was wearing, it was safe to assume my brains were exposed and were leaking down the side of my face.

Justin pulled himself up from the back seat and gingerly probed his fingers around the wound.

"What are you doing? It feels like you've got arsenic on your fingers," I fairly yelped at him.

"Well, to quote Monty Python, Dad, 'it's only a flesh wound.'" Justin said still messing around with a flap of skin attached to an exposed nerve bundle secured tightly at the base of my spine.

"Yeah, but if I remember right, the 'flesh wound' in that movie equated to a missing arm," I told him.

"I'm not sure it will even leave a scar," Travis threw his two cents into the mix.

"You guys aren't just saying this like they do in the movies are you? 'Oh Murphy, it'll be alright,' meanwhile the guy's guts are blown all over the beach."

"Wow, Mom did say you were a little dramatic," Travis laughed, "but I didn't really believe her, at least until now."

"You get shot in the head, smart ass, and then tell me who is being dramatic," I said as I finally mustered the courage to put a finger up by the grazing. The wound was shallow and about the width of the tip of my pinkie finger. I had once again cheated death. This hadn't been my closest call but it was in the top five. The black robed one would have to wait yet a while more. Could Death alter destiny to serve his needs? Or was he (it) merely one more cog in the vast machinations of fate? No more able to alter his course than a blade of grass in a swift running stream. Were any of our ends foretold, the time and date written on head stones, or were they fluid? Did Death wait for an 'expected' demise or was his arrival contingent on our passing?

I preferred to think that he was snapping his fingers in the familiar 'Damn, he got away' gesture rather than sitting back with a slated schedule and saying, 'Not yet, but SOON.' Giving Death the finger seemed WAY cooler.

After a couple of miles when I was fairly certain we had lost our dinner guests, I pulled over to the side of the road. The wound may have been shallow, but it would not stop bleeding and I might be entirely too thickheaded to know when to die but I'd passed out before and I did not want to suffer that indignity again. Perla jumped down from the fire truck with a white first aid kit.

"I'm so sorry Mike," she said as she came towards me.

I staggered out of the car, some was from blood loss, some for dramatic effect. Hey, it's not every day you get shot in the head, might as well milk it for something.

"Mike?" Tracy asked approaching hesitantly. Concern, care, and worry were all wrapped up in the one word question.

"I'm fine," I said leaning against the car heavily.

"It barely touched him," Travis said as he got out of the car to check the approach from our rear.

"Yeah, it's bleeding much worse than it actually is," Justin added as he reloaded a magazine.

Perla placed a hydrogen peroxide soaked cloth to my head pinkish foam oozed from my wound. The resulting sizzle sounded much like the Pop Rocks candy I had enjoyed in my youth. Who am I kidding, I had eaten a bag of the sugary goodness not a week before the zombies had come. I found them in a dollar store and bought the whole box. I had hidden them out in the garage, not willing to share nor divulge my secret stash.

I was trying to pull my head away from Perla's ministrations; she wasn't having any of it. She quickly placed some disinfectant on the wound and then wrapped my head in gauze. My head began to throb like I had spent the last three nights partying, but without the resulting fond memories of crazy actions performed.

"Good thing you jarheads have thick skulls," Brian said as he came over. "Left my damn rifle at the fire station."

"Doesn't surprise me," I told him. "I wouldn't think as an army dog you'd know how to shoot it anyway."

Brian looked at me sternly. I thought I might have crossed an imaginary boundary with him before he smiled. "You alright?" he asked seriously.

"Yeah, just feels like someone is tapping on my skull with a ball peen hammer."

"We still on then?" Jack asked from the ladder, watching the conversation from above.

"Your head is still bleeding, Uncle," Meredith said as the cloth around my head began to soak red throughout.

Gary came over to give me a quick once over. When he was confident I wasn't going to expire, he popped the hood. Chunks of gore ran towards the windshield as he raised it up. Tracy's car looked like it was in imminently more danger of going to the great beyond. The front end was caved in and the smell of caustic anti-freeze filled the air.

"Radiator is shot and the fan has cut through some electrical lines," Gary said mournfully as he stood back up, popping his back as he did so.

"Well, let's transfer the stuff out of there, we have plenty of room with the fire truck now," Tracy told him.

Fifteen minutes later we were back at the original overpass that overlooked the furniture store.

"This really looked better on paper," Jack said as we surveyed the throng of zombies.

"No it didn't," I told him frankly.

"Yeah you're probably right," he answered back.

"But that doesn't mean we aren't going to try. Isn't that right Mike?" BT asked. I nodded in reply. "See, do I know my crazy friend or what?" he said triumphantly.

"I think Eliza is here, I can feel her almost like an echo," I said almost imperceptibly.

"You can feel her?" Justin asked.

What was awesome was Justin couldn't. Did Easter's incantations really work?

"Eliza is here?" Tracy asked with alarm. "Then we should be anywhere but here!" she emphasized.

"If Eliza is here, so is Tommy, Mom," Travis said, linking all the pieces of the puzzle together.

"This sucks," I said. "This is just about a text book trap,"

"Brian?" Cindy asked.

I know what that implied; life right now was already difficult enough to hold onto without charging into a trap to rescue people they didn't even know.

"Guys, you owe us nothing," I told the group.

"What would you do, Mike? Honestly, if you were us what would you do in this situation?" Brian asked me.

"I'd leave," I told him.

"Bullshit," BT said. "You'd be the first in,"

"That's what I thought," Brian said, "Then we stay,"

"Ass," I turned to address BT.

"Anytime," he smiled.

"We should get moving then," Gary said. "Zombies are zombies, but zombies in the dark are a lot scarier."

"Agreed," I agreed.

The beeping from the fire truck as Brian backed it into the Wendy's parking lot was nerve racking. The zombies didn't even seem to pay it any attention. Brian backed the truck up as far as he could go; the rear tires were resting on the retaining wall. I was no expert on fire trucks and ladders, but I didn't see any way that the ladder was going to extend to that furniture store roof.

"Good to see you Mike!" Paul shouted from the far roof, his voice traveling considerably well over the thousands of quiet zombies below, and without any roadway traffic there was really only the sound of birds and insects to contend with.

"You too Paul, although I really wish we could have met in a bar with a pitcher of beer instead," I told him.

Even from this distance I could see him nod. Alex waved enthusiastically. I returned the gesture with an arm that felt more filled with Jell-o than muscle. Have I yet discussed my fear of heights?

"That going to reach?" Paul asked the question that was on everyone's mind.

"Find out in a minute," Jack shouted back.

The entire group, even the pain in the ass Deneaux, watched as Jack extended the ladder. Woefully short would have been an adequate description. There was a good twenty feet between the tip of the ladder and the lip of the roof. An Olympic jumper could not bridge that gap. I smirked a bit as I thought of Deneaux trying. She could have probably made it if she had her broom.

Jack came down from the ladder control box and walked around the ladder truck until he found what he considered a suitable portable ladder.

I looked at Jack as he grabbed the ladder and then looked to the furthest point of the extended ladder which was swaying in the light breeze. "No way," I breathed.

"Jack I don't think so," I said, voicing my concern.

Eliza and Tomas - Interlude

"Interesting," Eliza said as she watched the rescue attempt.

"No way," Durgan said as he watched the sway of the ladder. "They came up short. I say we take them out now!"

"We will do as We wish," Eliza said, nodding to Tomas. "What do you think we should do, dear Brother?"

Eliza asked as she stroked his cheek.

"Michael Talbot will find a way on to that roof, Sister. And then we will have them all in one place," Tomas answered as he looked through the window in the former store manager's office. Grief was etched on his features, but it was belied by the eagerness in his eyes.

"All you have to do is send your zombies up to that fire engine, Mistress, and this whole exercise will be over," Durgan said with a tone of exasperation.

Eliza grabbed a handful of Durgan's shirt and lifted the man who weighed nearly three times her body weight and thrust him against the far wall. A small picture and a framed award shattered to the floor as a dazed Durgan tried to regain his footing.

"Do not trouble me with what *you* want!" she shouted. "Do not presume to think that I care at all what petty thoughts run through that pathetic human brain! You will do as I command, WHEN I command it!"

Durgan was finally able to stand. He was certain that he had just suffered a mild concussion, but Eliza's words rang loud and clear through the accumulating fog in his brain. "Yes Mistress," he said meekly as he placed his hand up to a small wound on the back of his head. Tomas never turned around throughout the entire episode and that enflamed Durgan more than that little shit-eating grin the kid generally displayed around him.

"What are you doing, Brother?" Eliza asked as she joined Tomas back at the window. Durgan for the moment was completely forgotten.

'So, this is the joy of being in the company of immortals,' Durgan thought as he pulled up a chair, his head throbbing uncontrollably, his vision slightly blurred.

"I am sending zombies to the truck," Tomas answered matter-of-factly.

"When did you discover that you could control them?" Eliza asked with an arched eyebrow.

"Just now," Tomas answered, deep in concentration.

"I do not think that I like this new development, Brother."

"I would not think so," he told her, never wavering in his concentration.

CHAPTER 28 – Talbot Journal Entry 14

"Zombies have spotted us," Cindy said as she looked down from her perch on the fire engine's hood.

Perla began to question the wisdom of what Jack was trying to pull off.

"Jack, I think we should just get out of here. Those people on the roof, we don't even know them," Perla said, embarrassed when she realized that I was within earshot.

Jack looked over towards me and shrugged his shoulders as if to say 'She doesn't speak for me.'

"I've said it from the beginning," I told them. "You don't owe us anything,"

"We might not know you well now," Jack began. "But we will eventually, and I for one wouldn't be able to look myself in the mirror if we didn't do everything in our power to rescue them," he finished more to Perla than for me.

"You be careful," she said, putting her head on his shoulder.

"I made it through a tour in Afghanistan and one in Iraq. What's a little high wire act above a few thousand zombies in comparison?" he asked her with bravado.

"Not funny," she said as she mock punched his arm. The words did have the desired effect though, as she walked away from him with a slight smile.

"Jack, I think we should get out of here before the zombies make their way up to us and rethink this," I told him.

Gary was at my side, nodding as he looked at the outstretched ladder swaying gently in the breeze. "I wouldn't trust a monkey on that."

A rifle shot exploded through the relative stillness of the day. "Nice shot, Meredith!" Justin yelled.

"Fifty feet, Dad!" Travis yelled.

Now came the dilemma. If we tried this insane plan we were stuck here. It was an all or nothing proposal and to what end. Within seconds, we would all have to be on the fire truck or in our own vehicles getting the hell out of Dodge. The plus side had completely diminished as far as I could tell. The absolute best we could hope to accomplish at this point was to be stuck up on the roof with Paul and Alex, the worst would be being stuck in the fire truck. I didn't think it would be capable of pushing through a wall of zombies. Well scratch that, the absolute worst would be getting eaten. Yeah, that would take the cake.

"Twenty-five feet!" came the update.

"Let's get out of here!" I yelled. I'd made up my mind, there was no upside anymore.

"I can do this," Jack said as he began to climb the extended ladder with the mobile ladder.

"What's going on Mike?" BT asked.

"Zombies will be here in a few seconds," I told him.

"And then we're stuck," Tracy added, filling in the blanks.

Perla seemed relieved that her fiancé would not be making the attempt.

"Just let me try it once Mike?" Jack asked, never really stopping his ascent.

"Brian, he's not going to listen to me. You need to get him down so we can get out of here," I said. Gunshots from Meredith, Travis and Justin seemed to reiterate my point.

"Jack, he's right!" Brian yelled. "We've got to get out of here while the getting is good."

"Get the girls and get the hell out of here!" Jack said as he reached the end of the ladder.

"Can we just drive away with him on the ladder?" Perla asked, nervousness putting a tremor in her voice.

"He's having a hard enough time staying on as it is,

we hit a bump…" I let my frank answer trail off.

"We stay. Travis! I'll help you, let's grab the ammo cans, everyone else on the fire truck," I said with dejection. This was not how I had envisioned this moment.

I had no sooner handed up the last ammo can when the zombies came around the back of the truck. I scrambled up the truck quicker than I thought my bone-weary body could move.

Meredith started firing into the rapidly growing crowd around us. I placed my hand on her shoulder. "Save the ammo for when we're going to need it," I told her.

"That isn't now?" she asked me incredulously.

I just shook my head in negation.

I turned to watch Jack's progress. It was at this exact moment that I wished I had been forced to watch a 72 hour Glee marathon, anything but what I was about to witness. Jack had propped up the smaller ladder by jamming it through a couple of the much bigger ladder's rungs. Now he was trying to secure it with some cabling. But before he could do that, the swaying from the wind, the jostling of the truck from our movements, and the zombies bumping into the body of the truck began to jar the ladder loose. I saw the small aluminum ladder begin to slowly fall as Newton's law began to take effect. My first instinct was to tell him to let it go. I had always taught my kids that it was not worth injuring yourself to save ANY piece of equipment, get out of its way and let it fall where it may.

Jack did not adhere to those rules. He reached out and grabbed it with one hand. There was a moment where it appeared that he might be able to muscle the wayward steps back into place, but the centrifugal force of Mother Earth was just a bit stronger than him that day. Jack began to lift off the ladder as the levering action began to outweigh him.

I swear it seemed to happen in super slow motion, but before I could form the words 'Let it go!' he was already past the point of no return. Perla turned just in time to watch as he pitched head first into the throng of zombies below. The sound as his head crashed into a zombie's was sickening. Why had I told Meredith to stop shooting? At least it would have masked that cracking noise.

I ran up the ladder halfway. What I was expecting to see that would be any different from the reality of the event, who knows? It just seemed like the right thing to do. But it wasn't, Jack was lying prostrate on the pavement, blood pouring from a fissure in his skull. A zombie was lying next to him, at least he had taken one out with him. As I write that thought down, I can't decide if it's a crappy thought or a realist thought. A small circle of empty space formed around Jack and the zombie. There was more going on here than met the eye, but that always seemed to be the friggen' case.

"He's alive!" I yelled as I watched Jack's hand twitch. Although I was thinking that I should have maybe kept that thought to myself. It could have just been the spasms of death throes and even if he was alive, he was basically the last bottle of beer in a dry county.

"Jack!" Perla screamed from the base of the ladder.

Cindy was next to her with her arms around her shoulders.

"We're going to get you out of there!" Brian yelled.

'We are?' I thought. Hey, I was all for a rescue, but short of a helicopter, this was going to be a bit tricky.

BT was looking over Brian's head at me.

'No clue.' I mouthed.

Jack slowly turned over, his mouth full of blood. "Bufsted a few teef," he said as he gingerly pulled himself to a sitting position.

"No biggie, buddy," Brian said. "Don't need them to drink beer."

Jack gave him the thumbs up, but his head was hanging down.

From my elevated perch I watched as a path began to form from the front of the store right to Jack. I lifted my rifle. Something wicked this way came and I was going to blow it back to the corner of hell it had been let out of.

"Hi asshole!" Durgan yelled as he approached. "And put the damn gun down, you shoot me and Eliza sends zombies onto the roof, and you know what happens then. Friends get eaten, blood spurts everywhere, it's a mess!" he shouted gleefully. "Oh, what's the matter? You look like someone just dropped a big smelly log in your Cheerios! Bet you didn't know my Mistress was here, did you?"

I still hadn't said anything.

"Shoot him! If you don't, I will!" Paul yelled from the roof. "We'll take care of ourselves!"

Durgan hesitated, he hadn't been expecting that.

I loved Paul for that, but I'd been shooting with him before. If the target wasn't the size of an elephant and stationary, he would have a difficult time putting a bullet in it.

"Don't you dare!" Durgan shouted at me. I pulled the muzzle up just to see the asshole sweat a little.

"O mi dios!" I heard Marta scream.

"Zombies are banging on the door," Alex explained.

Durgan smiled. I lowered my gun, not willing to let the bluff get out of hand.

"Oh, and shithead, Eliza says if you try to leave on that fancy truck of yours, she will let me bust down that door and kill your friends."

That was of course if I even thought the truck could roll over this many deaders.

Paul picked up his rifle and started to pepper Durgan's general location. Zombies fell as bellies erupted and heads splintered. Zombies closed around Durgan like a shield, I could see the small bubble of protection as it weaved its way back to the safety of the store.

"Not a great idea!" I yelled to Paul.

"Screw him. Do you think they're really just going to let us go? I could have at least had the satisfaction of watching him die!" Paul yelled angrily back.

"I guess you've got a point there."

"How's he doing?" Paul asked of Jack.

"My heaf if killing me," Jack said as he shakily got to his feet.

I started firing into the zombies that began to tighten their circle back around Jack. His time on earth had come to an unmerciful end. Perla started running up the ladder which began to swing from the effort.

"I love you Perla!" Jack yelled just as the first of the zombies tore into his flesh. It came out more as 'I wove woo' but the man was about to die and I let him have his dignity back at least in this journal.

I kept firing into them long after his screams had died down. What was once Jack O'Donnell would now fit snugly in a lunch box with room for a thermos. Perla nearly pitched in after him, wrapped up in her grief as she was. Brian wasn't much better.

I slowly descended, bringing Perla with me so that Cindy could try and console her. The guilt that dropped onto my frame would weigh heavily for a long time.

BT met me at the controls to the ladder as I handed Perla off.

"You still going to try this?" he asked me.

"Got nothing better going on," I told him.

"Mike, come on man, its suicide," BT said seriously.

"It's only suicide if I take my own life, not if they do it."

"You know what I mean."

"I know what you mean, I just think I'd rather die up there than down here."

"Why don't we just run the squishy turds over and get out of here?"

"Eliza is not one for idle threats, we leave, they're dead." I said pointing up towards the roof.

"Mike, we stay, they're dead AND we're dead."

"Man, I know it, you know it, they know it," I said pointing to the front of the store.

"But you're still going to try, aren't you," BT stated in amazement.

"It's what I do man, I'm a helper."

"Durgan was right, you are an asswipe,"

"That hurts man, now help me get another ladder."

Tracy watched BT cover me as I reached down to unfasten another ladder. "What are you doing, Mike?" she asked, although she already knew. "You are not going to try that again," she said, pointing her finger to Jack's last perch.

I stood back up with the prize in my hands. The zombies watched me with a predatory gaze but they never made a move for me. I had been within reach as I bent down to retrieve the ladder but they had remained fairly civil.

"Mighty decent of them," BT said echoing my thoughts.

"I thought so. Maybe we could take a few of them out for drinks when this is all over," I told him.

"Don't you dare say it!" Tracy snapped.

"What?" BT asked in bewilderment.

"Fine, tell him," she said, turning towards me.

"We could get Zombies!" I said with a small smile.

BT still looked confused.

"Oh, you're ruining it, man. A Zombie is a drink we used to get at Chinese food restaurants," I explained.

"That's not a good joke, Mike," BT said seriously.

"It sounded way better in my head."

"What color are they?" he asked.

"Huh?"

"The drinks, what color are they?"

"Green," I told him.

"Man, they don't even sound good,"

"Well, they're not really. They're just really strong, supposed to make you feel like a zombie."

"Maybe we should just move on to the whole ladder thing," BT said, grabbing it from my hands.

"Mike, no," Tracy entreated me.

"Need some help?" Gary asked.

"Are all you Talbots insane?" Tracy asked.

"I'm not a Talbot," BT said indignantly.

"Oh, that makes it all better then!" Tracy yelled at him.

BT shrugged his shoulders and went back to his climb. I followed close behind.

Gary stayed down as the ladder began to dip under the added weight of BT and myself. In fairness, the downward slant of the ladder had more to do with BT's bulk than my own, although I'd never tell him that.

"What's the plan?" BT asked once we reached the top.

"You know how I feel about plans."

"Okay, what's your idea then?"

"Well, let's extend this bad boy as far as it will go, straight up, and then we'll try to do a controlled fall so that it hits the roof."

"And if it doesn't?"

"Then make sure you let it go before it falls into the crowd."

"Seems sane enough."

"Yeah, most of my ideas start off with great expectations, only to decay rapidly into…"

"Devastation," BT concluded.

"Well, I wasn't going to go that far, but whatever. Let's do this."

By the time we had the ladder fully extended, it looked about as sturdy as a pipe cleaner. The swaying of the main ladder and the resultant swinging of the one we were holding had my confidence ebbing faster than Superman's libido after putting on a kryptonite condom, that is providing of course that such a thing can be made. But IF it could be, it would be disastrous for him, and I guess Lois too.

"This seems safe," BT said as he tried to keep his footing while also steadying the ladder.

"You guys ready?" I yelled to Paul.

"What the hell do you want us to do?" Mrs. Deneaux shouted.

"Catch it!" I yelled back.

"Yeah, preferably with your face," BT muttered for my ears only.

"Good one, let's let it go."

It fell faster than I was expecting. The good news though was that we had about a foot and a half to spare as it slammed onto the roof. Our end kicked up a good foot from the shock of the contact. It missed me completely but caught BT squarely on the shin. It wasn't an injurious hit, but it had enough force to make him lose his balance. BT began to pinwheel his arms. I could hear the horrified cries from above and below as I reached out and grabbed the waist line of his pants. There was a shockingly long second where I thought we were both going over. BT wasn't a piece of equipment and I was *not* going to let him go.

We were frozen between absolute death and relative safety. A butterfly landing on BT's shoulder would have been enough to tip the scales. As it was, there was a slight breeze to my face that I think God issued just for us. The death détente was shattered by minutiae; the forces I applied pulled us back from the literal edge.

"Whew," BT said as he sat down, placing a tight grip on the ladder he sat on. "That was close."

I didn't say anything. I probably would have just vomited anyway. And that really would have just killed the heroic moment I was hoping to bask in for another minute or two while I got my heart rate under control.

"Mike, I can't…"

"Don't," I said putting my hand up. "I don't want to talk about it."

BT remained seated while he secured the ladder with some tie downs and a few bungee cords. "I don't think this would stand up to a regulatory inspection."

The whole assembly was bouncing around like Mexican jumping beans high on cocaine.

I eyed the climb as I psyched myself up.

"What are you doing?" BT said ominously, placing massive arm across my chest.

"Getting an ice cream cone. What the hell does it look like I'm doing?" I asked him.

"I'll go first," he said.

"BT, come on man, this won't hold you."

"So was that how you planned on getting rid of me? You all go up there and then I'm stuck down here by myself."

"I hadn't really planned it out," I told him honestly.

"Listen, this makes the most sense, IF this holds me then there's no doubt it will hold everybody else."

I started to protest.

"Shut up Mike, I know you're the Type A personality with control issues and a hero complex, but I'm doing this. It makes the most sense and now once a-friggen-gain, I owe you,"

"We're not keeping score, BT."

"Maybe you aren't, but I am. Just make sure your end doesn't come undone,"

"Fine, your funeral…oh man, I didn't mean that… that was a poor choice of words,"

"Actually it wasn't, just poor timing. Stop looking like you just swallowed a mouse, it's alright my friend." He fist bumped me and started up.

Paul and Alex each grabbed their respective ends of the ladder to keep it from shifting around too much, which was not an easy task with BT's weight. The real problem began to arise as BT was halfway through his climb, the bow in the ladder began to pull precious inches of aluminum from its perch on the roof. The eighteen inches he had started with had rapidly been reduced to less than two.

BT had not raised his head during the entire expedition, wise move. I don't think I would have either. He just stayed focused on the task at hand, hand to rung, foot to rung.

"Stop, BT," Paul said.

"I'd rather not." Although he did.

I had been so intent on watching BT, I did not realize

the drama happening up above. I looked up to Paul and instantly saw the issue.

"Foh!" I said.

"What, Mike?" BT asked without looking.

"I said that out loud? Apparently it's Shakespearean."

"Mike!" BT roared.

"Sorry man, your weight is pulling the skids of the ladder off the roof."

"How much more of a climb do I have?"

"Fifteen feet," I gauged.

"How much of the ladder is still on the roof?"

I looked up to Paul, he held up two fingers.

"Two inches," I told him, my heart sinking.

"Am I over halfway?"

"I'd say you're just about dead center,"

"What is it with you and bad word choices?" he asked.

"Huh? Oh man, I'm sorry," I said again.

"In for a dime, in for a dollar," as he reengaged his movements.

A third person who I had not seen previously came to the aid of Paul and Alex by getting in between them and reaching down to grab the top rung. I think that may have been what saved BT's ass. Looks like he was going to owe someone else big time. He was soooo not going to be happy about this.

"Ten feet BT!" I shouted.

"How much?" he asked in return.

I once again looked to Paul. He let go his hold with one hand to raise all his fingers.

"Five inches! That's awesome!" I said with jubilation.

"Maybe where you come from," BT said.

"Did he just make a dick joke?" Alex asked.

"I'll explain it to you later," I heard clearly from Mrs. Deneaux.

"Just get your ass on that roof," I told him. "Five feet, and no, I'm not telling you how many inches so that you can tell me 'That's more like it,'" I said, trying to do a reasonable facsimile of BT's deep voice.

"Don't quit your day job," BT growled as the new guy grabbed a fair amount of BT's shirt and pulled.

Considering that my day job consisted primarily of killing zombies, I didn't think that was going to be a problem.

I rested heavily once BT got his ass up and over the wall. I knew BT far outweighed everybody still on this side, but how in the hell was I going to be able to sit here and watch eight more people cross this suicidal bridge?

Travis was already clambering up to meet me. "I'll go next," he said with just a little too much excitement.

"Be careful," I said needlessly.

"No way, I'm going to do it standing up."

"Just be careful, smart ass." The minute it took him to make the climb was among the longest clock ticks I had ever known as a parent. If he slipped and fell, I would have dove in as if he had fallen into a swimming pool. There would have been no thought, no hesitation. My death to mirror his would have been much more preferable to soldiering on without him.

The new guy had found a rope and secured the top rung to something on his side. The ladder had barely bowed at all during Travis' climb.

"Alright here's the deal." I told those on the truck. "I'm heading up, Eliza will definitely kill them if I leave, but if any of you think that you can get this truck out of here safely than I strongly suggest you take that route."

Brian looked at the growing crowd of zombies surrounding the truck. "What do you figure the odds this thing could plow through them?" He asked me.

"Fifty fifty." I replied.

"Kind of optimistic, don't you think?" He asked gazing out among the throng. "We'll come with you."

I nodded, I was happy, we'd need as much fire power as possible.

Meredith climbed up the ladder next. She took a solid five minutes to make the climb, but besides that, nothing out of the ordinary took place. Justin went next; his trip was not as smooth. He had one foot slip and dangle dangerously over the precipice.

"Sorry," he said sheepishly when he got to the top. "I was trying to beat Trav's time."

"Yeah, that seems worth it," I said sarcastically.

It was pretty much Perla's turn, but she was having none of it. "I can't!" she cried into Cindy's shoulder. "He's gone!"

"He is, Perla," Cindy said consolingly. "But his memory isn't. He would want you to go on, Perla. You let me read the letters he sent you when he was in the thick of the war. He loved you more than anything. He was always telling you to not let your life go by unlived if anything should happen to him."

"Wait, you read his letters?" Brian asked, "Did she read mine?" he asked, pointing to Perla.

"What do you think?" Cindy answered, pulling Perla in closer.

"That was some pretty personal stuff," Brian said with some embarrassment.

"Don't worry, you're no poet," Cindy said.

"But there was a lot of love in them," Perla said, sobbing into her friend's shoulder.

"Please," Cindy said. "It was the only comfort we could give to each other while you were off fighting your wars."

"Fine, but I don't like it," Brian said as he turned away. I could only imagine that he was trying to desperately remember all that he had said and how many of his deepest secrets had been exposed.

I remember some of the letters I had written to Tracy when I was traipsing around the world in some of the least unsavory places on the planet. When you are under the belief that the day in which you are living is going to be your last, you tend to spill everything within you. Sometimes I had gushed such heartfelt sentiment that I had actually become embarrassed when I reflected back on it from a safer vantage point. If Tracy ever thought that perhaps I was becoming a girly-man, she never once brought it up or held it against me.

Perla did go next; she never once took her eyes off the spot where her fiancé dropped. I personally think it was the anger that spurred her on and not the fear. A pissed-off woman was always a good ally.

Brian grabbed a coil of rope that was housed at the bottom of the lift controls and brought it up. "Never know if we'll need it," he said.

By the time the rest of the troop had made it up the ladder I figure I had aged a good five years. It is a sucky feeling to feel so powerless (I would like to banish the word but impotent rings closer to the truth). It is the effect of being a man but unable to do the manly thing. No, I'm not talking sex; it was the inability to completely protect my family. I couldn't spot them on the ground if they should happen to slip and fall. I couldn't go up with them and hold them secure. I just had to wait and hope that a higher power was not calling any one I loved to be by His side just now.

Of course that is assuming that I believe in Someone or Something. I have wrestled seemingly my entire life with my belief system. A lot of time in my youth I believed only when it served me. As I have grown older (you'll note I did not say wiser) and I have spawned my legacy, I sometimes see Him and His Power shining through their eyes. But I waver as I look at the cruel black eyes of those that oppose us and wonder how an omnipotent being could ever find justice in the cruelty that the world afforded so eagerly. And I'm talking even before the zombies came, but if you really start to put all the pieces together, than perhaps it does fit. I'm not saying I like the picture that the puzzle is portraying, but who am I to say what is art? I can't stand Picasso either. But let's just say for the sake of argument that He gave us all free will to do as we pleased in His garden. And let's say that as the spoiled, greedy, egotistical, uncaring, brattish life forms that we are, we took a big shit on his prized Azaleas and maybe His way of disciplining his wayward children is this plague, this plague upon humanity. I have yet to see so much as ONE zombified lady bug, or dolphin, or even an ape who shares somewhere in the neighborhood of 98% of our genes. So there you have it, Beginner's Theology, Course 101.

So I've been stalling my inevitable climb up the ladder. I am no fan of heights. I was so wrapped up in everybody else's go at it, I guess I never figured my turn would come.

"Henry, it's just me and you. You ready for this?" I asked him. He didn't respond, he was too busy looking down at the zombies.

"Talbot, get your ass up here!" BT yelled.

"What about the truck?" I asked him needlessly.

"What about it?" Tracy asked in response.

"He's afraid of heights," Gary said, looking over the lip of the wall.

"Talbot? I watched him charge into machine gun fire," BT said disbelievingly.

"Our brother Glenn," Gary said, bowing his head and doing the Holy Trinity upon his chest (Catholicism dies hard), "once took him hiking to a place called Blue Hills when he was young,"

"Gary, you really don't need to tell that story right now!" I shouted from the truck.

"If you come up here I'll stop," Gary said with a wicked smile.

"That's kind of messed up," Meredith piped in.

"I agree with her!" I shouted. Just then the fire truck began to shake as zombies began to slam into the body. I almost pitched over the side long before I had a chance to go up that ladder.

"Continue," BT said.

"Mike never told me this story," Tracy said.

"He told me once," Paul said, "but we were pretty

drunk."

"This sucks," I said.

Gary turned from me and began up his narrative, "So Glenn," (Gary stopped for the Trinity again) "took him all the way up this Hill. How old were you Mike, ten, eleven?"

"Seven," I answered back.

"Wow, that young? Damn, no wonder you're so screwed up," Gary reflected.

"Just finish it up, will you!" I yelled at him.

"So on the top of this hill is a Ranger's station, looks a lot like a castle come to think of it. But anyway Glenn (yes the Trinity came again), one of his friends, and Mike go to the top of it. The stations were unmanned and unsupervised back then, I think that's probably changed since then. Do you know, Mike?" Gary asked.

"Never been back Gary, thank you very much. Please continue!" I told him.

"Well, Glenn," Gary started again with the cross upon his chest.

"God gets it!" I shouted at him.

"What? What are you talking about?" Gary asked.

He was completely oblivious about what he had been doing. Catholics were used to doing things by rote. If you have never been to a Mass, it consists of a lot of sitting, kneeling, bending and the damn shaking of strangers' hands. It's not the people that I can't stand nearly as much as the germs that they have on them. I'm concerned about where MY hands have been and I KNOW. Only God knows where Joe Schmoe's hands have been. Who knows, maybe he has an incurable case of pubic lice and he's been feverishly scratching his nether regions moments before he grasps your hand in mock friendship. I don't know, but that's what I'm thinking. I once saw a video on YouTube where a lady on a public train once shoved her hand down the crack of her ass and then pulled it out to give it a good licking. Yeah, you read my entry right, I wrote LICKING. Sniffing would be bad enough, but LICKING? Are you kidding me? I almost upchucked on my monitor. What if that bitch is sitting next to me in church! Still stalling about the climb up the ladder in case you hadn't noticed.

Gary had started back up while I was having my inner dialog. "… they're up on the top of this castle slash ranger station and Glenn (Sign of the Trinity – I sighed heavily) asks Mike if he wants a better view."

"This doesn't sound like it worked out well for you Mike!" BT shouted.

I flipped BT off. It had absolutely no effect on the big man as he laughed it off.

"So Glenn (SotT – guess what it stands for. I have to write this journal out with a pencil and I'm sick of repeating the same thing over and over) hoists Mike up."

My breathing started to accelerate just thinking about what was to come.

"Immediately flips him over and hangs him upside down by his ankles outside the window."

"Oh my God!" Tracy exclaimed.

"Glenn (SotT) was a wild man," Gary said with his head bowed.

"Damn Mike, I'm sorry I was messing with you. That would be a head fest for any one, especially a seven-year-old," BT said. "Now get your ass up here."

"Is that your version of tough love?" I asked him.

"There are zombies getting on the truck," the guy I hadn't met yet shouted.

Henry started barking, something he only does under extreme duress, and zombies closing in was apparently on his sliding scale of bark-worthy events, that and doggie ice cream treats, but I hadn't heard the ice cream man coming.

*   *   *

Eliza and Tomas Interlude

"Are you controlling the zombies' motor skills, Brother?"

"Yes, do you like it?"

Eliza did not answer her brother. For the first time in a very, very long time, an unfamiliar feeling jolted through her frozen veins. She thought it might be fear.

*   *   *

"Not much choice Mike!" Paul shouted, trying to motivate me.

I think it was a bit of overkill, what do you think? I had zombies climbing up the truck. They didn't give a damn about any of my myriad of phobias. I absolutely detest heights, but being eaten alive trumps even that. I was halfway up the truck ladder when the fastest of the zombies stepped onto the rungs. I watched him in disbelief as he tried to coordinate the placement of his hands and feet. He looked like a puppet controlled by an inept puppeteer, but that he was even trying this was a frightening new development.

"Brian, could you tie the end of that rope down and toss it to me?" I asked him.

He unslung it from his shoulder, retreated for a minute or two, and then tossed the rope into my face.

"Great idea Mike!" Tracy said in encouragement.

"She's not going to like this," I said softly to Henry.

I began to tie a make shift harness around Henry, kind of like what I've seen on Animal Planet when they have to hoist a cow out of a well or something.

"Oh for Christ's sakes Mike, what the hell are you doing?" Tracy asked with chagrin, "That damn dog."

"This damn dog saved your daughter's life and mine! I shouted back. She backed down but she was not a happy camper.

I no sooner got the harness as snug as possible when Henry brushed by me. He was either showing me the way or saving his ass, no sense in the both of us perishing here. Henry kept his gaze focused solely on the roof he was striding for. His paws splayed out as he stepped on the rungs;

he seemed pretty sure of himself. On second thought, I might have been better off using the rope myself. Although I don't know how Henry was going to climb the ladder once he got to the incline.

"Mike, why are they following you?" Alex asked.

"Really Alex? That's the question you're going to ask?" I asked sardonically, looking up at him.

He shrugged his shoulders.

"Any chance one of you guys could maybe shoot the zombies?" I asked. "Instead of watching."

"Sorry, Dad," Travis said. "I've just never seen them do that."

"I told you Mike was trouble," Mrs. Deneaux said to her audience.

Almost as one the group turned on her and told her in varying ways to shut the hell up. I would have savored it a lot more if I wasn't on a swaying ladder suspended above zombies, frozen by a phobia my crazy ass brother thrust upon me some thirty-eight years prior.

Travis' shot went wide of the zombie's forehead. I couldn't blame him, the wind had picked up and the ladder was moving a good twenty to twenty-four inches back and forth. The fact that he ripped the damn thing's ear off was impressive enough and the force of the bullet was enough to dislodge him from the ladder, which was just as effective as a kill. I climbed two more rungs when another shot rang out followed in quick succession by two more.

"Dad, they're getting better at climbing," Travis shouted.

"Don't turn around Mike," Paul said.

So of course the first thing I did was just that. A line of zombies was making the ascent and they were getting close enough that covering fire was going to be extremely difficult.

"You'd better get going," Brian said needlessly.

"And they always said Army guys were ignorant," I mumbled.

"I heard that," Brian said. "Now get up here so that we can settle this like gentlemen."

I was moving a little quicker but I was making Meredith's five minute snail pace seem pretty damn impressive.

"You've got a ten-foot cushion," BT said just as I made it to the junction from the fire truck ladder to our make-shift bridge.

"How's Henry doing?" I asked, too fearful to look up.

"Better than you," BT said.

'I'm screwed,' I thought to myself. As soon as two or three of the zombies got on the ladder with me, the added weight would pull the skids right off the roof.

"I'm not going to make it," I said looking up into my wife's eyes.

"You get moving Talbot or I'm coming down there to get you," she said, and she wasn't kidding. BT grabbed her elbow as she began to climb over the wall.

"Just wait, this isn't the way Mike goes out. It isn't climactic enough," BT reassured her.

"This isn't a movie or a book, BT, and last I checked you didn't have the power of precognizance!" she shouted in his face. "For all we know he could die on that ladder by scraping his hand and getting an infection. That wouldn't be climactic at all, in fact, I'd call that very anti-climactic, but it would still be a reality. Now let me go so that I can get my husband up here!"

"Don't you dare let her go!" I shouted to BT. "If I die here, it'll be alone!"

A thick rope almost toppled me off my perch. "Wrap that around your waist Mike!" Paul screamed. "Fast!!"

I was never great with knots, maybe I should have joined the Navy, but in a pinch I can tie a double granny like nobody's business.

"Now climb, if you fall we've got you!" Paul shouted. "Mad Jack, tie the other end off."

'Wait, didn't he tell me they would have me? Should

I really trust a man named Mad Jack to tie the other end of my life line off?'

"Henry's up!" Justin shouted.

'Damn, that was fast.' I looked up to verify and immediately wished I hadn't. Vertigo, like a physical force, pushed my face into the ladder. From my vantage point, with cool aluminum on my cheek, I could see the gamut of encouraging and disparaging (Marta's and Deneaux') faces. When the worst of the episode passed, I looked behind me. Mindless pursuit would not be the adjective I would have used to describe what approached. Relentless, yes, mindless, no. The zombie closest to me extended his hand. This was like my worst nightmare in church. If I let him get any closer I would have to take the proffered viral encrusted hand in celebration of a new bond between man and zombie. Yeah, that's it. I could be the ambassador, the one that broached peace between man and monster! I would be a national hero, heralded as the savior of all mankind! Or he'd gnaw through my fingers on his way to devouring my forearm. Yeah, that seemed much more probable. Still stalling.

I quickly unsnapped the tie down that was holding the ladder in place; the buffeting wind made it jump. I jumped on it before it could completely bounce off.

"Mike, what are you doing?" Paul asked in alarm, not sure if the nylon rope they had secured the ladder with would hold the entire weight should the ladder and I both go over.

I was four rungs up when I felt the ladder shift. Company had-joined me on this final leg of the journey.

I was halfway craning my neck to look back when BT's words struck me. "*Don't*," was all he said, and the tone was enough, I actually paid him heed.

The ladder was bowing something fierce. I looked up to watch as the top skids were a good fifteen or sixteen millimeters from losing contact with the roof. See how I did that, I changed from U.S. measurements to the Metric system. Maybe if we had just switched back in the seventies like they said we were going to, I would be able to feel much better about my predicament. Because fifteen or sixteen millimeters sounds WAY better than half an inch!

Another zombie joined us, or a particularly heady wind hit, or a damn butterfly landed on a palm frond somewhere on an island in the Pacific, didn't matter, the rear of the ladder came off the ladder truck. What had previously seemed like a good idea now truly sucked as I death gripped the rung I was on as we swung with velocity towards the wall. Memories flooded through my senses, I guess the mind feels the necessity to show events that are not life threatening when one is faced with a most certain demise. For the briefest of moments I was once again a fifteen-year-old enjoying a burgeoning beer buzz with my two best friends on the planet, Paul and Dennis, as we discovered a place called Indian Hills. My parents had left me alone for the weekend and I did what any respectable teenager would do if they wanted to hold on to their cool card, I had a raging party. The next morning as my two buddies and I cleaned up, we decided to hightail it from the premises before my mother came home. During the best of times she could give Deneaux a run for her money. With the hangover I was suffering from, I did not want to add her to the mix.

Paul, Dennis and I had grabbed a few beers and were reinvigorating the buzz we had so much enjoyed the previous evening. Our goal was an area that we had seen from a perch atop our local grocery store. We would come to find out that the area was known as Indian Hills. It was an Indian burial ground (no, really!). The place had become a sort of oasis for us as we had grown over the next three years. That it was mystical was beyond reproach. We had more than our fair share of adventures on that land, but that's a story for another journal.

The fingers of my right hand smashed against the wall as I had readjusted my grip from rung to rail. I'm not ashamed to admit I screamed. I'm pretty sure it was a good throaty man scream but I can't be sure, it might have been as intimidating as an eleven-year-old girl's. My immediate thought was better the right, I shoot lefty. And then all thought was washed away by the mind-blistering pain that ripped through my neurons. The pain peeled back quicker than I expected. I would learn later that the left side of the ladder had struck first, absorbing the majority of the strike. I would most likely lose all four fingernails on my right hand but that was a small price to pay for my life. I might have had some small micro-fractures in the tips of my fingers as well, but I'd left my Blue Cross Blue Shield card back in Colorado, and I figured that I was out of network anyway.

The haze in my mind burned off the moment I felt that hand wrap around my foot. So there we were, me and my new buddy, suspended thirty feet above the ground by a small rope attached to a ladder I wouldn't tie anything bigger than a Chihuahua to. The ladder swayed back and forth against the wall, I'm sure doing its best to cut through the nylon holding us in place just like in every movie I'd ever seen. Sure, I had a safety rope on, but it looked like it had seen better days.

My new buddy was really trying to climb up the ladder. His hand was wrapped like a vise and I could feel his full weight as he either was trying to pull me down or pull himself up to greet me properly. But he would bite me long before we could exchange banalities.

"Cut the rope!" I shouted. 'Did I just say that?' "For the ladder!!" I clarified quickly.

"We figured that much," BT said, looking over the rim of the wall.

"Just making sure, hurry, my buddy here is pretty hungry and he thinks I'm on the menu."

"What do you mean nobody has a knife?" I could hear Tracy ask irately.

I tried to shake my new buddy's hands free, but he was having none of it. His right hand gripped my calf. As soon as he pulled up and got his mouth into position, I was about to become his lunch. My arms strained as I supported the both of us.

"Not that one!" BT shouted.

'Are you kidding me?' I thought as I hung on, still grimly trying to shake my 'friend' loose.

"Let go of the ladder!" BT said, "Don't worry, bud, the rope will hold."

"The both of us?" I asked him.

"Probably," the one called Mad Jack said.

I pulled my hands back just as the ladder zipped by. The rope tied around my waist bit deep into my flesh as it absorbed all of our weight. I felt like I was being severed, and the added pressure as the group on top of the roof began to hoist me up only contributed to the strain. My biting buddy was still firmly entrenched like a fat deer tick, but without his feet planted on the ladder he was merely hanging on for his dearly departed life. I wasn't in any immediate danger of being bitten but rather torn in two like a convicted felon, drawn and quartered or, in this case, halved. To-MAY-toe, to-MAH-to, what's the difference?

"The rope is breaking!" April shouted.

"Shut up, fool!" Mrs. Deneaux snapped. I would like to think that perhaps it was to save me from the bad news of my upcoming demise, but more than likely it was to hide the surprise so she could relish the look of shock on my face as I plummeted earthward, the old bitch. There was a lurch in my stomach as I free fell a few feet. I quickly looked up.

BT was leaning as far over the wall as he could, fat droplets of sweat cascading down upon my face. Normally this would have grossed me out to no end, but since he was single-handedly pulling the rope up hand over fist, I would forgive him this transgression. The veins in his neck stood out thicker than the rope I was tied to. His teeth clenched together in a pressure I think could snap through a steel cable, his eyes squeezed shut in concentration and pain.

I wouldn't find out until I was safely on the roof, but the rope had snapped. BT had dived after it and just barely gripped the edge of the trailing rope. He and he alone had my lifeline in his hands. He hadn't even had enough cord to wrap it around his hands, he was just pulling two full grown men up the side of the building. Well, to be fair, the zombie looked a little on the underfed side and had decayed a substantial amount, but still!

As more of the rope became available, Paul and Alex gripped some and the pain in BT's features eased. But he never let go, even as the blood ran from his hands in droplets to rival those from his sweat.

I had never before been so willing to be embraced fully within a man hug. BT grabbed me under my armpits and basically manhandled me up. Travis got his rifle into position and blew my buddy's head in two. I looked over my shoulder as the zombie fell towards the ground. His friends greeted him gaily at first, hoping for a meal from the heavens. He was quickly trampled underfoot once as they realized he was tainted. Of all the things zombies were, it was a damn shame they weren't cannibals.

BT picked me up and placed me firmly on the roof. It took me a little longer to regain my wits.

"You can let go now, people are starting to stare," BT whispered in my ear.

I pulled back slowly. "Thanks, man." Those two words meant much, much more but the true sentiment was conveyed in my tone.

"You're welcome and we're even now," BT said with a smile.

I watched as he walked away looking for something to wrap his hands up in. Tracy came over to me and pointed out the blood that covered my armpits; his hands must have been flayed. He might think we're even, but the save-o-meter clearly pointed in his favor. Would it be against the rules if I staged a fake disaster and 'saved' him from a perilous fate? Just to swing the meter back in my favor, something minor, maybe a skateboard on the stairs or I could kill a malaria carrying mosquito before it bit him, something small. Just a scale tipper, that's all I'm looking for. Well, no real worries with the state of the world as it is, I'm sure an opportunity would present itself soon enough. But what if he saves my ass again? Then I'll be down by two. That could be a pretty big deficit to come back from. Maybe if I just up and chucked Deneaux off the side of the building, he would consider that a leveling of our score.

"You alright Talbot?" Tracy asked. She looked more nervous than I'd seen her in a long time.

I nodded slightly. The shock of the event still hadn't completely registered. I was betting there would be nights to come where I would dream BT hadn't made it to that rope and I had plunged backwards into a sea of sharp teethed zombies. Maybe even staying asleep long enough to feel them rend the flesh from my bones, elastic skin snapping as it was pulled free from my body. Veins and arteries popping as the sealed blood within arced out in red rainbows of death. Rein it in Talbot! I know my imagination can be like a three-year-old on Red Bull and still I feed it.

"How's your hand, buddy?" Paul said as he gripped it for a handshake.

"Hurts like hell," I said, ripping it from his grip.

"Dude, I am so sorry. I thought it was the other one," Paul said, moving in for a hug.

Erin smacked him on the shoulder. "We really are so glad to see you and your family Mike," Erin said, moving Paul aside so that she could get her own hug in. "Do you have a way to get us out of here?" she asked hopefully.

I looked back over the wall at a fire truck that was barely visible due to the swarm of zombies on it. Worse yet was the now thirty foot gap between us and the ladder.

Erin was still waiting for an answer. Paul helped me out and pointed at the way we had come up.

"But there are zombies all over that thing," she answered. "How will we get them off of there?" she asked, looking between me and Paul.

"That's something we might have been able to do with the guns. It's the gap that shuts that avenue down," I told her.

Zombie Fallout IV: The End…Has Come and Gone

"So now what?" April asked. "You bring him!" she spat, pointing to Justin, "but no way out!"

"April!" Joann exclaimed. "They came to help." She swore with a contemptuous wave of her finger.

"They've done nothing for us!" she screamed, "except bring us more troubles."

"Listen April!" I yelled, "I think you were in a world of crap long before we got here. All I did was risk my family and friends' lives so that we could help your ungrateful ass! I'll tell you what," I continued, "when I figure a way out of this, I'll make sure to leave you here."

"Mike, she didn't mean it," the new guy said, trying to placate me.

"Yes I did," she answered with fire in her eyes.

"Well, this is interesting," the new guy interjected. "My name is Mad Jack," he said as he extended his hand. I gripped it way tighter than I meant to, it hurt like hell.

"Nice to meet you," I growled.

"Likewise," MJ said, pulling his throbbing hand away.

"Hi Mike," Joann said next, trying her best to not get sucked into the argument. Marta barely managed a weak wave. The kid… Freddy? No, Eddy, was hidden behind Joann's legs. I didn't see his mother or siblings anywhere. There was no reason to ask where they were, if they weren't on this roof they were dead. Didn't much matter how.

BT came back with a rag wrapped around each hand. I couldn't help but ask what I did, it's ingrained in my genes. "You get some Bacitracin on those?" I asked pointing to his hands.

Without missing a beat BT responded. "Yeah, they got a first aid station on the other side, fixed me up just right."

I almost, I said ALMOST, looked over his shoulder to see if he was telling the truth. He said it so dead pan I figured he just might be.

"Would you like a cigarette Mike?" Mrs. Deneaux

asked me genially.

I might have taken it except for the murderous expression on Joann's face. "Bitch," she cursed before walking away.

I shook my head, damn thing was probably laced with poison. Deneaux shrugged her shoulders and lit the one that she had offered me, but she was smiling. I don't know what got her rocks off but whatever it was, I could bet it was mean spirited. It was looking more and more like she hadn't offered me that cigarette out of any sense of camaraderie, but rather to make a point of not giving one to Joann.

"Have you always been this way?" I asked her incredulously.

She responded by taking an extra-long drag on her smoke.

Marta had walked away to take care of her children she seemed to be warring internally with 'glad to see us' and 'why are you here'. April walked off with Marta.

"She's just under a lot of stress forget about her," Alex said. "It really is good to see you my friend." He clasped my hand. Did no one witness the ladder event? I pulled back sharply.

"I'm sorry," he apologized.

I told him it was alright, but it was close to an hour before the crippling pain dulled. Most of that time I hid it in my coat pocket lest it be further abused.

"How did you find us?" Paul asked.

"Eliza led the way," Justin said, coming up to us.

"She's here," I told them.

"Like *right* here?" Paul asked, not truly believing my words.

I nodded.

"I thought we were screwed, now I know we are," Paul said, his right hand going up to massage the dull ache in his temples that my news had obviously caused him. "You got anything Mike, any sort of idea?" he asked as he began to pace.

I shook my head.

"Why in the hell did you come up here then?" he asked angrily. Not that he was being ungrateful, only that we had clearly endangered ourselves in the process.

Perla, Cindy and Brian had stayed in a tight circle amongst themselves. There had been introductions, but like cliques in high school people began to peel off into their own familiar groups. Joann and Eddy stayed close to Marta and her two kids. Mad Jack was pretty much a clique unto himself, but April would not stray more than a few inches from his side no matter how obviously he tried to lose her. Tracy sat down on the roof, her back against the retaining wall. The past few events had drained her damn near dry. Travis sat with her. Gary was off looking at the door that led down into the store. I so wished that he would stop jiggling the handle.

Paul, BT, Alex, Justin and I stayed together. We were the planning committee, so far without a plan. Mrs. Deneaux merely watched every group, a few moments spent studying each one.

"Anything yet?" Gary asked, thankfully coming away from his door handle turning expedition.

"Still locked?" I asked him.

"Yup," he said straight faced. "And it's a good thing too."

"You think?" I asked him.

*   *   *

Gary hadn't been away from the door for more than a few minutes when it looked like it was beginning to bulge out. I thought I was seeing things at first, but it was tough not to hear the groan as the metal of the door began to stretch and pop.

"Incoming!" Brian shouted.

What were individual groups moments previously now became one discombobulated mass.

"Joann, you and Eddy might want to get behind the first line," I told her, motioning back. She looked terrified but she did it.

For all the pressure the door was under, it was kind of anti-climactic as it swung open gently. But what flooded through more than made up for the lackluster revealing. At first we could keep up with the zombies coming through the choke point. Zombies staggered in by ones and twos, then threes and fours, and like always they began to overrun our suppressive fire. So many zombies and so few bullets. It took me back for a moment to my time in the service when we were in class studying tactics.

When Iran and Iraq had been were having their Holy War (I always wondered if God truly approved of those that died in his name, whether you called him God, Allah, or Buddha, I doubt it. I can't imagine an omnipotent being creating his children in his image so that they could murder, rape and pillage each other in his name. To me it sounds like a bunch of spoiled brats that were in need of some heavy slapping upside the head. Once upon a time he released the flood waters to purge man, the zombies were the modern version of a scouring. Lord knows we needed it, no pun intended.) Back to my original tangent; if I go off on too many branches, I'll never find my path home. Iran was losing the war badly, so they did what any civilized country would do, they rounded up one million children, armed them only with the knowledge that Allah awaited them and then sent them in huge waves against the Iraqi machine gun nests.

So a million unarmed children running at full speed across the desert did what the entire Iranian army could not. They overtook the Iraqi positions. Oh, it wasn't that the Iraqis couldn't fire upon and kill children, it's just that they couldn't fire enough rounds to stop them, and that was what was happening to us. Although I could say I was eternally grateful I was shooting flesh eating zombies rather than innocent children who believed death by machine gun fire was a viable alternative to living in Iran.

We were yielding inches of precious footing on that roof and the zombies were taking feet.

"Hold tight!" I yelled, watching April. She looked like she was going to bolt followed by Joann. Where did the hell they think they were going to go?

Brass flew. I was burned more than a few times as the hot ejecta passed me by. We were so tightly grouped one hand grenade could have taken us all out. My drill sergeant would have kicked my ass if he could see me now. I wondered what happened to him. He was entirely too mean to die, probably scared the shit out of the Reaper when he came to collect him.

I dry fired my rifle, quickly feeling around for a replacement magazine that wasn't there.

"This sucks!" I shouted to the wind.

Gary looked over. He was placing well aimed shots center mass in the foreheads of our opponents. "What?" he yelled over the din.

"I'm pretty much out of ammo." I uttered the two words in battle I swore I would avoid at all costs. "Fix bayonets!"

"What the hell are you talking about?" BT asked, raising his cheek off of his stock.

I grabbed the Bowie knife I had strapped to my side. I didn't actually attach it to my rifle; it was just a play on words. Our position was tenuous to say the least. Our backs were against the wall (no, literally, they were). Zombies had completely taken over the roof. Some of the speeders were actually so close that my weapon could be of use. I'd never stabbed anyone in the head, until now that is. I figured a direct thrust into the forehead most likely wasn't the best idea. I was afraid that if my blade did penetrate, that it would get stuck and then I'd be down to hand-to-mouth combat. Or possibly, if I didn't get a straight enough push, the blade would glance harmlessly off the thing's skull. Sure, it would open up a wicked wound and rip the flesh clean off exposing the white bone beneath, but the zombie sure wouldn't care. I came in sideways striking home through the temple. I'd had a harder time cutting off pats of butter back in the day than I did driving that knife home. If anything, I went too deep scrambling that thing's blackened brain matter. It couldn't drop fast enough as I pulled my knife free.

"That's pretty gross," BT said, kicking one of the zombies away before placing a pistol shot in its skull.

We were so tightly packed together at the end, it was tough to tell where I ended and the next body began.

Tracy whispered in my ear, "I've always loved you, Mike, even after all these years."

"Even after all my idiosyncrasies?"

"Maybe even more so because of them; they make you who you are."

"So you pretty much thinking this is the end then?" I asked her as I pulled my blade free from its errant placement in a zombie's shoulder. Its teeth snapped dangerously close to my hand. Gary blew the side of its face off. Its exposed chattering teeth made it seem that much more dangerous. If it got a hold of my fingers now, I could watch it eat them and swallow. I know that would have been too much.

"You should be more careful Dad," Travis said, finishing the beast off.

I nodded my head in thanks.

"Just know that I love you," Tracy said behind me.

"The fat lady isn't singing just yet," BT said, eavesdropping on our conversation.

"This is an intimate moment right now, do you mind?" I asked.

"Not at all, take a moment, maybe go find a quiet area," he said, breathing heavily. He was also out of bullets and was using his rifle as a club.

Thank the stars he was so tall that when he swung, no one needed to duck.

"The fat lady might not be singing yet, but she sure is stuffing her face at the buffet table," Justin said between rounds.

"Is anyone *not* listening to our conversation?" I asked the group. I received no response. "Great," I said sarcastically.

My arms hurt from swinging and I only heard a few shots going off. The roof was covered in the detritus from zombie bodies, so much so I thought the roof might be in danger of collapsing under their combined weight. I knew it was only a matter of time. Nobody ever survives a zombie apocalypse, it just isn't in the cards. A speeder came up on me so fast I was only able to raise my knife in defense. I watched as his mouth closed down on the blade. His teeth splintered on the cold metal and his lips ripped where they made contact with the sharply honed blade. He shook his head from side to side. I guess he thought that he had struck a particularly tough piece of human gristle and if he shook hard enough and long enough he would be rewarded with the sweet, savory satisfaction of meat.

What the ass did succeed in doing was to pull my knife from my blood soaked hand. Not sure who finished the blade stealer off, but he let go of my knife at the same moment a bullet pierced his skull. The backward push on his brain bucket sent my knife into the air, not far mind you, but I was in a little bit of a sticky wicket. You know, being in the middle of a battle with nothing more than my wits was not a great place to be, considering my wife would probably tell you I'd be wholly unprepared for such a confrontation.

As I reached out to grab the knife and came back up to defend myself, I felt the press of teeth on my shoulder. 'What a way to go,' I thought to myself as I came completely up. "What the...!" is what I yelled.

Staring back at me, tongue lolling all over the place, was Red Neck Number One. Of course if you remember correctly, he was missing his jaw due to some heavy facial reconstruction from Henry. So Redneck Number One, for the third time, almost got the best of me. "Third time's the charm," I told him as I shoved the knife up through his soft palate. There would be no fourth encounter.

"Sorry man," BT said, "I missed him completely!" he shouted, blowing a few more zombies to their version of Kingdom Come.

"It's alright, this one was personal," I grimaced as I pulled my knife free. RN#1's cowboy-boot-wearing feet twitched a couple of times and then I lay to rest at least one of my nightmares. And then I prepared for more. The zombies stopped their approach at precisely the same time I heard my name spoken.

"Michael," Eliza's voice came silently but with force.

"That Eliza?" Paul asked.

"You heard that?" Justin asked him.

"I thought that was in my head," I said.

"Conversing with the enemy?" Alex asked.

If I thought we were tightly packed beforehand, I was now able to tell who had Chapstick in their pockets and who was just happy to see me.

"That's her?" Perla asked, the whites of her eyes more abundantly exposed as fear pulled her features taut.

"She doesn't sound so bad," Cindy said, trying to bolster her flagging spirits.

Just the sound of Eliza's voice was enough to suck the soul from a preacher and not many of us looked pious just now.

"Why are you keeping her waiting?" April asked anxiously.

"If you're in such a rush, why don't you go say 'Hi,'" BT told her heatedly.

Like a little kid April hid behind the petticoats of Mad Jack. That is, assuming that he had petticoats on, but you get the picture.

"See, I told you she only wanted him. El Diablo!" Marta screamed.

"El Diablo," Mrs. Deneaux mirrored. "That's rich!" as she took a puff off her cigarette.

"When the hell did you have enough time to light that?" I asked her.

"If I was to die I thought it only dignified that I do so with a Chesterfield in my mouth," Mrs. Deneaux said smoothly.

Not a bad ad campaign I thought. Pretty sure Chesterfield wouldn't have agreed.

Travis stood up precariously on the lip of the wall so that he could get a better angle over the tops of the zombies' heads. He blasted two rounds through the open door. We all hoped he got lucky.

Eliza's echoing laugh in the stairwell soon answered that question. A lone cataract-eyed zombie fell face first through the portal, his tongue hanging out inches below his open mouth. I was instantly transported back to Day One and Sir Licks A Lot. That was back when a zombie invasion was what it should be, all slow shufflers with no one to lead them. Ah, the Good Old Days.

"If your spawn deigns to live through the day I would suggest that he does not fire his rifle again," Eliza said, her voice traveling elusively in the acoustic laden stairwell, making it difficult to get a fix on her. But what do I know? It could be some Vampire trickery.

"Still though, it is a damn shame he missed," I told her.

I think she hissed, either that or a cat got its tail stepped on.

"I've got a surprise for you Michael," she lilted.

I quaked as I realized what her surprise most likely was. 'Oh, poor Tommy.' I was already mourning his passing.

"Michael?" a labored voice asked.

I looked over towards Tracy, whose interest was piqued as was BT's.

"Is Lawrence with you?" the voice struggled to ask.

Questioning looks passed throughout the group. This was a gravely serious time, but still I couldn't resist a small dig on my friend. Who knows? It could be my last time, might as well do it while you can… no regrets! "Hey Doc, yeah, BT is with us."

"BT's name is Lawrence?" Alex asked me.

BT looked at me like he was going to rip my spleen clean from my body.

"I'm here Doc," BT said.

"She's killed my wife," Doc said, choking back the tears.

"What about the kids, Doc?" I asked hesitantly.

"She... she hung her upside down and then slit her throat. She made Tommy drink all of her blood as it fell... oh God!" The doc was having a very difficult time reliving the event, but he kept on going.

"She turned Tommy," Justin said bowing his head in grief.

"Then, when the boy was done, she just let the zombies have the rest, like my beautiful wife was a side of beef." Doc was full on crying, "She made me watch the whole thing. She swore she would do that to my kids... I believed her. I had to do it!"

The doc was needlessly asking for our forgiveness. He did whatever he needed to do to protect the rest of his family. Who am I to judge, and I told him so.

"Doc, you did what you needed to," I said, putting as much commiseration into my words as I could.

"Mike..." he paused. "I saved her. I saved Eliza." He started crying again, or had he ever stopped?

"Are you not happy, Michael? I once again walk among the immortals," Eliza said gleefully.

We could hear the doc being removed from the scene.

"Where are those kids, Eliza?" I said menacingly.

"Where I wish them to be," she answered cryptically.

That ranged from a room downstairs to a zombie's belly.

"Eliza," I started.

"Silence!" she yelled. "I owe no answers to you!"

The force of her words pushed us all back a step or two. I noticed April looking down the wall again as that was a potential avenue of escape. Hell, so was I. Maybe the zombies would break our fall and we could run on top of their heads. It could work, I saw something like it in a cartoon.

"This ends tonight Michael," she said in a more even tone.

"About fucking time!" Travis yelled.

Tracy and I both turned to him. "No swearing!" we said together.

"Just get on with it Eliza. I figured you to be above the theatrics," I told her.

She was quiet. Any chance I ruffled her feathers? I could only hope.

"Very well, but one more thing. I have someone here who wishes to say hello."

"Hello Mr. T," Tommy said in the voice we had all come to love but that no longer carried any warmth within its timbre.

"Tommy?" I asked, hoping above and beyond any recognizable chance that it wasn't him.

"It's Tomas," he answered. The cold response sent shivers through me.

"Is there anything from the boy we love still in there?" I asked him unsteadily.

"Tommy died alone and in the dark, Mr. T."

"I'm sorry for that Tomas."

"So was he."

"What a touching family reunion," Eliza said, her voice as brittle as broken glass.

"Any chance of a one-on-one Eliza, me against you for the fate of our souls?" I asked. Rage burned through the fibers of my being like a wildfire sparked from a lightning strike.

"Mistress, let me be your champion!" Durgan shouted.

"He's still alive?" BT asked me quietly.

"Apparently," I said dejectedly.

"That could be amusing," Eliza said.

"As soon as you open that door, I'll blow a hole in his friggen' head," I said, meaning every word.

"Not very sporting of you, Michael," Eliza laughed.

"I don't much see any reason why I should get the snot beat out of me before I die," I told her.

"But yet you wish to fight with me. Surely you know that there is not a mortal on this world that can defeat me," Eliza said triumphantly.

"I would only agree to fight you if you let my family and friends go unharmed, to live out their lives as they see fit."

"Michael, the fun will be when I kill them all one by one as you watch. I could never let them go. Perhaps we can work out a different arrangement."

"I'm listening," What choice did I have?

"What if I allowed Durgan to fight you? If you best him, I would allow your family and friends to go unharmed."

"And what of my husband?" Tracy asked.

"Either way he dies, of course, and in front of his family," Eliza answered as if this were the most insane question she had ever heard.

"No, Talbot!" Tracy said thrusting a finger in my face.

"Tracy, I will do whatever I can to make sure that all of you are safe."

"What makes you think she will honor her end of the agreement?"

"What makes you think he could beat me?" Durgan yelled.

I hadn't thought about Eliza not following through with her promise but it wasn't like Vampires were noted for their honor.

"Eliza, how valid is your word?" I asked, although what was I expecting? If she lied about the first part, wouldn't she do the same with the second? Maybe some morality would bleed through. Yup, little known fact, soulless demons can't tell two lies in a row.

"Cross my heart and hope to die, Michael," Eliza said coolly.

"Mike, technically her heart doesn't beat and she is already dead," Gary cautioned.

"Thanks for that," I told him.

"Mike, let me fight Durgan, I've been wanting to bust his ass up forever," BT said with a smile that scared the hell out of me. "I'll fight that racist prick! I'll be Mike's champion!" BT yelled before I had a chance to tell him this was my fight.

"What is this, 1634?" I said, "I can fight my own damn battles."

"Who you kidding Mike? He'll kick your ass," BT said none too softly.

"Don't sugarcoat it man, tell me like it is," I replied, a little perturbed at his lack of faith in me.

"Oh hell man, you know what I meant," BT said, back peddling.

"Yeah, that he'd kick my ass," I told him crossly.

"That's what he said," Gary clarified.

"I have no beef with you!" Durgan shouted through the door, "But me and Mike have some reckoning to complete."

Durgan sounded like the coward that he was. He would only fight when the odds were clearly stacked in his favor. I was sort of surprised that he would even decide to go one on one. He probably figured that Eliza would have his back if I somehow got the upper hand. Although I doubted first that I would get the upper hand and second that Eliza cared anything about him.

"Did he say reckoning?" BT asked. "What kind of cracker ass speak is that?"

"I will allow it," Eliza said as if she controlled the entire production, which ultimately she did.

"Okay, so there's a lot going on right now. What exactly are you allowing?" Mad Jack asked her.

Damn, his balls must be the size of small boulders.

His stock just went up in my eyes.

"I will allow Durgan to fight Michael," Eliza intoned smugly.

BT shrugged his shoulders in frustration.

"Michael, if Durgan kills you," she started.

"When," Durgan said interrupting her.

"You do that again, I will rip your throat out," Eliza told Durgan.

"If Durgan kills you," she continued disdainfully, "those that you are with give themselves up willingly."

Murmurs of protests arose from the group. I couldn't blame them.

"I can't speak for the people around me," I told her.

"You will allow my zombies onto the roof with you during the fight so that I can be sure YOU hold up your end of the agreement."

"What if I say no?" I asked her.

"I will burn this building and everybody in it, or on it, to the ground."

"And when I win?" I said running my hand through my now sweating hair.

Durgan snorted in derision.

"If you should somehow best my champion," Eliza said mockingly, "I will allow everyone you are with to walk away from this site unharmed."

"I wouldn't trust her," Meredith whispered next to me.

"Will you allow them to live out their lives without your interference?" I asked.

"No," she answered.

"Most likely the first honest thing she's said," Alex said.

"I understand that you humans like to confer on matters of importance. I will give you one hour and then you will give me your decision," Eliza said. I could hear her entourage heading back down the stairs, her zombies following suit.

"Clearly the answer is no," Mrs. Deneaux was the first to pipe up.

"I'd really like to thank you, but I'm pretty sure it has nothing to do with my personal safety," I told her.

Mrs. Deneaux smirked at me.

"Should we take a vote?" I asked the group.

Deneaux shrugged.

"No," Tracy said.

"No," Justin echoed his mother. I looked at him sternly but the vote was already cast.

"Yes," Travis said. Tracy looked at him with a smoldering gaze that said that she was going to ground him for damn near forever.

"I don't see what choice we have. I say yes," Brian said. I nodded to him and received the same back.

"If Brian thinks it's a good idea than so do I," Cindy said firmly.

Perla was not dealing well with the whole proposal. Cindy went over to her and attempted to calm her down. "NO!" Perla shouted. "I am sick of seeing people die!"

I turned to Deneaux who had walked away to light another cigarette. "You already got my answer," she said, never turning back lest the oncoming breeze put out her lighter's flame.

"I will not place the fate of my children in the hands of him," Marta spat.

"Does that count as three votes?" Meredith asked the group.

I shook my head no.

Gary walked up and looked me in the eyes for a lot longer than I felt comfortable with. "I think he can do it. I vote yes."

"That was strange, but thanks for the vote of confidence… I think," I told him.

"Oh, I didn't see anything," Gary said. "I was just trying to instill some confidence in *you*."

"Again thanks, and don't tell me any more."

"Mike, I'll vote however you want me to," Paul said, coming up to me.

"I can't tell you how to vote. It's your lives on the line," I told him.

"I trust you like no other," Paul told me. "I vote yes."

Erin placed her arm around Paul's waist. "As do I," she said.

"Do you people not understand what you're doing?" Tracy screamed, "You are sentencing him to a certain death. Whether by Durgan or Eliza, Mike will not survive this!"

She was pissed. I briefly thought about going over to calm her down, but she'd just as likely pitch me over the side.

"We should all be fighting as one," she continued adamantly.

"Tracy, there won't be a fight," Alex said to her pacifying her a bit. "Eliza will merely burn this place down. I would think that Mike would be honored that some of us survive rather than all of us perish. I vote yes."

"You've all lost your minds," Tracy said bitterly before storming off.

"I agree with her Mike," BT said. "I say no."

April, who looked like a jackrabbit getting ready to bolt, slid a few inches behind Mad Jack. "No," she said meekly.

"Do I get a vote?" Eddy asked Joann.

She was about to say no. I stopped her. "It's his life too, he should have a say."

"Yes," Eddy said beaming. "The crazy man can beat anyone."

"Then I say no," Joann said, not looking as Eddy scowled at her.

I looked to a staunch ally, Meredith. She shook her head and ran to catch up to her aunt.

"Interesting," Mad Jack said. "I either decide the vote or tie it up."

"Really?" I asked. "I didn't think it was that close."

"Nine 'no's' and eight 'yes's'".

"Damn, I had no clue," I told him truthfully.

"Then how do you vote?" BT asked, rejoining the group.

"There is only one choice," Mad Jack said. "Logically speaking, Mike's willingness to fight Durgan is our only chance of escape. Albeit it sounds like it might be a slim one, it is a chance none the less."

"Don't shower all the confidence on me at one time," I told him. Mad Jack looked at me with a blank stare, he didn't get it.

"I vote yes," Mad Jack said.

"You're kidding me? So it's a tie?" I asked.

Mad Jack nodded in the affirmative.

"It looks like the decision is yours, Talbot. What will you do?" Tracy asked with a sheen of tears in her eyes. She already knew my answer.

"I will fight, because that is what I do," I told the group.

CHAPTER 29 - Tracy's Journal Entry 1

I cannot believe the pig-headed stubborn man that I married. My mother was right when she told me not to marry a Marine. 'Marry a Navy man,' she told me, 'they're much more pliable.' He's been huddled up with BT going over strategy on how to fight that steroid induced crazy bastard Durgan. He's barely even looked over at me. Good, I hope he knows I'm mad at him for what he's doing. I have absolutely no doubt that my husband will kill Durgan, but what good does that do his family, I ask you. Either way he dies. I'd rather burn with him, but not my babies, no, not that.

Eliza's coming!

CHAPTER 30 – Talbot Journal Entry 15

"What have you decided, Michael?" came Eliza's question. Her tone betrayed nothing of which way she wanted me to answer.

"My only condition as it has always been Eliza, is that if I agree to fight, when I win you honor your end," I told her.

"Will you believe what I have to say?" Eliza asked. That she had a small measure of mischief in her words was not in doubt.

"There is the locket," Tomas said.

"What locket?" Eliza and BT asked at the same time.

"The Blood Locket that Mr. T holds," Tomas answered.

Eliza's gasp of surprise was amplified in the small space she now inhabited.

"What do you have?" BT turned to me.

"My brother gave this to me before I left the house, he said he had no idea what it was for but that I might need it," I said as I pulled out a large white gold locket with a rose and a blood red jewel on its face.

"You possess the Blood Locket?" Eliza asked. It was the first time anyone had heard a tremor in her voice.

"It looks that way," I said, turning the locket over in my hands. I pulled away quickly as something snagged my finger. A fat bead of blood welled on my thumb, "Damn, again?" I questioned, sucking the wound. The locket opened to reveal an ancient picture of Eliza.

"You will give it to me now or die!" Eliza fairly shrieked.

"It looks like I'm going to do that anyway. So I don't necessarily see the reason to relinquish this," I said, thrilled that I had set Eliza back on her heels. "What does this locket do?" I asked the question of Eliza, but it was Tomas that had an answer forthcoming.

"She is bound to the locket…" Tomas started.

"Tomas, you are walking down a dangerous path," Eliza growled.

"No, Sister, you started down this path when you decided to open up your world to me."

"You will not betray me, Brother."

"I will do as I wish, Sister."

It was unclear what was happening behind the closed door, but it was Tomas who spoke next.

"Do not think that I cannot wrest control of these zombies from you Eliza."

A muffled thud and cry of pain carried through the steel door.

"Eliza, help me," a pain tinged plea came from Durgan.

"Fool!" she spat. "I did not tell you to attack him. I would always take side with a wayward brother over that of a slave."

"I was only and always trying to help Mistress," Durgan begged.

The door to the roof crashed open. Eliza strode through, Tomas right behind her. In the darkness of the hallway was the huddled form of Durgan.

"Michael, I will honor our arrangement," Eliza said with a rage fueled voice as she approached us.

BT discreetly grabbed the locket from my hand which had gone slack at the sight of Eliza. He clutched it close to his chest. I knew vamps had many more powers than mere humans. I hoped her sight wasn't too enhanced as I grabbed the truck keys in my pocket; this might work, they were sort of goldish.

"That's far enough, Eliza," I told her. Any closer and

Mr. Magoo would have caught my ruse. Eliza did not stop her forward progress. It had been a long time since she had taken any orders from anyone, least of all a sworn enemy. "Travis, give me your shotgun." Travis did not hesitate as he handed over his weapon. I dropped the locket (keys, careful to place my body and my foot in a way that made her viewing difficult, if she got a good look we were screwed) onto the roof and pointed the shotgun straight at the piece of jewelry. I had no idea if this ploy would work until Eliza stopped in mid-step.

"Will she die, Tomas, if I destroy this locket?" I asked. (Oh pretty please!)

"She will not be the same," Tomas answered.

I could tell Tomas was watching in amusement as the white around my knuckle spread with the incremental amounts of pressure I applied to the trigger. The inner debate waged within me.

It was Tomas' next words that stopped me from blowing that 'locket' to hell where it belonged. "I do not, however, think that you will like the outcome."

"What would that be?" I asked, never looking up.

"I would be in charge," Tomas told me solemnly.

"You're much more powerful, aren't you Tommy," I asked, but it was more of a statement.

"Yes."

"Is there anything of Tommy left in you?" I asked as a solitary tear was migrating down my cheek.

"No."

Eliza appeared to have missed the entire conversation; her complete attention was focused on the golden locket lying on the tarred roof. Durgan dizzily made his way onto the crowding roof as zombies began to pour through the opening. Eliza or Tomas still controlled them as they did not attack but made a ring around us, the stranded humans.

Eliza snapped out of her trance. "Do not be so confident, Tomas," she said to her brother. "Now Michael, I believe you have what is rightfully mine."

"I do, but I have decided on another set of terms," I told her.

"I grow weary of this," Eliza said. A cheetah would have been amazed at her speed as she grabbed the locket and was back in her original spot just as I blew a hole in the surface of the roof, damn near taking my foot off.

"I was expecting that. I just didn't think it would happen so fast."

"Kill them," Eliza said before she looked the piece of jewelry over.

The zombies began to close the circle up, hunger intensifying their movements. April fainted outright. It was Mrs. Deneaux that was the first to fire. The front line of zombies dropped quickly as the rest of the group took to arms. Rifle fire crackled, smoke rose into the air, human shaped monsters dropped by the dozens. Missed shots from fifteen feet were a rare occurrence, and then the zombies were eighteen feet away and then twenty. I held up my hand for a cease fire. It wasn't that the zombies were retreating, they just weren't advancing anymore.

"Clever Michael," Eliza said coolly.

"I watched Interview with a Vampire," I told her. "You vamps move pretty fast."

"Where is my locket?"

I shrugged my shoulders.

"I can still kill all of you now and then sort out the pieces later," she told me ominously.

"Do you really want to look through zombie offal for something you obviously value so much?" I asked her. Can a vampire be a germ-a-phobe? I mean I doubt it, they suck the blood out of people. Who's to say where that neck has been, or what disease is running rampant through that person's veins. "And it might not even be on us," I threw in for good measure.

"You lie, I can smell it on you," Eliza said.

"The lie or the locket?" I asked.

"Both. But you are right, I would rather you hand me the locket on your knees rather than search among these diseased vermin."

"Well at least we agree about the vermin part," I told her. "Let's make a straight up trade, all of us leave here and you get your locket."

"Where is the fun in that?" Eliza asked me.

"I think it sounds like a lot of fun," Mad Jack piped up.

"Me too actually," BT added.

Gary raised his hand in acknowledgement also.

"Enough!" Eliza said forcibly. "That is not an acceptable bargain. Someone must die here today."

"There's always you," Justin said a little louder than he intended.

"Oh my pet," Eliza said turning her head to face him. "You do not know what you have thrown asunder. I could have brought you on an incredible journey. You could have danced across the graves of everyone who has ever wronged you." Justin pulled his gaze from Eliza. She laughed. "Silly boy, it is a shame you will never see the dawn of a new day."

"I will fight Durgan," I said.

"No Talbot," Tracy said obstinately.

"Hush," I said, putting my finger to her lips and hoping she wouldn't bite it off. "I will fight Durgan but when I kill that asshole, we ALL leave unharmed and unpursued." (Now that I said and wrote that word I'm not sure if it's actually a Webster's Dictionary approved word. Oh well, it's not like anyone besides me will ever see this.)

"Those were not our original terms," Eliza said.

"It's called leverage Eliza. I have a little bit and I plan on using it."

"If anyone on your side should step in and alter the outcome, our agreement will be null," Eliza said, speaking directly to BT.

"No one will," I said turning to face my friend.

"What? I haven't even done anything," BT said

guiltily.

"And you won't, right?" I asked him.

"But what if he's beating the crap out of you, can't I at least kill him before they get us?" BT asked. I gave him the sternest look I could muster, but it didn't do much considering it was aimed at his sternum. "Alright, I won't do anything even if your spindly ass is getting spanked and or demolished," he grudgingly conceded.

"Thanks man," I said sarcastically. "Eliza, do you agree to this?"

"I will let everyone including yourself leave here unharmed, IF you kill him."

"What about not pursuing us?"

"That will be *my* leverage Michael. You can all leave here and I will let you go, but not forever."

"Don't take the deal, Dad," Travis entreated.

"I welcome the opportunity to put a spike through your chest, Eliza," I told her. Eliza sneered. "Swear it, Eliza."

"I swear it on the Blood Locket, Michael."

"Tomas?" I asked.

"She is bound," Tomas said.

I pulled the locket from the barrel of the shotgun where I had stowed it once the zombies stopped approaching. Eliza gasped.

"It would have been the first thing destroyed," I told her.

Eliza walked purposefully over to me and took the locket from my extended arm, making certain that her ice cold touch came in contact with my hand.

"We could still have some fun," Eliza told me as she kept her hand wrapped around my wrist.

"I've already dated enough cold heartless bitches in my lifetime, thank you very much," I said, trying to control the fear that was threatening to run away with my nerve.

"Very well. It is a beautiful day to die," she said as she released her grip.

"I'd actually prefer a good rainstorm, maybe some

hail and a crap load of lightning. It's that whole flair for the dramatic," I told her.

"Even at the end, you jest. You are a unique individual, Michael. I will almost miss you."

"My mother told me that once." It was the first thing I could think of.

"Dude?" Paul said.

"Too far?" I asked him.

"A little bit."

"You will surrender your weapons now," Eliza said as she stepped back next to Tomas.

"Whoa, that wasn't part of the agreement," I told her.

"Yes, as a matter of fact it was. When you die, the rest of your group will surrender to me. With their weapons they will not be so willing to follow through."

"I say we just go out fighting now Mike," Brian said.

A few others thought the same.

"We voted on this already, either we're all in or we're all out. I'm prepared to fight to the end by myself or with all of you by my side."

More zombies began to funnel through the breech point in response to Brian's call to arms.

"We've voted," Alex said. "With Mike we have a chance. I've said my piece and I am at peace with the decision. I am prepared to meet my Maker."

"I'm not sure if I should be honored or not with that comment Alex."

Alex shrugged his shoulders.

"Well at least you clarified that, buddy," I told him.

The small pile of rifles and pistols we produced could have kept a guerilla unit in Southern Peru stocked for a few years. I honestly don't know how we could have carried all this armament and still move effectively. Now I know why the ladder bowed so much under BT. Sure, a good part of it was his bulk, the rest had to do with the two rifles and three pistols he contributed to the pile, plus the five hundred or so rounds he had stashed on him at various locations on his body.

"Got anything else on you?" I asked him softly, pretty much just kidding.

When he smiled at me diffidently, I didn't even want to know where that one might be hidden, best not to think of things like that.

"I will give you some time to say your prayers to your false God," Eliza said as she strode back through the roof door, her entourage of zombies on her heels.

"That's not like her," BT mused, coming up beside me.

"I agree but there's no sense in trying to figure it out. A normal woman's motives would be impossible to figure out."

"And she's not normal," BT concluded.

"Let's start working on some contingency plans while we have a chance," I said, getting the group into a circle, except for April who had not yet decided to stop napping.

"What if Durgan beats you?" Perla asked.

"He won't," Tracy said.

"Okay, but what if he does?" Perla asked again, "We can't just leave our fates up to her."

"Personally, I'd rather let the zombies eat me," Cindy said.

That's how you know Eliza is one mean mother, when people would rather get eaten alive than spend any time with her.

"Could we survive a jump off the roof?" Joann asked, "I mean, we'd land on all those zombies below us."

"And then what?" BT asked peering over the edge. "Even if you didn't so much as bruise a muscle from the forty foot drop you'd still have to make it through close to a hundred feet of zombies."

"Plus I've got a feeling that we won't be anywhere near the edge," Mad Jack said, "Eliza'll have us surrounded."

"Okay, who's got what?" I asked the group as I pulled out a Glock 26 from a concealed holster.

BT hoisted out a seven inch barrel .357 Magnum. Erin had a stubby .22. Travis had a small .32 revolver, and Justin produced a sling shot. Hey it was a weapon, not a great one, but just ask Goliath how effective they could be.

"Sorry man," Brian said. "All I had was that rifle. We won't be able to put up much of a fight with these anyway," he said, getting depressed at the notion.

Mrs. Deneaux came into the center of the circle, a small Derringer in her hand. "It's not for them, sweetie," she said, placing the barrel up against April's head and her still prone body.

"That's even worse," Cindy said.

"Desperate times call for desperate measures," Mad Jack said.

"What will God think if we take our own lives? That is a mortal sin!" Perla was nearly crying again.

"The sin would be to allow Eliza to possess us," Marta said resignedly.

"Agreed," Paul said.

"You'd better beat him," Marta told me.

I'd bested him twice, but once was with a rifle and the other was while he was recovering from the first injury, not exactly a hand on hand combat situation. Sure, I had trained for this in the Corps but that was a LONG time ago. My philosophy was and still is that carrying more ammunition is your best bet.

The door to the roof opened slowly. All of our weapons raised. We tipped our hand; did this make the deal a no go? It was Tomas. I dropped my weapon down to my side but no one else followed suit.

"Mr. T, there is no time for this. Tell them to put their weapons down so that I may approach," Tomas said.

"Tommy?" I asked, hoping beyond hope.

"No," he shook his head. "I thought it would be easier for you to accept me if I reverted back to how he sounded."

"Put your guns down," I told them.

Tomas approached. "Eliza is enhancing Durgan. You

will not be able to defeat him with his new powers."

"Enhancing how?" I asked. The question wasn't fully out of my mouth before I stumbled upon the answer myself. "She's turning him into one of her, into one of you."

"Not quite, that would take too long and she doesn't want him to share her blood."

"Then how?" Gary asked.

"The same way she accelerated his healing and the same way I survived all these years, a half-bite."

"Like a nibble," Eddy said.

Tomas nearly smiled. I don't think that Tommy was as far gone as Tomas believed him to be.

"What does this do for Durgan?" Tracy asked.

"He'll be faster, stronger."

"Great, like he didn't already have that going for him," BT said.

"BT, I'm right here man," I said.

"Sorry man, I'm just saying. It's not like you didn't already know that."

"Yeah, I guess I just didn't need it vocalized from my own camp."

"My mom used to say the truth hurts," Eddy said.

I laughed. "Great, out of the mouths of babes."

"Why are you here Tomm… Tomas?" Tracy asked, "Is it just to tell us this?"

"I've come to give Michael the same opportunity that Durgan is receiving."

"Wait, you want to turn me into a half-vamp? I can't," I was panicking on the inside.

"It's the only way," Tomas said.

"Hear him out," Mad Jack said.

"And then after today? Then what? I watch as my family and my friends die. I watch as my children catch up to me in age and eventually die? I won't, I can't watch that, I can't be a part of that."

"Stop being a pansy," Mrs. Deneaux said. "Today is the only day that any of us has guaranteed. If it becomes too much of a burden then you can always fall on your sword. Of course it would have to be made of wood," she cackled.

"I thought you were relatively cool when you pulled that gun out. Now we're back to square one and I can't stand you."

She cackled louder.

"Every second we waste in discussion will be that much more time you will have to stay alive waiting for your own powers to increase," Tomas said.

"How much of a head start does Durgan have?" Justin asked. I was still pretty lost in my own thoughts to make any coherent cognitive thoughts.

"Five minutes," Tomas answered his old friend.

"Why bother at all," Mrs. Deneaux said. "He couldn't survive five minutes against the old Durgan, now with the new and improved model? Pah, we should have kept more guns."

"You should see if that gun has any rounds in it and hold it up to your eye. I'll pull the trigger for you," Alex said.

She "pahed" again.

"What of my soul?" I asked Tomas.

He shook his head in negation.

"I can never go to Heaven?"

"Only to the gates."

"I've been there," I said, burying my head in my hands. "It's a beautiful place, lonely but beautiful."

"Oh Mike," Tracy said, draping her body across mine like a shield against the worst of what the world had to offer.

"I'm not strong enough for this," I said as my body heaved.

"Our lives are not worth eternity," BT said as he wrapped Tracy and myself up in his own embrace.

"Eliza will discard all of your souls before she is done," Tomas said.

"Why are you doing this?" Meredith asked, "You play on the other team now, what do you care what happens to us?"

"I have my reasons," Tomas said evenly.

I looked around at the faces surrounding me, searching for an answer that only I could produce. It was Travis and Justin that solved my dilemma. Watching them die today was infinitely worse than watching them die at some mythical point in the future.

"Do it."

"Talbot! NO!" Tracy yelled.

"You sure man?" BT asked in disbelief.

"Do I look sure?" I asked him, my eyes red-rimmed.

"I don't think so," Gary said. "What? He asked!" Gary replied when BT looked at him sideways.

"Damn, I thought the whole Captain Obvious was *my* strong point," Justin said. "It must run deeper in the family than we thought."

Tomas came up beside me, "You will want to lie down."

"Is this going to hurt him?" Meredith asked.

"Extremely."

"Wicked pissah," I said.

Tracy walked away, her arms folded across her chest. I couldn't be sure from my position, but it looked like her shoulders were shaking with sobs.

I lay down, saying the Lord's Prayer in one last vain attempt to possibly keep a dialog open with the Big Guy.

BT held my hand tight. "Let's just go out guns blazing, Mike."

I looked over to my sons' very concerned faces. "I would if we were alone my friend."

"I get it, I do. I'm sorry it came to this, buddy," BT added.

Paul and Alex stood guard over my prone body as Tomas leaned in. It was Henry that almost stopped everything. Where he had been and what he had been doing I'm not sure, probably basking in the sun and sending out his own ozone melting flatulence.

He jumped across my chest, his back legs by my left

arm pit and his front paws down by my right side. Froth formed on his muzzle as he barked and growled incessantly as Tomas approached.

"I will kill him if you do not remove him," Tomas said, stopping his progress.

"You kill him and I will drill you in the eye with my Ka-Bar, Tomas," I told him.

"Perhaps you would Michael. Now move the dog so that we can get to the business at hand," Tomas said, still not moving, maybe because he was fearful of the dog or me.

Justin grabbed the big Bully and hefted him back. Travis stepped in to assist and still they almost lost control of Henry.

"Put this in your mouth," Tomas said as he handed me a piece of rubber roughly the size and shape of a cigar. "And do not concern yourself where it has been, germs will no longer be a problem of yours."

That almost made this whole scenario a worthwhile endeavor.

Tomas moved down to my neck. I had an instant of paranoia thinking that he merely wanted to get this close so that he could rip my throat out. And then he did, at least that's what it felt like. Sparks of pain ignited in my throat like my veins were igniter cables and the fuse had been lit. Fire spread through every portion of my body. I arched so hard only the heels of my feet and the back of my head still made contact with the roof.

So this is how your soul was removed, it was burned out. I could smell burning cordite as my teeth struggled to cut through the guard. Muscles spasmed with a force that put my body into contortions that must not have been anything near to normal. I couldn't register it then, but even BT was looking away, not able to stand what I was going through. Although I'll give him this, his hand never left mine and I know I must have put enough force on it to crush a normal man's.

"Th..th..thisss thu..thucks," I chattered to BT.

He squeezed my hand tighter. "It's no bargain on this side my friend," he said, still not looking down.

Tomas had strode away at some point, could have been five minutes or five hours. Having your soul seared kind of takes your mind off of time.

"Dad?" Travis asked.

I gave him a nod but there was no guarantee that I pulled it off. My muscles were firing independent of any messages I was sending them. For all I knew, I could have stuck my tongue out at him.

"You stupid, stupid bastard," Tracy said, cradling my head gently.

"Is it over?" I asked.

"You passed out a few minutes ago buddy," Paul said.

"You said "goodbye" right before you went under. We were scared," Alex said. "Do you know what you were referring to? Did you have a vision?"

I shook my head no, but I did know what I was referring to. It was the loss of my humanity, my mortality, my personage, my soul. I was less of a man now and more of a demon. And I had never felt weaker in my life.

"We need to clean his neck and stand him up before Eliza gets here," Paul said looking nervously towards the door. "Tomas said this would look too suspicious if you were on the ground," he said, looking at my confused face.

"I'm… I'm not sure I can stand yet, at least on my own," I said. I don't think I could have held up Eddy's slight frame in this condition.

"Just lean on me," BT said, picking me up like a rag doll.

"I think she will know something is up," Mrs. Deneaux said, "with you carrying him around like a ventriloquist's dummy."

BT had one arm wrapped around my waist and had me pulled into his side, this I could tell because my head, which seemed to weigh a thousand pounds, was pointed straight down. Like a new born baby I couldn't even hold my head up.

"At least I'll be able to see Durgan's boots as he kicks me with them," I said. Gallow's humor.

"Not funny man," BT said as he dragged me around the roof. I'm not sure what he was trying to achieve but he kept doing it. Pretty soon he was going to scrape the tips of my hiking boots clean off.

"I'm not a junkie. I don't think walking me around in circles making sure I stay awake is going to work in this situation," I said, still looking down at the rooftop.

"Can't think of anything else to do man, and I'm nervous as hell, so you get to go for a ride."

"Wheee," I said cheerlessly. "How much more time do you think we have?"

"Never enough," he answered.

I was able to finally move my head upwards by degrees as we heard Eliza coming up the stairs.

"I'm in trouble," I said, almost able to pull my head into a horizontal viewing position.

"If you're in trouble, we all are," BT said grimly.

"If I can't stand by the time she comes for me, make sure you save one of those bullets for me."

"Will that work? I mean now?" BT asked me.

"I think if an overzealous horsefly came right now, he could finish me off."

"Mike, you're not instilling me with confidence in our group decision."

"You think?"

"So you lose your soul but not your sarcasm?"

"That might have hurt if I could muster up the strength to care."

"Do you think this was a trick?" Gary asked.

I hadn't known it before but he was walking behind us the whole time.

"I mean, maybe he just weakened you so that you had absolutely no chance. I mean, it seemed like he set his sister up, maybe he did the same to you," Gary finished.

"Well, you're just full of good cheer," I told him. "Maybe he even injected me with a little zombie plague for shits and giggles."

"It's possible Mike," BT added.

"Nobody thought to voice these friggen' concerns before I let Bat Boy bite me?"

BT shrugged his shoulders but since I was attached to his hip my feet now dangled four inches off the ground as he made the gesture.

"Michael?" Eliza asked almost sweetly.

"Mike's not here!" Gary yelled.

I could feel BT's head turning around. "You kidding me?" he asked Gary.

"I mean, he's sleeping!" Gary told Eliza.

"Get him!" Eliza said with not a hint of her earlier merriment.

"I'll see what I can do," Gary said.

"Don't they have medication for what ails you Talbots?" BT asked.

"I'm still looking!" Gary yelled in a different direction to make it sound like he had moved.

"One minute, Michael, or the deal is off," Eliza said furiously.

"I'm here," I rasped.

"Has the shroud of death settled over you yet? It is a cold cloak, wet with the tears of mourning loved ones and broken dreams," Eliza asked.

"They don't make one in his size, bitch!" BT roared. "You should know that by now!"

"Durgan will be ready in ten minutes, will you?" Eliza laughed as her voice trailed behind her descent back down the stairs.

"I don't like her very much," BT said.

I would have agreed but I was in the midst of passing out again.

'*Michael, I have stalled as long as I possibly can, you*

need to get up.'

'Tomas? Oh no, you're in my head again.'

'My sister and Durgan will be on the roof in less than five minutes.'

'Was this a trick?'

'Get up!' Tomas shouted in my head.

Can someone go deaf from shouting WITHIN their head? *'I'm up!'* I shouted back, but the connection was broken.

"Michael, there are no surprises waiting for us are there?" Eliza asked suspiciously.

"I'm up!" I shouted again, this time vocally. "Sorry," I said to those around me as I sat up.

"Well, that's an improvement," BT said, "Can you do any better than that though? Unless of course Durgan wants to thumb wrestle you to death."

"Don't you have some nails you can chew or something?" I asked him. "Help me stand."

"Michael?" Eliza asked again.

"What?" I said testily. "Oh. No, there are no surprises, our original agreement is in effect."

"You won't mind then if I send some of my army in to verify that?" she asked.

"You sound awfully frightened for being the Lord of All You Survey," I rang out.

Mrs. Deneaux got a good chuckle out of that one. She tipped her cigarette to me.

"Go ahead, send in your smelly minions!" Gary yelled.

"You felt the need to invite them, did you?" Tracy asked him.

"No more than a hundred," I said to Eliza.

'Why?' BT mouthed.

"I'm hoping by having to count them it'll take longer," I told him.

"Michael, what trick are you trying to play?" Eliza asked, her dark eyes narrowing.

"No trick, I just want the fighting ring to be as big as possible," I told her.

"It's so the little faggot can run away like a screaming little bitch!" Durgan yelled.

"Someone got their 'roid injection today," BT said.

"Three hundred, Michael," Eliza said.

"Fine," I told her. "Even better," I said to BT. It would take longer.

After a few minutes of zombies filing in like students into an auditorium, Durgan pushed his way through the throng. Two of them fell on their faces, and he smashed his heel down onto one of the fallen zombie's temple. The sound was much like that of a large beetle being squished, it was not pleasant.

"That's going to mess up your count," I said, taunting him.

"Don't care, there's more of them, there's always more of them."

I could only agree.

"But me," he said, pointing to his chest, "there's only one of me."

"Thank the God above for that," BT said.

Again, I could only agree.

"You stay out of this, black man. I came here to kill Talbot."

"Damn Mike! Durgan has gone all PC on us," BT said admiringly.

"Must be the anger management classes," I said, holding on to BT's side, trying my best to make it look like that wasn't what I was doing.

"I'm going to make this slow, Talbot," Durgan said while grinding his fist into his palm.

"The slower the better," I told him.

"You're fucking nuts!" he yelled to me, clearly confused at my answer.

"Nucking futs," I said.

"What is wrong with him?" Durgan asked BT as if he

was going to get a valid response.

"Hopped up on bath salts," BT said.

"What are you talking about?" Durgan asked. These were not the responses he was expecting to receive and it was throwing him off his game.

"Bath salts," Gary said. "They're all the rage in Paris, haven't you ever tried them?"

"Paris is gone you idiots!" Durgan screamed.

"Oh, my poor pet," Eliza said coming up behind Durgan. "So strong in body, yet not in mind."

Durgan's rage subsided as Eliza stroked his face.

"Are you about ready for the void of life?" Eliza asked me impatiently.

"A cigarette?" I asked Eliza. She looked like she was about to respond in the negative.

"Come, Sister," Tomas said, stepping onto the roof. "We must be cultured, all condemned men are granted their final wish."

"Wait, then I would like to change my request."

"A cigarette then," Eliza said.

Mrs. Deneaux was a good ten feet away. I was positive I couldn't make it on my own and it wouldn't look good if BT dragged me over there.

"Mrs. Deneaux, would you do the honors?" BT asked, over-exaggerating with his head a 'come hither' motion.

At least she was quick on the uptake, and for once she didn't have anything snide to say as she came over and (thankfully) placed the cigarette in my mouth and lit it. I barely had enough steam to inhale and luckily none at all to cough.

"This is ridiculous!" Durgan cried. "How long can it take to smoke a cigarette? You have to finish that damn thing eventually and I'm going to make you pay for delaying the inevitable."

"Worse than death? You twit," Mrs. Deneaux said.

"I'll kill you just for fun you old hag," Durgan said to

her, pointing his finger.

Never skipping a beat Deneaux answered. "Worse than you have tried. Give it your best shot."

"All of a sudden I like you," I told Mrs. Deneaux as I gingerly crushed the cigarette under foot. If it had offered even the least resistance I would have toppled over.

"Michael, you don't look well," Tomas said.

'Thanks!' I wanted to yell at him.

"Nothing a case of the deads won't cure," Durgan said.

"The deads?" I asked.

"Make the black man move," Durgan said as he approached steadily, fists clenched by his sides.

Halfway to me and BT had not yet let go. I could feel him fighting within himself to throw me to the side and fight Durgan. It would be an awesome spectacle, just like when I was ten and my friend and I would watch Creature Double Feature on the UHF channel (if you don't know what UHF is, it's a dark time in our planet's history, when we only had about five or six channels to choose from; it was hideous. No 24/7 cartoons, sports or comedy. I shudder to remember the days.) Godzilla versus King Kong, it would have been awesome.

"Michael, if BT does not move, we are done here," Eliza said evenly.

"BT," I said.

"I can't man, he's going to kill you."

"What about that whole thing about death not having the right size for me and all."

"Oh, I was just saying that."

"You really suck man, now let me go."

"You sure?"

"Yes." 'No.'

"This is going to hurt you way more than me." Durgan said smiling.

"How are you walking so well?" I asked truly wondering not just stalling this time.

"I'm cured man!" Durgan shouted.

"How do you get 'cured' from an amputated leg?" Now I was really curious.

"Eliza…" Durgan was cut short as Eliza yelled at him to finish me.

Well that one name pretty much answered my question irregardless that it was a cut short answer.

For each step back that BT took, Durgan took two forward. I swayed back and forth like a tall reed in a soft summer breeze. The best thing that I could ask to happen was that I would be on the back bend when Durgan swung. The audible crack as my jaw burst echoed throughout my skull, the reverberations finally ending in my left pinkie toe, and no I do not know why.

I could vaguely hear Durgan screaming at me to get up so that he could finish me off. It was much more comfortable where I was. I could hear Tracy and Gary, pretty much everyone urging me up, their urgent cries ringing in my ears. But I was falling deeper; the red of pain was rapidly becoming the black of unconsciousness.

It was them that I held on for. Durgan would only wait so long to get from me what he felt I owed him. If I were to pass out, he would still finish me off, most likely starting with a few rib crushing kicks followed by some face pummeling blows, capped off with my head in his hands as he cracked my neck. I might not experience any of the pain involved, but my family and friends surely would.

My jaw rattled in my head, teeth grinding against teeth as I turned over trying to get leverage with arms that couldn't support Gumby. A fresh wave of nausea and pinpointing blackness threatened to thwart my best efforts as my arms gave. I collapsed, jaw first, onto the tarred roof.

"That's right, you piece of dung. Get up!" Durgan yelled, "What? No witty comeback you shithead?" His spittle rained down on me.

The thought of uttering anything more than a throaty moan made me wish for my mother, and I hadn't done that since I was six.

"If you don't get up in the next minute I'm going to start teaching your wife what it means to be with a real man," Durgan boasted.

"You even look at her funny and you'll be licking your own asshole!" BT yelled.

"You're welcome," BT said as I gave him the thumbs up sign, my face still buried in the roof.

Henry charged at Durgan. If I could have screamed at him to stop, I would have. Not that he would have listened. That's the sort of relationship we have, I give him cookies, he does as he pleases. Henry wrapped his muzzle around Durgan's lower leg. He must have put all his strength into it because Durgan screamed to the heavens, although they would have turned a blind eye to him as they had to me. He shook his leg violently and swatted Henry away. Henry yelped as he went tumbling twenty feet away. I was thankful to whatever was watching over me now that Durgan was only able to land a glancing blow. Henry came to a stop by the edge of the roof. I could tell his head was reeling as he looked up, eyes not focused on anything, but he'd be all right. More than I could say for me.

The pain in my jaw had begun to ebb. I attributed it to the high octane adrenaline injection from Durgan's threat. To threaten me was one thing, my family? Well, that takes on a whole new level, and to top it off the asshole hurt my dog!

"You don't understand now, Lawrence," Durgan sneered. "I can kill you too, just as easily as I can kill him," he said pointing over to my mostly prone body.

"He's not quite dead yet," Gary said, quoting Monty Python as I struggled to gain vertical-ability.

"Did you really just do that Uncle Gary?" Travis asked.

Gary smiled diffidently.

Durgan turned to see me. I was now resting on my knees. I probably could have stood at this point, but I was busy listening to the knitting of the bones in my mouth. It was disturbing. The grinding as molar scraped across canine was akin to biting down hard on fork tines.

Durgan looked at me in alarm as color began to wash back into my face, from winter pale to spring hale. He gave a quick glance to Eliza as if expecting direction, but none was forthcoming.

I put my left foot under me and stood up shakily. I wouldn't be scaring a Girl Scout, but Durgan looked like he was having second thoughts.

"I broke your jaw, Talbot. Now I'm going to break your spine," he said as he advanced again.

It hurt like hell to say it but it was worth every snap and pop as I moved my still healing facial bones. "Bring it," I said as I put my hands up in the old school boxing fashion, fists upside down and all.

I tried to dance around like Muhammad Ali, but I think I looked more like Whitney Houston (you know… can't dance).

Durgan bull rushed me. I was still operating on something close to seventy-five percent of the old Talbot, but it was way more than he was expecting. So when I side stepped his advance and put everything I could muster into his kidney, his heavy expulsion of air was all I needed to know that I had surprised him and potentially inflicted an iota of damage.

"You should have just stayed down," Durgan said as he turned. His eyes glowed with a festering heat of hatred and contempt. "I might have made it relatively painless," he said, advancing but much more slowly and warily.

And without warning he struck, like a cat let loose from a tight trash bag. I didn't think anything that big could move that fast. His ham-sized fist slammed into my temple. If it hadn't first caught my upraised fist he would have killed me. Upgrade or not, he would have caved my skull. For the second time I went down, this one with more force than the first. My jaw dislocated as the side of my face bounced from the impact.

"Fuck you Talbot!" Durgan shrieked, standing over my body with his fists by his side, veins bulging out on his neck, his arms throbbing with power.

The pain was intense, but something was happening within me. What started as a ten on the pain index and should have taken days and heavy doses of opiates to alleviate rapidly began to climb down the pain-o-meter. Ten became an eight, which in turn became a five, and then a distant memory at a one or a two.

"And to think I once thought you might be a tough opponent. You ain't shit!" he screamed.

"You talk too much," I said as I got my feet back up under me.

If Durgan's neurons would have just fired a little quicker and he never gave me the chance to get up, then my family would have been doomed. But he just kept watching in amazement as I got completely up onto my feet.

"You should be dead!" he yelled.

"But yet here I am," I said softly, trying my best to not engage my jaw. A lot easier written than said.

"This can't be. I'm five times the man I was. You should be dead!" he screamed in consternation, "Eliza, it's not working. I hit him with everything I had, you promised!"

Eliza looked over to Tomas who never betrayed anything, but the proof was in my unwillingness to die.

"I fear, my pet, that the rules to the game have been changed," Eliza said.

"What does that mean?" he asked her.

"It means that Michael has cheated and as such our agreement is void," Eliza said.

"Not true, Eliza," I said to her. "You said I could not accept help from anyone on this side. You said absolutely nothing about help from your side."

Eliza was trying to find a loophole in her agreement. I could see the machinations working behind her black eyes. "Very well," was her grudging response.

Durgan was being unbelievably slow on the uptake of

this new information. He could take as long as he desired. I wasn't waiting for him to figure it out. I swung a roundhouse that started somewhere south of Detroit and struck him flush in the nose. Blood blew in a circle away from the impact. His eyes immediately flooded with tears as he dropped down to his knees.

"Yeah!" BT shouted.

With my other arm I hooked an uppercut that shattered all of Durgan's front teeth, pieces of which intermingled with the growing puddle of blood pooling on the roof. Durgan began to sag forward. I kneed him in his already destroyed nose; shards of bone drilled into my knee as the impact also drove pieces up into his brain casing.

"Ris ran't ree happenin," Durgan said through a jumble of broken teeth.

"Oh, I assure you it is," I said, punching him in the back of the head as he began to pitch forward.

Durgan was face first on the ground, his ass still up in the air. It was a comical pose but it contained no humor in it.

"This is for Jed," I said as I reared back and kicked him square in the ribs. At least two snapped as he fell onto his side. "This is for shooting me!" as I kicked him flush in the stomach. The force of the strike rolled him over onto his back, a gale of wind fused with blood expelled from his mouth. "This is for Jen!" I said kicking him in his junk. I thought Jen would appreciate that, being the man hater that she was. I got a sick sort of satisfaction out of that.

"This is for the little kids at Carol's house!" I cried, bringing my heel up.

"Talbot!" my wife yelled.

I wavered in midair.

"That's enough! He's done."

He should have been dead, he really should have, but we weren't playing by the same rules any more. As if to prove my point, Durgan began to stir. In a few more minutes he'd probably be fine and I wouldn't be able to surprise him twice.

"He's got no choice," BT told Tracy as she turned her back on the horrific scenario.

I brought the heel of my boot down on the bridge of Durgan's nose. His skull snapped like a fragile egg, blood and brain matter splayed out across the ground.

"You're next Eliza!" I yelled, grinding my gore soaked boot even deeper into the recess of what once housed Durgan's mad melon.

At some point during the fracas, Eliza had left the rooftop unnoticed, taking her zombies with her.

Eliza and Tomas - Interlude

"You play a dangerous game Tomas," Eliza said, her anger running deep through her blackened vitality.

"I did nothing more than make an even fight," Tomas said.

"With our sworn enemy!" Eliza shrieked.

"No Sister, he is *your* sworn enemy," Tomas said evenly.

Eliza took a step back and took a moment to compose herself, even more angered that she had allowed her emotions to show. Emotions were for the weak-willed humans, not for her!

"To what end, Tomas, did you empower Michael?"

"I have my reasons, Eliza. It is not all a loss Sister, you have the Blood Locket in your possession now."

"Yes, there is that," she said, fingering the pendant that she now had safely tucked in her bodice. "We will not stray far from each other come the future. I do not trust what reasons you possess. I do not believe that we are walking the same pathways,"

Tomas smiled and walked away.

CHAPTER 31 – Talbot Journal Entry 16
The Group

The congratulations and celebrations were brief, mostly out of necessity but partly because I didn't much feel like it. I had just crushed a man's skull with my boot. I had trained for it a hundred times in the Marine Corps but had never actually done it. I don't think I'd ever get over that sensation of the initial impact as my leg shimmied ever so slightly as my heel came in contact with his bone. The impact as his body first resisted and then accepted, from hard outer shell to soft meat. I can say it was Durgan for the rest of my life, but it was still one of the most singular disgusting things I had ever done. Why am I still feeling guilt? I don't have a soul to stain.

If I thought Marta didn't like me before, now it was personal. She was yelling at Alex just because he wanted to come over and talk to me. I really couldn't blame her. I didn't really want to be with myself just now.

"So what now?" Brian asked me.

"I'm going home," I told him as I walked away.

"He wants to know if there's room," Cindy clarified.

"Cindy, I don't know if that's what I want to do," Perla said. "I mean, if we had never come across them, Jack would still be alive." She started to cry again.

"Mike, I cannot thank you enough for what you sacrificed and what you have done," Alex said as he finally broke free from Marta.

"I did what I had to do," I told him.

"No Mike, you went above and beyond what you *had* to do. I will never forget this, my friend," Alex said, his eyes watering.

"I can't see man tears right now Alex. Please tell me you just sat on your keys or something."

Alex quickly wiped any evidence away, but the red-rimmed eyes told a different story.

"Mike, we're not coming with you," Alex said sadly.

I didn't need psychic powers to see that coming. Marta was about twenty feet away going ballistic that he was even in my presence. I really wanted to look in a mirror to see if I had sprouted horns or something, maybe my skin was beginning to look brick oven red. I don't think my feet were becoming cloven, but I couldn't really see them and I wasn't touching my right boot any time soon, gray-black matter still clung to them in wet clumps. I was trailing pieces of Durgan's memories behind me.

Mrs. Deneaux came up and handed me another cigarette which I gratefully took. "I think maybe I'll ride the rest of this out with you," she said in her smoke ravaged voice.

My luck was getting better and better!

BT grabbed my shoulders and steered me away from the crowd. "How you doing my man?" he asked, truly concerned

"How does 'stepped on crap' sound?" I asked him.

"A lot like Durgan," he said with a small laugh.

"Man, I didn't even mean it like that. I guess I walked into that."

"Literally."

"This is supposed to be a serious talk, isn't it."

"I'm sorry, I'm still pretty hopped up," he said looking down at me. "So, the original question still stands."

"Pretty scared, big man. Everything I did I always weighed against how it would fly when I finally got to the Gates. Now I don't have to answer to anyone. Nobody should have that kind of power, least of all me."

BT was nodding his head. "Mike, you have the hardest person of all to answer to," he paused. "Yourself.

I've never come across another person who tried so hard (and mostly succeeded) to do the right thing in every situation. Don't worry about what the future may or may not hold, you did what you needed to do right now."

"Thanks man," I told him.

"You're going to be all right, Mike," he assured me.

I had my doubts, but I nodded at the appropriate time.

"Whenever you're ready to roll, we'll get going," BT said.

"Do you believe in the eternal soul?" Mad Jack asked me curiously.

Where the hell he came from I wasn't sure.

"I believe," I told him, not sure if this was the conversation I wanted to have right now.

"Because if you don't, then nothing could have been taken from you. I wish we had weighed you before and after Tomas bit you."

"What are you talking about?" I asked him testily.

"Well, I've read studies that the human soul has a tangibility to it. It can be measured and weighed on a scale."

"Would that have confirmed anything for you?" I asked.

"Well, there could be a myriad of other factors. Loss of blood, passage of gas, a bug alighting from your body, wind pushing down."

"So you wouldn't have believed even with evidence," I told him.

"I'm just saying it would have been interesting to say the least, and would have required more study."

"Listen, I don't really know you and I don't want to have to test out just how hard I can hit right now." He flinched. "So I'm going to be very specific. I've been there, twice as a matter of fact. It's more real to me than this thing we call reality, and I would trade this life a thousand times to just stand in those fields once more."

"Did you travel through a tunnel?" he asked.

"Yes."

"Studies have shown…"

"Get away from me," I told him, which he thankfully did.

"Mike, I can't tell you how bad I feel that we ever left you in the first place," Paul said. Erin was nodding behind him.

All I wanted to do was go see my family. This was like running the gauntlet.

"Buddy, you just wanted to see your family. I completely understand that. And that's exactly what I want to do," as I pointed over towards mine.

He nodded.

I walked over to where Tracy and the kids were (including Henry). Henry looked up at me funny. He knew something was different, but at least he didn't run away. I would have lost it if he had done that.

"You look like hell, Talbot," Tracy said as she stroked my cheek. I bowed my face down lower, the human contact felt so warm.

Justin came over to give me a hug. "I'm sorry, Dad."

He had had a taste of what I was in for and felt deeply for it. Like I needed any more reasons to love my kids.

"How's it feel Dad?" Travis asked.

"Empty, son, empty.'

CHAPTER 32 – Talbot Journal Entry 17
Final Note

When we began our journey back towards Maine, it was without Alex and his family. I could not believe April did not want to stay with Mad Jack, but apparently I was a bigger repelling force than he was an attraction. And the biggest surprise was Joann and Eddy. I'm pretty sure Eddy wanted to come with us, but at eight years old his vote did not count in this matter.

EPILOGUES
On the Road to find Paul and Alex
1

After a few hours on the road we finally holed up for the night. Gary is a wonderful orator. While getting ready for bed, he decided to share this gem. Why now, I'm not sure, maybe just to point out that the natural world has always been a part of the supernatural.

"Did I ever tell you the story about the Keenagh family in New Orleans?" he asked.

"Do I know them?" I asked.

"I doubt it."

"Is this scary, because I don't need anything else to lose sleep over at night," I warned him.

"It's not really scary. It just makes you think."

"So, is it a true story?"

"Supposedly."

"Okay, tell me it. But if it's scary, we'll be sharing your sleeping bag."

"But mine isn't big enough," he answered seriously.

"Then be careful with your story selection."

"Most people would be fine. You, I'm not so sure. So, there's this family down in New Orleans, the Keenaghs. They live in this small town right on the beach year round. There's a father, mother, and two young sons, Robbie and Sammie. It's mostly a tourist town, the majority of visitors come during the winter months and stay in rental cottages."

"Not scary so far," I told Gary, settling in for the rest.

"See, I told you. So all these families come for vacation and there are three other families in particular that also have little kids. The Keenaghs have a little boat they named the Sparrow, which they take out and just let everyone have a good time on. So these three families with their kids, Tabitha, David and Donnie become fast friends with the Keenagh's kids. Year after year, they come and spend the same two-week period together going out on this boat, fishing and swimming and just making memories. For

Robbie's twelfth birthday, his dad gives him the Sparrow. Robbie cannot believe it. He loves that boat, he and his friends damn near live on it during the summer. After another five years of hanging out, the kids who are all about fifteen to seventeen years old now realize that they are just about coming to the end of these trips with their families. They do what just about every kid does, they make pacts that they will still get together in the years to come. And like the vast majority of pacts, they never materialize. Two of the kids go off to college, one goes in the military and the other two just go on with their lives, but they always remember the great summers together."

"Sounds good so far."

"Well, about ten years go by and the older Keenagh brother lives in New York now, I think he's an investment broker or something like that. He's heading home from work one night and this guy robs him and stabs him to death for $35."

"That's screwed up, getting killed for $35."

Gary shrugged his shoulders in acknowledgement. "I know, some people have gotten killed for less. Anyway, so that same night Rob gets stabbed and died, the Sparrow slipped its moorings. After they bring Rob's body home and get him buried, the family spends the next week searching for their lost boat. They even asked the Coast Guard if they could keep a look out for it. The Sparrow had become Rob's pride and joy in those long ago summers, and Mrs. Keenagh, I think her name was Luci, couldn't stand that this remembrance of her son was now also gone. She used to be able to look out her kitchen window every morning and smile looking down on the small boat. Rob's first words every time he called home were, 'How's she doing?' Luci couldn't even look out the window any more, the loss of the boat a constant reminder of the loss of her son."

"Man, that sucks," I said honestly, "Who needs that kind of reminder?"

"I know," Gary said. "So a few more years go by and

the younger brother Sam is home visiting his folks for the holidays. He's out on the front porch sitting in a big rocking chair having a cold beer."

"Do you know what kind of beer it is, because that sounds really good right now."

"That's not really important to the story."

"Sorry."

"Can I go on?"

"Wait, did they ever find the boat?" I asked.

Gary shook his head.

"Any debris from a wreck then?"

Gary shook his head again. "Can I continue?"

I motioned with my hand that he could.

"So Sam is on the porch and this car pulled into the driveway. It's Tabitha, she was down in New Orleans taking her daughter to her new college for orientation and thought she would show her where she used to go on vacations with her family while she was down there. Before she can even come across the yard and hug Sam, this truck pulls up. Its David. He lived in LA but had to go to New Orleans for a conference. When it was done, he decided to go see the beach he had spent so much time on."

I was sitting up now.

"Sam, Tabitha, and David are all talking and hugging about what good fortune it is that they all came together at the same time when another car pulls into the driveway. It's Donnie, the youngest of the group. He had no reason whatsoever to make the drive from his home in Texas. He told them he just felt compelled to do it. So there they all are sitting on the front porch reminiscing when Mrs. Keenagh comes out the front door. She is sheet white. Her son Sam got up so fast he knocked his chair over."

"Did he spill his beer?"

"Do you want to hear the rest?"

"Well yes, I just figured that was the scary part, him spilling his beer and all."

"Mike!"

"Sorry."

"So Sam is pretty concerned for his mother and asked her if she's alright. She can barely talk she's so upset. 'It's the Sparrow,' his mom tells him, 'it's back.'"

"The Sparrow came back? Damn, that gave me goose bumps," I told Gary. "So they finally did honor their pact. And that's a true story?"

"Supposed to be."

"Damn."

* * *

2

"Okay, you want to hear another one?" Gary asked, "It's a little freaky-deakier."

"Deakier? I'm supposed to be the one that makes up words."

"All right, so there's this guy."

"Wait, is this true?"

"Yes."

"What is your source of information?"

"What are you talking about Mike?"

"I mean did you read this in a book or did you hear it from a friend of a friend whose uncle it happened to."

"I read this in a book about hauntings."

"I thought you said this wouldn't be scary?"

"It's not really," Gary said.

"But by its definition 'haunting' is a scary thing."

"It's not."

"You know, because I'm pretty maxed out already with this whole zombie thing. I don't need another genre to keep me awake at night."

"Mike, I don't remember you always being this difficult."

"I've been away for a long time Gary. I've developed all sorts of neuroses."

"Did you seek professional help?"

"Why? Do you think I need it?"

"You tell me. Can I get on with the story?"

"Don't let me stop you."

Gary looked at me with a sideways glance and began his story. "So there's this guy."

"What's his name?" I asked. Gary looked like he was going to hit me with his canteen. "I'm just saying, it's a lot easier for me to visualize the story if I know the people's names."

"Fine, his name is Rob."

"Really? He's got the same name as the kid in the last story?"

"JAMES, his name is James."

"Like Bond."

"Sure, whatever. So James is married to Tricia and they have a son together, his name is…" Gary paused trying to think of a name, "Mickey and they live in Wyoming."

I didn't agree with his name choice, but I let it go for the sake of the story.

"It's about five years later and the three of them are going through life as best they can when the dad gets laid off. He's falling behind on his bills and the mortgage and he panics and robs a bank."

"Damn, I thought you were going to say he robbed an investment banker for $35 and then stabbed him to death."

"No, it was a bank and he got caught. Spent the next seven years in prison. When he got out he got an apartment within the Cheyenne city limits. His wife and kid were about a half hour away. James had paid his debt to society and wanted to try and rebuild his family. He had visited Tricia and Mickey a few times and had asked her if she would be willing to take him back. His wife told him that it wasn't just her decision to make. They had been on their own for so long she would have to ask Mickey too. So she and her son went out the next day to do some hiking, clear their minds and talk about the decision they needed to make. While they were climbing up the hill, they came across an open crevice which led into an abandoned mine."

"That's not a good move if they went in."

"Afraid of being buried alive?"

"Who the hell isn't?" I asked, not believing that I wasn't on the side of the vast majority in this.

"They went in, they'd gone about ten feet when Mickey leans up against one of the support beams, problem is it's all rotted out and the ceiling gives. The cave-in was devastating. At the same time as the ceiling collapses, James hears a frantic knocking on his door. He immediately answers it and standing there is a bloodied battered and bruised Tricia screaming at him that she needs his help, Mickey is trapped in a mine collapse. James grabs some tools and hops in his truck with Tricia. They drive for forty-five minutes to get to the site and James starts digging like crazy to get to his son. He tells his wife that she needs to get to the roadway and get some more help. Sure enough, after about ten or fifteen minutes two guys come up in different cars. They are all helping each other and they finally find the pocket where Mickey is trapped. They dig out a hole big enough to pull him out and Mickey is screaming at his dad to go further, that his mom is a few feet past him. James is trying to tell him that his mother is safe, that she came and got him and that she's fine. Mickey is having none of it. He's frantic, starts digging at the rocks with his hands. James and the men who came to help start digging and in a few feet they come across Tricia's body."

"Holy shit," I said.

"Yeah, for the love of her son, she went to get the help of his father. What is really weird, when they interviewed the two other men, one of them said what he heard could have been the howling of the wind but felt compelled to check it out. The second one said he definitely heard a woman screaming for help."

"Man that just gave me the chills."

*   *   *

3

This was a different night with Gary but in its own way it was way scarier, at least to me.

"Do you want a drink?" Gary asked handing his canteen over.

"No, I'm fine man. I've got my own," I told him.

"This isn't water."

So I'm figuring Vodka or some other such libation. "I'm good, I don't want to drink. I've got watch in a few hours.

"Mike, it's Kool-Aid."

"I'm good," I said, feigning that I was getting ready for sleep.

"It's really good," he said, placing it under my nose coaxingly.

"Gary, I really don't want any."

"This was your favorite as a kid. I remember making it for you all the time. I especially got this for you."

"I appreciate that man, but I still don't want it."

"Oh hell, it's that whole germ-a-phobe thing isn't it? We're family, germs don't count."

I smiled wanly. I begged to differ.

"I haven't drunk from this since I made the mix."

"Since when do germs have a shelf life?" I asked him.

"You just take this canteen, let me get something to drink out of so I can have a little."

He handed the canteen to me which I accepted gingerly. Then he began to scour the area we were in, finally grabbing an old Coke bottle that was laying on its side. Dirt and possibly a small nest of dead bugs were on the inside and he scraped a small cobweb off the opening.

"What are you doing?" I asked, horrified beyond measure.

"Make-shift cup," he replied smiling.

"You can't be serious?" I asked, finding myself backing up unwittingly.

"The more germs the merrier," he said still smiling.

"Are you kidding me? Get away from me with that thing."

"Yes I'm serious, the more germs you introduce into your body the better it can cope with them. Sanitizing wipes are horrible for people."

"Bite your tongue! Are you the Anti-Christ?"

He wasn't messing with me. This wasn't the whole big brother teasing his younger brother with the spit-and-roll-up procedure. He grabbed the canteen from me and filled that bottle almost to the top. He didn't wash it out first, he just gulped it down, added protein and all. My stomach was roiling for the next eight hours. Every time I thought about what he did I thought I was going to heave. Gary on the other hand was as right as rain, so which of us has it right?

*   *   *

4

"I miss Glenn," Gary said to me pretty much out of the blue one night. We were about three hundred miles from the Maine border, and we were both homesick.

Glenn is/was our brother. The order went Ron, Gary, Glenn, Lyndsey and myself. I hadn't seen Glenn in years, but the pain of his loss was still acute.

"Me too," I told Gary noncommittally.

Gary looked at me askew. I think he caught more meaning in my answer than I had intended to give away.

"Do you think we should look for him while we're down here?" Gary asked, scrutinizing my face.

"We could, I guess."

"Alright, what gives?" Gary asked, standing up and coming over to me.

"Glenn's passed," I told him.

"I thought so, but you seem to know for sure. How?"

"Listen, you might think I'm nuts if I tell you."

"I might, but you can tell me anyway."

"Great, all right. I don't know if you know about this or not, or even if you believe in this sort of thing, but I can astral project." I stopped right there, looking at Gary for any indications that he was going to get me some heavy medication. When he sat back down, I took that as a sign that he wanted me to continue.

"Astral projection, that's where you float out of your body, right?"

"It's a little more complicated than that, but that's the basic idea. From what I've done and read there are two types of projections. The first is on the astral plane which has nothing to do with the world we live in, and the second is the ability to travel within our own world. I usually can't control it, and the night I found out about Glenn was no different. I had gone to sleep relatively early because I was pulling a late night shift on the ladders."

"The ladders?" Gary asked.

"Yeah, it was an early form of torture when I still lived at Little Turtle."

"What are you talking about?"

"I'm sorry, my legs cramp up every time I think of them. They were just crude guard towers we used to watch the walls at Little Turtle."

"Gotcha."

"So I'm lying in bed and as soon as I fell asleep I found myself in our old home on Cefalo Road."

"Really? Are you kidding me? What was it like?"

"To be honest, it was awesome," I told him, and it was. I hadn't been back to my childhood home, well, since my childhood.

"Was anyone there?" he asked.

"Not at first," I told him. I have never encountered anyone on my path when I am on the earthly planes, it just doesn't work that way for me. "The house was exactly as it had been when we were kids. I 'appeared' in Lyndsey's room on her bed. The same white bed with flowers she had when we were growing up." My sister's room was at the top of the stairwell and my parents' room was further to the left. To the immediate right was my brother Ron's room, and then there was an ell and then mine, Gary, and Glenn's room and then a bathroom.

"You're freaking me out," Gary said.

"Yeah, well, consider it payback for *your* stories."

"Was it day or night?" Gary asked.

"It's always a sort of twilight when I'm on these planes. Light enough to see but would probably be pretty difficult to read by. And that's another thing I need to make clear, when I'm on these journeys the great abundance of what 'leaves' my body is saturated in 'feeling' and 'instinct;' higher reasoning does not tend to make the transfer. I went on a 'trip' once and could not figure out how to work a doorknob."

"What did you do?" Gary asked fascinated.

"I went through it."

"Oh," Gary said cupping his chin with his hand. "That's possible?"

"I'm basically a living ghost, so yeah."

"That's kind of scary when you describe it that way. Can you get trapped outside your body, like maybe not be able to find your way home?"

"I don't think so. I've read some stuff that says it could be possible, but damn near almost everything else says it's completely impossible."

"Still, that would be pretty scary. It'd be like you were in a coma, only your spirit is wandering around the world aimlessly."

"Great, one more thing to worry about. Can I go on?"

Now it was his turn to motion me on.

"So I'm in our house and I'm thrilled. I loved that place, I never really got over that we moved away. I got up off of Lyndsey's bed and went downstairs, took a quick look in the kitchen and then went into the great room and from there into our playroom."

"Remember how we used to put Pledge on our socks and play hockey there?" Gary asked fondly.

"I remember up until the point that you broke Mom's lamp with your hockey stick and then threw me under the bus for it."

"You were younger, she wouldn't hit you as hard. I taught you a valuable lesson that day."

"What, not to trust anyone?"

"No, how to take one for the team."

"Great. So anyway, I'm down in the playroom and there was no broken lamp, at least that I could see, and I started to sense someone else was in the house."

"You said you don't encounter other people."

"I don't."

"Who was it?"

"It was Mom."

"Was she there about the lamp?"

"I don't think so. I didn't see her, I could only sense

that she was there. I could 'feel' her presence in her bedroom."

"Did she know you were there?"

I thought about that for a second, "No, I really get the impression that she had no idea whatsoever that I was there. So now I'm sitting on the floor in the playroom. I've got my back resting on the cellar door and I'm just looking around. I can tell that Mom is just sitting on her bed. She hadn't moved, she's just waiting."

"Waiting for Glenn."

I nodded. "After a few more minutes I began to sense his presence. He had not yet made it into the house. It was kind of like he got lost and Mom was there to lead him home."

"Damn, Mike."

"That's what I thought. Mom was bringing him to a familiar place we all had loved when we were kids."

"That's not just some elaborate dream, Mike?" Gary asked, his eyes a little wetter than normal.

"I swear to you Gary, it was as real to me as this conversation we're having now. I glimpsed something that I think very few on this side get to."

"How does that make you feel?"

"It makes me thrilled, brother, to have *proof* that there is more to this life, especially now. To know that we have a soul and that when we are gone from here we go into the loving arms of those who have gone before."

Good Luck!

"Gary, what are you doing?" I asked more peevishly than I should have.

"Reading the paper, did I really need to explain that?" he said as he turned the over-sized page.

Maybe it was the crinkling of the paper, the huge size of the medium or the fact that my friends were stranded on a roof top surrounded by zombies five miles away. But I was pacing around like I had smoked some crack and while I was waiting for it to kick in I had snorted a couple rails of coke.

"You know that paper is over four months old, right?" I stopped my pacing long enough to berate him with that fact.

My brother seemed to gain some sense of enjoyment from my discomfort. He sat back in his chair and put his feet up on the small metal table.

"How the hell can you read that thing anyway? It's too damn big."

"You know, little brother, not all of us had our noses shoved up the Internet's ass. The cultured prefer the news the old fashioned way."

"Yeah, stale and irrelevant," I replied

He smiled and kept on reading. "Wow, this guy took out a full page ad the night the zombies came."

I finally sat down, I was beginning to wear a groove into the floorboards. "Now I'm not really curious, but since there's nothing else going on, what the hell was so special about this ad?"

"How much do you think it costs to run a full page ad?"

"Really? You're going to make me jump through hoops before you answer me?"

Gary had a look of bemusement on his face.

"Fine, I know a dinky little one inch ad runs about five hundred bucks, so a full page ad..." I stopped to think. "Has to be close to four thousand bucks."

"Not much return on investment here then."

"Gary, there's a full rack of papers over there. First,

I'm going to grab a paper, find the friggen' ad you're talking about, decide for myself what I think about it. Then I'm going to roll it up and beat the living shit out of you with it."

"Man, I thought they were kidding when they said they put gun powder in the Marines' eggs. You're a mean man, Mike."

"That's it," I said pushing my chair away.

"And absolutely no patience, hold on."

I stopped.

"It's got a picture of this guy Rodney Carnahan on one knee, and he's holding a small boulder up to the photographer. Then there's a side picture of the bride-to-be, Amber Allaman. And it says and I quote, 'Amber, you came into my life when I needed someone like you the most. You've become my best friend and have given me a son who, like his momma, is the light of my world. Would you do me the honor of becoming my wife, Amber Marie Allaman, and not just my baby-momma? Love Rod.' Do you think she got to see it?"

"Man, I hope so," I said, looking over his shoulder. "Although we don't really know who this Amber girl is. I mean, sure she's very pretty, but you can't tell from a black and white still picture what's going on in that head of hers. Maybe, just maybe, the zombie-pocalypse saved the rest of Rodney's life."

"I'm telling your wife you said that."

"I'll drive that truck off a bridge with the both if us in it, if I even THINK you'd say anything. Have I made myself clear?"

(Super secret note just for Rodney – Please post the results on my Facebook page!)

(For everyone else, that was exactly what you're thinking it was!)

Pre-Zombie Apocalypse

A Talbot family get together is rife with one-liners and zingers. If you let your guard down for even a second, or show a moment of weakness, the others will descend on you like a pack of starving wolves on a fallen Caribou. Our family motto has always been "Kick 'em when they're down."

This is just one example. Gary, who is undeniably a great cook, started to describe how awesome his apple pie is. I told him that I'd also been working on my own, and after years of trial and error that I finally thought that I'd gotten it right. So my sister immediately shouts out 'Pie Off!' Gary and I thought it was an awesome idea. My daughter Nicole, who is okay in the kitchen, threw her hat in the ring. What the hell, I thought, the more people I beat, the sweeter the victory.

My sister, who can't make Jell-o, decided that this would be an opportune time to show off her skills (or lack thereof). "I want in too!" she shouted. Now, I don't know if she was just caught up in the excitement of the moment or what, but I grinned to myself. This was going to be like shooting fish in a barrel.

So Gary immediately says, "If it comes out of a box, it doesn't count." Many laughs ensued. I took it to another level. "Sis, I could show up with an apple and beat you." My brothers (and myself) were laughing so hard we had tears coming out of our eyes. My sister was not a happy camper. She told me she hated me. I just laughed harder. I had won that round.

The Blood Locket

"Severed Hand, what do the spirits divine for our hunt?" Chief Running Bear asked.

Severed Hand had spent the majority of the fall day secluded in his tepee with twigs of ash, elderberry bush, and sage smoking on an enclosed fire pit.

"It is not good, Running Bear. I cannot get a clear message from the spirits. I think that you should wait until I have been shown the path," Severed Hand told his exasperated Chief.

"That is the same message as yesterday and the same as it was the day before. If we wait much longer, the herds will be gone and our clan will suffer greatly come the approaching winter," the Chief said.

"I fear Running Bear that to leave now would endanger our people even more."

The Chief snorted in disagreement. He normally deferred to the spiritual leader as long as the Shaman spoke words the Chief wanted to hear. It wasn't that Chief Running Bear was too egotistical to listen to his advisor and friend, it was that he had sixty people in his clan that looked to him to make it through the harsh winters. If they did not secure at least three bison on this next hunt he would lose a great many people to disease and famine, and he loved them too much to let that happen.

"I will give you until the sun has risen tomorrow, Severed Hand, to coax an answer from the spirits."

"Chief, you of all people know that it does not work that way. The gods will tell me what they feel I should know when they feel I should know it."

"As long as it is by tomorrow," the Chief said, heading back to his tepee. The cold of the night was beginning to seep deep into his bones. 'A few more seasons and the younger bucks will need to prove who is worthy to lead us,' the Chief thought. 'But not yet.'

Severed Hand reentered his smoke filled hut. He sat cross legged on his stack of elk and bison furs breathing deeply of the aromatic smoke, controlling his breaths that he might achieve a state of heavy meditation. His eyes rolled up into the back of his head; his second sight was shrouded in a thin veil of black. A lone crow blacker than the veil stood on the other side, one flat black eye staring at him hungrily. It cawed once and as it jumped into the air and flew away, the veil was parted. The emptiness beyond was too much for the Shaman who passed out. It was several hours later when he awoke. The Chief and twenty of the tribe's braves were already gone on the hunt.

"What have I done?" Severed Hand lamented as he clutched the amulet tied around his neck.

The women, children and infirm gathered around the main fire at the center of their encampment like they were wont to do when the men went on their hunts. Severed Hand spent the day asking all of the spirit guides for as much protection as could be afforded for his people.

"Chief Screaming Hawk, we need to get the people to a safer location," Severed Hand implored the former leader of the clan.

"I am old, Shaman, the people no longer follow my rule," Screaming Hawk said as he stared deep into the fire, remembering a time when he was as fast as the animal he was named for.

"You are not so old that they do not listen to your words. Do not pretend to have gone soft in the head, your people need you," Severed Hand said forcibly.

"What would you have me do?" Screaming Hawk asked, angry that he had been disturbed from his reverie.

"I do not know, but I feel that this land that we stand on now is not safe."

"The spirits have said this?" Screaming Hawk asked curiously. Severed Hand had always been a trusted advisor while he had been the chief.

"Not in signs that I can divine, Chief, but that we should leave immediately I do not doubt."

"Leaping Frog," the old Chief said to a young boy

that was running around the fire. "Get your mother."

The boy stopped immediately. As the son of Chief Running Bear he was afforded special privileges. But to not do as an elder, and a former chief at that, asked was more trouble than he cared to find himself immersed in. Leaping Frog nodded and ran off.

Leaping Frog's mother, White Fawn, was headed towards where Screaming Hawk and Severed Hand were sitting by the fire. She shivered as the warm touch of the sun slid from her shoulders and behind the mountains. A preternatural chill rippled up her spine. She sped her step up but it was too late as she felt her flesh rip from her side to the bottom of her shoulder blade. She fell to her knees as her spine became exposed to the cool twilight air.

Severed Hand turned to watch as she fell face first into the soft dirt. The black abomination that straddled her prone body had the same flat black eyes as the crow he had seen in his vision. Severed Hand rose, quickly grabbing his staff and running towards the fallen woman. Screaming Hawk was just turning around as screams of fear and pain issued forth from around the camp.

The blackness had moved from White Fawn; blood poured forth from her wound. Severed Hand reached into his pouch, grabbing a handful of blended herbs that were proficient in stopping bleeding. He looked into White Fawn's eyes but they had already clouded over. He saved the herbs. Just then Leaping Frog sailed over his head. Severed Hand tried to jump and grab him, but it was too late as the young boy landed in the middle of the fire. His screams pierced the night as the flesh melted from his bones. His small charred body crawled a few feet, almost coming completely clear from the fire before collapsing.

Screaming Hawk took his small flint knife from his leg sheath and ran towards where the most intense screaming was coming from. His war cry stirred the air, it was the last sound he would ever make. Severed Hand found him the next day nailed through the throat to a tree with that same knife.

No matter where Severed Hand went that long night, it was always moments behind the plague that was tearing his people apart. He came across a little girl, he thought her name might have been Wading Brook. She had been torn in two, the ragged halves spread twenty feet apart. Deep Water, her mother, was lying in a pool of blood. Her head and spinal column had been detached from the rest of her body, her mouth still twitching.

When the dying had completed their destiny, a shadowy image appeared from beyond the fire.

"I see you demon!" Severed Hand shouted.

"As I see you, Medicine Man," Eliza said as she appeared to walk through the fire.

Fear clutched Severed Hand's heart as she approached.

"Why?" Severed Hand asked as he looked upon the blood soaked apparition before him.

"I was bored," she said with a small laugh.

"What are you?" Severed Hand asked in horror. Anger was beginning to take hold.

"I am Death," she replied proudly.

"You are not death. Death does not sow, it reaps."

"Clever Shaman, but I will give you no further information. I know how powerful names can be to those who know how to use them."

"Why not tell me who you are and then let me join those you have taken?"

"Very well, I had hoped to leave you alive so that you could tell others about me. I grow weary of always being in the shadows. It is time that people are afraid of me and not my legend. But I will grant your request. Perhaps it will be fun to take my time with you. Come, you and I will sit by the fire as I tell you my tale."

"No one will fear a demon that destroys women, children and the old," Severed Hand said defiantly.

"FOOL!" Eliza said, hitting Severed Hand with the back of her hand. He slid effortless across the ground. "Did you not understand the visions I sent to you?" Eliza was fairly shaking with rage.

The insult did as he had hoped. While he struggled to get up, he ripped free a deerskin pouch he had wrapped around his waist. "Your pride will be your end," Severed Hand murmured before standing up completely.

"Now, come sit by the fire. I have a story to tell you before you die," Eliza said, all of her earlier hostility seemingly dissipated.

Severed Hand rubbed his jaw. If he ever got to eat again, it would not be without some significant discomfort.

"My name is Eliza and this is my tale." For several hours, Eliza related her story to Severed Hand about cruelties interlaced with atrocities piled high atop destruction.

"The world has no need for the likes of you," the Medicine Man said gravely.

"It was this same world that produced me," Eliza said. "I am merely returning the favor."

"I could end your suffering," Severed Hand offered sincerely.

Eliza laughed, "I enjoy the turmoil I cause, sorcerer. I fear our time together grows short," she said as the eastern sky began to lighten.

"Do you fear seeing what devastation you have wrought?" Severed Hand asked as he glanced at the horizon Eliza was watching.

Eliza turned to him without saying anything. She gripped him around the neck and lifted him effortlessly off the ground. "Pity, I would have so enjoyed a few hours more of your time," Eliza said as she slowly closed her grip.

Severed Hand threw the contents of his right hand up into the air. As it rained down, wherever it made contact with Eliza, tiny wisps of smoke arose. Severed Hand grabbed a hold of a lock of Eliza's hair as her grip around his neck released. She reared back in pain.

"What have you done, witch doctor?" Eliza screamed.

"I know you for what you are, soulless one," Severed

Hand rasped, his throat on fire. "You will bother the Lakota no more. Every surviving member of my people will wear our skins infused with Hawthorn and Rowan."

Eliza's eyes gleamed at Severed Hand, "Our time now is done, but we have unfinished business," she warned as she left.

Severed Hand fell to his knees, dragging in breaths that seemed to ignite the coals placed in his throat. "You are right demon, we do have unfinished business," he said, looking at the strands of hair he had pried loose from her head.

For seven days and seven nights Severed Hand alternated between performing burial rituals, burying the dead of the tribe, and hunting for one particular type of gem stone. He only stopped long enough to gather more Hawthorn and Rowan and to take small drinks of water. The demon did not return. On the morning of the eighth day, Chief Running Bear and his braves returned triumphantly with five bison, confident in the fact that his people would make it through the winter, warm and fat.

The sight of the smoke from many funeral cairns at first stopped his advance and then made him speed up. His horse came to skidding stop at the hunched over body of Severed Hand who had just finished placing the last rock on the old Chief's cairn.

"What has happened here?" Chief Running Bear asked alighting from his horse, wildly looking around for his wife and his children, in fact, anyone.

"They are dead," Severed Hand said standing up, his hands nearly scraped clean of skin from his burial efforts.

"Who did this?" Running Bear asked, tears streaming down his face as he sought an enemy to lash out against.

"It is not a 'who.'" Severed Hand said. "And your spears and bows would do nothing against it. Mourn, Running Bear, then come and sit with me. I have a way in which we can strike out against the demon that destroyed our people."

Running Bear barely acknowledged the words of his Medicine Man, so lost was he in the depths of his loss, but still he nodded. Severed Hand rubbed a small amount of his mixture onto every warrior's head and clothes as they fell where they were, cries of despair rising as one lone sad song across the now accursed ground.

For three days the remaining members of the tribe grieved for their lost ones. On the night of the third, Chief Running Bear entered into Severed Hand's teepee. He was barely able to see the Medicine Man in the gloom, but he could see that he was beginning to shrivel away since he had not emerged to eat or drink in that whole time. The Chief sat across from Severed Hand who was only here in the physical sense, his spirit was walking the planes. The entire night the Chief merely sat and watched as the Shaman from time to time would shout out incoherent mutterings of warning and surprise.

"Hello, Running Bear," Severed Hand said exhaustedly as the sun arose, light spilling through the top of the teepee's smoke hole.

"Hello," Running Bear returned the greeting, a determined look set on his face. "Can this demon be destroyed?" he asked.

"My spirit guides have shown me a way, but I will need the tribe's help to achieve this. Even then I am not sure if we will be strong enough."

"You will have all the help you ask for," Running Bear said. "And if anger can be your source of energy, than you will have all you will need."

Severed Hand gave the Chief a list of items he would need for that night's spirit walk.

"Come old friend," the Chief said to Severed Hand. "You have not drank or eaten in three days' time. Let me get you something while we walk among the trees."

"I would welcome some water, Running Bear, but I fear I will never walk in the light of day again. What I do the spirits have told me requires a high price."

Running Bear nodded once, stood up and went to get his Shaman some water.

That night Running Bear was instructed by Severed Hand to bring ten of his strongest warriors into his teepee. The Chief did as he was told. They sat in a circle around the spiritual leader of the tribe. Kills Coyote handed over the peyote buttons in a ceremonial bowl. Running Bear watched in concern as Severed Hand ate five of the magic seeds. He had never seen him take more than two. After a few minutes of chanting, Severed Hand became violently ill, heaving up his spirit as an offering to the spirits. Kills Coyote took away the proffered bile in a wooden bowl.

Severed Hand began to rock back and forth. The eleven Lakotas around him joined hands, their chants joining his. Higher and higher his spirit rose, further than it had ever gone before. His spirit guide, the antlered Hawk, warned him that if he traveled too far he would not be able to find his way home and still Severed Hand soared. He passed those who did not know they were yet gone. Some watched as he went by, but most were too wrapped up in their own events to even notice. Up to the edge of the Spirits' Home he went, to Purgatory, the location of lost souls. Tears rained down from these tortured individuals, they had been cursed in one form or another. Some bargained their eternity away for a bit of fame and fortune that was gone in the blink of an eye from this vantage point. Most had committed mortal sins and were banished from any form of a spiritual nirvana. A select few had had their souls stripped from them, some willingly, most not.

"I seek the one named Eliza!" Severed Hand cried among the lonely souls surrounded on all sides by their brethren, but they no more acknowledged each other than leaves on a tree. "I believe that I have something of yours!" Severed Hand said, holding Eliza's hair high up in the air.

For long moments nothing happened and then off in the distance Severed Hand could see a parting of souls as one walked among them. Crevices had formed in the girl's face from the tears that never stopped running through them. Her mouth was open in a wide oval as if she were screaming yet no sound was heard. Her arms were outstretched as she beheld the locket of hair Severed Hand held.

"You are Eliza?" Severed Hand asked. It was difficult to compare the evil being that had destroyed his people with this hunched over, tortured young girl. He had a moment of regret for what he was about to do. At least here she could walk free, forever searching for the body that had given her away. Once in the blood stone she would be trapped fast, even her tears would not be able to flow.

Eliza walked quickly to where Severed Hand stood. She was desperate to touch anything that had once belonged to her. When she reached out to touch the hair, Severed Hand pulled it close to his body and with the other hand gripped her arm tightly. "NOW!" he screamed in the ethereal world as well as the real.

Chief Running Bear and the braves began chanting the words that Severed Hand had taught them earlier in the day. He felt his spirit being dragged back down even faster than he had risen. It was too fast and yet he kept speeding up. Severed Hand slammed back into his body, almost relinquishing his grip on Eliza's soul. Everyone but Running Bear gasped as they saw the vision before them of a white mist which formed the shape of a young woman in the grip of Severed Hand.

Kills Coyote ran towards Severed Hand and with a torch of burning sage swept it completely around the medicine man and the apparition. Severed Hand let go of Eliza who was trapped for the moment in the smoke of the Sage. He spoke a few words to the Spirits of the Ground. The Blood Stone shone from within, the red light illuminating the faces of those around it. Eliza was panic stricken as Severed Hand once again grabbed her; his spirit intermingled with hers as they both plunged into the stone. The light from within flashed brilliantly and then just as quickly died out. Severed Hand's body slumped forward to the ground.

"Is he dead?" one of the warriors asked Running Bear.

"No, he will live forever," Chief Running Bear said as he stood up and grabbed the red stone from the open hand of Severed Hand. He held the stone up to the light of the new morning; two minor blemishes deep in the depths of the stone stared back at him. "I will miss you, old friend," Running Bear said sadly as he placed the stone into a pouch that Severed Hand had given to him the day before.

*　　*　　*

"You do this for me, Colonel," Eliza said. "And I will return your family safely."

"What proof do I have that you have them? I can't just take my troops a hundred miles to the West and destroy an Indian tribe that has not so much as stolen a chicken," Colonel Broward said to the beautiful woman before him. He had been summoned by his sergeant to meet her in the town saloon. She said that she had word of his family.

"Would you not recognize the earrings that you bought your blushing bride?" Eliza asked.

"Of course I would…" Colonel Broward gasped as Eliza produced the earrings still attached to the ears that once worn them, "My God, my Mary! What have you done?" the Colonel said in shock, getting louder and nearly rising from his seat.

"Sit!" Eliza commanded, "If you do not, I will leave and you will never see the rest of your precious Mary," she fairly hissed out.

The Colonel sat, the white of shock spreading through his features, his eyes never wavering from the blood encrusted ears that Eliza left on the table.

'My… my children are safe?" the Colonel asked, finally pulling his gaze up from the macabre image before him.

Eliza nodded once.

"All I have to do is kill a few Indians and you will give me my family back?" the Colonel asked, nearly breaking down.

"That is the deal I am trying to broker with you," Eliza said amiably.

"Swear it!" the Colonel demanded. "Swear it on your accursed soul!"

"I swear it on my soul," Eliza laughed.

"I will leave tomorrow. We are done here," the Colonel said, rising to his feet. He was eager to get away from the abomination standing before him.

"Colonel, you will leave tonight," Eliza said as she stood up.

The Colonel nearly fell over as Eliza tossed his wife's ears at him. The last sound he heard was Eliza's laugh as the saloon doors swung open.

*   *   *

"Captain, get forty of your men. I want to do a long range patrol out to the western edge of the Lakota nation. I have heard rumors of an uprising," Colonel Broward told his captain.

"I have not heard any such thing. Have we received orders from Washington?" Captain Reynolds asked.

"Just get the men ready! If you question my orders again you will be cleaning latrines!" the Colonel shouted.

"Who will be leading the men?" the Captain asked, snapping to the position of attention.

"I will," the Colonel said resignedly. "Let me know the moment they are ready. You are dismissed."

"Colonel?" the Captain asked. This was not like his commanding officer, he was hoping to get an explanation.

"Go Captain," The Colonel said with less force. "Perhaps someday I will be able to tell you…"

"Yes sir," the Captain said, saluting and then turning around to do as he was told.

Five days later the weary cavalrymen, pushed to their limits, came across the remaining members of the Lakota tribe. Chief Running Bear, although caught completely by surprise, rallied a stout defense. The army lost ten of its best, but that Lakota tribe was erased from the annals of history that day.

The remaining soldiers picked through the dead looking for souvenirs to impress their girlfriends or friends back home.

Corporal Tenson was almost caught as he peered into the red jewel he had found among the possessions of the dead Indians.

"Corporal, I ordered everyone on burial detail. Get your ass over there!" Sergeant Clanton bellowed.

Corporal Tenson slid the stone into his pocket. He had never before been so happy digging a hole in his entire life. 'I'm rich,' was all he could think.

Colonel Broward returned home five days later. His two children and wife were home, but the light of life had been extinguished days previously. The stench of decay permeated his entire home, flies and maggots fought for position on the bodies. Colonel Broward placed his Colt .45 against his temple and joined his family in death, but not in spirit.

Check out these other titles in the Zombie Fallout Series

Zombie Fallout

It was a flu season like no other. With fears of contracting the H1N1 virus running rampant through the country, people lined up in droves to try and obtain one of the coveted vaccines. What was not known, was the effect this largely untested, rushed to market, inoculation was to have on the unsuspecting throngs.

Within days, feverish folk throughout the country, convulsed, collapsed and died, only to be re-born. With a taste for brains, blood and bodies, these modern day zombies scoured the lands for their next meal. Overnight the country became a killing ground for the hordes of zombies that ravaged the land.

This is the story of Michael Talbot, his family and his friends. When disaster strikes, Mike a self-proclaimed survivalist, does his best to ensure the safety and security of those he cares for. Can brains beat brain eaters? It's a battle for survival, winner take all!

Zombie Fallout 2: A Plague Upon Your Family

This story picks up exactly where book one left off. The Talbot family is evacuating their home amidst a zombie apocalypse. Mankind is on the edge of extinction as a new dominant, mindless opponent scours the landscape in search of food, which just so happens to be non-infected humans. In these pages, are the journal entries of Michael Talbot, his wife Tracy, their three kids Nicole, Justin and Travis. With them are Brendon, Nicole's fiancée and Tommy previously a Wal-Mart door greeter who may be more than he seems. Together they struggle against a ruthless, relentless enemy that has singled them out above all others. The Talbots have escaped Little Turtle but to what end, on the run they find themselves encountering a far vaster evil than the one that has already beset them. As they travel across the war-torn country side they soon learn that there are more than just zombies to be fearful of, with law and order a long distant memory some humans have decided to take any and all matters into their own hands. Can the Talbots come through unscathed or will they suffer the fate of so many countless millions before them. It's not just brains versus brain-eaters anymore. And the stakes may be higher than merely life and death with eternal souls on the line.

Zombie Fallout 3: The End...

Continues Michael Talbot's quest to be rid of the evil named Eliza that hunts him and his family across the country. As the world spirals even further down into the abyss of apocalypse one man struggles to keep those around him safe. Side by side Michael stands with his wife, their children, his friends and the wonder Bulldog Henry along with the Wal-Mart greeter Tommy who is infinitely more than he appears and whether he is leading them to salvation or death is only a measure of degrees.

As Justin continues to slip further into the abyss he receives help from an unexpected ally all of which leads up to the biggest battle thus far.

Dr. Hugh Mann – A Zombie Fallout Prequel 3.5

Dr Hugh Mann delves deeper into what caused the zombie invasion. Early in the 1900's Dr. Mann discovers a parasite that brings man to the brink of an early extinction. Come along on the journey with Jonathan Talbot is bride to be Marissa and the occasional visitations from the boy with the incredible baklava. Could there be a cure somewhere here and what part does the blood locket play?

Watch also for:

Mark Tufo is hooking up with Severed Press for a zombie novella entitled "Timothy"

http://severedpress.lefora.com/2011/04/12/mark-tufo/

Indian Hill

This first story is about an ordinary boy, who grows up in relatively normal times to find himself thrust into an extra-ordinary position. Growing up in suburban Boston he enjoys the trials and tribulations that all adolescents go through. From the seemingly tyrannical mother, to girl problems to run-ins with the law. From there he escapes to college out in Colorado with his best friend, Paul, where they begin to forge new relationships with those around them. It is one girl in particular that has caught the eye of Michael and he alternately pines for her and then laments ever meeting her.

It is on their true 'first' date that things go strangely askew. Mike soon finds himself captive aboard an alien vessel, fighting for his very survival. The aliens have devised gladiator type games. The games are of two-fold importance for the aliens. One reason, being for the entertainment value, the other reason being that they want to see how combative humans are, what our weaknesses and strengths are. They want to better learn how to attack and defeat us. The battles are to the death on varying terrains that are computer generated.

 Follow Mike as he battles for his life and Paul as he battles to keep main stream US safe.

Made in the USA
San Bernardino, CA
12 December 2012